Excerpt

"Did you have anything to do with this, other than what I already know you did?" she asked.

"What do you mean?"

"You were very adamant about stalling me when I wanted to get into Jensine's house. Why?"

"I didn't want you going in there. It was too dangerous."

"Did you know the house was going to blow up? Is that why you held me back?"

From Roman's expression, she knew he finally understood what she meant. "I had nothing to do with Jensine's death." His voice got louder. "I cannot believe you would think that I—"

"Why wouldn't I?" she cut him off, matching his volume and tone. "You're the one who reported her to The Great Order authorities. I told you she didn't even know of the Clandestine World, only me, and to keep that between us. You took it to the world. It was my personal business, between a friend and me. It had nothing to do with you. You had no right."

Roman, jaw and fists clenched, said, "I have rules I have to abide by, Atlanta. Rules put in place to make her safe and keep us safe. That doesn't mean I killed her!"

"You as good as did!"

"Why is it so impossible for you to understand the rules of my people?"

She threw her good arm up in the air in exasperation, "*Your* people? They're *my* people too! Or don't you see me as really being a part of the Clandestine World because I don't breathe to serve Prince Phoenix Keziah? I promise you this, if The Great Order had anything to do with her death, I'll make you pay. I'll make you all pay."

"You're taking my words and twisting them around. Of course, you're part of our world. I meant the Order's rules, Atlanta. You consider them archaic, ancient, and useless."

"In some ways, yes, I do. It's the Twentieth Century. You all need to rethink these rules you live by. They didn't work out so well for Jensine!" She realized she was yelling and took a deep breath.

Roman did the same and said, "I'm sorry your friend has died because of your involvement with us. I am. More will die in this war, Atlanta. You have to accept that."

"How dare you use that as an excuse?" It was a cop-out at best and it pissed her off. "I don't have to accept anything, not on my watch, not if I can help it."

Living Dead Girl; Book Two, The Windfire Series -- Copyright © 2012 by Tamsin L. Silver
Cover Art Copyright © 2012: Kathleen Baum / FMS Digital
First Edition: September 2012
First Print Edition: September 2012

Published in the United States of America.

Living Dead Girl

Book Two
Windfire Series

Tamsin L. Silver

Dedication

For my Mother. Who never told me I couldn't do something. In fact, she orders me to chase my dreams and has helped me do so. It's because of her "nagging" that I moved to New York City. She is my rock and example of what working hard and being happy means. Thank you for always believing in me! I love you so very much!

Acknowledgements

Nothing this large happens without a support system, and those people deserve recognition.

Large thanks to my editor, Chris Borhani—to the Brit with wit, Rachel Grundy—and all my Beta Readers—you are amazing and I couldn't do anything without you. Huge thank you to Anastasia Catris—woman, you are a goddess. Finally, a special thank you to two people. First, Josh Price, for his unwavering support and encouragement no matter what state he lives in or how busy he is. Second, to my mini-me, Lauren Steinmeyer. You, my darling girl, are always there when I need you for whatever life throws at us, be it fun, stressful, or just plain weird. You both are gifts from God. Thank you for all you do for me.

Thank you also to Lady Shyra and Tryskelion for the use of their Yule Ritual. You can find them at http://www.tryskelion.com/tryskelion/ Blessed Be, ladies.

Last but not least, to my family and friends all over the globe—from Michigan to the Carolinas, to NYC, Georgia, Colorado, California, and the UK—without your support and belief in me these books would never have seen the light of day.

Letter to the Reader

Welcome to the second book of *The Windfire Series*!

I began this saga in college, yearning to create a kick-ass female character and take her on a journey. I wanted to not only show her strengths, but expose her flaws. For I feel that the true love for a person stems from understanding and accepting both.

Shortly after I started the novel it became apparent to me that just like in life, my primary character wasn't whole without her support system, her friends—a team. So, the book altered from one person's story to an ensemble team of seven to whisk you off on an adventure. I hope you enjoy where they take you.

Originally, books one and two of *The Windfire Series* were one book known as "The Betrayal - A Living Dead Girl Novel." If you read that book, there have been changes. For instance, this series is now YA Fantasy vs. adult. However, the story is still the same and I would suggest you begin reading this new version with book three, entitled "Metamorphosis."

If interested in knowing more about me or the series, you can visit my website, www.tamsinsilver.com and/or blog, http://tamsinsilver.blogspot.com. There are pictures of characters as well as videos from the photo shoots and character information. You can also come follow me on Twitter (@tamsinsilver) and Facebook for more updates on the series as well as other books I'm working on.

Cheers! Tamsin L. Silver

Living Dead Girl

Clandestine History
Volume Two: 1997 to 1998

Living Dead Girl

Chapter One

The wind blowing past her face felt exhilarating as the galloping horse took charge. Glancing at the trees as they flew by, Atlanta realized they were the same trees repeatedly. For that matter, she was going in circles. Glancing down at the black horse she rode on, she found that though he was real and breathing, there was a pole shoved through him to hold him to the carousel they rode on. Horror stricken, she looked into his eyes, but they held no soul. An empty shell breathing as they spun round and round.

Noticing the wooden horn coming from his forehead, she touched it. With a jolt, the carousel's speed increased and a faint beeping could heard for each rotation. Looking for an explanation, Atlanta carefully inspected the area outside the carousel. Where there had only been trees, now stood people. First, she passed her best friend Grayson, then Roman, Jensine, and finally Sean.

As the carousel picked up speed again, the incessant beeping did its best to permeate her brain. Sparks flew from underneath the carousel catching fire to both itself and the ground surrounding it. Spreading like liquid flame, the fire moved toward her friends at an alarming rate.

"Run! Get away from me! It's not safe!" she screamed, coughing from the smoke.

No one moved. Petrified, Atlanta watched as the flames headed for Jensine first, engulfing her.

"Somebody save her!" Atlanta screamed to the others.

No one moved, except the horse. Without warning, his eyes lit from within and the pole disappeared, freeing him without injury. He knocked Atlanta to the floor as he breathed a puff of fire and sprouted wings. His front hooves became talons before her eyes and in a flash, he leapt from the ride, heading toward Jensine.

The beeping noise became louder as Atlanta watched the flying beast snatch up her friend and fly off with her. Keeping an eye on Jensine as she flew away, the scene faded, leaving only the beeping sound, over and over in the darkness.

The light coming through the lids of her eyes was the first sign to Atlanta that she'd left the dream behind her. She still heard the beeping, but now it was slow and steady, almost soothing. She smelled no smoke. Instead, she felt the weight of a blanket on her body while a waft an antiseptic odor washed over her. She wondered if Gray had cleaned the apartment.

Her head felt heavy, consciousness demanding to return. She had no idea where she was, but she heard voices. It sounded like Gray and Sean. With no idea she could hear them, they spoke of her freely.

"Like I told you, it'd be her choice. I wouldn't offer, but she's gonna need all her strength to deal with this situation."

"Are you just trying to make her stay attached to you?" Gray asked, his voice a little mad.

"Absolutely not! Hell, I don't care if it's Stephan or Roman. I just don't think they'd do this for her. Rules, you know."

"Rules. Those rules got us here in the first place."

"Yes." Sean's voice sounded strained.

Atlanta was confused. She tried to wake up and open her eyes, but she couldn't seem to will her body to be fully conscious.

"Just be careful with her," Gray advised. "I love her more than anything else in this world."

"My feelings for her aren't a joke. I know I haven't known her as long as you, but..."

Atlanta felt a hand lightly brush the side of her face. She knew it was Sean. How could she already know his touch that well?

Gray sighed. "She looks peaceful for the first time in months. So much pressure on one girl—it doesn't seem right."

"It's not fair she has to carry the burden of who she is. But Gray, I'm sure that the goddess Diana knew what she was doing. If she didn't think her chosen could find her way, she'd have sent someone else. This is something horrible for Atlanta to deal with, but obviously its part of the plan. I'm not one to preach but honestly, I think in time it'll all be clear."

"I wouldn't give that line to Atty when she wakes up...she might clobber you with her good arm."

"Do I look stupid? Don't answer that." He paused, then added, "That was pretty great of you. Telling the nurse that I'm Atty's boyfriend so I could come in with you. She's not my girlfriend you know."

"She is in your heart. And though she may not realize it yet, you're in her heart too. That's what matters to me."

Nurse? Was she in the hospital? Consciousness came much faster with that thought in her mind. Her eyes fluttered and she demanded them to open. Stirring slightly she moaned and finally found her voice, "Where am I?"

"Union Hospital, sweetie," Sean told her.

"What happened?"

Sean held up a hand to quiet Gray and took her right hand. "What do you remember?"

"We went to bed and now I'm waking up here. Did I sleep walk off the balcony or something? That's what I feel like. What time is it?"

"It's eight in the morning. What happened isn't important right now," Gray said. "You need to get some rest and we'll all talk about it later on."

She tried to remember, but it was all a haze. Thinking of the carousel she said, "What are you not telling me, Gray?"

Gray forced his best smile. "Do you trust me?" She did, so she nodded. "Then know you need your rest and we'll go over all of it later. Okay?"

"Sean?" He would tell her the truth.

"Oh, don't drag me into this...if I don't back his play he will be mad and if I do back his play you'll be mad. That's not fair."

"Okay, fine," she said through a yawn, the grogginess she'd pushed through trying to pull her under again. "But later on you better all fess up to what you're hiding or I'll kick your ass even with—" she looked down at her left arm. "—my broken arm? Oh man, not again."

"No doubt," Gray agreed.

"I'm going to go call the others and let them know you're okay. I'll be back," Gray told them. He kissed her forehead, and left the room.

As he left, she looked at Sean. "Can you climb up into this bed with me?"

"Sure, but you can explain to the nurse why," Sean laughed.

"The nurse can kiss my ass," she teased.

"Ooh, can I watch?"

She slapped him with her good arm that then tucked her head under his neck, burying her face into his chest. But before Gray could return, Atlanta fell asleep—oblivious to the pain that had put her there.

* * * *

Atlanta awoke in darkness permeated by a low glow from a bedside table lamp, with Sean still next to her. Curled up on her good side she stared at his face. Slowly he opened his eyes. The honey color of them was striking against his pale complexion. Add to it the wide curls the color of dark chocolate that framed his face and the sleepy smile he gave her, and she was breathless.

"Hi, hon. How do you feel?" he asked quietly.

"Little better. Still blank though."

He reached out and gently ran his thumb down her face. "Did you sleep well?"

"I feel better, so I'm guessing yes. I didn't dream, which seems odd."

"Probably better you didn't."

He didn't know how right that statement was. The last thing she wanted to think of was that horse creature. She paused and asked, "Sean, what happened?"

He shook his head and kissed her nose. "We need to wait for the others to get here. Gray should be coming with the gang shortly. He swung by your place to get you some clothes and your emergency bag."

"That's 'cause my best friend rocks!" she said with a big grin on her face. She hated to think of what she was wearing under the covers or what she looked like.

He smiled and touched her face again.

"What is it?"

"You should smile more. It lights up your whole face. I'm just embedding it into my brain so that when you're not with me I can see it."

"Sean, am I dying?"

"No! Sorry…I'm gonna shut up now."

She snuggled her head under his chin and he kissed the top of her head. Then he did something he hadn't done since the night in the car. He pulled her head back up to him and kissed her on the mouth, briefly. She heard him in her head, *"Remember that I'm here for you."*

She nodded and he carefully climbed out of the bed, pulled her covers up, and sat in the chair. Reaching over, he increased the amount of light the side lamp gave. He opened up a random magazine just as a light rapping came at her door.

"Come in," she said.

In walked Gray, Stephan, Roman, and the three witches, Celeste, Bianca, and Desi. They all looked exhausted. Using the button on the side of the bed, she brought herself into a sitting position as they surrounded the bed. Seeing their faces, she wondered if she really wanted to know what had happened. Maybe it would be better to stay blank. However, that would be running away and she wasn't that person.

"Wow, y'all look like hell." Gray took her hand. She figured they'd given him the job. "I'm a big girl Gray, just say it."

"Jensine is dead."

Her heart sank and her brain went blank. She must've heard him wrong. Then she remembered the dream and choked out a reply. "What? That's not possible."

"We think The Superior Order had her killed," Roman explained.

"*You* think The Superior Order had her killed," Sean clarified, barely glancing up from his magazine. "Some of us think otherwise."

Gray filled her in on exactly what had happened.

"This can't be. You're lying to me. This isn't real. Why would you all lie to me?"

In her head, she heard Stephan. *"Touch me, and I'll show you. But remember the consequences. You might be happier without the visual memories of last night."*

"If I can't remember what happened, I am no use in helping figure this all out," she said, looking right at Stephan, frantic to understand. *"Show me,"* she told him mentally, and reached for his hand.

Roman almost jumped over the bed, as he yelled out, "No!" But it was too late. She touched Stephan and all the images of the previous night filed into her head, but from his perspective. She watched the events wash past her, the emotional disconnect of it being someone else's memory caused it to feel more like a TV show, than real life. When the pictures ended, she let go of Stephan and covered her gaping mouth with her good hand.

The tears ran down her face but she made no sound. Sean's eyes showed her how lost he was, standing there next to her bed. Reaching for him, he took her hand. She glanced at each face staring at her. A mixture of sadness and anxiety shone back at her. She knew she had two options. She could collapse into tears or step up and take action.

The depth of pain she felt reverberated down to the core of her being. Shoving it aside for now, she asked, "What do we know at this point?"

"The police aren't sure it's Jensine's body," Celeste blurted out. "They're able to tell that the body was female and that it was about her age."

Atlanta thought about what she knew from TV shows like Law and Order. "What about dental records?" The room fell silent. It wasn't hard for her to derive a conclusion. "They haven't found the head, have they?"

"They will, don't worry," Celeste affirmed, looking forlorn.

Stephan pulled a video cassette out of his bag. "I found this in our mailbox at home. It wasn't mailed—only left there."

"What's on it?" she asked.

Stephan shared a glance with Grayson. "We should just show you. Gray?"

Gray pulled her living room VCR out of his other bag. "Who can help me set this up?"

"I can," Desi offered.

The screen was fuzzy at first, and then a picture came up of a hard wood floor. As it lifted up and panned back, Atlanta could tell by the furniture it was Jensine's living room.

"What are you doing, silly?" It was Jensine's voice.

"I got this new camera and I want to see how it works. It's rather amazing what the world has invented in my lifetime." A male voice—Devon.

Even though Roman and Stephan were Living Vampires and would show up on film, Made Vampires like Sean and Devon would not. This sparked a thought. "Why on earth would a Made Vampire get a video camera?" Atlanta asked aloud. He won't show up on it, nor will some of his friends."

"Devon has friends?" Sean asked.

"He's got a point there," Stephan murmured.

Jensine herself filled the screen, smiling a big stupid smile. She held a giant spoon and was wearing her apron that said "kiss the cook." Gray and she had mailed it to her the previous Christmas. Atlanta reached out and touched Gray and she saw his eyes were watering.

"Really, and how long is your lifetime, exactly?" Jensine prodded.

"You keep trying to get that out of me. I told you, I never reveal my age." The camera zoomed into close-up. Jensine was baking her famous chocolate chip cookies. Devon tightened the shot on her backside.

"Hey now, get that off my behind, mister!" she said with a laugh.

Devon laughed. "But I like your bum." The picture was now just the pattern of her top, and they heard kissing.

"This is our important video?" Atlanta asked aloud, meaning only to think it.

"Just wait," Stephan interjected.

Devon now panned around the apartment, over the rugs and wall hangings. "I love this little apartment you know. I hope to have a place like it someday."

"I think you have quite enough of a house," Jensine stated. With a laugh, she added, "You know, Atlanta and Gray made fun of your place when we first went there. They called it Norman Bates' Motel."

"Did they, now? Well, they're just jealous. The poor envy the rich."

"Actually, Atlanta is really well off." Jensine's tone became serious and sad. "Her mom passed away when she was little and her dad disappeared right afterwards. But they had a substantial life insurance policy."

Everyone in the room except Gray stole a quick glance at Atlanta. She kept her focus on the TV and ignored their looks.

"Why is she going to school and teaching then?" Devon asked as he then wandered into the bedroom and filmed some of it, stopping to put the camera down for a moment.

Jensine yelled the answer from the other room, "She likes to pretend she's normal, I think. Besides, she likes teaching and she's good at it."

They heard scuttling and whispering as Devon talked to himself under his breath. The camera was picked up again and they were back in the living room.

"It even came with this tri-pod. I'm going to see if I can figure this out."

"At your age you should be able to," Jensine chuckled.

"Oh shut it, you," he replied, his tone sweet and endearing as he lay the camera down.

"So I suppose I should tell you why I called you over here," Jensine pulled a tray of cookies in the oven.

"Sex?"

She shut the oven door. "Yes, but that's not all."

"Okay. What's the other reason?"

"I am going to be going off on a big investigation. It's top secret. I can't even tell Atlanta what I'm going to be doing, but I may be gone for awhile."

"Really? When do you leave?"

The camera made a ton of noise as Devon attached it to the tripod. "Any day now. I'm waiting on all the paperwork to go through." She turned away from the camera.

"She's lying," Atlanta said. She never can look at you when she lies. Why would she be lying?"

"Well, that sucks. We should totally have some fun since you'll be gone for awhile." His voice now fell in front of the camera, but they couldn't see him.

Jensine reached over and turned the oven off. Her apron seemed to come untied magically—meaning Devon had undone it. It flew over a kitchen chair, and from the sounds and movement of Jen's body his hands were wrapped around her as he kissed her neck.

"Please tell me we're not about to watch them have sex—"

Stephan held up a hand and shook his head. A glance at Gray showed how tense he was, and Atlanta had a feeling it wasn't the presumed oncoming sex scene.

Eyes back on the screen, Atlanta was in time to watch Jensine and Devon's reactions as glass shattered everywhere as something large and black streaked across the screen in a blur of movement. It attacked Devon, who screamed, as did a few in the hospital room. The image solidified into a black panther, which shifted into a human right in front of the lens.

"Oh my goddess," Atlanta said at a whisper.

Unfortunately, the face of the intruder was above the camera's radius as they ran across the room. They heard a huge crash, and then no more sound from Devon, who had been yelling for Jensine to run.

"Leave him alone!" Jensine screamed. Her body suddenly landing on the ground with a thud, her face pointed at the camera that lay on the floor with her. She struggled ferociously with her attacker until immense pain erupted in her face as she screamed in agony until someone dragged her away.

All of a sudden, the camera clicked off. When the picture returned, the picture was upright, showing Jensine tied to a chair, her lower leg bleeding. Behind her, all that was visible was the torso of whoever held a knife at Jensine's throat—jeans, huge black sweatshirt and black gloves. Then they heard a voice, which had been digitally garbled so they couldn't even tell if it was male or female.

"I have been ordered to end the human life. This is the price you pay for telling humans about our world. Let this be a lesson."

Jensine screamed and the video feed went black.

Chapter Two

Everyone sat in silence. Atlanta wiped tears from her face, and she wasn't the only one.

Sean finally spoke. "Why blow up the house if you've already killed her?"

"This way the police have no evidence," Roman stated. "We remove the scene of a crime so the human world can't figure anything out. Fire is the best way when it's an option. It burns away all of the unusual DNA. All Superior Order members were once Great Order, so they do the same."

"Actually, they don't," Sean said. "The Superior Order considers our race superior to the humans. They believe that we should rule the humans. With all that the Clandestine World does for this planet, The Superior Order believes we should get something in return for it. They're not as worried about covering up evidence. That's a Great Order thing."

An odd silence hovered. Even Roman under his cool exterior seemed rattled.

"I'm going to throw a couple of questions out," Atlanta said. "First question: is there a chance the body wasn't Jensine's? There is no proof it was her. My second question is what are the chances that The Great Order are the ones who did this?" When everyone started to speak at once, she put up a hand. Gratifyingly, her friends fell silent. "Sean, you first."

"As to figuring out if it's Jensine or not...all the evidence points to it being her. Of course, when all evidence points to something, it's usually a set up. As to your second question, I totally think it's possible. They're the only ones who knew that Jen knew anything. Devon is still on The Great Order Council."

She let Roman speak next. "I think it is a fifty-fifty chance as to whether it's her or not," he said. "As to whether The Great Order was involved? It's absurd. Devon is a conniving man, but have his girlfriend offed? I don't think even he would do that. Besides, why would The Great Order leave you proof it was them when they need you to fight on their side in this war?"

"But who really knows who I am, other than you all and Phoenix? No one."

Stephan raised his hand and she pointed at him. "This felt like a set up and a planned hit, Atlanta. Whether it was The Superior Order posing as The Great Order or someone *in* The Great Order straight on, it's hard to tell. I'd honestly put my bets on Valencia rattling our cages, or distracting us from her real project."

Roman's phone rang, and he answered. "Hello? Yes, sir. No sir, it's not confirmed. We have not seen him either. Yes, sir, tomorrow night. Good bye." He replaced his phone in his pocket, his expression wary. "That was Phoenix. He wants a meeting tomorrow night. It seems Devon is missing. He was to have a pre-trial meeting with Phoenix at sunset tonight and he hasn't shown. No one has seen him."

Sean spoke up before anyone else had processed the thought. "Either Devon is dead because he got in the way of the target, or it was a double hit."

"In the explosion? But no other bones were found," Gray reminded them.

Stephan shook his head. "His bones would have turned to ash immediately."

"The weasel deserved it," Roman muttered.

Sean continued. "OR he's hiding out again, like after Elizabeth. For all we know he was in on the whole thing."

"You think he helped with killing his girlfriend?" Celeste questioned. "I don't think he's that cold. I mean, he wasn't my favorite person, but I honestly can't see him offering up her life for anything."

"What if he didn't realize she was going to die? He's pretty gullible," Stephan suggested.

"I know this guy. If it was his ass or hers…" Roman shrugged expressively. "He has lived longer than most in this room because he'd stop at nothing to protect himself, to the point of amorality. He let Elizabeth die. For those of you who don't know, that's why he's on trial with The Great Order. For his exact involvement with the execution of my sister, Elizabeth, by The Superior Order."

"Oh, he's going to be tried?" Sean asked.

"Yes. If he's not dead, that is."

"Call me as a witness. He was in the dungeon with me. I can help put him away."

Roman was taken aback by this, and Atlanta thought his dislike for Sean lessened a bit. He only thanked him with a bow of his head though.

Atlanta felt both emotionally and physically weary. She wanted to deal with the events from the night before, but she also desperately wanted to be left alone to digest everything she'd learned. She thought again, maybe not *totally* alone. She really only wanted one person there. She yawned and Gray took the hint.

"Folks, let's let Atty get some rest. We can all pick up on this tomorrow."

Everyone made apologies and agreement and started to say their goodbye's with kisses on Atlanta's cheek and light hugs that didn't disrupt her casted arm. She whispered to Stephan, asking if he would find some blood for Sean and he agreed.

As they all slipped out of the room, Atlanta mentally spoke to Sean, *"Could you wait outside with Gray?"* Holding the door, he nodded circumspectly. Then she said aloud, "Roman, stay."

When everyone left, Roman spoke immediately. "Did you mean what you said at the house?"

She struggled to remember, clawing through Stephan's transmitted vision of the explosion, and all that followed it. The memory wasn't hard to locate as it seemed that Stephan was standing right there next to them when she said to Roman they were over.

"Did you have anything to do with this, other than what I already know you did?" she asked.

"What do you mean?"

"You were very adamant about stalling me when I wanted to get into Jensine's house. Why?"

"I didn't want you going in there. It was too dangerous."

"Did you know the house was going to blow up? Is that why you held me back?"

From Roman's expression, she knew he finally understood what she meant. "I had nothing to do with Jensine's death." His voice got louder. "I cannot believe you would think that I—"

"Why wouldn't I?" she cut him off, matching his volume and tone. "You're the one who reported her to The Great Order authorities. I told you she didn't even know of the Clandestine World, only me, and to keep that between us. You took it to the world. It was my personal business, between a friend and me. It had nothing to do with you. You had no right."

Roman, jaw and fists clenched, said, "I have rules I have to abide by, Atlanta. Rules put in place to make her safe and keep us safe. That doesn't mean I killed her!"

"You as good as did!"

"Why is it so impossible for you to understand the rules of my people?"

She threw her good arm up in the air in exasperation, "*Your* people? They're *my* people too! Or don't you see me as really being a part of the Clandestine World because I don't breathe to serve Prince Phoenix Keziah? I promise you this, if The Great Order had anything to do with her death, I'll make you pay. I'll make you all pay."

"You're taking my words and twisting them around. Of course, you're part of our world. I meant the Order's rules, Atlanta. You consider them archaic, ancient, and useless."

"In some ways, yes, I do. It's the Twentieth Century. You all need to rethink these rules you live by. They didn't work out so well for Jensine!" She realized she was yelling and took a deep breath.

Roman did the same and said, "I'm sorry your friend has died because of your involvement with us. I am. More will die in this war, Atlanta. You have to accept that."

"How dare you use that as an excuse?" It was a cop-out at best and it pissed her off. "I don't have to accept anything, not on my watch, not if I can help it." Tears started down her face again.

Roman walked over and tried to take her hand, but she pulled it away. "No one would've known but Gray and I if I'd lied to you. But I was doing what I felt a girlfriend should do. I told my boyfriend the truth. I now see where that got me—my oldest friend dead. You may not have ordered the hit but you very well may have caused it because you were following orders. I don't know anymore, Roman. I thought I was falling in love with you. I trusted you with my heart and my friends' lives. But now…"

"What are you saying?" he whispered.

She swallowed, wishing for water. There was no easy way to do this. "If I'd kept my mouth shut, hell, if you had just done what I asked, we'd not be here. I trusted you and you betrayed me—you betrayed *her*." She took a deep breath and tears returned. "I hate myself for trusting you. It's not something I can push past so yes, I meant what I said last night." Her voice hitched and she wiped tears from her face, trying not to sob uncontrollably. "I can't be with someone I can't trust. I'm sorry, Roman, I really am. But right now—I honestly can't even bear the sight of you. So no, we can't be together." Her control was slipping. "Jensine," she whispered as the sobs came in a rush of sorrow that hurt in her soul.

Roman stood beside the bed, looking like he wanted to fight for her but unaware of how. He tried to take her hand again. She yanked it away as if his hand were a burning ember.

He pulled a handkerchief out and set it on the bed. "I hope someday you can see that I was trying to keep her safe because of how I feel about you. I'm so very sorry it doesn't seem that way. I know you've made up your mind. I guess I ask that as things unfold you don't close your heart to my good intentions."

Atlanta reluctantly reached for the handkerchief. In that opening, Roman moved so fast, that he was able to get a hold of her hand in his before she could pull away. "Look at me," he demanded. It was said so passionately, she did. "I still love you. I suppose I ask...you try, in time, to understand my side of this."

"Do you think Jensine understands?" she snapped, yanking her hand back. She knew it was a low blow but she didn't care.

"I suppose not. I hope that someday you can at least forgive me, and more importantly, yourself." With that he put his hands in his pockets, defeated, and started to leave the room. With one look at her he added, "I know I broke your heart and I'm truly sorry. But you have broken mine, probably more than you know."

He opened the door and walked out. Before it shut she heard him say, "Take care of her."

It was Sean who answered, "I will."

Gray came in to her first. His face showed he'd heard everything.

She reached for him. She needed to grieve with him. "Gray..."

He rushed to her, sat on the edge of the bed, and wrapped his arms about her. She let herself cry on his shoulder until she felt empty of tears. She went to blow her nose in the handkerchief, but Gray handed her the Kleenex box. "You'll fill that in seconds, use these." He took one as well.

It took a while, but finally she got herself dried up and calmed down. "I can't breathe," she finally whined.

"I would think not, you've swollen up that pretty nose of yours." He touched her nose and tried to smile, wiping his own tears away before kissing the top of her head.

She tried to smile. "Thanks again for bringing my stuff."

"You're welcome, baby." He rested his forehead on her left temple. "And Roman is right. You can't beat yourself up for this forever."

"I know. I just feel like it's mostly my fault. If I'd had the balls to tell her in person instead of writing that letter—if I'd not told him—"

The tears started to run down her face again and she felt someone touch her leg. It was Sean. "Shhh...you need to stop talking and get some rest."

She nodded.

"I'm going to head out with Stephan, if it's okay with you, baby girl," Gray asked as he stood up.

She nodded again and wiped her eyes. Gray leaned down to kiss her nose and petted her hair. "I'll call you tomorrow. Your phone is over here and charged."

"Okay, thanks."

Gray left and she looked at Sean, whose skin held a warm glow. As he stepped closer to her, she reached up and touched his face and it was warm like a humans. "Wow, you feel alive."

"I got a blood pack while you were fighting with Roman."

She nodded and hit the remote to lay the bed down. She turned onto her right side and gazed at Sean. Through all this, she still wanted him near her. She wasn't sure how much of it was thrall and how much was just wanting him to hold her, to try to fill the hole clawed in her soul. "Care to join me up here again?" she asked him meekly.

"Thought you'd never ask." He switched the light off, removed his shoes, and climbed onto the bed.

"At least until a nurse kicks you out."

"Oh, they won't. It's a Clandestine floor. Different rules."

"I should've known."

He chuckled and she nuzzled her head under his warm chin.

"Sean?"

"Yeah?"

"I'm sure you heard my conversation with Roman."

He paused. "Sugar, we all did."

"Oh." She felt slightly embarrassed.

"And?" he asked.

"Well, I didn't do that because of...you know, thrall."

He smiled. "I know that."

"You do?"

He took her hand and kissed her fingers. "I spoke to Stephan. We agreed you're not in thrall anymore. Too many chemicals and fluids pumped into your system."

"What?" She pulled away from Sean so she could see his face.

"You heard me."

"Then..."

"What?"

"Nothing."

"Be honest with me, Atty. You're a witch. I can't read your mind unless you let me."

She needed to think. If it wasn't thrall, then she truly wanted him here. Not only that, but she wanted him there not just as a friend. The electricity she'd felt the day he'd stepped into Roman's house was there again as she reached to touch his face. He closed his eyes and leaned into her hand.

Sean wasn't her usual type: Roman was. They were night and day. Yet she couldn't ignore the pull to this man—this good man. She worried though that she was projecting.

"I only thought to say...that my wanting you here is genuine."

"You want someone here, or you want me here?"

"You." She let her thumb caress his cheekbone. "Do you feel that? The hum? Did you feel it the day you walked into the house?"

His eyes stayed closed as he only nodded.

She swallowed. "I thought it was just me."

His eyes opened and held a glow she'd not seen before. "I felt it. I feel it now."

"Is that why your eyes are glowing?"

He closed them. "Sorry, it's your touch."

She leaned in so her nose bumped his. "I'm not going to jump into a new relationship, Sean. I'm still figuring things out. Can you be patient with me? Can we…I don't know, spend time together? Take this slow? Oh man, that sounds stupid." She dropped her head down, her chest feeling tight.

He slowly kissed her forehead, letting his lips linger. He inhaled her scent before settling his cheek there instead. She felt his body shudder lightly. "It does not sound stupid. I'm here when you're ready—'cause you eventually will be. I can live with just time spent getting to know each other. I can. I really, really can."

Atlanta pulled back again to see his face so she could see if he was being genuine. Seeing his smile, the tightness in her chest faded and Atlanta tenderly ran her fingers through his curls. "Okay. Good."

She leaned in and kissed him on the mouth softly and slowly. It felt good. It wasn't more than a gentle kiss, but it felt full of heart.

He hummed a light whimper of pleasure before their lips parted and they said goodnight.

* * * *

Atlanta awoke to something tickling her nose. Reaching up, she touched her nose but nothing was there. The tickling returned, and this time she moved faster and caught him.

"Sean, stop tickling my nose with my hair."

"Morning."

"Not funny."

"Sorry. I needed to wake you up before the nurses come in the next half hour."

She opened one eye at him. "Why?"

"I have an offer I want you to think about."

She shut her eye. "Okay, what is it?"

"I can heal your arm."

"So can Desi once I let her get a water cast on this bad boy. It'll be in good shape in two weeks and normal in a month."

"I can heal it today."

Atlanta's one eye opened again. "Are you screwin' with me, Mr. Cameron?"

"No…but if you'd like…"

"Funny funny, ha ha." She fought off a smile.

"Sorry, couldn't resist. But no, I'm not kidding you either."

Both her eyes were open now and she started to wake up. "How?"

"It's no fun."

"Sometimes the stuff that needs to be done isn't fun. What do I have to do? Drink your blood?"

"Uh, yeah."

"Oh! I was kidding."

"Yeah, I'm not."

"That sounds gross, you know."

"I know. But your arm will heal today. We don't normally do this. It's frowned upon. But you need that arm at one hundred percent sooner than in a month."

"What about—"

"It doesn't cause thrall. You'll feel bonded to me, but not in a sexual way. It's my saliva in your blood that causes thrall."

"What other side effects are there?"

"Well, you'll be sensitive to the sun. It'll bother your eyes. You may have some extra strength and speed as well, only for today and tomorrow. Then it'll thin out in your system and be gone."

Atlanta thought this sounded like a win-win situation, which gave her pause. She took a moment to consider the offer. "What are the other drawbacks?"

He started to tick things off on his fingers. "Probably a craving for rare steak. Your sense of smell will become better, and that's not always a good thing, as will your hearing, which can also be annoying until you are accustomed to it."

"You're stalling. Spit it out, Sean."

"I am, aren't I? Okay. Here's the thing—it's a bit invasive. We'll each be able to feel the other person's soul. It'll hurt: me physically when the connection begins— you mentally, when the connection breaks."

Atlanta realized this was one more step from being normal. But if she was going to catch Jen's killer she needed to be in better shape than she was now. She took a deep breath, let it out, and said, "Okay. Let's do this then."

He touched her face. "Are you sure? I don't want you seeing me as some ungodly creature because of this."

"I won't."

"Ok." Sean took off his shirt and she touched his skin, which still held the heat of sleeping next to her. His chest, smooth and defined in all the right places, drew her attention more to his physical body than what he did at first.

He reached into his back pocket and pulled out a small twig that he'd broken in such a way that the end was sharp. Dragging it across his pectoral muscle, an inch or two below his collarbone, the skin opened up and blood welled up, trickling down his chest.

"It'll heal fast, so I need you to drink from me now."

"I cannot believe I'm going to do this," she muttered and looked into his eyes. Interestingly enough, she found strength in his gaze. If he would do this for her, she should be willing to do it for Jensine. She curled up on her side and he wrapped around her. As her lips approached his skin, she felt him brace himself and asked, "When will I have had enough?"

"I'll tell you."

And with that, she let her tongue touch his skin. He let out a small shuddering sigh and then she tasted the blood. It wasn't like human blood. Not coppery or bitter. Sort of sweet and warm like cider, but not too sweet. Her lips closed in on the wound and as she drank she felt his body give one big jolt and then he relaxed and wrapped around her. She could hear him in her head as if they were speaking mentally, but this was his body and mind speaking to her, not his thoughts. It was as if she were him.

It was a rush—emotional where the psychic sex had been physical. She knew in seconds the depth of how he cared for her, how he wanted to protect and provide for her. The love he felt overwhelmed her. Tears ran down her face as she drank and she felt like if she wanted, she had the power to work herself into his private thoughts and rummage around like one does with an old trunk of things. But she didn't want to be nosy.

She heard him mentally say, *"Thank you."* Then without warning he added, *"That's all you need."*

He pushed her away and the mental disconnection hurt, like a part of herself had been removed. Crying out, her eyes opened in time to see the opening on his chest close on its own, healing without a mark. She licked off the last of the blood on his chest and he shuddered again before he scooted down in the bed so that his face evened out with hers. He wiped her mouth a touch.

"You barely spilled any. You'd make a good vampire," he teased.

"Gee, thanks."

"How do you feel?"

She felt different, weird, but strong—very strong. It also wasn't as dark in the room anymore. Then she realized she heard a bit better too. "I can hear the nurses out front talking about the guy one of them is seeing…"

"Stop eavesdropping, missy!" he said with a wink, "I told you, it's something you have to get used to. You'll need to leave your arm in the cast for the rest of the day, but tonight we'll take it off."

"Okay."

Sean put his shirt on and took a stroll to the blood bank as the nurse came in to check her vitals. The nurse informed her that once the doctor signed off on it, she would recommend they let her leave.

Atlanta looked at the time. She'd barley been there over twenty-four hours, yet it felt like days. Not because she hated hospitals, but because of all that'd happened since she'd gotten there.

Stepping out into the sunlight Atlanta put her sunglasses on," Holy crap it's bright out!"

"Told ya. And you wondered why I always have a pair on."

"Wow—you really see it this bright. Man, it's almost painful."

Once home she followed the doctor's instructions to rest. Vampire blood in her veins or no, it felt good to sleep in her own bed and relax. Yet once she got to the meeting tonight at Phoenix's, it would be a completely new game.

* * * *

Valencia sat deep in thought. Things were going well, though not as she'd foreseen. On top of that, there were new recruits to deal with and train. First, there was a newly bitten human who was a nervous wreck of emotional trauma. Second, was a werewolf. He had attitude to spare and a questionable history.

"Young people. Always making their life dramatic. Nothing ever changes," she muttered with a sigh before picking up the phone to call to have them brought up to her chambers. Following which, she called Jonathan. He'd keep her sane.

"Where are you?" she demanded.

"I'm in the training room," he sounded out of breath. "How can I serve you?"

"Are we ready for tonight?"

"We are."

"Good. I am about to meet with the new recruits. Care to join me?"

"I would."

"Very well. Come up." She hung up the phone and pulled her hair into a loose ponytail, taking a seat in one of the big, green velvet chairs, to wait. Both of these new recruits were interesting. The young woman arrived with Jonathan last night here at the upstate New York headquarters. The young man was a referral of one of her best computer men up at Asmarahald, her primary base of operations located in the Quebec Providence of Canada.

Valencia flipped through their paperwork on her clipboard. She noticed the young woman's real name, but that she'd chosen a Clandestine World nickname. Most did. Mercury, her bi-colored eyed cougar, had been born Penelope. She'd felt that with her unique eyes, she deserved a more interesting name and had changed it. Like Mercury, Pip came to The Superior order a freshly bitten human, soon to be shape shifter.

The werewolf, on the other hand, had a slight rap sheet. He was reckless. Question was could he follow orders? They were one man short for tonight's job. She was considering adding him to the crew to see how he did. It would be a good test. Leafing through his paperwork, she saw his new name and thought how fitting it was.

General McMasters knocked on Valencia's door and without hesitation led the two new recruits into her office. As they sat on her couch without uttering a word, she noted that they both were on the shorter side of norm for their sexes. The girl ran her hand nervously over her shaved head. Her green-hazel eyes darted about the room taking everything in as she sat Indian style on the couch.

The young man sat on the edge of the couch. With elbows on knees, he leaned forward and stared at Valencia, making the sound you hear when someone is trying to suck food out of their teeth. Thus making it obvious he didn't feel like he needed to be there.

Valencia excused the General and spent a moment inspecting them. She addressed the young man first. "Greyhound, right?" His slanted catlike blue eyes only stared back at her without any confirmation or denial to the question. "I'll take that as a yes. So, Greyhound, I've reviewed your rap sheet here. I see you tend to be a little bit of trouble. My question is, are you the right kind of trouble for my team?" She focused then on the girl. "I'm not going to hurt you, you know. You can breathe normally and calm down. I can smell how scared you are. You're with family here, little one."

A knock at the door came and in walked Jonathan. His tall, lanky yet toned form, walked so smoothly across the room it seemed almost as if he glided.

"Ah, thank you for coming darling. I only just started."

"Glad to come." He sat in the other velvet chair, running a hand through his shoulder length white-blonde hair.

Every bone in the girl's petite body became tense. Her eyes darted to Jonathan and then Valencia.

Valencia's tone softened as she evaluated the young girl. "He's not going to hurt you. Neither am I. Relax."

The girl took a breath and slowly exhaled with what seemed like a conscious choice to try to appear less tense. It didn't work well for her.

"That's…better? Now, I understand you wish to go by the name Pip?" The girl nodded. "I understand you're healing from a panther bite, am I correct?" Again, the girl nodded. "Well, I know you must be scared but know you're home here with us."

"Who exactly is 'us'?" Greyhound finally asked, rubbing his short grey goatee, which matched his head of short silver-grey hair. "What exactly do you do?"

Valencia looked at his young face. "I'm glad you asked. My name is Mistress Valencia and I am the leader of a group called The Superior Order. We are part of something called the Clandestine World. You two are a part of that world now. Let me explain."

* * * *

Sean turned his motorcycle onto the Keziah property. Following the long paved road through the trees, he finally arrived at the driveway to mansion. He parked on the side about halfway up and helped Atlanta off the back.

Atlanta noticed quickly that much like Devon's mansion, the Keziah estate was large, with multiple levels, and made of a dark brick. However, where Devon's home had a large side yard with few trees perfect for rituals, the Keziah estate had no open space. Trees hugged the house almost at every corner.

Sean glanced at the sky. "The sun set only a few moments ago. We'll be early."

"Oh well, gives us a chance to look around," she said as they approached the door.

Atlanta was disappointed though, for the butler led them to the meeting room and left them there. The entire room was elegant yet felt quite business-like. It contained a black leather sofa with a glossy end table at each end. Matching leather chairs surrounded a long, smoky glassed conference table, and above it hung a tinted skylight. Exquisite oil paintings covered the walls. One of which caught her attention—three foot by five-foot portrait of a man who looked a bit like Phoenix and she wondered if it might be his father.

Another painting held Phoenix and his brother, Harmon, and a third painting contained a family portrait. Roman and two older men accompanied Phoenix and Harmon this time. The beautiful woman standing between the brothers she assumed to be Elizabeth. She was tall, with long blonde hair, and blue eyes like Roman's. Even Harmon was smiling, which she'd never seen him do. In fact, his hand wound around Elizabeth's waist.

Atlanta wondered how old these painting were. How many years had they all been close? Was she asking mountains to move by wanting Roman to not follow family rules? Did she have the right to expect that to change?

Sean's arm wound around her waist, his chin resting on her shoulder as her mind returned to the present. "They all seemed so happy then, didn't they?"

"Yeah…" her voice trail off. "I think they all loved her so dearly that her death ripped everyone's world apart. She sure was beautiful."

Sean's tone softened. "This doesn't even compare to her in person. Her eyes had this glow that no painting or photo can capture. Definitely one of the best people I ever knew. You remind me of her a bit. I wonder if anyone else has noticed that."

"More than one of us has," came a voice from behind them. Atlanta didn't need to turn around to know it was Roman.

Sean let go of her quickly, out of respect for him. She didn't think Roman even noticed the gesture as he was too busy gathering the right words. "You knew my sister? How the bloody hell could you have known her?"

Sean looked at Atlanta and then at Roman. She knew he was trying to figure out what exactly he could and couldn't say, still bound by his promise to Elizabeth. "She taught me to fight," he explained finally. "I was in captivity in the dungeons of The Superior Order when she was there. I was weak and lost and she gave me hope. Lizzie was an amazing woman. She is the reason I am who I am today. Your sister was a bright shining part of my life. She saved me."

Each of his sentences were true, but they were in the wrong order. He hadn't lied, really, only misled those to believe she taught him to fight after he was a vampire and captured. She thought Roman might pick apart his sentences, but instead he only said one word.

"Lizzie?"

The room went quiet for a second before Sean produced an answer. "Yes, she asked me to call her that. I understand you all prefer to call her Elizabeth. I'm sorry I slipped."

Roman walked closer to Sean. "I'm going to ask you one question and you better tell me the truth, or so help me goddess your body will not ever fit back together."

"Ok…?"

"Did you have anything to do with her death?"

Sean stiffened. Atlanta was pretty sure no one in the room was breathing. "I was there when she died, but I had no hand in it. I'd have given my life, in fact I tried to offer it in exchange for Liz…I mean Elizabeth's release. Sorry."

"No need to apologize. If she told you to call her Lizzie, you may." Roman placed a hand on Sean's shoulder. "You and I must talk more of this."

Sean finally relaxed and nodded. "Anything for Lizzie," Sean agreed.

Atlanta reached out to Stephan mentally. *"What's the big deal with the nickname?"*

"She only let family call her that. She was very strict about it. That says a lot to Roman about Sean."

"Then why does Roman call her Elizabeth?"

"It was sort of their little teasing game. If he called her Elizabeth when she wanted Liz or Lizzie, she would call him Ro or Rome, 'cause he likes the full sound of Roman."

Atlanta understood a lot more now. She understood why having Sean call him Ro or Rome hurt and annoyed him. She understood why Sean would have even thought of calling him either. Lastly, she understood that Roman now held respect for Sean seeing as his sister saw him as family.

She probably would've sat there pondering everyone's existence and what it meant if Phoenix hadn't entered the room and broken the trance. "Your sisters and Gray are coming up the drive now," he addressed to Atlanta. "As soon as they arrive we'll begin."

Chapter Three

They all sat around the table, Phoenix at the head. Desi was so tiny she needed to boost her chair up, making her feet not touch the ground. Atlanta smiled at her. Desi flipped her off. Gray laughed and Phoenix cleared his throat. "Let's begin."

Phoenix explained they'd searched everywhere for Devon, to no avail. It had been decided he died in the explosion and a service would be held for him next week. Atlanta felt it a bit hasty, but as they weren't torn up by the news, they all agreed. Celeste brought up his amazing house. Phoenix admitted to helping him pay for it so it would be Phoenix's now.

"Devon would've wanted his home enjoyed. My plan is to use it for the good of The Great Order—hold gatherings there, parties in the ballroom, and meetings. We also thought of turning the servants' quarters out back into a shelter of sorts. A place some of the younger Clandestine can stay when their family either goes to battle or must leave town for missions. The problem is that we need to staff all of this," Phoenix said. "Sean, we were wondering if you'd be interested in running the shelter. We feel your background and skills would benefit the Order greatly in this job."

"It will be a paid job, so you can stop squatting at the professor's home," Stephan pointed out.

Atlanta knew Sean was shocked and touched. His face sort of glowed. "Of course. I'd be honored to run that house."

"Fantastic," Phoenix said.

"Sounds wonderful!" Desi agreed with much glee, and everyone chimed in.

"What about the actual mansion?" Celeste asked.

"Well, I think having you ladies all scattered about the city is ridiculous—all the calling and driving. The house will be headquarters for everything we do for this war. It's set back from the street and almost unnoticeable. We'll have you four move in as soon as possible."

Gray piped up, "Hold on there, chief. I'm not leaving my girl, so we need to think of another plan."

"I thought you might feel that way, so I have arranged for you to be on the payroll as the ladies' assistant. If you'd like, you can also set up a hair salon. You could be the Great Order's official stylist." Phoenix grinned, pleased with his plan. It was clear from Gray's face he didn't hate the plan too much himself.

Phoenix went on, "The large house is already furnished, yet the floors you all will live on are being cleaned right now. As we speak, furniture for the small house is being ordered. The sale will not be final until Sean okays it all. Please see Crone Brenner of the Circle after you leave here," he said to Sean, who nodded. "I will admit that the servant house is a mess and needs cleaning. I trust you all won't mind saving The Great Order some money and doing that in exchange for getting to move into the biggest house in town, yes?"

Everyone agreed, of course, and when the excitement calmed down Phoenix turned a page in his book. "Now, about Jensine."

The room became very quiet and Sean touched Atlanta's knee under the table. She casually laid her hands in her lap and he took her hand.

"You know most of this already. C4 was set to go off in Mrs. Winter's apartment downstairs. Also, the police are not certain the remains are Jensine's. Build was the same but as they can't find the head, it's hard to tell. Atlanta, did Jensine have any injuries that we might use for identification?"

Atlanta shook her head. She felt nauseous at the thought of a head being removed from someone's body, and she was sure she turned a bit pale.

"I suspect that whoever did this broke the victim's neck first and then removed it so we couldn't identify the body. That said, the chance that Jensine isn't the victim is possible. We are not going to stop the search for her. The investigation stays open amongst us, but I want the police and The Superior Order to think it's an open and shut case. That is very important."

"Who was watching her at the time?" Atlanta asked.

"One of my shape shifters, but she is also missing. The last entry in her log says that Devon showed up and told her to go on a dinner break."

"Gee, your girl wouldn't happen to be a big shape-shifting cat, would she?" Gray asked through clenched teeth.

Atlanta braced herself and said what was on her mind. "I don't think this was a Superior Order hit. All the clues point to The Great Order. I suggest that you examine your own people, sir. I'm thinking that someone in this organization is dirty. If I find out who they are, they will die a slow and painful death, and they too will never be found. Do I make myself understood, Prince?"

Phoenix's expression held a mixture of compassion and irritation. "Atlanta, the only people who knew that Jensine was an informed human were those in this room, the Clandestine Protection Agency, and the few members of my protection squad who were watching her."

"And I rest my case."

"Atlanta, you're not suggesting one of us here at the table had anything to do with this do you?" Celeste asked, shocked.

She glanced from Roman to Phoenix and then focused on Celeste. "I honestly believe no one at this table had anything to do with it. We all may want to remember who we spoke to that might have taken matters into their own hands. I'm not saying it was done on purpose...yet. However, we all need to think about who knew and what we may have said within earshot of someone else, and so on. That's all I ask of the Council—to investigate itself as well as others."

Silence fell until Gray spoke. "Was Harmon around when you spoke to Phoenix, Roman?"

Roman spoke up. "Only if he eavesdropped. We didn't even know where he was at the time. But with Harmon that doesn't mean he wasn't nearby, listening. He's like that."

"I will investigate everyone, including the members of The Great Order. You have made a very good observation and it deserves recognition. I will investigate every possibility for you," Phoenix agreed.

To be honest, she thought he'd have put up a huge fight. That he agreed so easily made her wary. But she kept her mouth shut, for the moment. "Thank you, sir."

"Moving on, then," he said. "I would like to have this group meet once a week as we move forward into this war. I want all of you to start training. I know that the girls have been working with Atlanta—"

"Hey, Gray and I are not girls." Sean feigned mock irritation.

"Speak for yourself, honey." Gray snapped his finger and they all laughed.

"As I was saying, there has been some training, but I want you to have more. The CPA will be joining you on your workouts. Is your current spot big enough to add six more guys?"

"It's half the size of a high school gym in there. But we may not always be able to use it. There are dance lessons in there daily."

"What about getting some mats for the new house and use the ballroom," Atlanta suggested.

"Consider it done," Phoenix made a note. "Okay, so we have a lot of work to redo this house. Expect the CPA there tomorrow to start loading in weapons for the arsenal."

Atlanta looked at Gray and he mouthed "arsenal?"

"You are all to be trained on sword and bow as well as hand-to-hand combat and the Bo-Staff work you've been doing," Phoenix continued.

"What about guns? Don't these people use guns?" Gray asked.

"Guns don't kill vampires. A werewolf or a shape shifter can be killed with a gun, but the bullets must be silver. So the Clandestine World uses arrows with silver arrowheads in battle, or silver swords. To us, it's more civilized."

"A gun is simpler," Gray stated.

"And it's louder," Roman stated. "We like to keep a low profile."

"A war that's low profile...now this I gotta see," Gray teased. Sean, Stephan, and Atlanta all stifled a snicker.

"As we are speaking of weapons—I have a gift for the five ladies and Sean," Phoenix said with a smile for Gray, who seemed very pleased. "I had the head of the Wiccan house working with the werewolves on this one."

He lifted a small bag off of the floor and set it on the table, reaching in to pull out what looked like a tiny wooden stake. It couldn't have been more than six inches from tip to end. He placed six of them on the table.

"These are for our non-vampire fighters and Sean, as he's part of their team," he tossed one to each of the girls, Sean, and Gray. Standing up and backing away from the table, he demonstrated. "Watch first, and don't do this until you see how much space you need. Now, grasp it with your hand and hold it away from your body, like so. Don't point either end toward your body for this. Now, say 'expositus.'"

Magically, the tiny stake elongated to twelve inches.

"Damn," Gray said.

"That's not all, if you say 'expositus prolix'..." The stake jumped to the size of a Bo-staff with a pointy tip.

Now it was Atlanta's chance to be impressed, "Sweet!"

The girls, Gray, Sean, and Atlanta stood up and tried theirs out. For a few, they opened so fast the weapons fell to the floor, while others had trouble just getting them to open. After a bit of practice though, most had it down.

"They are made of wood, magically strengthened to withstand three times the amount of weight a normal Bo-Staff does," Phoenix told them. "The only person who can open or close it is the one holding it. You have to be touching it for it to work. Now, to shorten the staff to the stake you only need to say 'termino' and to close it all the way say 'termino omnis.'"

"Whatever happened to using English?" Gray inquired with a laugh.

"Latin is preferred by the old ones. Plus, if someone who's not of our world finds it, it's nothing but a tiny stake and they can't open it on accident."

"Point made. No pun intended," Gray added with a sheepish grin.

"Carry these at all times. If a war is coming then we need to be armed."

Everyone nodded in agreement.

"All right, with that I think we're done here. I want you all moved into the house in the next week. If you cannot get out of your lease, Atlanta, please call me and I'll have the Mayor make a call to your landlord."

"I actually own my apartment. It's paid for in full, so I'll put it on the market or rent it out." This broke her heart. She loved her apartment. Gray and she had many fun memories there. The thought of letting it go upset her.

With a sigh, Atlanta got up from the table to follow everyone out into the foyer. She glanced about for the butler, but she didn't see him. They all were talking frantically about the move.

"How long will it take for you two to get packed?" Stephan asked.

"I can be packed by the end of the week," Gray replied. "Not so sure about Ms. Pack Rat over there."

"Hey, I have a lot of books from school and old lesson plans. I may need them again, you never know."

"And the clothes you never wear?"

"Same."

"Okay, okay," Sean put a hand up. "We get it. Atlanta needs help getting packed up then?"

She huffed out a breath. She hated asking for help.

"I can help you," Celeste told her.

Desi and Bianca chimed in with the same.

"Thanks."

"Let me walk you all out," Phoenix offered as he opened the door.

Atlanta and Sean headed out into the front yard, getting almost to the bike when Roman started his car, an industrial song blaring as the car came to life. Atlanta was busy trying to place which song it was when it happened.

Ambush.

Arrows showered down over them from the trees above. Atlanta felt each arrowhead as it penetrated the skin on her back, and the pain that followed. A fourth shot went into her upper thigh before she found her wits and blocked them. She screamed out in pain and fear as she saw Gray stop, drop and roll under his Jeep. The girls, who'd been close to the door, grabbed Phoenix and pulled him inside. The air barrier she'd put up held both Sean and herself.

"Brace yourself," he told her and then pulled each arrow from her back.

Atlanta swore as she yanked an arrow out of her thigh. Turning her attention back to the assault, Atlanta noted that the arrows had stopped raining down. However, people now leapt from the trees, attacking her friends without missing a step.

"These will heal up in moments due to my blood in your system. You should be okay. How do you feel?"

Surprisingly she didn't hurt from any of the entry wounds. "You're right, I feel fine now that they're out." She looked around at the fight going on. "I can protect us all day, but—"

"The two best fighters not fighting is bad for everyone else," he interjected. "You okay to fight?"

She nodded and grabbed their new weapons from her bag, handed him his and opened the air barrier.

"Expositus Prolix!" She and Sean shouted at the same time, opening up their Bo-Staff's with the pointed tip.

"I have to get to Gray!" She yelled out and they both fought their way through the people trying to get toward the house where the Jeep sat. Gray now rolled out from under it and opened his stake. She watched as he dusted his attacker.

"They're vampires?" She asked in surprise. "Good to know." She tossed her bag off and under a car.

Sean and she then split up. He went to help the girls and Atlanta continued toward Gray, Roman, and Stephan. As she ran in that direction, Atlanta got sandwiched between two vampires. She felt strong and fast. It didn't take her long to stake the vamp behind her as she kicked the one in front of her.

They needed Roman and Stephan in the fight but they were trapped in their car, surrounded by vampires. Spinning the staff around she mentally yelled out to Stephan and Roman, *"Get ready to go out and up!"*

Running at full speed, which was faster than her usual, Atlanta ran up onto the hard top of the Jeep's hood. Seeing what she was doing, Sean worked at keeping the vamps at her feet from getting up to her. She concentrated hard on where she needed the air to go. But it was going to take more than just her.

"Ladies!" she yelled out.

Desi, Bianca, and Celeste had one vamp between them. Quickly, they fought him off and ran for the Jeep. As soon as they all were on top of the Jeep with her, hand on Atlanta's shoulders, she sent the air. It moved from outside into the windows of Roman's car and then shoved through the front windshield, spewing glass everywhere as the air held, protected and lifted Roman and Stephen through it and up into the air. She brought them down behind the vamps that'd been surrounding the car.

The minute they landed all the vamps, none of which she recognized from the club, that had been trying to get at Roman and Stephan turned their attention toward her and the girls. One dove at Atlanta and knocked her off the top of the Jeep, sending her staff rolling out of her grasp. She couldn't reach it so she decided to try her best at hand to hand with them.

Normally she was sure they'd be too strong for her, but with Sean's blood in her veins and her training, she was a decent match for the one that got to her. The vampire seemed surprised she was doing so well. He held his own well enough until she backhanded him with her cast, stunning him, and followed it up with a roundhouse kick. He landed far enough away that she was able to get her staff. When he charged her again, she dusted him, his clothes falling to the ground.

In the moment of quiet, she whirled about, staff ready, to see how everyone else was doing. With Stephan and Roman in the fight, they had fought through the rest of their attackers. They even had two prisoners. Then she noticed the front door was open.

"Phoenix," was all she said, and Roman and Stephan ran toward the house.

"Celeste, where did he go?" Roman called.

"Secret passage. He should be fine. The ones that ran in went up the stairs toward the library vault. Is there anything else in there they'd want?"

Roman and Stephan looked at each other. "Shit." They disappeared into the house at a run.

"Stay with these guys, I'm going after those two as their back up," Sean shouted as he ran into the house.

Atlanta would've protested but he was gone so fast it didn't matter. Instead, she went outside to Gray and the girls, staff in hand.

"You guys okay?"

Celeste stared at her strangely. "The question is, are you? Look at your arm!"

Atlanta hadn't noticed it in the fight, but it seemed her last hit to the vamp had shattered her cast and it was lying on the ground twenty feet away.

She winced, seeing the pieces of her cast in the driveway. "Yeah, about that—" she started to say but didn't finish as a knife was at her throat.

"Drop your staff, sweetheart. I ain't playin'. All of you, put them down or I slice her throat like a Thanksgiving turkey."

"Seriously?" Bianca asked, her tone lighter than Atlanta would've liked.

"So cliché," Celeste commented.

"Totally without class," Desi agreed.

The three girls all looked at each other and then back to him saying together, "Werewolf."

Atlanta was completely lost, wondering what they were doing, and trying not to freak out when she heard Bianca in her head, *"We got you, girl. Don't panic."*

Easy for them to say, she was totally panicking. Sean's blood in her or not, she didn't think she'd survive her throat being slashed. She tried to calm down, but she couldn't until she caught Celeste's eye and she smiled at her before closing her eyes and mumbling under her breath. She was going to do a spell.

The girls put their staffs down and stepped away. Atlanta did her best to place her hand between her captor's hand and her throat, but he was stronger than her by far.

"You think you can overpower me?" he taunted. "I'm the great—"

Atlanta felt a tiny shake, and put a shelf of air beneath her as the ground opened up and swallowed him, the knife nicking her chin as he went down. They all peered down at him, encased in a tube of earth.

"The great what, loser? Don't mess with witches, you moron," Bianca told him.

The all started laughing and Atlanta stepped onto solid concrete in front of the door to the mansion. That's when she felt it. Like a hot spear had been shoved into her side. She looked down and the blood started to pour out of a hole in the right of her abdomen.

Had she been shot? A look of confusion crossed her face as she dropped to her knees. A man came running out of the house, a gun in one hand, and a book in the other. He leapt over Atlanta easily and once he was a bit of a ways away, he turned, seeing her fallen yet still alive. Something between a smile and a grimace crossed his young face, which didn't match his short silver-gray hair.

He lifted the gun again and aimed. She froze. It all happened so fast she couldn't move. But someone else did. She felt her body lifted and rolled along the ground as the bullet hit the house instead of her. After they stopped rolling she looked up in time to see Roman running after the guy with the book. As he reached within ten feet of him though, the gray haired young man slammed something onto the ground, and he was gone in smoke, like the wicked witch in the Wizard of Oz.

Roman screamed out in anger, his arms slicing through the smoke to see if the man or the book were there. Movement by the door caught her attention. Running out of the house, carrying an injured Stephan, was Sean. That's when she realized it wasn't one of them who'd saved her. She turned to see who it was, and laying there next to her was Harmon.

* * * *

It took hours for everyone to get looked at by Dr. Boswell, who insisted they call him by his first name, Thomas. He was the Great Order's physician. He was a nice guy, tall and thin, and a mix of Asian and Caucasian. Though young to be a doctor, as a witch of the earth and water family he had a knack for healing the body. Stephan had been seen to first, as he had an arrow in his back that had lodged just under his heart. Thomas used a special machine to help him see which way the head of the arrow was twisted, so he could remove it without nicking the heart itself.

Sean and Atlanta had been having a very quiet but intense discussion about how it was going to be very apparent to Thomas, and everyone else, that she had vampire blood in her. The bullet had gone clean in and out, and the hole had healed up during the past hour. She'd have been priority but she wasn't bleeding. The only mark on her was a tiny spot on her stomach where the bullet had come out.

"He's going to know. The question is, will he make a big deal of it or just move on," Sean speculated.

"You're Atlanta?" Thomas asked as he approached them.

She felt her heart pick up the pace. "Yes."

"I need you to show me where you were injured. They told me you were shot in the side? Were you only grazed?"

"Must've been. I'm fine; you should probably attend to others."

"I can't do that ma'am, Phoenix's orders."

She internally groaned. That man and his orders were the bane of her existence. "I received three arrows in the back, one in the leg and a bullet went through my side."

Thomas' face showed shocked. He grabbed her wrist for a moment and then dropped it.

"I need you to take off your shirt. If you'd like, we can go into another room for privacy," Thomas offered.

"I'm fine doing it here." She was very happy she wasn't wearing a 'laundry day' bra all of a sudden. She pulled off her T-shirt and stood still in her black bra, letting the good doctor examine her back and side. He scribbled notes, then brought his machine over and looked at her internal organs. He scribbled some more.

"You can put your shirt on." She did so as he stared at his notes, his face pinched. Finally he spoke. "You are human."

It was a statement, not a question, but she answered him anyway, "I'm a witch."

"How is it all of your wounds are healing themselves? The gunshot wound is taking the longest, but as I looked on my screen, I saw all the internal tissue repairing as I watched. This is not something witch's blood can do." He stopped talking and she had no idea if she was to say anything or not.

Just then, Celeste, Bianca, and Desi sidled up. The only word that came to Atlanta's mind was, "damn."

But instead, Celeste stared her down and said, "Yes, it is only something vampire blood can do."

Atlanta took Sean's hand in hers and squeezed it. She had no idea what to do and needed to be honest, but it wasn't she that would be in trouble.

Sean, being the man he was, spoke up. "It's my blood healing her." Her friends stared at him silently, hands on hips. Sean let out a sigh. "I gave her some of my blood when we were in the hospital this morning so her arm would heal faster. We can't have our leader with a broken arm—" Desi started to interrupt but Sean cut her off, his voice rising. "—even for two weeks with a water cast. You know I'm right. Besides, if I hadn't done that she'd be in the hospital again right now, or dead. The arrows were only aimed at her. Did anyone else notice that? But, if you all want to yell at me, it's okay. I'll accept that consequence for saving her life today."

Atlanta squeezed his hand, then kissed it. The girls stood there looking very unhappy, but she could see they understood the logic of it all.

Bianca spoke up first. "I'm cool with it. Circumstances, I think, warrant leniency of some of The Great Order laws. But that's me. What do you think, Dez?"

"I think a cast like before would've been fine—if we'd not been ambushed. In hindsight it's a lucky break for Atty—and us, really."

"Desi, can you and Thomas come over here?" Gray yelled from across the room.

Desi went to the other side of the foyer with Bianca, who gave Atlanta a smile and a wink. Thomas followed, his face still pinched. Celeste knelt down in front of Sean and Atlanta, sitting on her feet.

"This is a dangerous slope. Sean, you have to tell her the rules about these things."

"This was a one-time thing, Celeste," Atlanta said.

"You say that now, but you've done it once and chances are you'll do it again. You can't do it three times too close together or you'll change. Please remember that."

This she hadn't known, but it wasn't too surprising. There had to be a catch, or vampires would do this for all humans who were ill or injured. Celeste stood up, kissed her on the forehead, and walked off.

The idea of becoming a vampire gave her goose bumps and not in a good way. She had no desire to be the undead, for multiple reasons. Primarily the blood drinking part. She still wasn't comfortable watching someone else drink it, let alone it be her.

She shuddered. "You should've told me that. But I understand why you didn't. You honestly plan on it being a one-time thing."

"Yes. I'd never damn you to this sort of life," he said, brushing a lock of her hair out of her face. "Besides, I'd miss seeing your eyes in the sunlight."

She leaned in and kissed him on the cheek, then rested her head on his shoulder. They watched the rest of the commotion around them. And it was a lot of commotion. Since Phoenix had been attacked and his book taken, the whole Boston Council of The Great Order were in house.

"Think we could sneak outta here without anyone noticing?" Sean asked.

"Nope."

"So we're stuck here."

"Yep."

"Lovely."

Across the room, Phoenix was having a long discussion with Harmon. Atlanta worried about what they were talking about. She tried to use the air to bring their conversation to her and instead of being able to hear them, she heard everyone in the room all at the same decibel. Harmon may have saved her life, yet somehow she knew it wasn't for her benefit, but for his own. He had an agenda, she could tell. She just wished she knew what it was. Suddenly she thought of something. "They promised me they'd keep my identity from Harmon. If they don't—"

"If they don't I will not fight for them. If they put you in extra danger I'm out."

"You'd leave?" She asked, as she lifted her head off his shoulder.

He touched her hair and then her face. "No, I would stay and protect you, but I wouldn't fight for The Great Order or do their bidding."

"Even the house for kids?"

He stopped to think about it. "I'd stay and do that so I could be near you to keep you safe, but I wouldn't be going off into battle."

"Now that, Mr. Cameron, is an acceptable answer."

He laughed.

Phoenix proved himself true to his word. As soon as the injured were seen to, they were all pulled back into the meeting room, except Harmon. It was explained to them that the Book of Great Order History was stolen.

This honestly didn't seem like that big of a deal to Atlanta, but to them it was a tragedy. As they spoke, she came to understand that everything was in this book. It was a collection of all that they'd done for decades. The volume stolen, the most recent, was full of information they'd not want The Superior Order to have.

There were always two guards assigned to these books. One had been killed by the other, a Superior Order mole, so to speak, and he'd helped the gray haired one get out with the book. The mole was who Celeste had captured in the earth.

Phoenix told them he could think of nothing he'd put into the book they'd want specifically. He would review his backup disk, to be sure. His significant look to her, told Atlanta her identity wasn't mentioned in the book. She nodded back at him once with a small smile.

All pass codes to the secret entrances and locks would have to be changed. The schedule of guards would have to be updated, new guards trained—the list went on and on. By the time the meeting was over it was very late and Atlanta was almost asleep on her feet. They all were escorted out of the mansion with full-armed guards. Sean and she were about to get on the bike when Celeste's car pulled up next to them.

"Tomorrow night, why don't we all meet up at the new Great Order house and take a look at what we need to furnish the rooms not yet renovated."

"And pick our bedrooms in the big house!" Desi suggested with a huge grin plastered on her face.

Sean smiled. It was obvious he'd forgotten that tiny ray of sunshine until now. "Of course.

We'll see you all there at six?"

"Deal. Drive safe, you two!" Celeste said. They waved as they pulled out.

Sean pulled out as well and headed out onto the main road. "Where to?"

"Home, please. I really want to get some rest. Tomorrow is a long day." She wrapped her arms around his waist and buried her cheek into his back.

"You got it." And they rode silently home.

Chapter Four

Yule

Atlanta slammed the heel of her hand onto the dashboard of Gray's Jeep as she drove toward the University. "You piece of shit heater! Come on! Of course, you choose today to stop working. Thank God it's not super freezing cold."

December twentieth was the last day of the semester as well as the day before Yule. Atlanta needed to go pick up the things from her office as she was done with both classes and her teaching for the year. Happily the snow had stopped, for it had been coming down steadily for days now, giving them a beautiful white blanket for the holidays.

Shivering in Gray's Jeep, she thought about the past several weeks. It had been crazy. Between getting packed, moving, unpacking, learning more Wicca, teaching her classes, giving exams, and spending any free time she had with Sean, Atlanta was surprised she had time for sleep. Not that she wanted to sleep. Most nights she dreamt of Jensine, the house exploding, and her friend burning to death. She was just happy Sean was there next to her when she woke up screaming. He never became irritated, which Atlanta though must be one of his super in-human powers.

Parking the vehicle, she pulled on a hat and scarf, and then swiftly headed toward the English building. The sun would be down soon and the campus Christmas decorations were starting to come on. Down in the valley there would be quite a display. As she walked, she considered going down to see them.

Halfway through her trudge to the building though, she felt a tingle up her spine. Then she smelled him and started to laugh aloud. "Come out, come out wherever you are."

Sean stepped out from behind the building. "Damn. No fun if I can't sneak up on you." He stuck his elbow out for her to take.

"Remember? The wind talks to me. I smelled you." They began to walk.

"Ma'am, that's vampire sense," he said in a mock-formal tone.

"Oh, really?"

"If I didn't know better I'd assume you were spending too much time with the living dead. I may have to call you my little Living Dead Girl."

"Will you now?"

He tilted his imaginary hat at her, "Yes, ma'am. Consider it my term of endearment, if you will."

"I will then," she said and kissed him on the cheek.

A smile spread across his face, and he said in his regular voice, "You done for the day?"

"I'm done, period. Other than fetching my boxes and doing my thesis paper, that is. Care to help? I'll take you to look at pretty lit up Christmas decorations afterward if you do." She gave him a big, cheesy grin.

"How can I resist manual labor paid with Christmas lights? Let's go."

With Sean, it took less time to load her things into the Jeep. Watching him finish arranging boxes in the back, she thought about how great he looked in the sun. Turned out, tanning was one of the other benefits of the magick ring he wore. The one Valencia had put on him in a Wiccan ceremony before he escaped her fortress with it. Not only could he be in the sun without turning to ash, he could obtain a slight bit of color, making him look more human.

"This is a nice surprise," she told him as they locked up, "I take it you are on a break from working on the Clandestine Shelter?"

"Yup. The furniture folks are loading it all in right now. I have Celeste telling them where everything belongs."

"Nice."

They wandered down to the valley and took a seat on one of the benches in the middle of the quad in time to watch all the Christmas lights come on.

"What is the plan for Yule?" he asked.

"Well, we witchy folks are going to do something small in the afternoon and then that night is the big ceremony, out in nature."

"Outside?" he asked in mock horror.

"Yes, outside."

"Brrr...too cold."

She laughed and playfully hit him in the stomach, "You vampires don't feel the cold...what's with the bitchin'?"

"Isn't it cold for you all, though?"

"Nope. The fire witches heat up the circle really quickly."

"Is this going to happen in the woods or in the clearing next to our house?"

"Probably next to the house. Fires in the woods are not legal. Not to mention that there's a big ol' feast afterward and having the house right there for it makes more sense."

"What about Christmas?"

"I don't know. The girls talked of having a Kris Kringle party."

"And that is...?"

"Oh, where we all choose names and get a gift for that person, then we have a party on the twenty-fifth and exchange them, cook some good food...well, food for us."

"Funny, ha ha. Just so you know, I'm damn good at cookin' a turkey."

Secretly she loved learning silly things like this about him. "I'll keep that in mind. If I tell Celeste, you'll be stuck cooking on Yule afternoon. But actually, I feel bad about staying in town for Yule."

"Why? It's your first one!"

"I know, but I feel bad not spending it with my Grandma. I mean, it's the first year I have her in my life on Christmas. I don't know. Besides, I'd like to spend my last real vacation with my boyfriend and my grandparents. I thought this morning maybe Phoenix would let us use his private jet. We could surprise them. The do Yule there too, but they sit on the beach in the warm Carolina air."

"You know, I'll be at Yule here. Just because I don't eat, doesn't mean I won't drink some blood wine and spend time with you and the rest of the gang."

"You don't want to meet my grandparents?"

"Stop reading into what I say, silly. Of course I'd like to meet your grandparents." He rubbed her arm and they sat in silence for a moment.

"You said the B word," he casually informed her.

"Huh? What?"

He smiled and touched her nose with his finger. "You called me your boyfriend."

She wasn't being coy. She honestly hadn't noticed. Until now. "I did, didn't I?"

"Yep."

"Huh."

It was silent again. She stood up and stepped out into the snowy field.

"What are you thinking?"

"I'm doing what any female would do, I'm overanalyzing it in my head," she said with a smile, her back still to him.

Atlanta then felt a snowball hit her in the shoulder. She spun around and Sean attacked, tickling her as she tried to fight him, but he was stronger by far. Finally, she gained some distance from him and hid behind the manger scene. She threw a snowball at him and missed. After a bit of snowball fighting he finally tackled her to the ground and rolled her in the snow, tickling her until she finally yelled uncle.

He lay on top of her and wiped some snow out of her hair. At first he rested his forehead on hers, drinking her in. Finally, he took off his gloves, and caressed her face.

Atlanta brushed his hair out of his golden eyes. "What?"

"You called me your boyyyyyfriend," he teased.

"I did, I did...I'll admit I did," she said, giving into the playful peer pressure.

It was silent again for a moment as he looked at her face. "I love you."

If a heart could melt, hers would have, right there on campus, all over the ground, the red soaking into the white snow. Before she knew it, she said it. If she were honest with herself, she would say she knew it before now, but hadn't wanted to admit it. "I love you, too."

He leaned in and for the first time since that day in the car, she let him really kiss her. No more pecks or brief kisses. It was better than even when she'd been under vampire thrall. It was honest to goodness real emotion, not chemical lust that they'd had before. The cold in her fingers and toes from the chill in the air went away and it was Sean...just Sean. And for the first time since Halloween before Harmon showed up, she felt at peace.

* * * *

"How am I to protect you if you don't keep me in the know about what is going on with The Order? You've changed all the lock codes and so many other things," Harmon complained, plopping down into a chair.

It was December twenty first, about one in the morning. Roman stood in a secret passage between the outdoors and Phoenix's office watching and listening in on the meeting under Phoenix's orders.

"There are questions as to where your allegiance lies, Harmon." Phoenix glanced over the top of his paper at his brother. "Too many people who we need in this war said they would walk out if you were kept privy to important information. So you are on suspension from the Board, like Elizabeth was, for now. Keep your arse out of trouble and you'll be back in no time. They just need to see you support our side, that's all. Once they feel comfortable about that, you can come back."

Harmon didn't say anything except, "Bollocks."

"I'm sorry, but you brought this on yourself, brother. You entered the enemy camp without the go-ahead of The Great Order, and just because you're my brother does not mean you get separate rules. This is not the time for me to have to answer questions about you. If you're not in the loop, my answers to 'Could it be Harmon?' are simply 'no' and we can move on. If I let you stay on the Board, then everything The Superior Order does will make everyone scrutinize the Prince's own family. I cannot allow it." He went back to his paper.

"But—"

"End of discussion."

Harmon let out a grunt of irritation. From their past, Roman knew Harmon would understand that his brother meant it and there'd be no changing his mind. He stood up and left the study, slamming the door behind him. Roman slipped out to the driveway and into the bushes. He watched as guards led Harmon to the front doors where the butler held it open for him.

"Will you be leaving now sir?"

"Yeah, I'm going—what's the point of staying?" Harmon's voice was curt.

"Well Master Harmon, if you require any of your things, please call and I'll arrange an escort for you." He paused and then added, "I'm so sorry, sir."

"Escorted out of my own home," he muttered to himself. "I won't be back."

The butler shut the door with a sad nod.

Roman watched Harmon for a moment and then said, "Yet you could've prevented this if you'd only been honest."

Harmon spun toward the bushes. "Who's there?"

Roman stepped out from the darkness.

"I should've known. My brother's lap dog. What do you want?"

"Why would you assume I want something?"

"'Cause it's you. Did you say you wouldn't fight in the war if I was privy to information?"

"No. The people that laid down that ultimatum are protected by the Veil Law, you know that. However, I'll tell you, I wasn't one of them. You have to admit, Harmon, what you did was risky."

"I had to know who was responsible for her death, us or them."

This is what Roman needed, information. "And did you find out?"

"Yes."

"And?"

"Why should I tell you?"

"Because I'm trying to figure out who is responsible for the death of another young girl, us or them."

"Jensine, you mean?"

Roman looked at Harmon, not hiding his surprise. "You know about her?"

"Of course I do. Both sides are blaming the other. Like Elizabeth's death, Jensine's will be the kindling in which this war begins to take root. You wait and see."

"What else do you know about it? You hang in both camps. Don't tell me you don't know who really was to blame."

Harmon ran his hand through his blond hair, sat down on the hood of his car. "What would you do if I even told you? I mean, if I told you it was an ordered hit by Phoenix you'd say I was lying and tell him my accusations. If I told you it was The Superior Order you'd ask why I didn't stop it."

Roman went to say something, but stopped himself. He was at a loss for words.

"See, you know I'm right. Why does it matter to you anyway? It's not like that bitch Atlanta is your girlfriend anymore. You don't have to pretend to care about her friends."

Before Harmon could blink, Roman was in front of him, his hand on Harmon's throat. Harmon started to laugh. "Touchy, touchy, aren't we? Do you still care for her?"

"You leave her out of this."

"Oh, but brother, she's all over this, isn't she?" Harmon broke Roman's hold on him and stood up, bringing them nose to nose. "She's the whole reason you're even here. You want to know if you are responsible for Jensine's death by opening your mouth to Phoenix, don't you? You think you can win Atlanta back if it wasn't your fault."

Roman held his gaze for a moment, and then dropped it, stepping back. "Yes, I need to know."

"You should stay away from that girl. It'll only get you killed. Valencia shows a lot of interest in her. I'd hate for you to end up like Elizabeth." Harmon opened the door to his sports car and slid in behind the wheel.

"What does Elizabeth have to do with Atlanta or Jensine?"

Harmon turned on the engine and revved it a few times. "Let's just say that all their deaths, in the end, will have been ordered by the same people. Open your eyes, brother. Open them wide, or keep them shut and stay in bliss. It's your decision." With that, Harmon drove away.

Roman stood still, thinking about what Harmon was getting at. He said people, not person. He checked the time. "Bloody hell." He needed to head in for a meeting with Phoenix. He went through the hidden entrance that led to the secret observation room and then entered Phoenix's study.

Phoenix was still lying on the chaise lounge, reading the paper. "Did he tell you anything else?"

"No. He doesn't trust me any more than he trusts you."

"Well, it was a good try. Now, let's talk business."

* * * *

"What smells like it's burning?" Desi asked.

"Oh no!" Celeste ran for the kitchen.

40

Bianca started to laugh.

"Leave her be...she tries!" Desi smiled, putting on a Celtic Christmas CD.

"That poor girl always burns the bread," Bianca explained to Atlanta through a snort of laughter.

"Every year?" Atlanta asked.

"Every holiday," Desi replied, fighting a chuckle.

Other than the burning bread, the parlor was beginning to smell like Christmas Day to Atlanta. Between the scent of the huge pine tree that had taken the place of the stuffed black bear and Sean cooking the Yule afternoon turkey for mansion residents and their friends, it brought back memories of her childhood. There would be an enormous formal feast after the midnight ceremony, but thankfully, they had a chef and his team working on that in the big kitchen on the other side of the house.

Atlanta looked at Sean accusingly as Celeste ran out. "Hey, don't look at me, I'm here to baste and carve the turkey," he said, hands up in the air.

"Which reminds me," Atlanta said, leaning into him, nose to nose, "When did you love on your bird last?"

"Well, my chickadee—" he said, leaning in to kiss her, "about fifteen hours ago—if you remember correctly—"

Bianca and Desi made a gagging noise and then Bianca enlightened him, "Not her you idiot, the bird we *eat!*"

"Oh—*that* bird—well—" he checked his watch, "about thirty minutes ago. I'd better go baste her again. Be back."

He kissed Atlanta again and left for the kitchen. It took only seconds for the two girls to swoop in on her, vulture-like. Atlanta went to open her mouth and Celeste walked in.

"I put a new batch in. I set the timer this time," she assured them, then she noticed she walked in on something fun. "What's going on?"

"We were just going to ask little chickadee that," Desi prompted with a sly grin.

"It's not what you think," Atlanta replied.

"You still haven't slept with him?" Bianca asked.

"Nope."

"You're joking, right?" Desi whined.

"Not joking. No sex. We fooled around a bit, for the first time last night, but no sex. I'm not rushing into this. We had a nice night. No interruptions. It was very romantic."

The girls only stared at her, eyebrows raised—waiting.

Atlanta let out a sigh. "Fine. We decided we're girlfriend and boyfriend. That's the big news, if you must know."

The girls all squealed a bit and Desi clapped her hands repeatedly.

"It's about time," Celeste remarked, sitting down on the couch.

"The bird is looking amazing!" Sean let them know as he walked into the room. "And what girlie chatter did I walk in on?"

"Nothing," everyone chimed in.

"Yeah, okay. Suuure." The gong rang. "Saved by the...gong. Maybe some more men will arrive. I'm feeling a bit overpowered by the estrogen." He headed toward the door muttering something about fixing that doorbell.

"Don't even let him lie to you," Atlanta told the ladies. "He likes hanging out with women more than men. He had three sisters."

A ruckus of voices exploded at the door and Atlanta got up to check it out. There, hugging Sean, was her grandma. "Holy shit!" she said before she could stop herself.

"Surprise, dear!" Greta said, seeing her.

Atlanta was dumbfounded as she hugged her grandmother. Then Liam appeared in the doorway as well. "There's our little girl! Happy Yule and Merry Christmas, sweetie!"

"Obviously you've met Sean?" Atlanta asked Greta.

"Oh, don't be mad at him," she said.

"I'm not. I'm openly confused and impressed. How'd this happen?"

Sean didn't look nearly sheepish enough. "I borrowed your phone a week ago when you were in the shower and called them. I wanted them to surprise you."

Atlanta then realized why he'd wanted them to stay here for Yule when she'd suggested they go to the Carolinas. She walked over to him and wrapped her arms around him, kissing him and then rubbing his nose with hers. "You're amazing."

He beamed. "I did good?"

"Yes, you did good." She released him and went over to hug her grandma again. "It's really good to see you!"

"You have a very sweet boyfriend there, young lady," she whispered to her.

"I know. How'd you get tickets at the last minute?"

"He bought them for us. I have no idea."

Atlanta shot Sean a glance. He was busy talking with Liam, but he felt her looking at him, turned, and mouthed, "Merry Christmas."

Once all the excitement surrounding her family's arrival died down, they all meandered back into the parlor. Bianca got the fire going nice and warm and, before they knew it, the house was full of people. Gray showed up shortly after her grandparents, and found her as she poured herself a glass from the pitcher of spiked-homemade cider.

"You want one?" she asked him.

"Sure. Who made it?"

"Desi and Celeste did. It's amazing!" She poured him a glass and returned the cider to the fridge. "How you liking Yule?"

"It's like Christmas but without my annoying Uncle Roy drunk on the floor while mom yells at him."

"Your family is a mess."

"Tell me about it! Why do you think I adopted yours?"

"Oh, and mine is so much more normal?"

"*My* family is normal. That's why they suck. This is so much better! Wish Stephan could've come."

"He could've, but he'd have had to stay away from the windows."

"Good point. You know, we should see if we can get windows for this place like Phoenix has at his. Then he could come here without me pulling all the drapes."

"That's a good idea. I'll ask Phoenix tonight."

"Cool. By the way," he leaned against the counter, "I heard rumor…"

"Oh, you have, have you?"

"He's the boyfriend now?"

"Ah...*that* rumor. Yes, he is."

"Did we...?"

"No."

"What? Giving up your whorish ways? I *so* don't approve!"

She laughed. "That's only 'cause you want dish on how he is in bed!"

"Well duh. You say that like it's a bad thing!"

"I want to wait till it feels right."

"Girl, you've been broken up with Roman for almost two months. I think you can move forward."

"It's not because of Roman," she said. Gray gave her a skeptical look. "Okay, it's only partially because of Roman."

"You're a big girl, honey. Just go with the flow. Unless you still have feelings for TDH?"

She hadn't heard their acronyms in awhile so she smiled and said, "Tall Dark and Handsome broke my trust. Feelings or not, I can't be with him."

"So you do still have feelings?"

"I love Sean. I can trust him and he treats me like I deserve to be treated."

Gray pushed off the counter and walked toward her, wiggling his finger in her face playfully. "That does not answer my question."

She pretended to try and bite his finger. "It's the closest thing to an answer you're going to get. I'm with VWA now."

"Not sure that Vampire With Attitude still fits him...maybe we should call him WVL?"

"What's that stand for?"

"The Whipped Vampire of Love."

She hit Gray playfully as Sean walked into the kitchen. "Bite him, he's being an ass!" she said.

"His boyfriend would kill me," Sean teased.

"Oh yeah, my man is such a fighter," Gray said flatly.

They all laughed, remembering how in the past weeks of fight training Stephan had his ass handed to him by Sean a couple of times.

"Grandma is asking for you and the girls to come to the parlor," Sean told her.

"Okay. I'm on my way."

Gray sent her a look that said they'd finish their discussion later. She headed, hand in hand with Sean, into the parlor where Grandma had set out four matching boxes. They were square and silver with different colored ribbons on them.

Greta directed each of them to sit on the ground near a specific box. "Now, I would make you wait until Yule evening to open these, but I thought maybe prior to the ceremony would be better. Go ahead, open them up!"

They all were hesitant for a moment and then, with giggles, tore into their gifts. Inside were matching outfits—a different color for each of them. Atlanta immediately fell in love with the material. It was like nothing she had ever felt before: soft as cotton, warm like flannel, and yet flowed like rayon. Each top sported elegant silver stitching. Around the collar were small pentacles in circles while at the wrist were triquetra knots. What made each unique though, was the symbol stitched over the heart.

"What are these made of, Grandma?"

"What are these cool symbols on the chest?" Desi asked.

"They are Cabbalistic Mysticist context symbols for the four elements. Each of you has your particular element on your outfit." She grinned mischievously. "The material is a spandex polyester mix lined with a magick spell."

"Magick spell?" Bianca asked, with a wiggle of her eyebrows.

"It's made to keep your body at the perfect temperature, no matter the weather. Not only that but it is water, dirt, fire resistant, and tear proof."

"Damn the man, that's wicked cool Mrs. C." Bianca declared.

"Where did you get these?" Celeste asked, holding the shirt up to her chest to check sizing.

"I had them made for you and did the spell with Liam. We've tested them."

"I'm sure Liam looked great in this!" Atlanta teased. The girls all laughed.

"Hey now, you'd be surprised how great my legs are in spandex," Liam protested, dancing about in a circle doing an Irish jig.

"Spandex, it's a privilege, not a right!" Gray said, snapping his fingers. Atlanta rolled her eyes and laughed as he quoted the famous movie line.

"I thought you might wear them tonight for the ceremony, since you're leading it. That's why I wanted to give them to you now. There's one more box for each of you. Liam, did you bring them in?"

"Yes, here they are," he said, laying long boxes in front of each of them, similarly wrapped.

"Open them," she told them.

They all ripped open the gifts to find two more pieces to go with the outfits. One was a pair of leather knee high black boots and the other was a cape. When Atlanta wrapped it around her, it warmed her up almost instantly. "You outdid yourself, Grandma," she said, shoving a boot on to find it fit perfectly.

All the girls chimed in with the same sentiments.

"Your parents and I were working together on this for you all since Samhain. So I don't get all of the credit. I just had them made and blessed."

Atlanta stood up and hugged her. "Thank you Grandma, they're wonderful!"

Everyone hugged Greta. People filled their drinks, and then they ate. Atlanta then gave her gift to the girls and was happy they liked the handmade journals she'd had a fellow teacher friend in the university's art department make for them. She'd also had one made for Stephan, Roman, Sean, and Grayson. "I thought we should all document our journey," she told them. "It'll make a great story someday."

Everyone loved the idea and chatted about it as they exchanged their gifts too. Before she knew it, the gong sounded. She heard the door open and felt his presence before she saw or heard him.

"It's your boyfriend," Atlanta whispered to Gray. Gray looked at her sharply as he got up to go to the door. He knew that what she had felt was Roman. She hoped she'd covered it from everyone else, including Sean.

First to enter the parlor were Phoenix and Harmon. Phoenix looked dashing as usual, his shoulder length dark hair loose and his grey eyes lit with holiday cheer. Harmon, on the other hand, looked as if he had smelled some sour milk and got stuck that way.

Next came Gray with Stephan and his best friend Kat. She was a petite girl with short black hair whose bangs were dyed bright pink. Atlanta wondered if Kat still disliked Sean for capturing her and locking her in the trunk a few months back. When she shot a nasty look their way, Atlanta had her answer.

Following in behind them was Roman, but he was not alone. A short, pretty girl Atlanta didn't recognize seemed attached to him at the hip. Atlanta guessed her to be a vampire. She had deep purple hair and a silver hoop pierced on the side of her nose. Atlanta quickly realized he'd brought a date.

Clever little man. This was a test.

Roman and the aforementioned date walked right over to Atlanta and Sean. She was introduced as Pepper.

How appropriate, Atlanta thought. "Just Pepper?"

"Pepper Cotswald."

"I'm Atlanta Hart."

"Hi, it's nice to meet you," she said with a genuine smile that made her olive green eyes shine. "My friends call me P.J." Pepper put out her hand to Atlanta.

Atlanta wanted to say something snarky, calling her Pepper instead, as she saw no way they could be friends. Not when she shows up as her ex's date to a party in her own home. But she let it go and took Pepper's hand and said, "Welcome, P.J."

"Nice to meet you," Sean said, putting out his hand. "I'm Sean Cameron. Is this your first Yule with this group?"

She took his hand, and looked flush. "Yes, it is. I just got into the area from Maine, actually. Roman and I met and it just sorta moved on from there. He was nice enough to introduce me to Stephan and I'm staying with them until I find a place." She was still shaking Sean's hand. When he noticed, he took it back. "Oh, sorry. It's only that, well, I've heard stories about you."

"They're not all true," Atlanta informed her.

"She's right, I'm not a horrible person—"

"Speak for yourself," they heard Kat mumble.

"Unless you ask Kat. She hates me—with good reason," Sean disclosed.

"No," Pepper said. "I mean, you're *the* Sean Cameron, the famous vampire Hunter?"

Atlanta looked at him and chuckled. He playfully tickled her. "You'll have to excuse my girlfriend. She is insensitive to my pride."

"Oh bullshit," Atlanta squawked, his tickling getting the better of her. Poor Pepper seemed quite confused and Atlanta took pity. "Yes, he's the famous vampire Hunter."

"I was a vampire Hunter before I became a vampire," Sean told her good-humoredly. "But even then I only killed bad vampires."

"In Maine you're a legend. When we were teens we got stories from our parents that would say if we were bad little boys and girls Sean Cameron would come to kill us in our beds."

Atlanta looked at Sean in disbelief and then back at Pepper.

"Really?" He and Atlanta said at the same time.

"Really. That was the tale I was told for years."

"How old are you, P.J.?" Atlanta looked her short, curvy figure up and down. She was about five foot two, busty with ski slope nose and a heart shaped face.

"Oh, I'm only twenty-five. I'm a Living Vampire. And you're a witch, yes?"

Atlanta wasn't sure where this was going, but answered, "Yes, I'm a witch."

"How do you two deal with that?"

"Deal with what?" Atlanta asked, oblivious to the insinuation.

"The fact that you'll age and he won't."

"You know," Atlanta said, "I never even thought of that." And she hadn't. "Not even when I dated Roman." She knew it was a cheap shot, but she didn't care.

"Don't be mean," Sean said in her head.

"She started it. That comment was rude."

Sean smiled. "That's 'cause it doesn't matter."

"You won't be ruined when she gets old and passes away?"

"I'm going to smack her pretty face," Atlanta warned.

"Ok, change of topic," Sean said, laying a hand on Atlanta's leg.

"Sorry. It's just that I was in love with a sweet witch boy back home and he broke up with me because of it."

"It's okay," Sean said. "We have our own reasons why it works."

Atlanta saw Celeste stand up, and before Sean could tell their whole story, she thought she'd send this gal on her way. "Celeste!" she called. "Come meet a new recruit!" She introduced Pepper to Celeste and suggested she take Pepper to get a drink.

"Wow...she's like twenty five going on eighteen," Sean said.

"No joke." Atlanta took a careful drink of her cider. "Her comments were uncalled for, but she's right. We never have thought of that."

"Honestly, I don't care how old you get or how wrinkled. I'd be by your side no matter what. I don't plan to live forever anyway. Let's live through the war first. Then let's think about this. Deal?"

She touched his face. "Deal." In her head she was remembering her dream in the bloody field, where she died young. Obviously that was why she'd never even worried about it—she knew how this all ended already. With a shudder she let it go, not wanting to remind him of the dream.

Before the ceremony, she and the girls went upstairs to change into their new outfits. The fire and water witches had worked hard that afternoon to clear a large circle so people would not have to stand in the snow. In the center of the clearing were the altar and a large bonfire, erected like at Samhain. Around the perimeter of the circle, where onlookers would stand, were more small fires ready to be lit to help keep the area warm.

By midnight, more than a couple hundred people had collected around the circle. This time Atlanta wasn't as nervous, she was prepared and excited. As they all were situated in the circle, Greta stepped forward to address the group, which surprised Atlanta before she realized she'd planned it.

"This is the night of the solstice, the longest night of the year tis right. Now darkness triumphs, and yet, gives way and changes into light. Yet, we are awake in the night and we turn the wheel to bring the light. We call the sun from the womb of night. Blessed Be!"

Everyone answered, "Blessed Be!"

Bianca stepped forward and pointed at each mini bonfire. As she did, it burst into flames, adding more heat to the area already warmed a good fifteen degrees by magick spells done earlier that day. Everyone cheered. Then the four of them each took their place at a cardinal point of the circle.

Atlanta grabbed her Bo-staff, a six-foot long martial arts fighting rod, and pointed it at the sky. "Spirit of the East, Power of Air! With your gifts of light and clarity, we hail you and invite you to join our Circle this Solstice Eve. By the Air that is *her* breath send forth your light and bless us with your presence!"

Bianca pointed her staff at the sky. "Spirit of the South, Power of Fire! With your gifts of passion and love, we hail you and invite you to join our Circle this Solstice Eve. By the fire that is *her* spirit send forth your flame and bless us with your presence!"

Desi followed suit, saying, "Spirit of the West, Power of Water! With your gifts of depth and feeling, we hail you and invite you to join our Circle this Solstice Eve. By the waters of *her* living womb send forth your flow and bless us with your presence!"

Celeste stepped forth and with her staff high in the air; she called the final corner, "Spirit of the North, Power of Earth! With your gifts of substance and life, we hail you and invite you to join our Circle this Solstice Eve. By the earth that is *her* body send forth your strength and bless us with your presence!"

The four of them moved to the center and surrounded Greta, the tips of their Bo-staffs touching above her head. In unison they cried, "We invoke you, Great Mother, to be with us this night. We ask you to guard and to bless our Solstice Circle. We ask, too, for your guidance in helping us keep our hearts open and joyful, to those in our community, to people all over the world, to all of creation. Blessed Be."

Atlanta knew the plan now was to lead the circle in song, but Greta began to glow. A voice came out of her that was not her own—Atlanta had heard it before. It was Diana.

"Now let flame of Yule flare forth this night through death and darkness deep. Tonight the Sun King is reborn. Say the chant for his rebirth with me."

Greta put her arms out in front of her, a log of wood appeared there and burst into flame. The four girls knelt in the middle of the circle at the feet of Diana. "The night is dark," they chanted, "the sun is gone, yet we know the wheel turns on. Through midnight's hour, solid dark, within our hearts remains a spark."

Diana answered, "Lord in Heaven, Father of all, hear us as our voices call, send your fire back to Earth as we will the Sun's rebirth."

The entire group was entranced as they continued to speak together. "The night is dark, the sun is gone, yet we know the wheel turns on. Through midnight's hour, solid dark, within our hearts remains a spark."

Diana continued. "Who will light the sacred fire, bringing back our heart's desire? Sacred fire, kindled bright, leads us back into the light."

The hundred's replied, "The night is dark, the sun is gone, yet we know the wheel turns on. Through midnight's hour, solid dark, within our hearts remains a spark."

Diana finished the chant alone. "As the flames around us glow, so may love within us grow. Waken Sun King, be reborn! Bring us light this Yuletide morn!"

Everyone watched as the log became a young male baby. Naked, he squirmed in her arms, glowing like the sun. Diana lifted him into the air for all to see and the Circle cheered aloud. She placed him on the top of the large bonfire in the middle of the Circle, where he lay happy and wiggling.

"We have rid ourselves of the burdens and obstacles which hold us back and weigh us down," Diana said. "Let us now light our candles in the world and speak our blessings, reflections, words of wisdom we wish to share with this Solstice Circle."

One representative from each family stepped forward and lit their votive candle from the main bonfire, then took that flame back to the others to light from. Slowly, but surely, each member of the Circle had a lit candle held in front of them.

Atlanta remembered her readings. The large bonfire itself represented the goddess, the god, and the earth with all its elements. By the head of each family taking some of the fire to their family members, they were sharing in the light of the god and the goddess in both love and unity.

"Sing with me," Diana requested.

They all sang a Solstice song, to the tune of Silent Night. It was the voices of hundreds of people rising as one into the night air surrounded by light. It felt both beautiful and majestic.

Once they were done with the song, Diana took the newly born Sun King from the fire and held him in her arms and smiled. "Speak your blessings, reflections, words of wisdom. Share with this Solstice Circle."

This was a time for people to step into the Circle and speak of what they may have learned from the good or the bad of the past year. The goddess walked about the Circle with the Sun King in her arms, receiving testimony, and when she reached Sean, he stepped forth.

"There are no words for the goodness the goddess has brought to my life this year. Last year at this time, I sat in a dark cell in the bowels of The Superior Order's dungeon wishing to die. I didn't understand why the goddess had abandoned me, but you didn't, did you?

"Today I stand before you a new man from a year ago. I mainly have my wonderful girlfriend to thank for that. If it wasn't for Atlanta, I am sure I'd still be very angry and have no goals in my life. But the love she has shown me and others makes me want to be a better man, for her and for the Order. Phoenix has begun a project that is also close to my heart that I am thankful to be a part of."

Atlanta looked at Sean and felt her heart pound heavy in her chest. Tears came to her eyes and her fears concerning him seemed to dissipate. Phoenix stepped forth to say something, but Celeste cut him off.

"I too want to bless the arrival of our Air Witch. Her heart is bigger than many women I've known and, though she is my elder in years, she treats me and the rest of us as if we are all equal. Goddess bless the day she came back to the Clandestine World and into my life. I trust her and honor her."

After Desi and Bianca each made similar statements, Diana came to Atlanta and put her arm around her. It was warm both physically and emotionally, holding the impression of unconditional love. Atlanta felt a bit embarrassed and knew her face was probably flush.

"Is there anyone else here who feels that the addition of this child has been a blessing upon the Circle? If she has affected your life in a positive way since her arrival, please, step forward."

Atlanta was amazed by the response. People she barely knew as well as those she did stepped forth. Even Roman came forward. She'd have expected Roman to stay back, like Harmon did, so his step forward warmed her heart.

Diana leaned in and kissed her on the forehead. "You are loved for your heart and your loving actions to your fellow man and woman. I give you three calls. Just ask for me, and I will be there, my loving child."

"Thank you, Diana," Atlanta whispered.

She smiled at her and caressed Atlanta's face. "It is time."

Atlanta nodded and stood, saying, "Great goddess, Diana divine. Your presence has held us, protected us, guided us, and blessed us this night in our celebration of the Sun's return. We thank you for your many blessings, for your grace and goodness, for your beauty and wisdom. Stay if you will, go if you must. Blessed Be."

Diana smiled and reached out to hug Atlanta, and as she embraced her, the glowing child disappeared and she became Greta again. She let go of Atlanta and touched her face again, this time as a human.

"Blessed Be indeed!" Greta exclaimed. "Close the Circle, ladies."

With a not, the four of them went to their appointed areas in the circle from the start of the ceremony.

"Spirit of the North, Power of Earth! Your presence with us this night has anchored and strengthened us. We thank you for your many blessings. Stay if you will, go if you must. Blessed Be," Celeste said.

"Spirit of the West, Power of Water! Your presence this night has soothed and cradled us and connected us to our first home – the sea. We thank you for your many blessings. Stay if you will, go if you must. Blessed Be," Desi said.

"Spirit of the South, Power of Fire! Your presence this night has opened our hearts to life and to love. We thank you for your many blessings. Stay if you will, go if you must. Blessed Be," Bianca said.

Across the Circle Atlanta saw Sean, his face looking at her with such unconditional love and trust that her heart leapt in her chest again. "Spirit of the East," she called, "Power of Air! Your presence this night has brought the first stirrings of the new sun. We thank you for your many blessings. Stay if you will, go if you must. Blessed Be."

A loud cheer erupted and then, as in tradition, candles were set down around the Circle and the members all took hands and spoke in unison:

May the spirit of Yule
Remain with us all
For the whole next year.
May our obstacles and snares vanish
May our seeds take root and flourish
May we be blessed by spirit

Each and every one

Living Dead Girl

The circle is closed, but not unbroken.
Merry meet, merry part, and merry meet again.

Blessed Be!

The four of them closed the staffs, put them in the pocket of their capes, and went to join hands with their friends. As Atlanta took Sean's hand with her right hand and Greta's with her left, she felt solid and sure of so many things. Then one person led the group off, and they were making a long line, everyone still holding hands, and dancing in a serpent pattern across the yard to the house, singing Deck the Halls.

* * * *

"What a wonderful night!" Atlanta said to herself. And it had been. Full of singing by the piano in the parlor, great food made by the house chef, and the entire Circle sitting around chatting and drinking. Atlanta drank a lot of meade and found herself wrapped up in the fun of it all. Yule reminded her of a mix of Christmas and New Years rolled into one.

It felt like a new day for her. She not only saw herself in a new light, but Sean as well. Though she was definitely uncomfortable with Pepper sitting on Roman's lap, she didn't care as much as she thought she would. Even Pepper's flirtation with Sean held no worry. Not that the jealous monster in her head even had the chance to rear itself up, because Sean's lack of interest was apparent. Without a doubt, Sean had been focused on her all night. A touch here, a touch there—her leg, her hand, her hair—never for a moment did she question his focus.

The fun and beautiful evening made her realize she needed to stop holding back. She needed to live her life to the fullest, however long it would be. She couldn't second-guess things anymore. Yes, she'd make mistakes, but she'd learn and work her way through them and come out the better for it.

It was almost sunrise when the head of the Coven went out to make sure all signs of the ceremony were gone. Sean went to help while Atlanta showed her Grandparents their room and hugged them goodnight. Gray left with Stephan, Roman, and Pepper thirty minutes earlier to escape the oncoming sun and everyone else who lived in or was staying at the house for the holiday were also in bed.

Atlanta decided a hot shower sounded wonderful since her hair smelled like the bonfire. She went and changed out of her new outfit and got into the shower. The room she'd chosen for her bedroom was on the second floor, with a large room that overlooked the front yard. The French doors inside the room led to a private, large bathroom holding both a dual showerhead glass enclosed shower stall and a large tub that contained jacuzzi spouts in it. It was one of the rooms Devon had updated and she loved it.

Once she was done, she put on Sean's gift from earlier that night. It was a dark green satin nightgown that fell to just above her knees, and a robe to match. As she brushed out her long, wet hair, she heard a noise in the bedroom. Leaning back to peer through the one open door she saw that it was Sean. He took off his jewelry and shirt before sitting on the edge of the bed to remove his combat boots and socks.

Atlanta washed her face and brushed her teeth while wondering how to play this. It was a big step. Was she seriously ready to let go of the past with Roman? *Damn it, she had to be,* she thought and spit toothpaste out and rinsed. She had to move on. She knew that. However, that didn't stop the butterflies from flying about her stomach as Sean walked into the bathroom just then, black jeans still on but undone at the top.

Seeing her outfit, he stopped. "Wow, don't you look beautiful." His voice was almost breathless and it warmed her all over.

Realizing she probably had toothpaste on her face, she quickly wiped it off with the towel and coyly said, "Some wonderful man gave it to me. You like?"

Playing along he walked up behind her and slid his arms around her waist. Placing his chin on her shoulder, he pulled her against him and looked at her in the mirror. "You'll have to thank him for me, you look ravishing."

She turned to face him. "Oh, I plan to thank him. I hope you don't mind."

Lifting her up to sit on the long counter Sean said, "Do you now? And how might you do that?"

Atlanta wrapped her legs around his waist and laid her hands on his bare chest. Softly she dragged them across his pectoral muscles and down his arms. Sliding her eyes from his waistline to his eyes, she winked. "I'm sure I can think of something." Leaning in she kissed his neck, letting her teeth nip his skin lightly here and there.

He groaned lightly, his hands sliding from her knees up over the soft material of her nightgown to grasp her hips as his mouth found hers and devoured her with the twisting of passionate lips, teeth, and tongues that had her heart racing.

When they came up for air she said, "Take me to bed."

He paused and Atlanta hoped he understood her meaning.

"Are you sure?" he finally asked, obviously catching the truth of her request.

With a settling breath, she nodded. "I'm sure."

The look that filled his face was one of awe. The tenderness in his eyes was almost delicate. Slowly she reached for his face and caressed the side of it. The kiss that followed was soft and slow as her free hand reached to the wall and hit the light switch.

In the dark, he leaned back and untied her robe slowly, all the while his gaze drinking every inch of her in. Parting it carefully, he slid the robe from her shoulders, dragging his fingers lightly down the bare skin of her back, revealed by the spaghetti strapped nightgown. Enfolding her arms around his neck, she held on with her legs as he lifted her up and carried her into the bedroom.

Seeing the look on her face as they entered, a tiny smile touching his lips. "You like?"

Atlanta laughed. "You are amazing. When did you do this?"

"You take awhile to get ready for bed."

She couldn't help but laugh at herself before saying, "Not *that* long."

"Long enough."

Every candle had been lit, filling the room with soft, romantic light as a favorite CD of hers played from the stereo.

"*You* are wonderful," she breathed in his ear.

He laid her down slowly on top of the bed, his weight on top of her as both of his hands cupped her face. "Just trying to give me an advantage. Ya never know, I might be bad at this. It's been a long time," he said, eyes glowing in the candlelight.

"How long?"

"Remember, I've been in a prison for five years."

"Well, you could've fooled me."

He took her hand and kissed the palm of it, placing it on his cheek, all the while holding eye contact. She pulled his face to hers and as their lips met, Atlanta knew she had never felt so cherished.

Chapter Five

The New Year came and went, more snow came down, and life was quiet. It was the end of March and like most days, Atlanta sat in the parlor by the big fire Sean made for her each morning. She was working on her thesis paper so she could graduate with honors while Sean worked with the CPA on the yard and both houses. So far, a jungle gym had been put in next to the shelter in case younger children stayed with them and a basketball hoop had been added to the garage front.

Today the CPA were installing vampire glass in all the windows. Gray would be thrilled. That meant he and Stephan could spend more time together at the mansion. Atlanta like that too, for she didn't see as much of Gray lately as she would've liked.

A breeze from open or missing windows blew through the room and she shivered. Getting up off the chaise she padded on into the kitchen for more hot tea. On her way back into the parlor a crash of glass caused her to almost drop her mug, which would've really pissed her off because she'd already dropped one that week. It seemed Jay of the CPA, who went by Big Daddy Jay, was sort of a klutz.

The first time he broke a window she'd been walking from the kitchen to the parlor and dropped the mug, shattering it to the floor. The mug she had now was from Jensine and said, "Just when the caterpillar thought the world was over, it became a butterfly." She'd rather it stayed whole.

This time she only flinched, sighed, and took a sip of her tea before sitting back down on the chaise. Hearing the back door open and shut, she turned her attention to the kitchen. Someone washed their hands in the sink.

"In here, baby," she yelled out, rising up so as to go over to the stereo to switch CDs.

"Of course you are," he yelled out from the kitchen.

She stretched out on the chaise lounge, throwing her red blanket over her as he came into the room. His blue jeans and black T-shirt looked mildly dusty, his face too, proving he'd been working hard. He proceeded to come over and lie on top of her.

"Why hello," she grunted with a smile. "You're getting my blanket dirty."

"I'll wash it," he said, kissing her. He then laid his head on her chest.

"Those aren't pillows."

"You coulda fooled me."

She laughed. "You tired?"

"A bit."

The other big project Sean had been assigned to was an underground facility. With his knowledge of Asmarahald, Valencia's fortress, he was vital to helping The Great Order build one of their own. Normally they'd have had to wait until spring, Celeste did a ceremony after the New Year and they asked the earth for permission to tunnel through her. She'd agreed, so they were working on a full training facility underground, as well as secret tunnels and passages that connected the main house and the above ground shelter.

"We've been moving equipment into the tunnels all day," Sean told her. We have to work around the window people. Did you hear Jay break another window?"

She chuckled. "Yeah, I hope that was an old window, not one of the new expensive ones."

"It was, but man, they're leaving a mess for me to clean!"

"Awe, poor baby," she said, because she knew that's all he wanted to hear.

He snuggled into her and let out a deep sigh.

"Gonna nap there?"

"Was thinking about it."

She grabbed her book and got comfy. "Go ahead. If I go numb I'll wake you up."

"Sounds good," he mumbled, and was out. He could sleep anywhere. In his defense, he hadn't slept last night because a pipe burst under the house. Then the police chief, who was Clandestine, showed up with a kid, so Sean sat with him.

He was a ten year old shape shifter whose home life wasn't great so he'd run away. By the time Sean finished with paperwork and water cleanup, the window guys and CPA had arrived to work.

Atlanta found she dozed off as well because the next thing she knew she was awakened by Sean having some sort of nightmare. He was twitching, and shouted out the word "No!" It woke him up as well. Realizing where he was, his head dropped onto her chest.

"Are you okay?"

She knew he'd gone through a lot of torture the five years he was in the dungeons of The Superior Order. That alone would cause nightmares. He had also watched his family die at the hands of evil vampires. His sleeping troubles were therefore normal, like hers were. But lately he'd seemed to have a similar dream over and over.

"Are you ready to tell me yet?"

He shook his head.

"Sean, obviously you're stressing over something. If you'd share it with me…"

"I can't," he said, his head still down.

"You can't or you won't?" She felt him shudder. She wrapped her arms around him and kissed the top of his head. "I can't help you heal what's wrong unless you tell me."

"I'm not ready."

"Ok." She didn't want to push it, but this was getting crazy. If they were to be a couple, she felt she deserved to know what was wrong. Maybe it had to do with her.

"I just get scared it's about me and that I've done something…"

He looked up at her quickly. "Oh baby, it's not you."

"Then why can't you tell me?"

He hesitated. "Because it's embarrassing and humiliating—and I'm afraid if I approach this subject you'll think I'm crazy, or it'll put a wedge between us."

"But that's your perspective. Why not let me decide."

He reached up and tucked a loose hair behind her ear and she saw him make a decision. "Do you want children?"

She about choked on her tongue. "What?"

"You heard me."

"Uh, well, I don't think about that. I am too busy concentrating on training and the upcoming war, thank you. I wouldn't want to bring a child into the world until I see how all that turns out. But you know this, why are you asking me?"

"Cause I can't give you one."

"I know that. I've always known that. What does this have to do with your nightmares?"

He swallowed and then took a deep breath and slowly let it out. "Before Valencia turns any person into a vampire, she does a medical procedure. You don't know about it unless someone who does know tells you. You wake up groggy and in a cell and then after she changes you…if she wants information from you…she uses this power to control you."

"I'm sort of following. Can you be more specific? What is the medical procedure?"

"Can't you guess?"

Again, Atlanta thought about it and her head dropped sideways onto the couch and she looked at him, finally understanding. "She collects your sperm."

"Bingo."

"So…then…you could have kids someday if you can get your stuff back," she said with a smile at the word "stuff."

He shook his head.

"Why not?"

"The dream I keep having is about Elizabeth. Valencia threatened to dump mine down the toilet unless I helped her catch Elizabeth."

"You didn't…"

"Of course not. I mean, I didn't think I'd ever be free anyway, so I didn't see what good it'd do to sacrifice my only friend. But she was able to use someone else to get to her."

"Devon."

"Yes. And because I didn't help, she threw my jar over the edge of the castle. As my punishment."

"Why would you be dreaming about this now?"

"Well, you and I have started a sexual relationship. We don't have to use protection because my body can't get or give any diseases and I can't get you pregnant. That doesn't mean my psyche knows all the info. My DNA tells me one thing and my mind tells me another and then…I saw the way you looked at the baby that came into the home two weeks ago and I just started having the dreams."

She ran her hand through his hair affectionately. "And you're worried I will want kids and leave you."

He nodded. "I feel stupid."

"Let me scoot down so I can be face to face with you." He lifted himself up and she lined herself up with him and put her arms around him again. She was about to reassure him, but he spoke up first.

"Roman is a living vampire. He could give you kids if they ever allow that sort of mixing again," he said, putting his forehead on hers.

She kissed him. "First off, you're being silly. Children are not on my radar. I'll be twenty-five in July, Sean. I am not in any way thinking about kids."

"But someday you might."

"And if that happens...we have options. I can be artificially inseminated and we can adopt and so on and so forth. Hey, we could have Gray donate sperm!"

He laughed reluctantly.

"And quit thinking about Roman," she muttered.

"He still has feelings for you."

"I know."

"You still have feelings for him."

She knew lying was pointless. "Sometimes. But I can't be with someone like him and you know why. Besides, feelings for someone aren't the same thing as loving someone. I love you. You'd remember that if you'd stop over-thinking this baby thing! Yeesh!"

He looked as if her words weren't enough. "I know you love me. But I love you more than my own life, and I want you to have everything that this world has to offer."

"You want me to be happy."

"More importantly, I want to be the one who makes you happy."

"You do make me happy. And truthfully, you personally being able to give me a child—not an issue, or a reason I'd ever use to let you go."

"Honestly?"

"I don't lie to you. I never have had to. I never will."

"If you change your mind I'll—"

She shut him up by kissing him. He kissed her deeply. Afterwards he curled back up on her chest with a sigh.

Atlanta dragged her nailed through his hair to put him back to sleep. As he did, she thought about what he'd said. Honestly, the thought of not having children didn't bother her. Besides, she wasn't going to live to be old enough for those things to matter. She knew that in the depths of her being. Did she tell Sean she knew she'd die young? No. It would've only given him more to worry about.

The thing that hurt was being honest with him about Roman. Sean was a vampire though, so even though he couldn't read her thoughts unless she let him, he could sense her feelings. This is why she hadn't lied. She knew her connection to Roman hurt him and to see Sean hurt was like being hurt herself.

* * * *

The rest of March and April were quiet. In May, Atlanta finished her paper early and turned it into her professor. As long as it didn't get a failing grade, she would graduate in June with honors and an MFA in English. Her grandparents and adoptive parents would be so proud and happy to watch her get the diploma. Atlanta currently was trying to decide if she would introduce them or not. How would that conversation go? She shuddered at the thought.

However, today was not for deciding that. Today was the big reveal of the underground facility to the upper members of The Clandestine Council and affiliates from all over the United States. As her eyes scanned the group that had gathered in the ballroom, she saw few she recognized. Thankfully, Harmon was not there. Atlanta decided that the Prince's brother still must be suspended from the council.

Most were talking amongst themselves at a dull roar until Phoenix approached the podium. Those who weren't sitting already took their seats, quieting themselves out of respect. The prince was in one of his nicest pinstriped suits. His dark hair that usually touched his shoulders was slicked back, pulled into a tiny ponytail, and his grey eyes were serious and commanding.

"Good evening," Phoenix said. "Thank you all for coming. Today I have much to cover with you. As we've noticed, The Superior Order has been very quiet since the holidays—or shall I say, since they got hold of the book. I am going to admit to you today that I have someone on the inside. This person is a complete secret to all but the Occultus."

Everyone in the room started to whisper and chatter. Atlanta leaned over to Sean just as he leaned into her and their heads hit. Before they could even laugh it off Phoenix continued. "I put this into motion shortly after Halloween. This person has become one of Valencia's new foot soldiers, alongside Harmon, who is still acting as a plant within The Superior Order. For their safety, I cannot say who it is. They are not even listed on my database."

Roman raised his hand.

"Yes?"

"But they are listed in the Occultus, you said?"

"Yes. Obviously, in the occurrence of my death, I'd hate for this person to be stuck there. So far they are feeding me back small pits of information when they can. Valencia hasn't taken this person into her confidence yet, but they know something big is in the works. Our mole has seen the book we lost, and knows Valencia is planning some kind of high-security infiltration based on something in the book. I have been going over my notes from the past year and nothing has jumped out at me, but I promise to keep scouring them. As more information comes to me, I will keep you posted.

"All in this room are bound to secrecy. As you leave this room, a spell has been put on the doorway. If you breathe a word of this to anyone not in this room, it will alert the witch that set the spell and you will be dealt with accordingly. I did want the heads of this Order informed though. Now, Sean, are you ready to come up here?"

"Yes, sir." Sean stepped up to the podium. She was so proud of him. He looked all businesslike in his suit with a clipboard of notes. "Good evening. Phoenix has asked me to tell you all about our underground facility. Some of you know about it, most don't. I'm here to educate you on it all."

He went into detail as to what they were constructing under the grounds on Devon's property, how many it would hold and who would be considered for living there in case of an emergency.

One of the members of the board who she didn't know that well raised their hand. "Why have we been building all of this?"

"Phoenix, do you want to take it from here?"

"Yes, thank you, Sean."

Sean grabbed his things and came to sit with Atlanta again. He put his arm around her and she put her hand on his leg and gave it a squeeze as if to say, "good job."

"The reason for this facility is to keep members of The Order safe," Phoenix told the room. "When the war begins, we can't have Valencia killing off everyone on our side. She has underground facilities, now we do too. As Sean knows how hers are constructed he helped us do the same, if not better."

He pulled down the sheet that covered the wall behind him, revealing a large draft drawing of the facility in question. Phoenix then pulled out a laser pointer and took his time explaining all the details.

* * * *

The girl with the shaved head rolled over on her cot. It was extremely uncomfortable. She let out a groan followed by a heavy sigh. Sleep was pointless. She sat up and rubbed her head, still not used to having almost no hair. She threw her legs over the side of the bunk and looked around. The barracks were quiet. It seemed she was the only one awake. With a sigh, she stretched and looked around the barracks.

That's when she saw him, the guy she'd arrived at The Superior Order with. He was standing by the window smoking a cigarette and writing something on paper. The moonlight was shining off his short silvery grey hair. She figured what the hell.

Standing up she padded across the room in her military sleeping attire they all were given—army green knit pants and a matching T-shirt—and sat down at the opposite end of the long window sill from him. "Care if I bum one of those?"

He didn't say anything or even look up at her. He did, however, pick up the pack and hold it out for her to take one.

"Thanks." She took a cigarette. "You got a—" he handed her a lighter. "Thanks." She lit the cigarette and handed him the lighter back. He put it on the window sill and went back to writing.

She smoked quietly next to him, blowing the smoke out the cracked open window while trying to peer over to see what he was writing. His handwriting however was hard to make out without really obviously looking over his shoulder. After a while, she asked. "What you writing?"

He didn't answer. She wasn't one to give up that easily, though.

"I see you writing all the time. Would it kill you to tell me what you're writing?"

He paused. "It might."

With a light sigh, she lifted her eyes to the ceiling as if it would give her patience. "I highly doubt it. Come on, I can't sleep, you can't sleep, you might as well make some conversation."

Finally, he looked up at her, his cat-like blue eyes meeting hers. "Why don't you piss off?"

"Why don't you kiss my ass," she said with a smile.

She could see he tried to stay stern, but he broke and laughed.

"That's better," she said.

"You're a bitch, I like that."

"I will take that as a compliment."

"You should."

She thought about how she was before all this happened. She'd been far from being a bitch, or one to stand up for herself. It was like when the shape shifter DNA mixed with her it made her character stronger, more powerful. She was still learning how to use all these new powers, yet, she'd be damned if she would go through it alone. She'd been sent here for a reason but that didn't mean she couldn't make friends. Not everyone here was bad, she'd seen that. She'd even told Phoenix that. This guy seemed like he could go either way.

"So, what are you writing?"

He seemed to contemplate his answer for a minute and then said, "Lyrics."

"Lyrics? You a singer?"

He laughed, "No, I'm tone deaf most of the time. I rap though. I write my own stuff. Do you listen to hip hop?"

She blushed. "I am sorry to say I know very little about hip hop culture. I remember when Run DMC was popular…I like the Beastie Boys…does that count?"

He smiled. It was genuine and forgiving. "It's okay. You didn't strike me as the hip hop type-a girl." He flicked his cigarette out the window.

Watching it hit the grounds outside she commented, "She's gonna yell at you for that."

"Screw her."

"Not one for authority, are ya?"

"Gee, am I that transparent?" he joked.

She laughed. "Yes. Yes you are."

He set his pen and paper down and got out another cigarette and lit it. "So, girl whose name eludes me, what is your story?"

Oh, how she wished she could tell the whole truth, but the story Phoenix had her learn, though a bit altered to fit her new unplanned physical changes, was a better option. Safer. "I was a human girl until a couple months ago. Then I was attacked by a member of The Great Order for knowing too much, and now I'm here. What I don't understand is why all of us recruits are in these barracks instead of a nice room somewhere. This estate is huge."

"Trust."

"What?" She flicked her finished cigarette out the window like he had.

With a grin he clarified, "She doesn't trust you, me or any of the people in this bunker yet. So we're under heavy guard. That's why we're still in this room."

"But didn't she send you on a task? You'd think you'd have gotten some better lodgings by now."

"I got the book for her but she was pissed I shot that girl."

She felt her eyes widen in shock and fear. "Who did you shoot?" she asked, trying to sound calm.

"That Air Witch the Great Order has. Valencia was pissed. She put me in isolation for a week after that. Apparently that girl must not be harmed."

"I find that odd."

"As do I, but that woman has got her reasons. Hence, I'm still in these barracks with you losers." He looked at her and winked.

She waited a moment before asking, trying not to look too interested. "Did the girl live?"

"From what I know, yeah. That's why I'm not dead," he said.

Against her will, she let air out of her lungs in relief and then covered it up as best she could, "Glad you aren't in trouble anymore."

"I'm Greyhound by the way," he said, putting his hand out.

"Pip," she answered, shaking his hand. "Is Greyhound your real name?"

"Naw, it's my stage name. Grey hair and all. Been grey since I was in junior high."

"How old are you now?"

"I'm twenty-one. You?"

"I'm an old lady of twenty-five."

He laughed then asked. "What kind of name is Pip?"

"Oh, it's not my real name either. I chose that after the change. Valencia said some people here do that. We had this black cat growing up. She was a crazy cat!" She laughed. "One minute she was your friend and the next she was clawing you to shreds. My maker was a black panther, so I am as well, and seeing as I'm two kinds of creatures like Pip was, I thought it fit."

"Word," he said, as an affirmation of her thought.

A pause lingered for a moment and then he leaned over and whispered in her ear. "My real name is Hunter."

She leaned over and playfully bumped his shoulder and whispered back.

"Nice to meet you, Hunter. I'm Jensine."

* * * *

Valencia had Jonathan wait in the hallway until General McMasters left her office. Had he heard his brother's name in their discussion? She hoped not. She couldn't pull off this op if he got in the way. It was for him, damn it, but he'd never see it that way.

He entered, hair pulled back, long strides showing her hopes were shot to shit. He'd heard. "What were you talking about?"

"Nothing you need to worry about, darling," she cooed, placating him.

"I don't like him," Jonathan looked toward the door. "McMasters is a buffoon."

"He is a means to an end. Come now, shut the door, lover." She rose from behind her desk headed over to her filing cabinet.

"What's with the normal-person outfit?"

Valencia had foregone her usual gowns and corsets in favor of jeans and a t-shirt. "I'm running a team down to Massachusetts."

"What?! You never go on missions."

"I know."

"Why did I hear my brother's name mentioned? What are you doing?"

"Nothing that concerns you."

He strode to her. "If it concerns my brother it concerns me. You made me a promise when I began working for you."

Valencia knew now wasn't the time to tell him her plans. "I know."

"Are you going back on that promise?"

"That depends."

"On what?"

"On whether you can go through with my last and biggest task for you."

"Which is?"

"It's not time to put it in front of you. It will be soon enough."

Jonathan grunted in frustration and flopped onto one of the big chairs.

She wanted to calm his fears, but it would have to wait. "Can you head up to Canada and keep things in order there while I'm out? I've never been away this long and everyone knows you're my right hand."

Jonathan's face pinched, but he nodded.

"Good. My jet will take you as soon as you can be ready. If everything stays in order, when I return you can keep the second ring."

This got Jonathan's attention. "Sorry?"

"The sunlight ring you were using to kill off the members of the Great Order council—it will be yours."

He saw a sunlight ring on her hand. It was different than the one he or Sean wore, smaller, more feminine. "I see you made a third."

"I made a few more."

"Who are they for?"

"Ah, that I cannot say, I am sorry. If my plan goes as I hope, it will be for someone very, very special."

He yanked out his hair tie and began redoing it. "You used to tell me everything."

He was right. She did. That was until things became difficult. "And your brother used to also, until Sean alerted them that you were working for me. As you are not privy to their info anymore, I can't have you totally privy to mine. Just in case."

Jonathan stood. "Valencia, you know my allegiance is here with you."

She sat on the corner of her desk nearest to him. "Is it?"

He drifted toward her. "It is."

"We'll know soon enough." She stood and kissed him. "I will see you soon. Don't let me down!" She grabbed her dark green trench coat and opened the office door. "Nothing you might want to snoop for is in either of my offices. When I return I promise, you'll know everything—if you're good and keep your ass at Asmarahald and keep things in order. Understand?"

"Understand."

"See you later, lover," she said with a wink and then shut the door. Before walking away she heard him say one thing.

"Bugger."

Chapter Six

"You want anything to drink?" Sean yelled over the music.

"What?" Atlanta yelled back.

"Do you want something? I'm going to the bar," she heard in her head.

"My usual," she answered.

Roman and Stephan had ordered them all out to The Barn to celebrate Phoenix's birthday. She kept her eye on Sean as he headed up to the bar to get their drinks when she felt someone take her hand.

"Gray!" She hugged him. He looked tired but good. His hair held a pound of gel to spike it, then to make sure it never moved again during this lifetime he'd sprayed it blue. His eyeliner matched the hair as did his blue velvet choker necklace.

He'd been out of town for a few weeks doing something with the CPA. Due to their main computer tech guy, Brad, going missing they had asked Gray, who was pretty good with computers, to help them on a mission. From what she could tell, they'd all become good friends while they were gone.

The Clandestine Protection Agency consisted of Jason "J.J." Marcus, their Alpha, and a martial artist like Sean. Then they had David Hade, aka 2Doggz, a pressure point fighter and Beta of the pack. The two biggest brutes of the bunch were Lance Khan and Jay Gallagher, aka The Great Khan and Big Daddy Jay, respectively. Those boys were seen as "the muscle" of the group. Last would be Erik Caldwell. From what Gray told her, he was demolitions. All of the CPA were werewolves, except Lance. He was a Tiger Shape Shifter. From what she'd heard, possibly the last of his breed.

"You look great!" Gray shouted to her. "That new?"

"You like huh?" She and Celeste had gone club shopped and tonight Atlanta thought was a perfect occasion for a new outfit. The skirt was long and fitted with silver spikes along the sides and a high, cinched in waist to show curves. , a see through purple mesh with a black bra underneath that contained silver studs on it, and silver platform Doc Martens that made her tower over Sean, which he loved.

After they'd danced a few songs Gray led her out onto the patio for a smoke. He handed her a cigarette and lit it for her. "You miss me?" he asked, lighting his own cigarette.

"Like the desert misses the rain."

"Awe, I'm loved."

"You are."

"I missed you all, though if I must say it, those boys can party! Damn!"

She laughed. The CPA were well known for their crazy behavior.

He inhaled and blew the smoke skyward. "How are things?"

"Things?" she asked.

He tilted his head. "Things."

"Oh, those *things*...good. Roman and I avoid each other and Sean tries to ignore the fact that Roman and I have really strong chemistry and it is what it is."

"Not fun."

"Nope."

This time the pause created came from her long inhale and exhale.

"Have the nightmares about her stopped?" His tone was casual, but she heard the concern under it.

She blew out the smoke. No point lying to Gray. "No. But I don't have them as often. Probably only have dreams about her skin burning off her bones once every two weeks instead of every night. Take that for what it's worth."

"Does Sean know?"

"How can he not? I wake up screaming as I try to put out the fire on him." She took another drag. "He's great, Gray. He doesn't get upset, only wraps his arms around me and rubs my temples and tells me it's okay."

"He's a good man, Atty."

"I know."

"You need to let go of this thing for Roman."

"I wish I could. Trust me, I know it's just physical attraction, like a moth to a flame. Chemistry—it'll get you in trouble."

"Can I have an Amen?" Gray said, followed by a sip of his beer.

"Have no fear, I am happy with Sean and that's where I'm staying."

"Good. Just remember what happens to moths that go into the flame."

"Yeah...I know."

"Hey! What are you two doing out here?" Stephan interrupted, popping his head out onto the patio.

"Is it time for the cake and gifts?" she asked.

"Yes indeed!"

"Fantastic!" Atlanta put out her cigarette.

"Cake? Vampires eat cake?" Gray said as she walked into the club.

"Tell Sean I'll be right there, I have to use the ladies room."

"Okay."

Gray and Stephan walked toward the area they'd procured by the door. She headed into the ladies room, did her business, washed her hands and headed toward the door and before she could even react she was grabbed from behind and a needle went into her neck. She thought she heard a familiar female voice say, "I'm sorry."

Then everything went black.

* * * *

They were waiting on Atlanta to light the candles on the cake, so when she didn't return from the ladies room they sent Kat to go see where she was. With a grumble about how she wasn't a babysitter, Kat headed toward the bathroom, only getting halfway when screaming erupted. Screaming, that is, from the non-Clandestine people in the club. Kat stopped mid stride as she came face to face with a golden cougar, one blue eye, and one green eye.

Unfortunately, that wasn't the only large cat on the premises. A large black panther emerged right behind her from the direction of the ladies room. Humans started running in droves out the back and side doors and Gray saw why. A large pack of wolves had taken the stage.

"Shit," Sean muttered.

"This is going to get ugly," Stephan whisper in Gray's ear. "You may wanna get the outta here."

Gray pulled the wooden stake from Phoenix out of his pocket, opened it up to full length, put the new attachment on the tip which was made of silver, and answered with, "Hell no, I'm not. I'm heading to that bathroom to find Atlanta."

Roman started to move Phoenix toward the front entrance. Unfortunately, as he did, a huge group of vampires came in that way. Each exit becoming blocked either by wolves, cats or vamps, and Gray could tell they were there for a full out fight.

Everyone in both The Superior Order and The Great Order held their ground as the humans were running out of the building, and The Superior Order let them. As Gray approached the stage, which was near the bathrooms, he glanced at the formation the wolves stood in. His time with the CPA now became useful. Scanning the formation, he was able to pick out the alpha of this pack. He was a large wolf that was silver gray with a black undercoat.

Phoenix was the first to speak. "So this is where it begins."

Though not a question, the voice of a woman answered him. "Yes, Phoenix, this is where it begins."

Her voice came from above, and like everyone else, Gray looked up to see a beautiful woman hovering in mid air, with large red curly hair. He knew right away she was an Air Witch like Atlanta and, even before Sean spoke next, he'd figured out who it had to be.

"Finally gonna get your hands dirty in person are ya, Vee?" Sean yelled out.

"Sean, I gave you an amazing gift. A polite or nicer person would've thanked me."

"What can I say? I'm not a polite or nice person," Sean commented, shrugging his shoulders, pulling out a vial from under his shirt that hung on a necklace. He opened it, and drank its contents.

"That's true," Roman said.

"See? Even Roman agrees with me!"

Valencia motioned toward Sean's hand and nothing happened. Sean started to laugh. "Looky there—I think that's a big ol' fuck you," he taunted, giving Valencia the finger. "Ya can't take it off me can ya? See, that's what happens when a more powerful witch than you puts a spell over the top of it. So why don't you kiss— my—ass!"

Her tone stayed polite though her smile was as cold as ice. "We can take the hand if you'd rather."

"I'd like to see *we* try!"

"Your wish is my command."

"Bring it, bitch."

Sean flew up to fight Valencia in the air, triggering everyone else to advance on each other. Seeing that Sean could manipulate air, Gray realized that what Sean must've drank was a vial of Atlanta's blood. As it wasn't much, he'd not have access to her powers for long. Five minutes, maybe, possibly ten. Anything helped. If Sean could keep her busy while The Great Order fought Superior Order foot soldiers on the ground, they might have a chance of gaining the high ground, so to speak.

Gray tried to focus. He thought, *What do we need to win?* He saw the bathroom door and muttered, "We need Atty."

With that, he spun about, facing the ladies room. One step in that direction however, and the silver wolf stepped into his way. He coiled to sprint when a black panther, the same one that'd come from the ladies room, stepped between him and the wolf. The wolf growled and snapped and the panther hissed back, and shook its head. The wolf examined her, and then went after someone else.

The cat turned to Gray, its green hazel eyes looked at him and then at his staff, and for a moment he sensed something—but then the panther turned away and the connection was gone. It positioned itself in front of the women's restroom and sat on its haunches.

Gray took a deep, steadying breath, and figured what the hell, and he cautiously approached the black panther. "Okay pretty kitty, I need to get in there. Can ya let me pass?"

The cat shook its head at him. Gray twirled his Bo-staff and the panther hissed, showing its teeth and crouching into attack stance. Gray realized either this cat wanted to kill him itself, or the reason it protected him earlier was something else, and he would have to figure it out. "Great...I've gotta play twenty questions with an overgrown cat."

He glanced behind him. On the other side of the room, it was an all-out brawl. Primarily each breed fought its own kind with minor switch over. It was organized chaos. Sean fought Valencia up on the upper level and held his own. Except landing on a member of The Superior Order, knocking them out.

He cussed and got up just as an arrow flew toward Roman. Sean shoved Roman out of the way—taking the arrow himself in the right side of the chest. He dropped to his knees as the second arrow headed toward Roman and Phoenix. Kat jumped up to deflect it and it hit her in the neck, going straight through. Falling to the floor, she didn't move.

"Kat!" Roman yelled out as he went to her.

In doing so, he let his guard down and a vamp slid in behind him, staking him. Roman went down, a scream on his lips, but he didn't turn to dust.

Valencia was now free to fight from the air without anything to stop her and Gray knew the battle wasn't turning in their favor. He needed to get Atty. Where was she?

He turned back to the panther. "What the hell. Is Atlanta in there?" he asked the panther.

The cat nodded.

"Will you let me pass?"

It shook its head.

"Is she okay?"

The panther nodded and Gray heaved a sigh of relief.

"If you're not here to hurt her or take her, what are you here for?"

The panther tilted its head as if to remind him that it couldn't talk.

"You remind me of a girl I knew—stop giving me that face! Let me through to her!"

The cat shook its head again and he contemplated attacking, but then he noticed the utter silence behind him. Everyone in the fight zone was frozen. Gray had seen Atty do this. The air around them had solidified and they couldn't move.

Valencia floated down from the top of the room to hover above Phoenix. She motioned to a cougar not far from the group and it changed into a tall woman with short blonde hair. She sprinted over to the bar and reached under the ledge. She pulled out a syringe and held it up in the air. Valencia motioned and it flew toward her. Grabbing it, she flipped upside down and with no trouble at all injected its contents into Phoenix's neck.

Loosening the air around him she hooked an arm around him and began to lift him into the air. With her free hand, she pulled at the air coming from open doors and windows and threw it at the ceiling. The thin roof of the old bar exploded open and she flew out the hole she had created and into the night, with a Prince of The Great Order in her arms while everyone stared in horror.

Seeing this, Gray switched focus to the black panther, now ready to kill it so as to get to Atlanta. Before he made a move though, the panther jumped on him, knocking him over, putting its face in his. Its gaze bore into his and the face of the panther seemed to go soft. Gray thought for sure it would bite him. Instead, it licked his face, giving him what Jensine would've called a "moose kiss," and leapt off of him, following the silver wolf out the door with the rest of The Superior Order. Gray stood up and ran into the bathroom to find Atlanta on the floor, out cold. Next to her lay a tiny brown paper lunch bag that said one thing on the outside: "Gray."

He picked up the bag and opened it. All that lay inside was a syringe. He took it out and for a second he worried it would kill her, but something told him if Valencia wanted his best friend dead, she already would be. He pulled up the sleeve of her shirt and stuck her with the needle, dispensing the yellow liquid. Immediately her eyes fluttered open.

"Where am I?"

"The bathroom floor, cause it obviously looks comfy."

"Gray, you ass. Help me up, I feel—icky."

"You were drugged. Can you walk? We have an emergency. I need you out in the club, like *now*."

"What happened? I feel woozy. I'll need your help."

"Yes, ma'am." He rushed her as fast as possible out into the main room where everyone still stood frozen.

"What happened here?" she asked utterly confused.

"Valencia has them stuck somehow."

"She turned the air solid. That's not fair fighting."

"Cause she seems like the poster child for fair."

Atlanta concentrated on the air. "It's like what I put around Roman at Jensine's house. It freezes and protects you. It's tricky because you leave a small bubble of breathable air inside. The fact that she can do one this size is amazing." Working quickly she reached out and pulled the walls down in sections, causing wind to whip around the room until she finished.

The first thing Atlanta did was look for Sean. He stood, pulling arrows out of his body and she rushed over, Gray on her heels.

"Are you, are you okay?" she sputtered, her voice frantic.

"Yeah. It's Roman and Kat I'm worried about."

Atlanta scanned the damage. Seeing both, she hurdled over people and tables to get to them. Roman currently lay on top of Kat, a stake in his back on the left side. Stephan stopped her. "Don't move him, it could be so close to his heart."

Tears welled up in her eyes, but she agreed.

Desi ran over to him and put her hand on Roman's body. "It's close, but you should be able to pull it out."

"How can you tell?" Gray asked.

"Water. The body, even a vampire's body, is still made of a lot of water. It can talk to me."

Sean gently put his hand around the stake. "Which way should I pull, Desi?"

"Straight up and out. Tip is nestled on the right side of his heart."

Sean counted to three and pulled it out. Lance lifted Roman up and laid him on the long party table, his feet in what was left of the cake. As bad as he was, Gray could tell everyone knew he'd live. It was what lay underneath him that broke his heart.

"Kat? Can you hear me, baby?" Stephan said, kneeling down next to her.

She'd shifted into human form with the arrow still stuck in her neck, the floor covered in her blood. Desi touched her body and closed her eyes. When they opened Gray saw true sadness in Desi's face. She looked at everyone and shook her head. "The wound never closed since the arrow is still in there."

Gray understood the unspoken sentence. Kat had bled out too fast to save her.

"Stephan?" Kat whispered.

Stephan knelt by her. "Yes, baby, it's me."

Gray came up and stood behind him, his hand on Stephan's shoulders.

"Magick arrow. I couldn't change back at first. Couldn't move."

"Shhh…no need to explain.

"It doesn't hurt. It's okay."

"Her body is going numb," Desi whispered.

"Is Roman okay?" Kat whispered.

"He's going to be fine, you did a good job, Kat," Celeste said.

Stephan took her hands in his, "You're going to be fine too, baby."

A slight smile touched the corner of her mouth. "You never were a good liar," she said, trying to swallow.

Tears started to run down Stephan's face.

"It's all right. I did what I was trained to do. Protect him. I may be the first to fall in this war, but I will not be the last. Fight for what I died for. Freedom and safety for the humans and our kind."

Stephan nodded, he was crying too hard to speak.

"We will," Bianca said.

"Tell him I loved him till the end."

Atlanta's breath stilled in her throat and Gray caught her eye. He knew she understood, as he now did, why Kat had never liked her. She was the ex-girlfriend he'd stopped seeing when Elizabeth had died.

Tears ran down Atlanta's face and seeing it, Gray took her hand.

"I will baby," Stephan said, finally finding his voice. "He'll know everything. I promise. I love you so much."

"I love you too..." Kat's voice trailed off, her eyes appearing glassy and flat.

Stephan collapsed over her body and sobbed, petting her black and pink hair. Gray let go of Atlanta with a hand squeeze and knelt next to Stephan, his arm around him, as they all stood there with tears running down their faces.

After a few moments Atlanta asked, "Where is Phoenix?"

* * * *

"I breaking news tonight, large wild animals were discovered at a nightclub in the city causing pandemonium, injuries, and one fatality. Brian Bowman has more information for us on the scene...Brian?"

"Yes, thank you Patty. Behind me, you will see The Barn Nightclub. Originally a farm barn in the early 1900's, tonight this building received animals it never intended to house. According to eyewitness statements, wolves, panthers, and cougars were just some of the animals seen on the premises.

"It is unclear how they got in or where they went. The city is on high alert tonight as the police department has officers on patrol in the area for resident's safety. They are asking everyone in the vicinity to please stay indoors tonight. If you see something suspicious, call 911 immediately.

"The owner of the club, Phoenix Keziah, was unavailable for comment but the co-owner, Lance Khan, was. He stated the number of those injured was minimal. Sadly, one young woman was killed in this bizarre attack. No names were given at this time but it is a sincere tragedy surrounded by extremely bizarre circumstances.

"Will The Barn be looking at a lawsuit? Mr. Khan didn't believe so. It will, however, be closed tomorrow for repairs, opening back up on Saturday. This is Brian Bowman reporting for Channel Five News. Back to you Patty."

"Thank you Brian. A tragedy indeed. If you have any information surrounding the events tonight at The Barn Nightclub, please call 911 or the number at the bottom of your screen. This is Patty Cordal with Channel Five Special News Update. We now return you to your regularly scheduled program..."

A football hit the TV and turned it off.

"I hate them."

"Yes, darlin'. I know," Atlanta said, patting Gray's leg.

Thomas was attending to wounds in the mansion's parlor and the crowded room was very quiet. In the study on the second floor, Stephan was calling Kat's family. Gray tried to offer to make the call, but Stephan said they needed to hear it from him—he was her best friend.

Sean, Atlanta, and Gray were sitting on the hearth of the fireplace getting warm.

They had spent an hour at the scene answering questions for the police. Luckily, the police chief was of Clandestine decent and the news crews were given little information. It would blow over in a few days and no one would think of it again— at least, in the human world. In their world it would be all they'd be able to think of for a while.

When Stephan returned, he looked paler than normal.

Gray rose and went to him. "Were you able to reach her family?"

He nodded and pulled Gray into his arms.

The silence grasped the room again as Roman walked in. He still had a bandage wrapped around his bare chest from when he'd been seen by on scene paramedics. The wooden stake had been in him long enough that the wound was taking a little more time than normal to heal. He only wore the pair of black pants he'd had on that night, which were still covered with blood and remnants of cake.

He addressed everyone in the room. "I need us all to figure out exactly how this happened. Is there anyone who had a full view of the kidnapping?"

Gray pulled away from Stephan and raised her hand. "I did."

"What happened?"

Gray told them every last detail.

Roman spun toward Sean and Atlanta. "And where were you?"

"In the middle of the fight, dude," Sean shot back. "You know that."

"No offense, Sean. I wasn't talking to you."

Sean went to say something and Atlanta touched his arm to stop him. "I was attacked in the bathroom before anything even happened. Someone grabbed me from behind and stuck a needle in my neck. I don't remember anything until I woke up to find Gray hovering over me."

Roman pursed his lips together and took a breath in. He stayed silent for a moment and then he gave her a deadening stare. "So this is your fault."

This caused an eruption from Sean, Gray, and the girls.

"Silence!" Atlanta yelled. Everyone stared at her and the sinking feeling Roman might be right hit her. Atlanta needed to hold her ground and stared him down. "How is this my fault? Please, educate me, Roman."

"You were sloppy and pre-occupied and let down your guard. Because of that, the Prince is gone. Valencia didn't have an Air Witch to combat her skills. You may as well have handed her Phoenix. Or maybe that was the plan."

At this she stood up. "Seriously? You really believe that?"

"It's no secret you aren't fond of our old ways. Ever since you arrived The Superior Order seems to be getting exactly what they want."

"That's Harmon's fault, not mine!" she yelled, moving closer to him.

He matched her tone and movement. "What is the point of all the training we've been doing if you don't use it, Atlanta? You let this happen!" He put his finger in her face and as he yelled, his voice getting louder and louder. "You let them take you out of the game and Kat is dead and Phoenix is who knows where because you weren't paying attention!" He threw his hands in the air on the end of his rant, letting them land crossed over his chest with a slight wince of pain.

Tears welled up in her eyes. The deep down feeling that it *was* her fault, and the anger at herself that came with it, ate at her soul. Yet, for Roman to air this dirty laundry for everyone took her pain and anger to a boiling point. So much so, that the windows began to tremble.

"Not the new windows Atlanta," she heard inside her head from Sean. *"Control the anger."*

She took a deep breath and the windows stopped shaking. In a low, quiet voice Atlanta answered him. "You are his bodyguard. If you wanna put blame on me because you failed—fine. If the pain of losing Kat is more than you can deal with on your own—fine. I'll take the blame." Atlanta stared in the face of everyone else in the room, one by one with a sweeping turn. Their faces were a mix of pain and sorrow. She hurt inside for what she'd let happen. But it wasn't only her fault and she knew that.

"I will take the fucking blame!" she yelled. "Is that what you all need? To put blame somewhere? That's fine. I'll carry it for all of us, if it'll make you all sleep tonight." Sean reached for her but his touch felt like fire on her skin. She wasn't in the state to be consoled yet, nor was she finished speaking. Again she let her voice calm down and continued, "But this is all of our doing. Not just mine, not just Roman's. *All.* We all knew something was coming and instead of taking precautions we got sloppy, me included. We did exactly what she knew we'd do."

"Oh, you now know how she thinks, do you?" Roman blurted out, placing a hand on her shoulder and spinning her to face him.

Sean stood up. "Hands off her, Pierce. Now."

Roman took his hand back.

"She's right," Sean said. "We played right into her plan. She needs Phoenix for something. The question is, what does she need him for?"

"I don't recall asking you!" Roman shouted.

"I so don't care if you asked me. Shit, Roman, I'm the one that was stuck with that psycho for years, not you. I think I have a better idea of what type of things may go through her head."

"Maybe you are working for her."

"Are you kidding me?" Sean took a step toward Roman.

Atlanta moved to stand between them. "We do not need to be fighting amongst ourselves," she pointed out. "He's gone and we have to figure out how to get him back."

"Yeah, he's gone!" Roman cried out, tears starting to run down his face. "We trusted you and you did nothing! She's dead—both wonderful girls are dead and you did nothing—*we* did nothing—we just let them die—"

Roman dropped to his knees in the middle of his crying ramble and Atlanta finally understood the depth of his anger and pain. He was pairing Elizabeth with Kat in his mind. She stepped toward him and put her hand on his head. He let his head fall onto her waist, wrapped his arms around her and he cried like she'd never seen. Sean gave her a nod of understanding. Roman was not only feeling guilty for Phoenix's kidnapping, but Kat's death had him reliving Elizabeth's.

Once he had cried out all his anger, Roman let Gray and Stephan help him up and escort him to one of the bedrooms on the second floor. Celeste made some tea to help him sleep and they left her with him and came back downstairs. Once they were in the parlor and let everyone know Roman was sleeping, Atlanta took the floor.

"Roman is right about one thing—we did let our guards down. It can't happen anymore. We all need to be ready and cautious at all times. Not only that, but we can't be the defensive team, we need to be the offensive team. We need to attack, not just be attacked. We need to figure out where her key people are and take them out."

"I am down with that!" Bianca said.

"But how are we supposed to do that?" Celeste asked, wincing in pain as she entered the room. Her leg had gotten slashed open. "Don't get me wrong, I'm all for us kicking some Superior Order ass, but our leader is gone and we have no idea how to find him."

"She's right, Atty," Desi agreed.

It was time to sink or swim. Atlanta saw that. She also knew who needed to lead the team to shore. It scared her, but it also seemed to feel effortless and right. It was her time to step up into her birthright and do what she was meant to do. She'd stated she would take no side. By stepping forward to do this she would be.

Atlanta looked at the faces of those in the room. They all were so used to following Phoenix, to have him gone and his second in command consumed by grief; they were like a lifeboat without oars. She caught Sean's eye and even without any mental conversation they seemed to understand what needed to be done.

"Sean, you know who many of her key people are, right? I mean, you lived there for years—the people in the prison must've talked."

"I do know who a lot of her people are, I just don't know *where* they are," Sean said.

For the first time a member of the CPA stepped forward. "With the right recon we can find them," J.J. said.

"Good. Okay. So, tonight let's all get some rest. We'll meet here tomorrow evening and everyone needs to bring ideas to the table. One hour after sundown. Here in the parlor. Everybody in?"

"Am I to understand you are going to take point, pick your side?" Stephan inquired, lifting his head from Gray's shoulder.

"I am. Are you all with me? Yes or no? Now's the time to jump on board or run for safety. I'll not judge you either way. You just need to pick which way you will go. So, are you with me?"

Everyone either nodded or said yes.

"Good. Now please, go home, get rest. The sun will be up shortly, so vampires, you either need to crash here or go home. If you want to stay here, please let me know and I'll show you to a room."

Most people wanted their own beds and left. A few, like Pepper and Stephan, stayed with them. Atlanta wanted her room as well but Stephan stopped her, pulling her into a hug.

"We'll make her pay for this, I promise," she said in his ear.

Stephan pulled away from her, put his hands on her shoulders, and said, "You know he didn't mean it."

"Of course," she agreed flippantly.

"He didn't mean it," he professed again.

"I know," she said again but she felt the tears coming.

"He didn't mean it, Atlanta. It's not your fault."

The tears pushed free of the hold she'd had on them. Through the blur of them she kept her eyes on his and nodded.

"We all have faith in you. We all knew people were going to die in this fight. You can't save everyone and you can't be the only one whose shoulders this war falls on."

She stared at the floor. "But I'm the chosen one who's supposed to—"

He lifted her head up, finger on chin, to look at him. "You are not Jesus Christ. You are not perfect. You'll have victories and you'll have losses. It's how you handle your losses that define you, not your victories. Tomorrow is a new day. Get some rest."

Atlanta nodded and wiped tears from her face. He kissed her on the forehead and walked off toward Gray's room. Gray hugged her, too. He didn't say anything because he didn't have to. He only needed to give her that Gray smile. He planted a kiss on her cheek and went off to join Stephan. She felt someone take her hand. It was Sean. Her bottom lip trembled as more tears ran down her face.

He leaned his forehead onto her temple. "I love you."

It took the wind out of her and she let her head fall onto his shoulder. He picked her up and carried her to bed. He made love to her and then let her fall asleep in his arms.

Chapter Seven

"Ouch!"

"Stand still, you wuss," Jensine ordered.

"Yo, you coulda warned me you were gonna throw alcohol on that!" Hunter complained.

A sly smile touched Jensine's lips. "I'm trying to stitch ya closed but you keep moving. Sit still!"

"Yes mom."

Jensine glared at Hunter with narrow eyes.

"Hey, that's a compliment. My mom is fantastic." Jensine started to stitch up his left arm. "Can I ask you somethin'?"

Resituating in her seat, Jensine tried to remember their class on sutures. "Sure."

"Why didn't you let me jump that tall skinny kid with the sprayed blue hair?"

She glanced up at Hunter's face and then down at her work on his arm. "He used to be a friend—he *is* a friend."

"He has an odd way of showing it. He's not even Clandestine and he's fighting with them? Why is he not here with you?"

"He thinks I'm dead. He thinks that this is the side that killed me, so he fights against them."

"But that's not true. Jonathan saved you from The Great Order."

"So it would seem. But he doesn't know that."

"Well, tell him!"

"Valencia said I can't, yet." Jensine put the last stitch in and started to tie it off.

"What was your job then?"

She grabbed the scissors. "All she wanted me to do was drug the witch girl and guard her so no one could wake her until we had the package."

"You've become a good fighter. I have no idea why she gave you such a menial job."

"It was a test, I'm sure." She cut the stitch thread. "There, you're done."

Hunter looked down at it. "Nice job. Think I'll get a scar from that stupid silver tipped Bo-staff?"

"Maybe. Who hit you anyways?"

"Really tall blonde chick. Witch was faster than I thought she'd be. I got her, though, a nice slice on the thigh. It'll leave a scar."

It almost made her choke, but Jensine said it anyway, "Good for you."

"Thanks! Now come on, I'm starving. Let's get some food before she calls us for debriefing. She said she'd open the cafeteria for an hour in honor of our good job."

"I'm not real hungry," Jensine admitted. To be honest, she was nauseous.

"Ya sure?"

"Yeah." Jensine wished she could explain how her stomach was in knots; how the one person in The Great Order who *knew* she was here was the one man they'd captured that night.

She'd had no time to warn Phoenix of the attack. When they'd suited up, they thought it was only for an exercise, not the real thing. Not until they were on the plane did the squad leader tell them the deal. She wasn't wearing the ring she used to talk to Phoenix, because it was rather large and she had to be careful of where she wore it.

"You ok?"

"Huh?" She muttered, climbing out of her head and into the real world.

"You seemed to have checked out there for second."

"Sorry, told you, not feeling good."

"Go lay down in the barracks. I'll come fetch you for the debriefing."

She smiled. "Thanks."

Hunter pointed at his arm. "No, thank you."

He walked off to the cafeteria and Jensine decided to take his advice and head on over to the barracks. She took a hot shower, changed into civilian clothing, and lay down on her bunk to attempt to figure out what to do next. She woke to a touch on her arm and swiftly sat upright, swinging. Luckily, she missed.

"Whoa, calm down there, Jen, it's only me."

Jensine took a deep breath and let it out slowly. "Sorry Hunter, I'm on edge a lot lately. It's all the training," she lied.

"I snuck you out some chicken soup and a roll. Here, eat it. You'll feel better."

Jensine thought to refuse it, but realized she never knew when she'd be running. Eating when she could was probably wise. "Thanks."

"No problem."

Hunter hung out while Jensine ate. As she finished, an announcement came over the speakers. "All Bravo company please report to the lab. All Bravo company to the lab."

Hunter jumped up. "That's our call."

"Yes, it is."

They both headed across the courtyard and then down the elevator. Hunter hit the button for the lab and as the doors were about to close a few other members of Bravo stepped in.

"Yo, Greyhound...Pip...what's up?" the young boy asked.

Jensine wasn't sure of his name but she thought it might be Toby.

"You two lookin' forward to this as much as I am?" Toby asked, bouncing on the balls of his feet as the doors to the elevator closed.

"This is gonna be quite a show, I'm sure!" the girl that'd gotten in with Toby added.

"How so?" Jensine asked.

"Anyone else notice that Jonathan wasn't on the mission?" Toby asked.

"She never does anything without him, you're right," Hunter agreed with a nod. "Wonder why this was different."

Jensine felt the soup in her stomach vying to come up. Other than Valencia and the General, was she the only one in The Superior Order who knew Jonathan's true identity was Harmon Keziah. He was Phoenix's fraternal twin brother. If Valencia kidnapped Phoenix without Jonathan's knowledge, either this would be the best showing of self-restraint ever, or Jonathan was going to go ballistic.

* * * *

Valencia came out of the medical ward as Jonathan approached the interrogation room. She peeled off her gloves and threw them away in the biohazard bin. "Hello lover, did you miss me?"

"Of course, always," Jonathan said, leaning in and kissing her.

"I got you a gift. Go ahead into the interrogation room. We'll join you in a moment."

"Who is it?"

"You'll see. Now be a good boy and go on in."

Jonathan walked into the room and Valencia returned to the medical suite. With a simple motion from her, the guards picked up a groggy Phoenix, and dragged him into the interrogation room. She watched Jonathan stand up so quickly his chair tipped over, anger engulfing his face.

Using vampire wire, a special rope woven with thin slivers of wood and steel wire, Valencia's guards tied Phoenix to the steel chair in the room that was bolted to the floor. Phoenix was so drowsy that tying him down was quick and easy.

Jonathan walked over and hit the switch so that the observation booth couldn't hear him. Through clenched teeth he said, "What the hell is this?"

She put her hands on her hips in a coy manner. "What, you're not happy? I go all the way into town to get you this gift myself and you're not happy?"

"Happy? Why the hell would I be happy that you kidnapped my brother?"

She placed a hand on Jonathan's chest. "You're pretty, but thick in the head, honestly. With him out of the way you can be Prince. We had a deal." She poked him in the chest with her finger. "I'm holding up my part of the bargain. A year ago you wanted his head on a platter for handing Elizabeth over to me. Now you what, feel bad? Get over it." She went over to stand next to Phoenix. "This man is a monster. He talks pretty, he looks pretty, and he acts like The Great Order is righteous, but you and I know they're not."

Valencia could both see and feel Jonathan was at war within himself. It was true; she was only keeping her side of the promise. Did he really think she'd keep her end without his brother facing the truth? Was it possible Jonathan wasn't ready to torture his flesh and blood? No. He was. He just needed to get over the shock, warm up to it. Walking over she took Phoenix's chin in her hand roughly and spat out, "What's holding you back?"

"We didn't agree to this," he complained as he pointed at the audience of Bravo Company.

She let go of Phoenix's chin. "What does it matter? It's not like they don't know. The Great Order plays dirty, dirtier than we do by far. You and I agreed that in order for The Superior Order to take control of the Clandestine World and save this Earth from the humans destroying it, he needed to go. You need to take his place."

He sighed and sat on the corner of the table. "There's a hole in your plan."

"How so?"

"Now is not the time for this. By now my brother has contacted the King, and if not, he's at least called our cousin Javin. There is no way they'll let me assume control without a full investigation. An investigation we cannot afford right now."

"By law they have no choice," she argued.

"That law is old and, I can promise you that with circumstances as they are, the investigation will take precedence."

"Oh, so you'd like me to be able to capture him again, later."

Jonathan leaned into her. "No, I'd like you to kill him later. Let him die a hero to his people and I will be welcomed with open arms. But right now? I won't be the one they choose to lead them with him gone. I can guarantee it."

"Oh really? Who else would they choose? Roman? He's not fit to lead everyone. The man is an emotional train wreck."

"He's not the one they'll look to."

* * * *

"Okay," Atlanta said, quietly yet firmly. "This is supposedly where one of Valencia's top officers hangs out when she's not at Asmarahald in Canada. Her name is Alicia Cane."

"Hey, if she were a stripper she could go by Candy!" J.J. shouted.

Only 2Doggz, his tall, broad-shouldered figure, shook with laughter.

"Werewolves," Atlanta muttered. "She is our first target. Remember, this is a capture, not a kill. We can't learn from her if she's dead, people. Ok?" Everyone muttered an agreement of choice. "Are there any questions before we head over?"

They all were standing in a park in New York City, on Avenue A. Down two blocks, was a dance club called The Pyramid. That was their destination. They had a team of ten prepared to go in and find Alicia Cane, the first solid lead they'd found to Valencia. The team consisted of Sean, Atlanta, Celeste, Desi, Bianca, Roman, Gray, Stephan, J.J. and 2Doggz.

The werewolves were along with them for multiple reasons. One of which was because they had a safe house in Brooklyn tucked amongst some old deserted loft buildings. Second, they owned the long dark van they'd traveled to New York City in. Plus, she thought, the plan would go smoother with ten.

"I have a question, boss," Gray said, raising his hand like a kid in school. "What's the plan again?"

"Smart ass! Now let's head to the bar."

Gray started to laugh.

Atlanta knew he understood the plan just fine. "J.J.? 2Doggz? Your guest bartending shift starts in minutes. We paid good money for these spots. Get your asses in gear."

"Everyone got their C.L. workin'?" J.J. asked.

They couldn't know if Alicia would be listening in on their telepathy, so they all had on these cool new devices J.J. gave them. They looked like com-links from

Star Trek and worked like a mini walkie-talkie's. Touch it to talk, don't touch it to listen, or you could leave it open to talk and listen simultaneously, which they all decided on.

After a systems check J.J. ran off to the club to work the upstairs bar. 2Doggz wasn't far behind as he was supposed to be arriving at "work" now, too, in the downstairs bar. Atlanta thought it should be a simple mission with full witch and vamp backup. However, she was nervous anyways. You never knew what could go wrong.

They entered the bar in small, staggered groups. The first two groups to go in were Atlanta and Sean, followed by Gray and Stephan. Each couple paid their five bucks and headed over to the long bar on the right. J.J. was behind the long counter pouring a beer for a customer. He looked like a professional.

Atlanta let her gaze travel past the long hallway of bar toward the black box of a room where people danced. It was still early and only a few littered the dance floor, talking more than dancing. Leaving Sean at the bar, she headed toward the back. At the end of the bar, she noticed a door across from it, with stairs that led down to where 2Doggz would be working.

Seeing the three girls had entered, she leaned against the wall and spoke quietly into the com-link. "Bianca, Desi, and Celeste, let's have you three head downstairs."

"Sure thing!" Bianca agreed, obviously anxious for some dancing, her fire engine red hair already glowing in the bar lighting.

Once they headed down, Atlanta maneuvered into the main room. It reminded her of The Barn slightly, with its stage and dance floor with benches along the wall. Since the club was fairly empty still, Atlanta searched around for the girl she'd gotten a sketch of. Alicia Cane had long dark hair and pale skin—like most women in New York City. This was going to be difficult if she didn't get some inside help. That's when she saw the warm-up DJ was spinning, leaving the main DJ hanging out at the bar.

Thankfully, he felt like chatting with her before he started his set.

"Ms. Cane? Hotness is what I call her."

Atlanta gave him a look that said she needed more information.

"I mean, yeah—like, I know her, she's a regular all right. She's really into music. Sings too. Anyways, she usually shows up around one or so. Why you lookin' for her?"

Doing her best British accent Atlanta explained, "Oh, my brother happens to own a recording company. We'd heard through the grapevine she's a catch."

"Really? I mean, she's been trying to get her stuff out there but she works a lot."

Atlanta muttered, "I bet she does."

The DJ kept talking, "I keep telling her if she doesn't do something with her music now while she's young, her youth will pass her by."

"Somehow, I doubt that'll happen," Atlanta said sarcastically.

She heard people chuckling in her earpiece. Roman took his cue and, acting like a playboy music producer as best he could, slinked up to Atlanta and kissed one cheek and then the other.

"Patricia—darling—so good to see you love, any luck finding Ms. Cane?" he queried.

"This wonderful young man told me her hotness will be here around one."

"Her hotness?"

"She's smokin', man," the DJ clarified.

"Well, then, I may have to really get to know this girl when she arrives," Roman purred smoothly. "Set up a chance for her to sing in the studio."

"I always play her favorite song when I see her arrive, so listen for 'Send Me An Angel' by Real Life. I'll even point her out to you."

"That'd be excellent Chet," Atlanta said.

"It's Chip."

"Yes, sorry," she said, in character. "Had a cat named Chet once."

Roman pulled a twenty-dollar bill out of his pocket. "For your trouble?"

"No trouble at all," Chip said, taking the twenty. He then glanced at the clock behind the bar. "I'm up. Listen for her song and then come over this way."

"Excellent! Cheers!" Roman said, putting his arm around Atlanta and leading her away.

"Seriously? Patricia? Do I look like a Patricia?" she muttered so only Roman could hear.

"Well, actually—" she heard Gray in her earpiece about to comment.

She cut him off. "I know where you sleep, Stoltz." He cut off whatever he was going to say so she went back to speaking to Roman. "How was the accent? I didn't suck too bad, did I?" she whispered.

"You sounded a lot like Elizabeth. It's a bit creepy."

"I'll take that as a good sign."

Roman laughed and looked down into her eyes, and for a moment, it honestly felt like there'd never been bad blood between them. Then she saw him remember reality and slowly pull his arm away. He pretended to go get them drinks at the bar while she situated herself on the edge of the stage.

"Couldn't you have tried to get his name right?" Celeste teased in her earpiece.

"Not as much fun that way, Cee!" Atlanta said with a laugh. Celeste laughed too and Atlanta heard her go up to 2Doggz downstairs and order a drink. "How is it down there?"

"It's completely different from up there, let's just put it that way. It's sorta musty down here too."

"I thought Earth Witches liked the smell of the wet earth."

"We do. We don't like the smell of moldy earth so much though."

"Ah…I see."

"The music down here is heavier. Not mainstream stuff at all. The folks down here obviously all know each other. Not a place a vamp would hunt—the humans would notice someone was missing too fast."

"Okay—well, if our lady comes your way, we'll let you know. It's starting to get busy up here."

"Drink?" Sean said, sliding a vodka cranberry into Atlanta's hand.

"Thank you, dear," she said, kissing him.

Celeste's voice came out of the earpieces. "Do I hear pleasure mixing with work up there?"

"Nope," they both said at the same time.

"Liars, all of ya!"

"I hate to interrupt, but I think our lady just walked in the door," Gray said.

"You sure?" Atlanta asked.

"Pretty sure," Stephan said. "She made a large entrance, she and her entourage—one of which looks to be the meal ticket."

"Human toy on arm?" Roman asked.

Atlanta heard someone sniff the air and then J.J. spoke up as he gave Roman a glass of white wine. "Yep. He's human."

Roman sipped his wine and turned casually to glance at the entourage coming his way. "He better looking than me?"

"Nope," Stephan spoke up this time. Atlanta couldn't see where he was, but she figured he and Gray were near the entrance.

"Then we're still golden," Roman said, sipping his wine.

"Ego check is next to the coat check, Roman," Celeste teased.

They heard Bianca and Desi laugh and Atlanta about snorted her drink.

"Ha ha—I'm just doing that 'in character' thing." He swirled his wine in the glass to aspirate it.

"Sure you are, sir, sure you are," Stephan commented.

"Sod off, all of you," Roman sassed, but Atlanta saw he was smiling. She'd not seem him do that in a long time. It made her smile too.

"Where is she headed?" Atlanta asked.

"Straight back to you all in the main dance floor," Gray said quietly. "We're coming up right behind her. Look for—hell, you can't miss her."

Atlanta had no trouble spotting her. "Oh my."

"What?" Sean asked, then said, "Never mind. Dominatrix spotted." He let out a low whistle. "Hey baby, you got anything like that?" He turned to Atlanta.

With a playful shove at him she said, "Pervert." Pausing long enough that he'd pout she added, "Maybe."

"Eww...stop there," Gray teased. "Are we here to work?"

"Fill us downstairs people in!" Bianca begged.

"Target acquired. Woman with long, straight dark hair pulled back severely, wearing leather pants, see-through shirt, black bra, a patten leather waist cincher with spikes and cuffs, and serious black heels."

"Damn," Celeste blurted out.

Alicia handed what looked like a long leather jacket to her human toy.

"Celeste, boy toy is coming down to you. See what you can do to make him find his way home, would you? He's a cute guy...dark hair in a ponytail...scruffy trimmed facial hair..."

"I see him. Consider it done. Come on, girls. No man can resist three witches at once."

"So not fair," 2Doggz whined. "I want three witches at once."

"In your dreams 2Doggz!" the girls all said at the same time.

Atlanta realized the song "Send Me an Angel" had started playing and looked across the room at Roman. "It's time to go throw on the British charm there, pretty boy!"

"I'll do my best." Roman left the bar and walked to Atlanta. "Shall we go and see Chuck?" He gave her a wink as they headed to the DJ booth.

"It's Chip!" Everyone yelled into their headsets.

Atlanta laughed as she and Roman reached the DJ. He lifted her up into the booth. "Hi there—is she the girl with the…uh…leather?"

"Yeah, that's my hot girl."

"Thank you, Chuck," she said and leaned in and gave him a kiss on the side of his neck. She blew air into his ear, muttering words of a spell, and his eyes glassed over.

As Roman lowered her down, the DJ said in a far-off voice, "It's Chip."

"He'll remember nothing in three, two, one—"

"Hey folks, did you wanna request something?" Chip asked, coming over to the side of the booth, looking down at them like he'd never spoken to them in his life.

"Thanks, I'd love to hear some Nine Inch Nails if you have it?"

"Do I ever—what's your name?"

She smiled. "Alice."

"Like Alice in Wonderland…but, uh, without the blonde hair I guess."

She smiled. He blushed and tottered over to his equipment.

"You're mean," Roman said as they wandered off.

"How so?"

"Now I paid that man twenty dollars for no reason."

"Think of it this way, it's the first time I've used that spell, so we'll see if it lasts. If it doesn't, at least you gave him money to be quiet. And if it did work it's possible I just erased his whole day, so I think twenty bucks is probably all his day was worth."

"Sadly, you're probably right. Poor guy."

"So, shall we go and introduce you to our lady?"

"She seems to be surrounded by the other people in her entourage," they heard Gray say on the headset.

Smoke started to pour onto the dance floor making it a perfect time to move closer.

"Let's move in," she said and started to head in Alicia's direction to dance.

"Has she noticed her boy toy hasn't returned?" Bianca asked in her earpiece.

"Not yet," Atlanta said. "Doesn't seem to care too much."

"Wonderful."

"No need for her to worry." Stephan clarified, as he and Gray appeared at the edge of the dance floor. "She's got a whole bar full of humans to pick from."

"How are you going to get her alone? She's dancing with two girls who follow her everywhere," Gray observed.

"You and Gray are two boys. Go snag those girls," Atlanta suggested.

Through the smoke she saw them look at each other and then say in unison, "We're gay."

Atlanta sighed. "Thank you Captain Obvious! They don't know that. Play it straight for the night, gentlemen. If you have to, use Gray as bait."

"It's actually a brilliant idea," Sean said. "If she guesses they are gay, Stephan can convince them Gray is dinner and they all can share."

"What's that noise?" J.J. suddenly asked.

"Oops!" They heard Desi say. There was a moment of silence before they all realized that she was in the bathroom peeing and had forgotten to turn her com-link off. Everyone burst out laughing.

"Moving on…" Atlanta said.

"Yes, moving on, we're on our way—" Roman said and whisked himself toward Alicia, with Atlanta in tow.

They started dancing toward her. Soon, Atlanta took one side of her and Roman took the other. Alicia noticed Roman pretty quickly, and moved in his general direction. Atlanta hoped that the spell she'd put on him would last long enough. The spell gave him warmth to the touch and a stronger heartbeat, so she'd think he was human. She quickly started dancing with him. All it'd taken was a smile and eye contact.

"Wow, she's easy," Sean commented.

"Or hungry," Atlanta suggested.

"I like the idea of her being easy more," 2Doggz offered.

"I second that!" J.J. added.

Atlanta groaned. "Her friends are looking bored."

"On our way," Gray said. "Removing com-link seeing as I don't have long hair to hide it.

Stephan and Gray walked on into the dance floor area and over to the hot girls. They leaned against the stage and watched them for a bit. Atlanta blew a little air with a spell on it toward the girls and they went from being bored to noticing two pretty boys. And she had to admit, Stephan and Gray were doing a good job so far at pretending not to be gay. Quickly Atlanta cast the same spell on Stephan as she'd done on Roman just in case. The girls picked up on the scent of Gray and moved on in. Through Stephan's com-links they all heard bits and pieces of the conversation.

"Wow, they're dull," Desi observed.

"Ah, you're back, how was the bathroom?" Sean asked.

"Ha ha. It's gross. Anyway, I'm letting you know that Celeste was able to get the boy to switch focus."

"Celeste?" Atlanta asked in surprise. She never was the aggressor.

"Yeah, once we wiped him clear of Alicia he zoned in on Celeste and is really putting on the moves. He's cute for a human boy, actually."

"He's got a rough charm about him," Bianca agreed.

"She needs to get him to leave. The last thing we want is him in the way as we try to take our lady down," Atlanta reminded them.

"I hear ya loud and clear boss," Celeste confirmed. "He went to get us drinks. 2Doggz, slip that herb I gave you into his beer, would you? He'll be feeling a bit ill shortly."

"You got it, gorgeous!"

"Thank you."

"Make sure to get him a cab and pay for it," Atlanta told the girls.

"No problem. I'll come back online when we're done. Gotta go, here he comes."

"Desi and Bianca, follow them out, make sure he gets outta here okay."

"No problem."

Atlanta stole a glance at Alicia. She was really putting the moves on Roman, who didn't seem to mind at all. Roman whispered in her ear and Atlanta realized he'd removed his link. Alicia smiled and took his hand and they walked over to the bar. She jumped up to lean across the bar and Atlanta could hear her through J.J.'s com-link.

"Hey bartender!" she yelled. J.J. walked over to her. "Where's Dirk?"

"He's on vacation."

"I'm Alicia. Did he tell you about me?"

"Maybe." He wiped a glass out and pretended she wasn't important.

"I keep my wine back there. I'd love a glass of it. Did he show you?"

J.J. gave her a sly smile. "He sure did ma'am. Hold on and I'll be right back. Anything for you, sir?"

"I'll have a Heineken," Roman ordered.

"Comin' right up!"

J.J. brought Roman his beer and Alicia a glass of the drugged blood wine they'd replaced her usual blood wine with. They toasted each other, and she started asking him questions about himself, doing the "want to get to know you" routine. Atlanta wondered how often she did this, how much time she put into getting to know someone before she killed them. It made her stomach turn a bit.

Sean joined Atlanta on the dance floor. "Hey good lookin', wanna dance? We've got some time to kill, since that drug takes about thirty minutes to work."

She stopped watching Roman enjoy Alicia's company and brought her attention to where it belonged. "I'd love to!"

Half hour later Alicia was showing signs of the wine taking effect and Roman's link came back on.

"It's so loud in here," Alicia's voice slurred out.

"We could go for a walk outside," Roman offered.

"It's a chilly night though."

"Can I gag yet?" Atlanta asked. Nobody responded.

"I have a nice big…van, we could go in there…it'll be warmer in there…"

"Perfect," she purred. "You sure you don't want some of my wine?" she asked.

"Oh, I can't. Red grapes make me break out in hives."

"Nice one!" Bianca threw out there. They saw Roman smile at the praise—or was it because Alicia reached up and ran her hands through his hair?

"Bartender!" Alicia yelled out, "I'd like to take my bottle with me!"

"As you wish, ma'am," J.J. said, very politely, then handed Alicia the wine bottle.

That was when Atlanta realized she hadn't seen Gray and Stephan in a bit. "Gray? Stephan?"

No answer.

"Gray! Stephan!"

Still no answer.

"Crap. Everyone look for Gray and Stephan. Sean and I are running out the front door right behind Alicia and Roman."

"My van is this way," they heard Roman say.

"Roman, we'll be right behind you acting drunk and stupid and we'll be outside the van. If we stop hearing you, we're coming in," Sean let him know.

"Ok," Roman said, then after a long pause, "here's my van."

Laughing loudly in drunken fashion, Sean and Atlanta stumbled arm in arm down the sidewalk, pretending to help each other stay vertical. As Roman opened the van door and let Alicia in first, they continued this ruse. He gave them a nod as if he would to any stranger and they giggled. Sean tickled Atlanta until he had her back against the building near the van. Roman went in and shut the door. They continued talking as Sean started kissing her.

"Those two out there have the right idea," Alicia said, "don't you think?" She'd have sounded very seductive if she hadn't sounded so tired.

"Then come over here," Roman said.

All Atlanta could hear now were the sounds of the pair in the van making out. She was about to make some funny comment about it when a breathless Stephen came online. "Holy cow. We're back. Woo! That was a ride!"

"Where have you two been?" she hissed.

"Girlfriend, we've got a story for you!" Gray said.

"Where are you?" she asked.

"Two blocks away. Sorry, we were outta range."

"I'm exiting the bar," J.J. told them. "What's the status of the couple in the van?"

Atlanta had forgotten about the van for a moment. Looking over, she noticed the van lurch and they all heard heavy breathing in their com-link's that was either a fight or seriously kinky foreplay.

"Looks like we've got a fight going on in there!" Sean told them. "Good thing she's drugged, he should have her pinned in seconds."

"When the van is a-rockin', please come a-knockin'!" J.J. said.

"Roman?" Atlanta asked. No answer. "His link has probably fallen off. Everyone surround the van. I'll go on top."

Atlanta heard Sean mutter something about her being on top and she slapped his arm before she flew up to the top of the van. She needed to create a magickal visual block so onlookers wouldn't see anything. Sean went to open the van door and it was locked.

"J.J.?" Sean put his hands up.

J.J. tossed Sean the keys and he opened the door.

When it opened, Sean found the two of them fighting. Roman was on top and had her pinned down, but Atlanta could tell Alicia had given him a run for his money.

"Man, I can't have sex with my girlfriend in here if you're screwing Cruella DeVille," Sean joked.

"But Sean, I thought you'd want in on this," Roman said, playing along.

"Oh, how I do!"

With that, Roman leaned back enough to let Sean hit her in the face, and knock her out.

"Nice work there, Cameron," J.J. said.

"I hate this girl. She's one of the vamps that caught me. She's a strong, feisty little bitch, ain't she, Roman?"

"Even drugged, she was strong."

"Quick, let's get her tied up and into the back before the spell Atlanta's doing wears off."

Gray, Stephan and the girls appeared. Celeste gave Atlanta the thumbs up and she let the magick wall down. They all got into the van and J.J. started it up.

"How is it one punch and Sean knocks her out, but you only could get her pinned, sir?" Stephan teased.

"I don't like hitting girls."

"It was probably just the sedative finally kicking in," Sean suggested, giving a look to Roman.

The van started up and they pulled into traffic. "We're off like a prom dress!" Gray said and they headed away from The Pyramid and toward Brooklyn.

* * * *

"She's securely fastened and coming to. Who wants to be in there with her first?" J.J. asked, coming out of the interrogation room, his hand running through his chin length, light brown hair.

Atlanta adjusted her now more comfortable attire, long sleeved T-shirt and jeans. "I think all of us up here can go on in."

J.J. nodded and headed on downstairs to the main entrance where he and 2Doggz were to stand guard. Stephan and Gray had taken the van for supplies, as they were out of blood and food. It left Atlanta, the girls, Roman, and Sean to talk to Alicia.

"I honestly think it might be better to let the men do this, Atty," Celeste said. "Keep our faces unknown."

Atlanta pondered this. "You three can stay out here if you want, but I'm going in. We'll bring you in if you're needed. That work?"

They all either yawned or mumbled an agreement as Roman, Sean, and Atlanta wandered into the interrogation room. It was small, with no windows or ventilation and had soundproofing along the walls. Alicia sat in a steel chair in the corner farthest from the door, shackled into the chair in multiple places. The rest of them sat at a long table on the other side of the room.

Atlanta inspected Alicia. She didn't seem like a mass murderer, but looks were deceiving and probably the reason she was such a good hit man for Valencia. Attached to her temples were electrodes that she'd been told would emit a high frequency if she attempted to reach out mentally to touch anyone's thoughts. Next to the chair stood a floor lamp turned up to half. Above the chair hung a tanning lamp bulb whose UV rays could seriously hurt her, if they needed it.

Roman went over and opened the velvet pouch on the table in front of her. Inside were knives. One was silver, one gold, and one that seemed to be made of wood. Next to them lay a syringe filled with pink liquid and a small plastic container about the shape and size of a tube of Chap Stick. Atlanta had never seen either of these last two items before, yet figured now wasn't the time to ask questions.

"She'll be able to see you," Roman reminded them as he sat in the chair facing the subject.

"That's fine," Atlanta said, as Sean and Atlanta walked to the chairs at the other end of the room and took a seat. Roman opened the small plastic container that looked like Chap Stick, leaned forward and waved it under Alicia's nose. This caused her to wake up rather quickly.

"Where am I?" was the first thing she mumbled.

"I thought I'd bring you home so we could get to know each other better," Roman said.

Her eyes focused on Roman's face and it all seemed to come back to her. "You know, it's not nice to drug a girl just so you can take her home and have your way with her."

Roman smiled. "Nice girls get treated nicely. You're not a nice girl."

"Oh, you're a clever one aren't ya?" she said, mimicking Roman's accent badly.

"I am." He stood up.

She sniffed the air and Atlanta wondered how long the spell on Roman would hold. She looked at him and sniffed the air again. "You smell human, but now that there's no flashing lights and smoke I can see you don't move like a human. And I smell others…ah, there you are. I see you."

"They are not your concern. I am." He put a ring of some kind on his right hand.

"So, what is your real name? I'm assuming it's not Mark."

"No, it's not."

Alicia started to laugh but the laugh became a scream of pain. Atlanta turned to Sean and he touched his temples. She understood then—Alicia had tried to read Roman's thoughts and discovered the electrodes.

Roman leaned down into her face. "Uh, uh, uh—no going into my head. We don't look too kindly upon going where you're not invited. Speaking of which, let's talk about The Barn party."

Alicia collected herself from the shock and pain she'd experienced. "What party? I like a good party."

The slap came so fast Atlanta didn't see it. She knew Sean did. There had been a blur of movement and then her head reacted and a red line of blood formed on her face. She started to laugh.

"Let's try this again," Roman said, leaning in a bit toward her as he lifted his right hand, prepared to strike her again. "Valencia took Phoenix. Where and why—that's all we need to know."

"Phoenix Keziah? The leader of the Empire?" she mocked.

This time the blur of movement resulted in a few more hits and more lines of torn flesh on her face produced blood.

"Oh sweetheart, I didn't know you were into the rough stuff. Bring it on," she said.

This time Roman leaned into her face full on and grabbed her throat. "Tell me where Phoenix is or I will give you more than you want."

"Oh stop, you know exactly where he is," she choked out. "You know she took him, you know where her location is, just ask her spy."

"Her spy?"

"Yes. Her spy. Sean Cameron."

Chapter Eight

The room erupted in noise.

Sean vaulted up. "That's a lie!"

"I swear to the goddess that if you are the reason Phoenix was taken I will burn you alive myself!" Roman yelled back at him.

"You honestly believe I work for that bitch? Are you serious? Come on!"

"Everyone calm down!" Atlanta yelled, stepping between him and Roman, doing her best to keep them apart as they both screamed at each other. Feeling as if hell would erupt through the floorboards at any moment, Atlanta mentally called out to the girls who rushed in and helped break Roman and Sean apart.

"What is going on?" Celeste demanded. "Roman, back off from Sean!"

Then they heard it—laughter. It stopped everyone at once. There sat Alicia, her face bleeding and healing at the same time, and she'd broken out of the arm cuffs and was standing up, blood dripping off her fingertips to the floor. Atlanta was pretty sure she'd break the chair in a moment and be gone.

"Roman Pierce. Wow, the head of the vampire sect of The Great Order, interrogating me. I must be important, or you all must be desperate."

Atlanta noticed Celeste had left the door open so she didn't hesitate. Using the air from the open window in the other room she wrapped Alicia in it.

"Well looky, looky there," she taunted, twitching at the binding. "You have an Air Witch too. How convenient."

"Screw you," Atlanta yelled.

"I see she has a mouth on her like the other Air Witch too."

Atlanta lifted the syringe on the tray into the air and pulled the cap off the needle. She allowed it to penetrate the air barrier and let it touch Alicia's skin. For the first time, she saw fear on Alicia's face.

"Atlanta, put that down. She's no good to us dead," Celeste told her, but the blood rushing in her ears made it hard to hear.

"I want the truth," she said. "This needle will give me the truth, will it not?"

"Yeah, but it'll kill her too," Roman said. "A slow and painful death at that."

Atlanta walked over toward Alicia, putting the tip of her nose barely above Alicia's and looked into her eyes. "I think it's funny how the dead are afraid to die. You are scared by this thing, aren't you, Alicia?" She felt Roman come up behind her. "Back off, Roman! Touch me and I'll inject her."

"I'm backing off."

"What an interesting dynamic we have here." Alicia said with a strained voice, "What do you want to know, witch?"

"You made a comment that has all of us fighting. Negate it, or prove it, or I will kill your ass right here and now. No more parties. No more innocent boys to drink from. Nothing."

Alicia paused and Atlanta let the needle go through another few layers of the vampire's skin, causing her to scream.

"It was a lie! Sean's wanted by The Superior Order. There was a price on his head, but ever since the werewolf was killed in the library, the order was lifted. Valencia didn't say why. All I could tell was that once she heard he was with you, she let him be."

Atlanta reached into the air around Alicia, placed her hand on the vamp's head and looked inside, pushing past the electrodes. The psychic contact hurt, like a high-pitched migraine, yet Atlanta was able to shove it aside and listen. She was telling the truth, at least to her knowledge. Atlanta took her hand back and removed the needle from Alicia's neck. She put it on the table and used the air to sit Alicia down in the chair.

"Roman, refasten her to that chair. She's telling the truth."

Roman, lips pursed and face radiating anger, held his tongue. She allowed him into the air field around her so as to tie Alicia up. Once she was, Atlanta let the airfield off her and left the room, giving Sean a quick hug on the way out. "I need fresh air," she said over her shoulder.

All she heard behind her was silence.

* * * *

"Pip! Wait up!" came Hunter's voice.

Jensine was getting used to the name. She set her bag down and wiped the back of her neck with her towel. She was a sweaty mess from training.

Hunter jogged over to her with a friend—a guy around Hunter's height, with a head of short, thick, dark hair, and ice blue eyes.

"Greyhound, what's up?" she asked, trying to make it sound like they were acquaintances instead of friends.

"Pip, this is Kamitted, aka Josh Brooks. Josh, this is my girl Pip. She's the one I told you about."

"Great to meet you," Josh said, putting his hand out.

"You too," she said apprehensively as she shook his hand. "How do you know Greyhound?"

"Josh raps with me in my group back home in the Carolinas. His street name is Kamitted, like mine is Greyhound."

She nodded and let go of his hand. "I get it. Nice to meet you, Josh."

Hunter stuffed his hands in his pockets. "What are you doing now?"

"I was going to grab a shower. PT kicked my ass."

"I meant after that."

"Oh…well, thought I'd go into town and get a steak and see a movie or something."

"Cool, who's all going to the movies?" Hunter asked.

Jensine looked down at the ground, "Uh…just me…I figured I'd go…you know, get off the base for a few hours." Jensine looked up again. "She did give us all twenty-four hours leave, right?"

"She sure did! Care if we join you?"

Jensine was taken aback for a second. "Um...sure. That'd be great!" she stammered, trying not to sound as excited as she felt.

"Sounds perfect. Got stuff to fill you in on over dinner," Hunter said with a wink.

"About what?" Jensine asked.

"You'll see."

"Ok then. So, it'll be the three of us?"

"Yeah."

Josh's phone buzzed. "Actually no. My girl's in town."

Hunter nodded. "She is? Word."

"Yeah, seems she just got in."

"Fantastic," Jensine said. "Well, let me get cleaned up. I'll meet you by the bus at seventeen-hundred hours."

Hunter smiled. "Great!"

The boys went off to their locker room and Jensine went to hers. As she showered, feeling the hot water hit her face she became lost in thought. She asked herself, "Is this a double date?" She answered herself with a resounding "No," telling herself Hunter didn't see her that way. Or, at least she didn't think he did. Hell, she didn't even know how she felt about Hunter, so it was a moot point to even contemplate.

After drying off she went to the barracks and decided to make herself look presentable. She put on a nice pair of jeans and a thin green sweater that always pulled the green in her hazel eyes out nicely. She put on her light trench coat for even though it was June, it was raining and it'd be a touch chillier than she'd like.

She stepped outside the barracks and was hit with rain. She opened up her umbrella and quickly headed over to the parking lot where buses stood to take members of her squad into town. Hunter, Josh, and a girl with a purple trench coat and black hat were getting on the bus.

"Hey!" Jensine yelled out, "Wait for me, ass!"

Hunter stopped and turned with a smile. "Come on woman!"

Jensine caught up and they got on the bus. Josh's girlfriend took off her hat and shook the water off of it.

"Wow! Your hair!" Jensine gushed, staring at its color.

"You like?" the girl asked.

"Yeah. I wish I had enough hair to do that with."

"Once you're done with basic training she'll let you grow your hair back," the girl said.

"Thank goodness!" Jensine said, pulling her cute cap down a bit. "I feel like I look like a dude."

Hunter laughed uproariously.

Jensine smacked his shoulder. "Shut up! It's not funny!"

"Hey now! I'm laughing 'cause no one would ever confuse your curves for a dude." He rolled his shoulder. "Woman's got a good swing!"

The bus started to pull out of the parking lot.

After giving Hunter a scowl she turned to Josh's girlfriend. "So how long have you been in the army here?"

"For a while, actually. I just happened to meet Josh one day 'cause I was teaching a class in combat when the regular instructor was out sick."

Jensine shook water off her umbrella in the bus aisle. "I was gonna say, I haven't seen you around."

"I've been on assignment actually. I still am. I got lucky and was able to leave for a bit to come see Josh and my brother Gabe. I have to go back out into the field after this weekend or I could blow my cover."

Jensine let that sink in, but didn't let it show in her tone as she said, "I'm glad you could get away. By the way, I'm Pip. It's great to meet you."

"Same here. I'm Pepper...but my friends call me P.J."

* * * *

The night air felt crisp for an early June night. As a shiver passed through her, Atlanta wished she'd brought her coat with her. But she refused to go downstairs, and decided to deal with it as she stood on the rooftop of the building in Brooklyn. She lit a cigarette and stared out over the buildings. In the distance she could see Manhattan all lit up. The twin towers stood above the rest, glowing. Atlanta always used to wonder what New York City's power bill must be. She took a long inhale on the cigarette and blew it up toward the stars.

"Those things will kill you, ya know," she heard a voice say behind her, jovial yet strained.

It was Roman. She glared at him as he stood at the door to the rooftop, and then went back to her skyline. The silence was so long that for a moment she thought maybe he'd gone back downstairs, until she heard him light up a cigarette.

She considered asking him what he wanted, but she knew that wouldn't be all that came out of her mouth. So she kept smoking her cigarette and staring out over the rooftops.

"I love this city," he finally interjected into the silence. "The nightlife here is as busy as the day life. It makes sense that a lot of vampires are here. You don't end up feeling like you've lost anything by missing the daylight. To be honest, a lot of humans here live the life of a vampire. People who get to work before sun up and leave after sun down like we do.

"Actually, I knew a Dead Vampire that worked on Wall Street with those hours. It was easy for him to blend with the humans that way. He only ended up leaving the job because he wasn't aging, and people were starting to notice after he'd been there a long time. He was able to push it off as great genes until he was reaching an age where it really wouldn't matter how great your genes were. He still misses that job."

"How long ago was that?" she managed to say. If he was going to try, she would too.

"Blimey—a long time ago," he said, walking over to her and leaning on the waist high wall that surrounded the rooftop. "I think he started working there in the early 1900's and left after World War II. He didn't need the money and he wanted to open up jobs for men coming back from the war. He retired early, so to speak. I think he told them he had a terminal disease and he left New York. Did you know that the Wall Street Stock Exchange began in 1790?" Roman asked her as he mindlessly messed with the cuff of his jacket.

Atlanta shook her head as she rubbed her arms. "I never was a history buff, sorry."

"My father was. Loved it. In fact, he first came over here around that time. I can hear him now. 'Son, did you know New York City was the first capital of the states in September of 1788? Then, in 1789 George Washington inaugurated at Federal Hall on Wall Street.'" He chuckled, stopped, slipped his coat off and draped it over her shoulders.

Atlanta opened her mouth to reject it but he continued to walk past her to the corner of the roof. Instead, she snubbed out her cigarette on the brick wall and tossed it into a coffee can that looked like it had been up there for ten years. While she waited, she slipped her arms into the coat.

He took a long drag, exhaled, and continued, "My dad would drill me on this stuff. He had watched how this country grew and was excited. What we now call NYU was created in 1831 and after he married Elizabeth's mum he applied to teach History. He was hired in 1916."

"He taught night classes, I take it," she asked.

Roman laughed and turned around to face her again, "Yes. Night classes. He told them he needed to stay home during the day with my sister, she was one year old so they believed him."

"Elizabeth's mom? Isn't she your mom as well?"

Roman's eyes locked with hers. "No. Same dad, different mums. My mother, her name was Joelle, was my father's second wife. They were married in 1923. I was born in 1922."

"Ooh, the scandal," she said with a smile.

"Oh yes," he smiled back at her. You see, my mum was previously married as well. She even had two sons in her previous marriage and because of her first husband's affiliation to politics she too was heavily involved. Times were changing and things in the Clandestine World were unstable. They desperately needed a great amount of order to keep those who were pressing legalities to their utmost limits in the name of superiority. So you see, my mum and her first husband started The Great Order."

"So, if you were born in 1922 you're...?" She did the math in her head. "Holy crap! You're seventy-five years old!"

He smiled wide enough to accentuate his dimples. "In human years, yes. But in Clandestine years, I'm only thirty-four."

Atlanta chuckled slightly and then remembered something else he'd said. "I noticed you mentioned having half-brothers. Is that right?"

"Yes, I do. Joelle had two sons—fraternal twins—with husband number one. Those boys were, are, my half-brothers. Due to their father's profession they came to live with their mother and took to being my big brothers instantly, teaching me all they knew, taking care of me."

It suddenly became clear as day. Atlanta stepped closer to him saying, "Phoenix and Harmon are your half-brothers, aren't they?"

"You are correct. Joelle's previously married sir name was Keziah."

Atlanta found she was nodding. Pieces of the puzzle were falling into place.

"There was a great fire in 1935 here in New York. Did you know that?" Roman asked, followed by another deep inhaling of his cigarette. He leaned back onto the roof ledge with both elbows. "About 700 buildings were lost in lower Manhattan. Being thirteen I was prone to adventure. I happened to be in one of those buildings at the time. Harmon got me out before I was killed."

He let that hang in the air a moment as he snubbed out his cigarette on the bricks before he continued. "It took him a while to heal from the damage he sustained doing that. Elizabeth took care of him. They didn't actually get together for years after that, because she was out trying to build The Great Order. But I always knew he liked her, and she him."

"But if they're—"

"Not blood related. She's the daughter of my father and another woman. The boys are sons of my mum and another man. So, they're only siblings though marriage. I'm the only one related to them all."

"And you are telling me all this now because…?" she asked, taking his cigarette butt and tossing it into the tin can.

Roman took a deep breath and took her hands quickly so she couldn't pull away and faced her dead on. "I'm sorry I was stupid enough to believe that bitch, even for a second. She played me like a piper and I fell for it. Down deep, I know there's no way Sean is working for Valencia. However, do understand, the rest of my family are dead. My half-brothers are all I have left."

He seemed to search her face for what else needed to be said, weighing it before he continued. "Of what's left of my family, one of them is in anguish and missing, while the other, who we all count on to keep us from chaos in our world, has been taken. So, other than Stephan, there's no one else I love left here except—" He cut himself off, as if he was deciding if he should finish or move on.

He didn't need to finish. She knew the answer. "Me."

He nodded. "You. And just because we didn't work out and you're with Sean, that hasn't changed—even though I know it should have. When she said Sean was the spy it sent my head reeling. Even though I knew better, I didn't—if that makes any sense at all. I really am sorry."

Atlanta squeezed his hands. "He's a good man, Roman. He's always honest, and I come first to him. That's what I need right now."

"I know." he said, letting go of her hands and turning his back to her. He raked his hands through his hair and added, "I can't help how I feel. My heart says one thing and my head says another."

Now it was her turn to go to him. She stood next to him, leaning on the roof wall edge with him, letting their arms touch. "What about that girl you brought to Solstice? Pepper?"

He paused. "I like her. She's really great. I guess we've been dating a bit, but she knows how I still feel about you and so she's cool with taking it slow. It's just nice to have a date for things. Because sometimes seeing you with Sean is harder than it should be."

Atlanta wanted him to know she felt the same way, but she didn't want to give him hope. She had no plans on breaking up with Sean. Then she considered lying, telling him she didn't feel that way so maybe he could move on. But she hated being lied to, so she couldn't do it to him. "If it makes you feel any better," she finally said as her heart pounded away in her chest. "I feel the same way sometimes. But I love Sean. He's really earned it."

"Ouch," he said, mockingly.

"You know what I mean."

"I do. I'm a mess, Atty. I really am a mess. I keep telling Pepper I'm not good for anyone, but she is very patient. I'm going to see what happens I suppose."

They were both still leaning on the edge of the roof when she reached over and took his hand, lacing her fingers with his. He squeezed her hand and she leaned over and kissed him on the cheek.

She felt a shiver go through his body, though he tried not to show it. His skin on her felt wonderful. But chemistry isn't everything she'd learned. Yet, for that moment, it felt good to let his head rest on the top of hers as they both looked out over Brooklyn, holding hands.

"Come on," he finally said. "I told your man I was coming up here to apologize. Let's get downstairs and chat some more with Ms. Cane, shall we?"

"Sounds like a plan."

* * * *

"So, Josh and I have a plan," Hunter whispered over the restaurant table.

"About?" Jensine whispered back. They were alone for the moment, seeing as Pepper had gone to make a call and Josh went to wash his hands as the food would be arriving soon.

"About you getting in to see Phoenix," he said through his teeth.

Jensine about choked on her soda. A day ago she and Hunter had been sitting out by the water and he'd really pressed to know what was bothering her. She'd caved. She gave a story saying she really needed to talk to Phoenix to get clarification as to what happened to her, see if he'd really ordered her death and so on. Hunter had acted like it wasn't possible, yet now he was saying otherwise.

She squeaked out one word. "Really?"

"Yeah, I wanted to talk to you about it, but I don't know Pepper and I don't know what her assignment is, so I don't trust her. Besides, the less people that know what we're up to, the better. Turns out Josh now has a split duty shift. He spends time working on The Superior Order's computers."

"He does?"

"Yeah, he's a computer whiz kid. Anyway, his job is to maintain cameras and other electronic equipment in the fortress. He's helping set up a new state-of-the-art system."

"And that helps us how?" she whispered.

Hunter leaned in and so did she. "All new systems have glitches. Maybe the cameras go dark for a few minutes while Josh lets you in to Phoenix's cell. Maybe it gets fixed after you've left."

"You are brilliant!" she said louder than she'd planned.

"Shhh! This I know, but we'll talk about it more after Pepper goes back to her job."

"What is her job?"

"No idea. All I know is she's doing undercover stuff. Josh isn't real thrilled with it. He knows she has to get close to some guy for information. He's jealous."

"I would be too. She seems to compartmentalize it easy enough."

"I think she's older than she looks."

"Oh, she's a vamp. Gotcha. What is Josh?"

"What am I what?" Josh interrupted, arriving at the table.

Jensine blushed. "I'm sorry. I was asking what classification you were."

"I'm complicated." Josh sat down in the side of the booth across from Jensine. "I'm a shape shifter by birth. But my mother was injured while she was pregnant, and her best friend Clare, who's a vampire, saved her life and mine by giving her some of her blood. So I suppose you could say my DNA is a bit screwed up."

"It gives him a super connection with anything electronic," Hunter said.

"What do you mean?" Jensine asked.

"He can look at anything mechanical and work it with his mind," Pepper said, sliding in next to Josh. "He's rare and beautiful. Valencia will have so many wonderful uses for you." Pepper leaned in and gave him a kiss.

"I do hope so," Josh said.

"Who had the rare steak?" The waitress asked.

"That'd be me," Hunter admitted with a grin. The waitress put the medium rare one and a milkshake in front of Jensine, and gave Josh his salmon.

"Fantastic!" Josh said, "I'm starving."

"You sure you don't want anything, miss?" The waitress asked.

Pepper shook her head. "I ate before we left the house, thanks though. I could use another coffee."

"Can do." She left them.

"Did you check on Gabe?" Josh inquired with a side glance at Pepper as he squeezed lemon on his salmon.

She smiled and clarified for Jensine, "My little brother runs my mom crazy with me gone. He's a handful. It helps if I call."

"You're close?" Jensine asked, cutting into her steak.

"Here's your coffee."

"Thanks." When the waitress left Pepper leaned in. "Yes, very. So, what were you two whispering about while I was gone?"

For some reason her smile made Jensine nervous. Vampires. They always made her feel like a deer in headlights of an oncoming semi-truck. "Nothing. Just Josh."

"What do you wanna know, darlin'?" Josh asked, biting into his fish.

"Where are you from? What is your animal? How do you know Greyhound?" Jensine asked, taking a sip of her milkshake.

"Well, I'm from Charlotte, North Carolina, and we know each other from college—UNC Charlotte. Both of us were in theatre. We had a hip hop group up there."

"Dynasty, baby!" Hunter said.

Jensine laughed. She'd heard Hunter use this term before. He used it in place of someone else saying "awesome" or words like that. "So what cool animal are you?" Jensine asked.

"He's a bird," Hunter jeered with a snicker.

"I can fly, what can you do, ass?"

"I can grow to be almost seven foot tall and eat a bear," Hunter bragged as he ripped a piece of the steak off with his teeth.

Josh rolled his eyes. "You werewolves are barbarians sometimes, you know that?"

"Says the romantic," Hunter mocked in a girlish voice.

"Hey, there's nothing wrong with a romantic man," Pepper defended, leaning in on Josh.

"You're a bird? I've never heard of that."

"We're rare. The power of flight isn't for all families," Josh taunted, obviously meaning this as a dig at Hunter.

He laughed at Josh's joke a bit harder than you'd have thought needed. "Oh now it's 'we're greater than you mammals' is it? We'll see who says that when you're in the jaws of one of us lowly mammals."

Pepper smiled and picked up her coffee. "You think you can outsmart a hawk? I'd like to see that!"

"You're a hawk? How fascinating! What kind?"

"A Red Shouldered Hawk."

"A hawk who can work computers…nobody would believe me if I told them!" Jensine laughed.

"Hey, I can type about twenty words a minute with my beak…don't knock it!"

The whole table started to laugh and for the first moment since she arrived in Canada, Jensine felt at home. She smiled at the thought of this and took a sip of her shake again. Life wasn't so bad after all. She was making friends, she was going to get to talk to Phoenix, and everything would be okay. Right? She glanced at Pepper again though, and got a bad vibe. Was it because she's a vampire or was it more than that?

Time would tell.

Chapter Nine

"Damn it's hot," Hunter whined.

"I second that," Jensine said. "Amazing how the weather here jumps about. Aren't you hot too Josh?"

"I'm good. Doesn't feel hot to me at all," he said, a stupid grin on his face.

"Beast versus Bird—big difference in body temperature," Hunter explained

Jensine glanced at Josh. "Does it make a difference?"

"No, Hunter's just a wuss. We should probably talk business before he melts."

Hunter hit him in the arm and Jensine spoke up to keep it from moving on from there. "Ok—so far I understand that the new system is being installed into the entire facility today and goes live tomorrow at noon...and there will be a five minute window between one system coming down and the new system coming online?"

"Yes, and no," Josh said. "The switch from old to new will be instantaneous. However...I can do a five minute blackout on the camera and mics around Phoenix's cell area. I've already told Jonathan that not all areas may come online at the same time. I have set up for a few other areas to be down too. You have the map there, yes?"

"Yes."

"You can see how to get to his cell easily?"

"I can."

"Okay. I need you to get out to the lounge tomorrow and pose with your book at like 10am. I will start the video loop of you reading at 11:45am seeing as we're supposed to go live at noon. It'll give you fifteen minutes to get from the lounge to the hallway of the dungeon entrance."

"I can do that."

"Good. I snagged an access card from some witch girl who's sick with mono or something. You only need to return it to her somehow."

Jensine shrugged. "Not a problem."

"You sure you need to do this?" Hunter prodded.

"Yes. I really need to talk to him."

Josh nodded. "There's only one catch."

Hunter laughed. "Just one?"

"The girl in the cell next to him. Her name is Alicia Cane. She's a bitch. She'd turn you in to get her freedom."

"And how do we get rid of her?"

"I've scheduled her bi-weekly shower for that afternoon."

"Bi-weekly?"

"Yeah. She's a vampire. They don't have the same odor issue humans do, so Valencia allows them a shower twice a month. I just happened to schedule her shower during our camera outage time."

"You can do all this from inside the computer area?"

"Darlin', computers will run it all someday," Josh stated.

"That's scary."

"I'm with you on that," Hunter agreed.

"My only worry is you, actually, Josh," Jensine told him.

"Oh, no worries for me needed. I'm doing all this under another sign-on name, plus I'll be hacking in from a location in town. I've got myself covered."

"If you say so I believe you," she replied. "Now, how do we get the disguise into place behind the couch?"

"Oh, easy. Hunter is gonna plant it."

"You gonna strip and forget your clothes?" Jensine asked, raising one eyebrow at him.

"More like 'not need' my clothes—" Hunter said and Josh gave him a high five.

"Oh." Jensine said, understanding now that Hunter planned to use sex as his alibi. Typical.

"I gotsta have me an alibi, too, ya know. Nothing better than a person who can verify I was busy—and I do mean to get busy," he added with a wiggle of his eyebrows.

"I'm not an idiot, boys. No need to explain it to me. But I am *not* sitting and reading on the couch you had sex on!" Jensine demanded, slapping Hunter's arm.

"I'm only gonna remove my clothes there and we'll slip into one of the side rooms."

"So, all of us will be accounted for in case someone sees you or suspects something," Josh said.

"In theory it all will work."

Hunter put his arm around Jensine's shoulders. "Girl, everything works in theory. It's in practice that it don't."

"We're going to think positive here, boys. Positive."

They agreed. Though she sounded optimistic, she was realizing all the ways this could go very wrong.

* * * *

It was after sunset on Friday night and the house was coming alive again. Atlanta woke up early, leaving Sean to sleep, and grabbed a shower so as to do her hair before anyone else would be lining up for the bathroom. She quietly headed downstairs to make some tea and could hear people's alarm clocks going off. A door opened, a door closed, a shower came on, a door opened, a door closed, and so on.

The others were starting to rise so as to get ready for their evening of interrogation. Atlanta was in the midst of trying to reach the top shelf where the tea was when she heard a voice behind her. "Let me get that for you."

Atlanta felt his body barely rest against her as he reached over her head and grabbed the tea for her.

"Thanks Roman." *God he smelled good!*

He handed it to her and nodded. She looked at the countertop so he wouldn't see her face blush as he moved away from her. He grabbed the teakettle and started to fill it with water.

"You don't need to do that—I can—"

"I know you can."

"Ok." Atlanta didn't know what else to say so she worked at opening the plastic on the new box of tea and got out a bag. "Did you want one?"

"Please."

She pulled out a second bag and went to the other cupboard to get two mugs down. But as she went to do so he'd beaten her to it. "Huh. Ya know? Your speed is sometimes a bit unnerving."

Roman leaned against the counter. "I don't mean to be."

He seemed so out of place as they both stood in the U-shaped kitchen, an area only big enough for two people to move about in. His blue eyes seemed to be calmer than she'd seen them in a long time. Atlanta secretly wondered if that was because of their talk last night.

She soon realized they were just staring at each other so she dropped her head and pulled herself up to sit on the counter. "Can I ask you something?"

"Of course." He turned from her to set the kettle on the stove and put the burner on.

"Your mom, Joelle, right? He hummed in agreement. "What happened to her and your dad?" He didn't say anything so she nervously went on. "I mean, you told me all you have left are your half-brothers so I was wondering—you don't have to tell me if you don't want to, it just sort of came to mind…"

A sly grin touched his face. Atlanta was sure he was enjoying her nervous behavior. "They both passed away years ago in London. Mum in the winter of 1940, Dad in the spring of 1941."

"I'm not a huge history buff, but even I know what that was—The Blitz on England by Hitler."

He nodded once. "As we've discussed before, human and Clandestine conflict tend to run neck and neck as we try to help. This time though…well, this was the uprising of The Superior Order. No one noticed the massive fights and destruction as The Blitz was going on. My mother was a key voter on the board of The Great Order and was taken out of play. My father voted in her stead. He was also killed, but only the goddess knows if it was the Germans or The Superior Order."

"Your mother stood for The Great Oder and he stood for her. Very Romeo and Juliet."

"Agreed," he said, his eyes caught hers again and where she thought they'd be sad, instead they seemed to twinkle back at her. He then laughed lightly, catching her off guard. "My mum would've found the irony of it all very amusing."

"Your father must have been loved her very much to head to London at that time."

Roman stepped toward her. "He was, even more so because he'd listened to her. He'd stayed in America with me, causing their last years together to be spent apart. You see, she'd told him we'd be safer here. We all were of an age to take care of ourselves, plus I was starting college as I was eighteen. She felt we'd be targets if we were in Britain."

He stopped for a moment. Atlanta lightly bit her tongue to keep from asking more questions. Finally he continued, "But, once she died, my dad, Phoenix and Harmon ended up going to England anyways. He took a leave of absence from the university and they headed home. I was old enough to understand what my mother had died for, but not allowed to go back for her funeral."

Without thinking she reached for him, placing her hand on his arm. "I'm so sorry."

He kissed the hand that had been at his chin and touched her hand. "I've missed that. You'd stopped touching me."

Atlanta didn't know what to say. Instead she sat there biting her bottom lip looking at him, leaving her hand where it was. He moved a hair closer to her, inches from her face when the tea kettle started to whistle. The trance was broken and she took her hand back slowly. He gave her a guilty grin and turned back to the kettle to pour their tea.

Her head was screaming with embarrassment and with the struggle that comes when you're at a loss for words. At last she thought of something. "You went to England in May when it was over I take it?"

Roman put the kettle back on the stove. "Milk?"

"Huh? Oh! Sure." she was sitting next to the refrigerator so she opened it up and got the milk for him.

"Thanks." He put a dash into each of their mugs and gave it back. "Yes. I did get to return to bury him. Sugar?"

"Please."

Roman opened a drawer to grab a spoon. He then placed a tablespoon of sugar from the sugar canister into each mug. "Our home was hit at the end of The Blitz. I was told he died instantly. Phoenix and Harmon weren't home at the time, luckily. Here." He handed Atlanta her tea.

"Thank you."

He nodded and came to sit on the counter next to her. "Funny thing is, we had a bunker built. He should've been able to get to it in time. Phoenix and I believe he didn't want to live without my mum for over a hundred years. His kids were all grown up and he was ready to go."

"Ready to go?"

"Living vampires do age you know. Just really slowly. Even though we slow down at thirty, males can produce offspring their whole lives unlike living female vampires." He took a sip of his tea. "My father was quite old. He'd grown weary of his life."

"He never remarried?"

"A third marriage? Ha! Not *my* father. He hated that he had to have two. A vampire female leaving her man is very unheard of in our culture, especially back then. I do believe Elizabeth found the reason why but she never told me. Either way, my father had lost two wives and that was enough for him."

"You say a vampire female leaving her man is unheard of—why?"

"Much like werewolves and shape shifters, the animal within us has us mate for life. Once we fall in love with someone it's rather hard to change course."

Again she felt his eyes on her. She knew she shouldn't turn to look at him, but she did. His face was so close she felt his breath. It would only take for her to move a few inches and his lips would be on hers. Atlanta knew he wanted to kiss her and she wasn't so sure she didn't want him to. But it wasn't about her, and it wasn't about him, it was about loyalty.

So she leaned in and kissed his cheek, and he hers, their faces lingering close for a moment before she found the strength to pull away and drink her tea. She could see out of the corner of her eye that he did the same. They then heard someone coming down the stairs.

"Good morning!"

"It's night time Stephan," she pontificated.

"It's morning to me."

Atlanta laughed and slipped down off the counter and walked over to him. "There's still some hot water left if you want tea."

"Splendid." He rubbed his hands together.

She turned to Roman praying her face wasn't as flush as she thought. "I'm going to run upstairs and see what's keeping the girls. I know they wanted to do research on a spell to help get Alicia to open up."

"Sounds good to me." Roman too got down off the counter.

She stopped at the bottom of the stairs. "Oh, and Roman? Thanks."

"Of course. You're more than welcome."

There was a slight moment where without words, mental or otherwise, they understood the implication of what they'd said, besides there obvious meanings. Atlanta saw Stephan look from her to Roman and then back to her.

"Did I miss something?"

That was her cue. She headed up the stairs. The last thing she heard of that conversation was Roman telling Stephan how he was giving her a history lesson.

History indeed. So, vampires mated for life. She sighed and stopped at the top of the stairs, leaning against the wall, tea in hand. Was he telling her he would be in love with her forever? How did she get into this mess? Oh yes, now she remembered. Deep down, underneath being the "chosen one" and all—she was just a stupid human girl.

With a slight bang of her head on the wall to knock some sense into herself she headed toward the room Celeste, Bianca and Desi were in while she pushed her thoughts of self loathing aside to focus on what really mattered right now—getting Alicia to talk and finding Phoenix.

* * * *

Alicia stayed tight lipped the night they'd picked her up. By now they'd kept her in their custody for nearly twenty four hours and it was Atlanta's chance to take a crack at her. Mainly because Atlanta was the one who could come closest to reading Alicia's mind.

Atlanta set up her stuff, which included a glass of wine for herself and a glass of blood wine for her captive in case she cooperated. Sitting in the chair opposite Alicia, they inspected each other and Atlanta sipped some wine and picked up a book. She could feel Alicia getting irritated as she sat bound to the chair, by both her ankles and hands with vampire cuffs, as the minutes ticked away and she got thirstier.

As Atlanta read, she heard the wind blowing outside. The weather report had said they were in for some rain tonight. She focused on the fireplace and pushed with her mind, watching the fire jump as the logs caught on fire. Then she went back to reading.

After about an hour Alicia finally snapped. "What are you reading?"

Atlanta didn't look up. "Oh, just an L.J. Smith novel. I love her stuff. Very inventive." She sipped her wine again and continued to read.

"Are you going to give me any of that blood wine or is it for show?"

"That depends," Atlanta said, still looking at her book.

"On?"

"On if you give me any useful information," she told her, finally looking up at Alicia.

"I really think you have the wrong person here," she said.

Atlanta returned to her book, "Uh huh, sure we do. Meanwhile, we'll watch you dry up like a prune."

Atlanta saw Alicia begin to realize—the fire, no windows, no blood or water in hours—she definitely was in danger of drying out. She tried to see her watch and realized it was gone. "What time is it?"

"It's Friday night. From my calculations you have about an hour left until your throat starts to hurt, and then your body starts to dry out. We can sit here until you go through all that, or you can answer questions for me. Who knows, you give me enough info and you can drink the whole glass!" she bubbled with faked enthusiasm.

"You remind me of her, you know."

"Of who?"

"Valencia."

"I am nothing like her."

"I disagree. Same eyes."

"The eye color is a trait of Air Witches, so I'm not too surprised," she said, and lifted her book.

"It's more than that—"

Atlanta sighed loudly, putting her book down again. "If you have nothing useful to say," she stood and moved into Alicia's face, "say nothing at all." She stood and turned her back on the prisoner.

"Not sure why Sean would like you. Unless he has Stockholm Syndrome."

The fire in the fireplace got bigger as Atlanta's patience was gone. She spun about, the back of her hand connecting with Alicia's face. "Keep it up, bitch. Let's see how soon you go into withdrawal." With a glance at the fire it roared even more, the room's heat intensifying.

Beads of pink sweat start to form on her Alicia's forehead, and knew she would get her right where she wanted. But, it was hot for her too, so she pulled off her sweater to expose a tank cami beneath.

Returning to the table she rummaged through her bag for something to pin up her hair. Finding a scrunchi she pulled it up into a top ponytail. As she did she heard Alicia do a sharp intake of breath and flipped around. "What?"

"Oh my goddess—it's you—you're her—now it all makes sense." Her head fell backward as she started talking more to herself than Atlanta. "I can't do this—but I have to—"

Atlanta's stomach clenched. It should have been impossible for her to see the emblem on the back of her neck, unless— "I'm sorry, what are you talking about?" Atlanta asked, doing her best poker face.

"You're the daughter of Diana—the mark—it's there, on your neck—"

"Excuse me a moment!" Atlanta held up a finger and whisked out of the room and shut the door behind her. All the boys playing poker looked up.

"How you doing in there, Atty? She spillin' anything yet?" J.J. asked.

"The prophecy says that those in darkness cannot see my mark, right?"

"Yes. Only the good at heart can see it," Roman said.

"She can see it."

"Bullshit," Stephan said.

"No, really. I pinned my hair up in there and she was in shock."

Sean put his cards down. "Well, that changes things a bit. I'm coming in. Gentlemen, deal me out for this next set." Sean stood up and followed her into the room. "God Almighty it's hot in here!" he said.

"That's the idea," Atlanta clarified, going to the glass of blood wine and giving a sip to their prisoner.

Sean sat on the chair in front of Alicia. "Why or how are you claiming this girl is the daughter of Diana?"

"You can't see the mark?" Alicia asked, in a voice that sounded as if she were truly concerned.

"I'm the one asking questions here," he ordered, leaning forward, lacing his fingers. "Now, answer my question. Why do you think she is the daughter of Diana?"

She went to say something and then closed her mouth tightly.

"Staying quiet is not going to help your cause. I'll let her kill you before I let you take your notion to Valencia."

In the silence, her face contorted. A tear finally fell down her face.

"What is it, Alicia?"

She shook her head.

"You're going to die here unless you tell us what the hell is going on," Sean said matter-of-factly.

"I can't," was all she was able to squeak out.

Sean waited for a moment and then he picked up the syringe from before and stuck it into her leg in one fast motion. He didn't, however, inject, he pulled blood.

"If I inject this with your blood already mixed, it'll hit your system faster. You'll talk faster—you'll be dead sooner—it all works out for everyone involved."

Her bottom lip started to quiver and she shook her head. Sean reached for the syringe and was about to push the liquid into her thigh when she cried out.

"Please no! I can't say anything or she'll kill her. Please, you have to believe me! You have to let me go—if you kill me she's dead too—"

"Kill who?"

"My sister—please—"

Sean looked at Atlanta, extremely confused, and Atlanta stepped forward and kneeled next to Alicia, who had pink tears running down her face.

"I promised to do this but—oh goddess—either way, my sister is dead. Please let me go—I won't say anything, I promise—we can forget I was even here—"

"Alicia, you know that isn't possible. You either talk or we'll get answers from you anyways," she said, wiping a tear from her face.

Sean sat again. "Alicia—you need to talk to us."

"I'm not Alicia," she said. "Alicia is my identical twin sister. My name is Amanda."

* * * *

In all the ruckus about Amanda, dinner ended up burned, so the group ordered a few pizzas. In the living room of the safe house, everyone ate and listened to the whole story. Amanda, now untied and with her hair down, was obviously nervous and very uncomfortable being put on the spot.

"It all started six months ago. I was arrested at an animal rights protest, and the person who came to bail me out was this tall blond guy with grey eyes. He said his name was Jonathan and that he'd bail me out but I had to agree to come with him. Well, I knew my parents didn't have the money so I agreed. He drove me to the airport and injected me with something. I woke up hours later in another car, driving along the ocean."

"Ah, leave it to Harmon," Atlanta thought aloud, "To whisk a girl away against her will."

"Hey—we drugged her and brought her here," Gray pointed out.

"Yeah, but we didn't transport her from California to Canada!"

"Please continue, Amanda," Roman encouraged.

"I was put up in a nice room and anything I asked for was done for me. It was this way for a day, and then he brought me to an office. There was a short woman with red hair there, and as it turns out she is the one who paid my bail. Which, if you ask me, was way high for a silly protest infraction. We only wanted to make our point about animal testing. I don't see—"

"And what did this woman ask of you?" Sean said, trying to keep her focused.

"She said that my sister worked for her, and I told her, there was no way Alicia would work for anyone and she must be mistaken. I wanted to know why and how and..." Amanda was visibly getting worked up so Atlanta put a hand on her arm and she took a deep breath. Her hands were fiddling with the hair tie that'd held her hair up.

Roman threw on the charming smile. "Continue, Amanda."

"She took me down to this holding area. It looked like those old fashioned dungeons you hear of, ya know? I could see my sister through glass in the floor. She was badly beaten. The woman, Valencia, explained that Alicia broke code and would be put to death unless I promised to do something for her."

Atlanta leaned over to Sean and asked, "Code?"

"Valencia has a code of conduct. It's punishable by death or imprisonment. She has no trouble keeping people in line with it because she never wavers. It can be as simple as if you are asked to kill someone for the cause and you fail. Or you are asked to go on a mission to obtain information and you don't get it due to your own stupidity. It's your funeral."

"And she asked you to what? Pretend to be your sister?"

"In a nutshell—yes. I was to go to her usual hang outs in the city and just be seen, so that Alicia was seen around town and nothing seemed out of place with the vampire community. I was to collect dues and deal with issues for her, but as my sister. I'd go to events. Pretend to be her. Then I was to report my findings to Valencia."

"This is starting to make sense." Roman rubbed his chin. "From what we know, Alicia is basically to Valencia as I am to Phoenix: head of the vampire sect but for The Superior Order. To kill her off or imprison her, there must be a trial. However, Valencia needed your sister out of the way so this is how she did it."

"All I know is that I was told that as long as I did as she requested my sister, would live...and if I did a good job she'd let my sister go."

"Bullshit." Sean fake-sneezed out the word.

"Sean," Atlanta scolded.

"What? You know darn well that woman ain't gonna let Alicia go or she would tell the world about what's been going on. This replacement is permanent. Or Valencia will have them both killed and she'll move Jonathan into their spot."

Atlanta stood up and wandered over to the window that looked out onto the Brooklyn street. She watched some kid who must've been returning home from the bar. He barely got up the stairs. How she envied him. He seemed to not have a care in the world other than to get up the stairs to bed.

"Maybe. Maybe not," Roman said. "It all really depends on her plans for Phoenix. If she keeps him or kills him, the throne goes to his brother. That, more likely, is her angle. But she must know that no one in The Great Order would allow Harmon to be in charge right now, so this is not the best time for Phoenix to be removed if that's what she wants."

Atlanta turned around and faced the group, sitting on the windowsill. "If they were to kill or keep Phoenix and the Council doesn't see fit to allow Harmon to take over, who would?"

"Any of their children, made or created."

"Created?" Atlanta asked.

"Yes. Children created by either way can be considered for being heirs to the throne. They did this due to how short the span is that living vampire women can have children. A child chosen to be made, by transfer of blood, is considered equally important. Thing is, neither of them have done either so it'd be a vote of the council. It's not a democracy. They will put names on the table and decide…there is no running for office. It's a birthright."

Amanda sat forward in her chair. "Harmon is a Keziah, yes? I remember my teachings somewhat. He's Phoenix's younger brother, am I right?"

"By about five minutes," Roman informed them all.

Atlanta then added, "Who you know as Jonathan."

"Damn," was all she said and she leaned back.

"What we need to concentrate on is how we can use this new discovery to our advantage." Gray said.

Amanda seemed near to tears. "I just want my sister back. If Valencia finds out you know any of this she'll kill her and maybe me. Can't you just let me go?"

Celeste kneeled at her feet and took her hands. "Not until we figure out what to do to keep you and your sister safe."

"She emails me stuff daily and I have to respond. That's part of the way I keep Alicia alive. Do you have a computer here?"

"It's in the room next door," Celeste replied. "Come, let's go do that so you can calm down a bit."

Amanda nodded and wiped the tears from her face, then followed Celeste into the other room. Atlanta let her head drop onto the window glass. She felt a hand slide onto the small of her back and a kiss on her shoulder.

"It'll be okay," Sean said. "We'll find a way to use this information."

"She's so scared for her sister, but part of me thinks that Alicia isn't someone to feel sorry for and we should just let Valencia kill her. I know we need to really think this out, though. Plus, is it just me, or does she totally not seem like the kinda spitfire that'd go to a protest? I'm surprised she even has the spine to stand. That is, unless she's acting like her sister, then she's a rock."

"I agree. She's a bit scattered. I think though that as soon as Celeste sees what's going on in that email we'll be a step closer. It's actually a big help. I know we wanted to get Alicia, but this might be better."

Atlanta shrugged. "Maybe."

"I agree with Sean," Roman said.

"Somebody save me, I think my heart has stopped beating!" Gray pretended to swoon.

"Gray, behave," Atlanta scolded.

"Okay mom!"

"No, really, all joking aside," Roman said. "I think this is good luck."

No sooner had he spoken than a blood curdling scream came from the computer room followed by a thud. Everyone rushed into the room. Celeste was standing there, really pissed off, holding her neck, with blood coming through her fingers. On the floor lay Amanda, who held her head and rambling in a high pitched tone.

J.J. laughed. "Now that's funny!"

"What the hell happened?" Atlanta asked Celeste.

"That bitch bit me and tried to jump out the window!" Celeste explained.

2Doggz now howled with laughter as well. .

Gray smacked 2Doggz on the ass. "Care to share what is so funny?"

"Hey!" 2Doggz tried to say through his laughter.

J.J. laughed harder, wiping tears from his eyes and put a hand on 2Doggz to steady himself. "Doggz? You tell 'em."

"That's not a real window," he explained through fits of laughter, running his hand through his short, dark hair. "It's a spell. It was a gift to Brad by some hot witch who he was doing last year. It changes with the time of day, but it's not real. She basically tried to jump through the wall!"

Atlanta tried not to laugh, but she couldn't help it.

"Hey, I'm bitten here, people!"

"Oh, sorry," Atlanta apologized, hustling over to Celeste and blowing on it to stop the bleeding.

Stephan cut his finger with a bite and walked over and wiped it on her neck. The holes disappeared completely.

"Somebody help her up. Celeste, did we at least get into the email?" Atlanta requested.

"Yeah. She got me in and then bam, she was eating my neck."

"We totally shouldn't have sent you in here alone with her, sorry. She's not eaten in a while. I'm sure that didn't help. Can we get a full glass of blood from the fridge for her?" Atlanta asked to no one in particular.

"I can get it," Bianca offered.

"Thanks. Now...come on, Amanda, up we go." Atlanta offered her a hand up.

Amanda took the hand and stood up, still holding her head. "I feel woozy."

"I bet you do. Come on, sit down." Atlanta helped her into the chair next to the desk.

"I noticed something when she bit me that might be of use."

"Yeah?"

"I think she's under a spell. Her memories were all garbled. They jumped order. Usually, you experience things from the vampire's life when they bite you, but her stream was in no order. Her head's been messed with."

"No surprise there," Sean stated.

Bianca entered with a mug of blood. "Here you go."

Atlanta reached for it. "Is it warm?"

Bianca held the cup between her two hands for a moment. "It is now."

"Thank you." Atlanta took the mug and gave it to Amanda.

"You shoulda made her drink it cold," Celeste whined under her breath.

As Amanda drank, her face flushed with color and the glaze over her eyes started to clear.

"If what you say is true, and she's all messed up in the head, that'd explain a lot. Can we reverse it?" Sean asked.

Roman sat on the arm of the small couch. "Probably. But she'll need to give permission for Atlanta to rifle around in her head."

"Me? Why me?"

"Cause it's an Air Witch spell. Probably similar to the one you used on Chuck last night."

"Chip!" The three witches said.

Roman smiled. He obviously was trying to lighten the mood.

Atlanta dragged her hands through her hair. "Makes sense. When should we try that?"

"No time like the present?" Roman tried.

"But I have no idea what I'm looking for."

"I might," Celeste said. "Come take a look at this, but don't read it."

Atlanta walked over to stand behind Celeste and examine the information on the computer screen. The email held words like a poem, or in this case—a spell.

"She is reinforcing her spell with an email that keeps the spell she did strong," Celeste showed them.

"So that means it's not as strong on its own. I could probably do a simple reversal spell. Desi, could you go run a bath for me with sea salt? Celeste, we'll need your herb kit. J.J., do you have red and black candles?"

Desi nodded and headed off. Celeste started to follow but J.J. stopped her and smiled.

"You two, come with me."

Atlanta and Celeste followed J.J. down into the wickedly dark basement. Atlanta thought she might fall until J.J. pulled a cord, popping a light bulb on. It swung slightly, casting lights and shadows, as J.J. moved a wall rug to the side. Behind it stood a door. He opened it and motioned them follow him in. Again he pulled a cord and a light bulb came on in the middle of a room the size of a walk in closet, full of herbs, candles and other witchy items.

"Why would werewolves have this?" Atlanta asked, a smile plastered to her face.

"It's a safe house for Clandestine, not just werewolves. You probably didn't notice that the windows are made of that special glass."

"I slept all day today, so I didn't notice."

"Atlanta? Celeste? You down there?"

"Yes, Bianca, did you get the book?" Celeste yelled up.

"I did."

"Well come on down here, we'll need your help with collecting the ingredients."

They heard Bianca say something about basements and mold.

Celeste ragged her. "It's not gonna kill ya...get down here."

"I'm comin', I'm comin'!"

"What's with her?" J.J. asked.

"Fire Witch. Hates it damp," Celeste rolled her eyes and shook her head.

"Ah. No Seattle living for her then."

Bianca walked into the room. "Wow! This is almost as much as we have at the mansion!"

"I know. Okay, we need incense candles, parchment, oil, a free flowing ink pen—Desi already has the sea salt in the bath."

The three witches gathered all they needed and headed upstairs.

"Okay boys, time to leave the girls to do what they do," Desi said, as they led Amanda into the bathroom.

"Fine, but we'll be out here, just in case," Sean said.

"My hero!" Atlanta kissed him.

The four of them took Amanda into the bathroom, stripped her down and helped her into the tub. While Atlanta wrote the spell on the parchment Bianca lit the incense and covered the candles in the blessed oil. Celeste hit the lights and the four of them stood each holding a candle.

Atlanta ran the paper through the smoke of the incense. "Ready?"

"You sure this is going to work?" Amanda asked.

"No, but it's a good starting point," Celeste told her.

Atlanta held out the parchment so they all could see it. "The question is, are *you* ready?"

Amanda sounded apprehensive. "Am I allowed to say no?"

"Nope," the four said.

"Okay ladies, we need to repeat it three times and then burn the parchment," Atlanta explained. "Here we go…"

They called upon the four corners and the god and the goddess to attend their circle and repeated the spell she'd put on the wall three times, in unison. As they finished saying it the third time, the four of them placed their candles under the parchment. They held it as it burned and then Atlanta made it levitate above the water until all of it became ash, floating into the water.

They then helped Amanda out of the bath and wrapped her in a fuzzy bathrobe. As they drained the water they said, "Return to the elements from which thou camest!"

As Atlanta spoke, she repeated the spell in Amanda's ear and blew some air at the end of it. When the last of the water drained away. Something flashed in Amanda's eyes and she collapsed.

Celeste grabbed her and Atlanta assisted.

"We gotcha," Celeste assured her.

"Let's get her to a bed. This could take till morning," Bianca suggested.

They opened the door and Roman picked her up and took her to a room on the third floor. He was going to sit with her in case she tried anything else. It was easily about five in the morning and they all decided to get some rest. Atlanta put on her warm pajamas and curled up on Sean's shoulder.

"Think it'll work?"

"No idea. Depends how embedded it is."

"Guess we'll see." He kissed her ear and then move down her neck.

"Sean, we're guests in someone's home."

His kisses continued to her shoulder. "No we're not—this is owned by the same people who own our home."

"Well, when you put it that way—" she said, and then immediately forgot all about Miss Amanda Cane—for a while.

Chapter Ten

Atlanta knocked softly on the door and walked in. Roman was asleep in the chair next to Amanda's bed. She set the two mugs and her book down on the old dresser and tiptoed over to him. She lightly touched his arm and his eyes shot open.

"My shift. Go get some real sleep," she whispered.

"You sure?"

"Yes, silly. It's eleven in the morning. Go to bed."

He nodded and slowly pulled his tall frame into a standing position. He started to collapse and she caught him.

"How long has it been since you fed?"

"I don't remember."

"That's what I thought. Sit down." She lowered him into the seat and fetched one of the mugs. She brought it to him and placed it in his hands. "Vampire bedtime snack."

"Thanks."

He took a sip of the warm blood and his cheeks flushed. She always loved to watch that. Sitting on the bed next to Amanda's legs she asked, "Did she even move at all?"

"Nope. She's in a deep sleep. I'm just hoping she wakes up. Has Celeste gone through the emails?"

"She stayed up late doing that and is at it again now. She's printing them all up and then we have to do a spell over them making the words just words. Then we can read it all so they're not potent."

"Words in an email can hold her spell?"

"Sometimes. That's what Celeste says."

He shook his head and stood up, steady this time. "I'll take this out to the kitchen. Thanks."

She nodded and he left the room, quietly shutting the door behind him. Atlanta sat in the rocking chair and rocked, looking out the window at the brick wall next door. "So much for the New York view," she muttered.

After about an hour Atlanta thought she saw Amanda's eyelids flutter. Marking her spot in her book, she crouched next to her on the bed and saw it again. A tiny flutter, but enough this time that she knew she saw it for sure. Atlanta wanted to reach out and touch her arm, but she knew Amanda needed to wake up on her own. So she sat there, staring at her flawless face.

Vampire skin is smooth with pores so small they're invisible to the human eye. They show no scars, blemishes, or even discoloration. Just pale and pretty, both the men and the women.

Atlanta's eyes flicked over the restraints that used to tie her to the bed. Though they hated to do it, there was no way to know for sure who she'd be when she woke up. And she was waking for sure. Her eyes opened and blinked a couple times, trying to figure out where she was. Then she saw Atlanta.

"You're awake."

"Barely."

"How do you feel? Do you know who and where you are?"

Amanda's brow furrowed. "Why? Did you do a memory loss spell on me or something?"

Atlanta laughed. "No, I happen to have no idea what spell I pulled off you."

"I remember small parts of last night. I remember you the clearest. I remember the interrogation, the spell, the smell of pizza, biting some girl—"

"That was Celeste."

"She okay?"

"Yeah, she's fine—though she might be a bit upset you bit her as she's also a witch."

"Yeah, witches aren't fond of sharing their blood."

"I've done it to help someone."

"That you loved?"

"Not at the time."

"Interesting."

"What else do you remember?"

"It's all in bits and pieces. My last clear memory, before it's all scattered, is a jail cell in California. The stuff from then to now is in sections, and they don't seem to go in the right order."

"Valencia's spell messed with your memory and altered your personality."

"I hate that woman. If I could kill her legally—"

"Get in line, sister. You're not the only one."

Amanda blinked a few times. "It's really bright in here."

"It's about noon. Very sunny Saturday."

Amanda looked with confusion at the light coming through the window.

"Vampire glass. You're in a Great Order safe house in Brooklyn."

She nodded. "So no going out for a bit, I see. Can I at least be untied?"

"Sure. As soon as I have backup," she explained, standing up and heading to the door.

"Don't trust me yet."

"Nope. You'll earn that though, I think."

Atlanta went to get Sean and J.J. As they entered, Amanda smiled. "Sean Cameron—how the hell did you get away from Valencia?"

"You know her?" Atlanta asked him.

"Oh, he doesn't know me, I just know of him. Everyone knows about Sean Cameron—if you're a vampire, that is. Vampire Hunter turned vampire always makes the news. It's gotta suck for you, huh?"

"I can add you to my list if you keep yappin' about it," Sean snapped.

"Sean!"

"Sorry," he apologized to Atlanta, arms crossed, as he stayed by the door.

Atlanta cut the binds and Amanda sat up, leaning her against the headboard. "Whew—little woozy."

"Celeste is bringing you some blood. If she's in a forgiving mood, she'll heat it for you."

Amanda's eyebrows went up, "We got snitty all of a sudden, didn't we."

Celeste opened the door and handed the blood to Sean, then exited with a nasty look at Amanda. Sean passed Atlanta the mug. It was cold.

"You stop picking on my boyfriend and I'll stop being snitty," Atlanta clarified, "Here's your blood. Looks like Celeste hasn't forgiven you."

Amanda took the cold mug and her head dropped a bit. But she quickly recovered and said, without any sarcasm, "Thanks. I've had worse so, thank you."

"You're welcome."

"Sorry about the comment about Sean. I didn't realize. Not many witches will date a vampire."

Atlanta gave her a quick nod and then touched her mug and whispered words she'd heard Bianca say before and felt the mug warm up a bit.

Amanda's eyes grew a bit. "I thought you were an Air Witch."

"My grandfather was a Fire Witch so I have a little talent with it. I have to really work at it, though. I'd drink that quickly before it cools again."

Amanda drank about half of the mug's contents before she put the cup down. As her face flushed she looked much better. Amanda finished the mug quickly.

"Better?"

"Yeah."

"You feel well enough to come out into the other room to talk to everyone, or do you want to stay in here and only talk to me and Sean?"

Amanda thought about that one. She spoke to Atlanta mentally, *"I want to say talk to everyone 'cause I'm not afraid of doing that, but honestly I'd rather stay in here for a bit if that's okay."*

Atlanta nodded and motioned Sean over.

"Any funny stuff and I'll dust you here in this room." He made clear, coming toward the bed.

"I'm faster than you, Cameron," she said, leaning forward.

Sean pulled out his stake.

"Ease up, Cam...I'm just messin' with ya. Where would I go anyways?" She pointed at the sunlight coming in through the window.

"A. You're not faster than me. B. You have a point."

"Okay then."

Atlanta gave him her seat in the chair and she sat on the bed. Sean pulled the chair closer to the bed so his knees almost touched it. She wondered why until he put his hand on Atlanta's leg, then she understood. He wanted to touch her. She loved that about him. He rubbed her leg with his one hand while his other held the stake very firmly. It always amazed her how he could be soft and yet rough at the same time.

Amanda seemed to notice that too and she smiled a bit. "I'm not sure where to begin. Maybe a year ago would be a good place."

* * * *

"A year ago today, where was I?" Jensine thought, as she lay on the couch, pretending to read her book, as planned. She was too nervous to actually read, though. Turning pages was about the best she could do. "Oh yes, I was in London. I was doing a piece on the anniversary of Diana's death. That seems so long ago. What time is it? Ugh—eleven-thirty in the morning. Fifteen minutes to go. Okay—go over plan in head."

Jensine thought out everything Josh had told her and waited. At eleven-forty-five, she saw the light on the camera in the room flicker and she knew the recording had come on. She got up, put the book under the couch, and grabbed the clothing.

"One black hoodie? Check. One matching pair of sweat pants? Check. One girl's bra? Nice, Hunter. Very nice," she said, tossing it to the floor.

Jensine threw on the sweats over her own clothes and headed out the door, hands in pockets and hood up so her face couldn't be seen. It only took her five minutes to reach the corner where the camera was. She waited. It felt like forever. She watched her clock and then, right at noon, the red light went off and she was on the move.

She moved down the hall to the door. She pulled out the swipe card and used it. The door unlocked and she went through it and down the hall to the end of the first part of the maze. Jensine pulled out her map and saw she needed to go right. She turned and headed on down.

"Shit," she muttered, seeing a guard with a prisoner coming that way.

Quickly she ducked into the hall and around a corner until they passed. Silently, she slipped into the hall she needed and moved to the end where she had an X that marked the spot. She saw him lying there, looking extremely filthy and exhausted.

"Phoenix," Jensine whispered.

He didn't move.

"Phoenix!" she said louder.

Finally he lifted his head and stared at her, his eyes squinting, his face dirty and covered by his hair.

"It's Jensine. Wake up, I don't have much time!"

This opened his eyes. "What are you doing here? The cameras—"

"They're off for five minutes while the new system goes online. I overheard someone in my class talking. Did you really think I wouldn't find a way to you? You're the only one who knows I'm here and why...and now you're here...I need to know what you need me to do."

"You need to get out of here."

"Oh, yeah, that's a great idea—like I hadn't thought of that. How, Phoenix?"

"Just turn around and return to your barracks."

She realized he was only talking about getting out of the dungeons. "But what about my life? You never said I'd be...*changed.* Did you try to have me killed? Talk to me! Was it all a lie?"

"Jen, you can't help me. You need to stay safe and when you have information that is imperative to the Order you need to leave the fortress and get it to Roman. Do you remember the plan?"

"Yes."

Phoenix sat up slightly, his dark hair hiding his face to where a bit of his nose and mouth showed along with his grey eyes. "What was the plan, Jen? Have you done as requested?"

"Yes. I've observed Harmon...you know that. Do I need to run now? Wouldn't that be better? Atlanta needs to know I'm okay and that you're here!"

"No, not yet," Phoenix said, his voice dry and raspy.

"Maybe I can get you out."

"No. Does Harmon know I wanted you here?"

She shook her head. "No one knows."

"Good. Keep it that way. Now, how'd you get down here?"

Jensine held up the card. "I stole this from a sick worker when I overheard someone talking about the computer upgrade glitch."

"No one helped you?"

Jensine thought this question odd. "Why does that matter?"

"You can't trust people here, Jensine. I'm only looking out for you. Who were they?"

Jensine realized time was almost up, and she had no idea if the microphones came on first. So she lied. "No one. My friends know nothing. I'm here on my own."

"Then you'll take the punishment on your own. Hope you can sleep well with that. *Guards!*"

Phoenix stood, pulling his dark hair off. It was Jonathan. She'd been set up. She went to run in one direction, but it was blocked. She'd looked at the map so many times that as the adrenaline pushed through her veins she saw it in her head. In doing so she realized where she needed to go and she ran. However guards came in the other direction, too.

As she ran she allowed herself to change into the black panther. The transformation happened as she reached the other guard. Running under his legs she sent him flying into the air. As she rounded the bend the door to freedom was in sight. She had no idea where she'd go once she was free, but she'd tackle it once she was out. If she had to jump into the water and swim for it she would.

"Get her!" a guard yelled.

She skidded to a stop and shifted into her human form—she needed hands to swipe the access card hanging around her neck. The door opened, and she returned to panther form and ran as fast as she could. The alarm sounded as she reached the door to the cove. She half-changed and attempted to use the door but it didn't budge. The alarm triggered its lock.

Jensine never tapped into her half-breed strength before, but she figured now wasn't a bad time to try it out. She let her body morph into half human, half cat. Grabbing the bench in the hall she hurled it at the large window. It shattered and she stepped through. Changing into the panther she ran at full speed for the cove.

She could see and smell the water. She was almost there. She could out swim most everyone here. Her paws hit the water, and morphed into half-breed form again and started the swim for the ocean. As she hit her stride she felt it—an electrocution from a stun gun arrow. Normally this wouldn't have slowed her down, but with her body in the water, it fully electrocuted her. Losing control, her body reverted to her human form. She saw Jonathan standing above her, wigless but still in the rags he'd worn in Phoenix's cell. And with that last image Jensine passed out.

* * * *

"Come on, answer your phone!" Hunter cursed aloud as Josh's phone rang and rang without an answer.

The alarm blaring, Hunter jumped into his uniform and ran for the courtyard. He wasn't supposed to have his phone, but he had to know if this alarm had to do with Jensine.

"Shit!" Hunter blurted when the voicemail answered again. He waited for the tone then said, "Yo, dude. Where you at? You need to call me. You know why."

He hung up the phone and shoved it into the side pocket of his camouflage jump pants. Pulling his cap on, he reached the courtyard where Bravo Company was taking formation. He stopped running so he'd walk into the group, seeming calm. All across the field members of both companies were coming into the area and lining up. Suddenly a large bird flew right at him and he held out his arm. The hawk landed and it had a piece of paper in its beak. Hunter took it and let the hawk climb up to his shoulder as he opened the note.

H - It wasn't me dude. I swear. Meet me at 1900 hours at the cove dock. –J

Hunter looked at the hawk. "Dude—you sure?"

Josh squawked at him and pecked his forehead.

"Ow! Okay, okay—we'll talk at seven. I'll be there. But you better have answers."

The hawk's head bobbed once and flew off.

"This can't be good."

* * * *

The smell was horrible, like dirty zoo cages. Jensine's eyes slowly came open further to see she was in the shape shifter cell block of the dungeon. She wore nothing. Not even her dog tags. She shivered and huddled into the corner. She tried to change into a panther to stay warm, but she'd been drugged, making the change impossible. As she adjusted to the light she saw a rough wool blanket over on the bench. She crawled over and wrapped herself in it, lying down on the straw floor to wait for the drugs to wear off.

As soon as she got warm enough to start to doze off, she heard heavy footsteps coming in her direction. She decided to lie still, pulling the blanket over her head and hoped they weren't coming for her.

The steps got closer and closer until she could smell him outside her cage and her insides began to quiver. The gate lock clicked and the door slid open.

"Get up."

She didn't move.

"I said get up."

It was Jonathan's voice.

"Screw you," she said.

"Don't offer what you don't plan to give freely, sweetheart. Now get up."

Jensine pulled the blanket down so she could see him. "What do you want?"

"It's not what I want. It's what *she* wants. So get up. You've pissed off the big dogs, so I hope you can take it like one."

"What?"

"I said get up!" he screamed as he reached down, grabbed her by the arm and lifted her into the air. The blanket fell off. Her nose was inches from his face as her feet dangled above the ground.

The adrenaline rush this gave Jensine was enough to get claws to come out of the hand he didn't have a hold of, and she shoved them into his stomach and pulled upwards. She could feel the blood flow over her hand. He threw her against the wall.

"You whore!" He kicked her in the stomach. As he did so, she shoved her claws into his calf and pulled him down. She thought she had the upper hand but as he landed he pulled something out of his pocket and stuck her with it. Quickly, her nails retracted and she became sedated again.

* * * *

Hunter worked his way into the observation room along with the rest of Bravo Company, snagging a seat at the front. Below him sat Jensine dressed in an army green prisoner jump suit and shackles on her ankles and wrists, holding her to the chair on one side of the table. Jonathan's shirt was blood stained and torn, as were his pants.

The speaker was on, so they heard Jonathan and Valencia. "She was able to fight back before I got the syringe into her," Jonathan explained as he showed the damage to Valencia.

Valencia backhanded Jensine across the face. All of Bravo Company jumped, Hunter more so than the rest. Yet Jensine didn't react as she was still drugged up.

"We can't have her knocked out for this portion," Valencia said, pulling yet another syringe out of her pocket and sticking Jensine with it.

Jensine's eyes came open and she seemed very aware of her surroundings. Realizing where she was she stared up at observation, and for a moment his eyes locked with hers. But she looked away from him quickly.

"So, as you can see, I brought your entire team in here to hear how you've been lying to them all along. Do you want to tell them or shall I?"

Hunter saw Jensine's jaw clench shut while she stared straight ahead, ignoring Valencia.

"Fine. Suit yourself. Ladies and gentlemen of Bravo Company, before you sits a traitor to the cause. The shape shifter you knew as Pip is really Jensine Blackensdale. You are asking yourself, who is that? Well, let me tell you. She is best friends with our enemy. We thought she understood we'd saved her, taken her in for protection from The Great Order. Seems though, she was sent here to spy on our beloved Jonathan—and the rest of you. She was sent here to kill us all and then run to The Great Order with all she'd learned from us. It was only a matter of time. She had dirt on so many of you that if she'd even had another day or two, you may have found yourself on The Great Order kill list. As it is, she killed poor Caroline for her badge so she could sneak into the jail cells to meet with Phoenix to get her next assignment. She is a traitor to The Superior Order and we will treat her as such."

Hunter found these accusations hard to believe. He knew for a fact that Jensine hadn't killed Caroline for the card, which made him suspicious of the rest of the tale.

Jensine broke her silence. "You have quite the imagination there."

Valencia smacked her across the face again. Hunter knew from past experience with Valencia that Jensine was in a lot of pain, but she held it together.

Jensine brought her head back to center. "I am not here to kill anyone and I didn't murder Caroline."

"But you were found with her card and she was found dead. If you didn't kill her, then who gave it to you?"

"She gave it to me freely," Jensine lied. "I asked to borrow it."

"So you could sneak in to talk to Phoenix."

"Yes."

"Because you are working for him here?"

"I wanted answers!" she yelled. "Why do you ask? You know the answer to these questions. I'm sure your little boy toy told you all about how he impersonated his brother—"Another smack to Jensine's face flew. This time all Jensine did was spit blood out onto the table.

Hunter realized two things at that point. First off, they were being watched for reaction and he needed to stay calm. Second, he realized Jensine was talking to him more so than to Valencia when she gave information.

Valencia hit her again. "Who else worked with you to get you in? Who was in on this?"

"No one."

Valencia shoved Jensine's head down onto the table. Hunter heard the cracking sound, even up in the booth through the speakers, of Jensine's nose breaking. Valencia lifted Jensine up by the little hair Jensine had. Blood ran down her face along with tears.

"Let's try that again. Who was working with you?"

"Are you as deaf as you are dumb? Nobody helped me, you stupid whore."

The hit this time came from Jonathan, and it was a good fist punch to the face, splitting the skin under her right eye. Jensine shook that off as her eyes ran again. She tilted her head back and as she looked up, Hunter caught her gaze again. Unconsciously he moved closer to the glass, closed his eyes, and reached out mentally to her. Normally he wouldn't be able to do this; werewolves couldn't mentally speak to shape shifters or vice versa, only to their own kind. But Hunter could.

"How could you lie to me?" he asked her, trying to keep his tone level.

He opened his eyes now that he'd established connection. He saw for an instant her confusion on hearing his voice in her mind.

"I didn't. I told you that it was complicated. I wanted to tell you the truth. I planned to, after I spoke to Phoenix."

"Don't lie anymore!"

"I'm not. If I was here to damage you and the others I'd have turned you in by now to save my own ass, wouldn't I've? I didn't hurt Caroline either and you know that! If that poor girl is really dead, Valencia or one of her goons did it, not me, so she could frame me."

But that's all the time she got to talk to him. She was jolted up from her seat and her face thrown up against the wall. Valencia ripped open the back of the jumpsuit with a knife. A man entered and handed her a short whip. She lengthened it out and made it snap. "You're going to tell me what I want to know, or die in the process."

Hunter's stomach churned as one vampire grasped Jensine's right arm as Jonathan held the left one. Valencia let the whip go and it sliced into Jensine's back, a line of red appearing immediately as Jensine's scream pierced his eardrums. Hunter leaned back in his seat, his teeth clenched as his mind raced on what she'd said. Who was telling the truth?

"Tell me who told you about the computer system switching over."

"No one told me anything. I overheard some of the I.T. guys chatting about it a day or two ago. They said there would probably be a delay in camera time so I took my chances. I only wanted the truth!"

The whip cracked, and she screamed out. Hunter's head dropped into his hands, like many of the others in the room, this was painful to watch.

"It's the truth, I acted alone! I had no help!"

"Then where'd you get the clothes you were sneaking about in?"

"I found them behind the couch in the lounge, next to a bra and a woman's shirt. I have no idea who they belong to."

The whip cracked one more time and Jensine screamed in pain. That was all Hunter could take. He had to stop this. He stood up and pounded on the glass. The intercom was next to his seat so he leaned over and pressed the talk button. "Where were the clothes found?"

Valencia grabbed the back of Jensine's neck. "Tell him."

"I found them in the Bravo Company's lounge behind the sofa."

Hunter thought for a moment of lying, but he couldn't. "They were my clothes, ma'am. I was on a date with a girl and we left them in there around oh-five-hundred. We got a bit busy after that and when I went to retrieve them this afternoon, they were gone. My clothes, not the girl's, ma'am. It was a black hoodie and sweat pants. Is that what she had?"

Valencia looked up at Hunter. "What's your name, private?"

Hunter thought this odd as she knew exactly who he was. He answered her anyway. "Greyhound, ma'am."

"Well, Greyhound, thank you for your honesty. Guards, please show him to my office. Find this girl he speaks of so she can verify his story."

With that, the guards in the observation deck grabbed Hunter as he spoke to Jensine mentally one last time. *"I will come for you."*

* * * *

Jensine had never been in this much pain in her life. Thankfully, just as she thought she couldn't take any more, the whipping had ceased. A sob escaped her lips before she could pull it back. Biting down on her lip she held back the next. She refused to give Valencia what she wanted.

Jonathan let go of Jensine's arm and shoved her toward the other man who had helped hold her still for the lashing. He was a Hispanic man, strong for his size so she assumed he was a vampire. He caught Jensine and though she wanted to stand tall in front of her peers, she went limp in his arms. Without hesitation, he lifted her up and over his shoulder.

"See if you can find a way to get more information from her Eddie," Valencia ordered, picking up a syringe from the table Pulling the cap off she stuck the needle in Jensine's behind and dispensed the liquid. "This will keep her from changing." Valencia paused then added, "Do whatever it takes—she must pay a price for silence."

"Yes, Mistress," Eddie said and left the room.

As she lay across his shoulder, her back screaming in pain with each step taken, Jensine knew he'd take her back to her cell. Did Valencia think she'd tell him what she hadn't told her? Yes, she could save herself further torment if she gave up Josh and Hunter's name. Yet Hunter's last words to her rang in her mind. Any ounce of consideration toward the easy path vanished. She would not say a word.

As they entered her cell, she noted it had been cleaned out. A new blanket lay on the cot along with a thin but usable pillow and a pair of drawstring pants and a large top, both made of dyed muslin. They were the usual attire of those in the dungeon. The guard laid her down, undid her shackles, and helped her out of her blood soaked jumpsuit. This left her sitting there in a sports bra and underwear. He looked at her and smiled.

He turned her about, cut his finger on his tooth, and wiped his blood on her whip marks, causing them to heal. Spinning her to face him, he squatted in front of her and did the same to her lip and the skin under her eye. Then placed his hands on either side of her nose and with a quick movement reset it.

Jensine wailed. Her face screamed in agony as tears flooded her eyes. She tried to breathe but could only pant as she cupped her nose, rocking back and forth. Feeling her nose begin to heal, she mumbled a thank you.

"I did something for you, now you need to do something for me," he said.

"Like what?"

"You need to tell me what you wouldn't tell her. She knows someone helped you inside I.T. Your sentence is death unless you tell me who."

Death? Was he serious? Was her keeping silent worth her life? Quickly she decided only when death was a definite would she come back to that question. "I didn't have any help, sir."

"Oh, I think you did. I think you're going to tell me what I need to know. And until I get what I need—I'll do what I want. Compredé?"

"I have nothing to tell you," she pushed through the tears.

He grabbed her around the throat and lifted her up to look him in the face. "I can renew your injuries, little one. When she said nothing, he tossed her into the corner of the steel-walled cell.

Jensine fall to the floor and tried to change into the panther, but couldn't. Panic set in as she stared at her human hands, willing them to grow claws.

Seeing her distress, Eddie laughed. "It's a chemical that prevents changing form…if she'd given it to you as a cat, you'd be stuck that way for a while. She actually gave you a decent dose so I figure we have an hour together." He pressed his tongue into the center of his bottom lip and ran it back and forth with a laugh. "That is, unless you will behave."

Fear swept over her, but so did relief. She'd not lost the ability to shift permanently. This reaction startled her. Jensine hadn't realized she'd become accustom to her new abilities. Sadly, only now did she appreciate what used to make her feel ruined. Relying on that inner strength of that knowledge she said, "I did this alone. Comredé?"

He rubbed his hands together as his eyes judged her from head to toe, as if she were a painter's bare canvas. "The beauty is now I can decorate you as mine."

Before Jensine could react to what her brain was telling her, he grabbed her arm and spun her into him, her back pressed into his chest with her arm twisted painfully between them. Encircling his arm around her neck, he squeezed, causing Jensine to gasp for aim. "Tell me."

"Nothing to tell," she squeaked out."

Eddie spun her away from him, but backhanded her the minute her face was visible. Her lip split again and he grinned. Then, at vampire speed, he attacked. Jensine barely was able to block. Though her shape shifter DNA made her stronger, it did not make faster.

Blows from fists and feet rained down on her like lightning strikes. She blocked and pivoted in the tiny space as best as she could, calling on her training to help. But it only could do so much against his speed. With the wind knocked out of her she stumbled backwards into a corner. Taking this opportunity, Eddie balled up his fists and used her as a punching bag, slamming his fist into her face so many times Jensine thought for sure bones were broken and tears fell without reservation.

Grabbing her arms, he spun her about, slamming her face into the wall. He pinned both arms behind her, leaned into her ear, and breathed, "Tell me you're sorry."

Jensine started to sob.

"Tell me you're sorry!" he yelled.

"I'm sorry," she barely could say through tears that ran down her face, stinging the open wounds.

"Are you going to tell me what I want to know?"

Jensine knew she couldn't betray those who hadn't betrayed her. Besides, he'd still hurt her either way. She knew it.

"There's nothing to tell you," she whimpered. "Please don't—" she started to say but instead of finishing her plea, she screamed as Eddie broke both of her arms.

* * * *

Amanda held a pillow tight to her chest as if doing so would give her the strength to tell her story.

"I was dating this guy named Eduardo Martinez…Eddie is what he went by. He was a vampire at my college. I had a big crush on him and to make a long story short? He's a very bad man."

"There's always some man that has messed up some girl's life," Sean said.

"You ever messed up some poor girl's life?" Amanda asked flippantly.

Atlanta saw a dark look cross over his face. "You are not the man that messed up Elizabeth's life, so don't you even try to take the blame for that. You know better."

"I know," he said. "It just feels like I had a hand in it."

"Devon had a hand in it, and he's dead, so he got his."

Sean looked at Amanda. "You were saying?"

Amanda paused for a moment but continued. "Anyways, after I told him I couldn't see him anymore he decided my sister was the next best thing. I tried to warn her about him but she's—well—she's a bit rougher than me—walks a bit more on the dark side, so to speak. I knew she liked him, even when I was dating him. Needless to say she was happy to jump at the chance to date him after me."

"So you two aren't close, is what you're saying," Sean interjected.

Amanda looked at Sean as if to say, "duh." "We never were those twins that hung out together and liked similar stuff. It was like she was the dark half and I was the light half—no in betweens for us. Other than our looks and bad taste in men we're radically different. That said, she ran off with Eddie and I got involved with the animal rights activists to keep busy—I even started doing some song writing—joined a band to kill some time. That's all I was doing when I was arrested. The rest you know."

"Where is she now?"

"Probably still in the dungeon I last saw her in. She's not one to repent or anything."

"What about this Eddie guy?" Sean asked.

"Oh, he works for Valencia now. That's how Alicia got wrapped up with that horrible woman. See, he used to be this wonderful guy on the outside and all the while he wasn't too stable on the inside." Amanda's eyes glazed over as she continued to talk. "I think his good-guy front, something I liked to call his tattered mask, came apart while he was with Alicia. Maybe he got too much of what he wanted, or maybe Valencia gave him an outlet for what raged inside him—I have no idea.

"I tried to warn Alicia. She only saw his pretty mask of smiles and his tender gestures, not the glint in his eye of what really was beneath—violence. Not just in the bedroom, but ready to show up anytime. If I wasn't a vampire and healed quickly…God, I prayed she never had to see how he really was." The tears started to run down Amanda's face. "I am so horrible—I let her go off with him—I should've stopped her. I feel so horrible—I'm so guilty—I'm sure that it's his fault my sister is in prison and it's my fault she ever got mixed up with him."

She started to cry harder and Atlanta let Amanda lean on her. She felt Sean get up and leave the room. He returned quickly with a box of tissues, sat in the chair, and waited until she asked for one. As her sobbing slowed down Atlanta gave her a tissue. She thanked them, wiped her face, and blew her nose.

"You don't need to feel guilty for what he did," Sean said. "He's a bad man and now on my short list of those who need to meet their maker."

"I am guilty though, don't you see? I could've killed him more than once but I didn't have the guts to do it—I tried—I honestly tried. But I couldn't. He creates this mental hold over your mind...and what's worse—" Another sob hit her and she about choked out the next sentence, "I was secretly glad he left with her so I could be free. Who wishes that on their sibling? Oh goddess, forgive me!"

Amanda collapsed in sobs onto Atlanta's lap. With one hand she rubbed her back, letting her get it out of her system, as with her other hand Atlanta gripped Sean's hand tight.

Chapter Eleven

Atlanta checked her watch. Almost seven o'clock on Saturday night and she was sitting outside a dilapidated building in Brooklyn that you could drive by and not even notice, which was the point. It was an underground blood bank for the Clandestine people. Sean was inside getting fresh supplies for the safe house. At least this got her outside for a bit.

"Coming out, pretty lady—open the van door—this stuff is cumbersome to carry," she heard in her head.

Quickly she stepped out of the van, opened the side door, and he exited the building. He carried a cooler on each shoulder.

"Want some help with that, baby, or are you trying to impress me?" she yelled out.

"You impressed?"

"I am!"

"Good, now help me out."

"My pleasure. Taking the one on your left." She motioned to the cooler, levitating it over to the van, gently setting it down on the second row back seat.

Sean dropped the other one onto the first row back seat and smiled. "Thank you, my dear," he said, giving her a quick kiss. "Ya know, next time I should probably send you in. Maybe he'd charge us less if you showed off your legs and levitated him into the air for fun."

"You really think the price would go down by me going in there?"

Sean thought about it and looked her up and down, his eyes staying on her breasts. "Yes, ma'am."

She smacked him. "Men."

He laughed. "What can I say? As a species sometimes we're single minded."

"No…you jest," she said flatly. "Now really, would it have cost less?"

"Who knows. I hate that guy. He's such a prick," Sean admitted while shutting the side door of the van.

"Then why do they use him?"

He got into the driver's seat. "From what I gather, he's trustworthy and dependable."

She got in on the passenger side and shut the door. "Trustworthy, dependable, yet a prick…gee, ya just can't find nice men to steal blood for you these days."

Sean laughed as he turned the key and revved the engine. "Exactly." He pulled out onto the street. "He did, however, give me his brother-in-law's card." Sean handed it to her and she looked at it. It was a white card with nothing on it.

"I can see how this'd be helpful," she said sarcastically.

"Oh right, you don't know a vamp card."

"A vamp card?"

"Yes, ma'am. That there is the card of one of the best witches in New York, and I figured since we were in town, you and I might pay him a visit."

"What for?"

Sean smiled as he turned onto Metropolitan Ave.

"Mr. Cameron, stop smiling and tell me how to read this card."

"He makes magickal weapons. If you can think it up, he can create it. Thought we might go have a pow-wow with him and see what he could do for us."

"That's fantastic! How'd you hear of him?"

"J.J. told me about him the other night. Seems prick boy and his cool brother-in-law owe J.J. a favor, so I was able to get the card and a visit with him when I call."

"But there's nothing on this card."

"There is if you wipe blood on it. He's in love with the blood, that man, or so I've been told. Married a vampire himself, actually. You wipe blood on the shiny surface and his name and number will appear."

"This I gotta see!"

They pulled up to a stop light and Sean turned the overhead light on, bit his finger and rubbed it on the card.

"Low and behold, look at that!" she said as red lettering appeared that spelled out "Bernard W. Cauthen III, Warlock" followed by a 212 phone number. "That is fantastic! By the way, the light's green."

"Oops." Sean turned the overhead light off and drove.

"Warlock?"

"Yeah, some male witches prefer that word. No idea why it matters."

"When do we want to see him?"

"I was thinking we'd call him tonight and see when is best for him."

"Sounds good to me. I don't think we'll be in New York much longer, so the sooner we do this, the better."

* * * *

Hunter paced back and forth on the docks at the cove. Looking at his watch he say it was almost seven. "I hate waiting," he muttered.

"You're always impatient so I won't take it personally," came Josh's voice.

"You're here. Fantastic!"

"Come on, let's head back this way, out of sight and outta this wind!"

It was a cool night. Hunter had thrown a light sweater on over his usual white T-shirt. Josh even had on his thin leather coat. Hunter followed Josh back to the area of the docks that held the doors that led to the storage areas for the shipments. It was pitch black in this area as there were no electric lights. This also meant no cameras. In fact, the only light came from a tall metal garbage can with a fire in it. A few people were standing around it drinking a bottle they seemed to be passing around.

"This weather is crazy huh? Hot yesterday and cool tonight. We must have a storm coming toward us from out in the ocean."

"Come on, let's step in here shall we?" Josh suggested.

"Sure but…I don't trust…"

Josh leaned over and whispered into Hunter's ear, "They're on break for five more minutes and then they head in to work. We have about fifteen minutes until the next swarm come out."

Josh and Hunter walked over to the fire and warmed their hands and didn't really say much of anything. One of the tall guys standing around looked at Josh and elbowed his friend.

"Looky what we have here," said a tall, burly man with a thick accent Hunter couldn't place exactly. "Newbies."

"Nice—very nice," a shorter guy agreed, his accent the same.

Josh looked up and smiled at them, "How y'all doin' tonight?" he let his North Carolina accent sound stronger than it normally was.

"Can't complain—you new?" The big guy asked.

"We sure are—we came to meet with the boss here," Hunter played along.

"Excellent! You two look like good chaps! Care for a little hair of the dog?" The shorter one asked, handing Hunter the small pint in a brown bag he'd been holding.

"Well, hell. Sure, why not? I'm normally a forty ounce drinker, but this'll do just fine!" Hunter took the bottle with a nod and took a swig of liquid. He coughed extremely hard and handed it to Josh. "I'd say I'd have coughed it up, but I think it evaporated on the way down! What is that?"

"Homemade moooonshine. Werewolves make the best moonshine—isn't it great?" The shorter said, slapping Hunter on the back.

"Hell yeah—damn—it'll grow some hair on your chest that will!" Hunter joked.

The two guys caught the werewolf joke and laughed. Josh took a drink and he about brought up a lung, but he kept it down. "Woo-wee boys! That's some stout shit!"

"Helps keep us warm in the winter and happy enough to ignore the heat in the summer." The big guy explained, taking the bottle.

A bell rang in the distance.

"Well, that's the end of our break. Good luck to ya. Hope to see you around here again!" The smaller of the two said. They both touched their ball cap bills at Hunter and Josh and left for their shift in the warehouse.

As they were way out of earshot Hunter said, "Wow! That was some serious moonshine, man! I thought my esophagus was going to be eaten clear through!"

"No kidding! Whew! I couldn't work here, I'd be three sheets to the wind all the time and falling asleep in the machinery!"

The two of them laughed and warmed their hands over the garbage can fire and stood in silence for a moment. Finally Hunter spoke. "How bad is it?"

"Really bad."

"Why? You think she's gonna break and expose us? Did she really kill Caroline? What happened, dude?"

"She'd never give us up. You know that. Besides, you really didn't do anything other than lead her to me. I'm the one in danger here, not you."

"I suppose that's sorta true."

"She didn't kill Caroline. Hell, she didn't even know the girl, Hunter. I'm the one that stole her card. Caroline's dating a guy in my wing, along with like one guy from every wing, so I flirted with her. She was sick the next day so she never noticed I nicked her card." He paused. "So you see, Jen is tellin' the truth."

"Why would Valencia say she did, then?"

"To turn her whole company against her, I'm guessing."

"That makes no sense."

"No one will try and save her if they think she was here to kill them."

Hunter rubbed his face. "Good point. But why is she here? Did she really come here to watch Jonathan? I find that odd. She only got her powers from an attack recently...or she's the best actress ever."

"I found the tapes and yes, she's here to watch Jonathan...he's Phoenix's blood brother, and she was to report on him."

"Well, that'd explain his anger and her freak out when Phoenix was captured."

"It's worse than that."

"How?"

"Valencia knows someone in I.T. helped her, so she's got Eddie working her."

Hunter was as new here as Jensine so the name didn't ring a bell. "Who's he?"

"He's bad news. He's a sociopath for sure..."

"She can handle him. She's a tough girl, Josh."

"He drugs the girls so they have no muscle control."

"She won't fall for his mind games, Josh, she's—"

Josh cut him off. "He beats them, Hunter. He drugs them up so they can't shift and he beats them to a bloody pulp—repeatedly. He then heals them with his blood so he can do it all again."

Hunter's face went pale and he felt his knees buckle. He sat on the stone bench near the entrance. "Has he seen her yet?" Hunter asked, his voice catching on itself.

"He's the guy who carried her out of the interrogation room after they took you for questioning."

Hunter looked at him skeptically.

"I saw the tapes. She made us all watch them, hoping to see one of us crack."

"You didn't have to watch him beat her, did you?"

"We were forced to watch up until a certain point. I saw enough that I almost vomited in front of the group. Luckily for me, Dean, the guy in her regiment, he threw up first and they dragged him off for questioning, while I was able to hold back until she let us leave."

"I promised her I'd come for her. I have to get her out, Josh. How do I get her out?" Hunter pleaded, his voice filled with panic and anguish.

"I don't know."

Hunter stood up and stepped to Josh, his eyes red with the tears he fought back. "We have to figure out a way. She's in there for protecting us. We have to figure it out or by God we need to come clean so as to stop the torture—please Josh. Think of something."

Josh put his arm around him. "We will get her out of there somehow, I promise. But if we 'fess up, Valencia will put us away and we'll never see her again. We have to keep our heads about us."

Hunter nodded, trying to take deep breaths in order to keep his panic from getting the best of him. He went back to the bench and sat down. "I have no idea what to do, Josh—I need to talk to her—but—"

"We just went down that road with her and now she's in jail," Josh said, finishing Hunter's sentence as he sat next to him.

They sat there in silence for a few minutes.

"Your girl leave this morning?"

"Yeah, she had to head back down to Massachusetts. That's all I'm allowed to know."

Hunter all of a sudden sat up straight and looked at Josh. "Yo dude, you didn't tell her about the plan we had for Jensine, did you?"

"Of course not, man. Besides, you really think Pepper would tattle on us?"

"She's a mole, Josh. With a career choice like that do you think she wouldn't?"

Josh sat back and let his head rest against the cold stone wall. He then rolled his head to his right to look at Hunter. "I want to defend my girl and say there's no way, but you're right, if she heard us at any point it's possible she'd say something to Valencia."

"If I find out she's the reason Jensine's in a cell getting pounded on a daily basis, I'll hurt her, Josh."

"You'd have to beat me to it," he said dryly. They sat in silence again and then Josh took in a sharp breath. "What if you got a job working for the dungeon?"

Hunter lifted his head, "The only people who do work there are the ones not smart or talented enough to be part of the attack force. That's why we make fun of them. Plus, working there sucks."

"It's all access to prisoners, though. I didn't say you needed to keep the job."

"Valencia would never allow me to have two jobs."

"Good point."

Again they sat there.

"I suppose..." Josh said, letting his voice trail off.

"Yes?"

"I could make you a fake ID. You still got the J.R. wig from college?"

Hunter started to laugh and said, "You want J.R. to get a job in the prison?"

"That was my idea."

"Well, hell yeah," he said in a very heavy southern red-neck style voice, "let's bring good ol' J.R. to the world shall we?"

"No one is in my office tonight, so we should be able to get in there. Go to your bunk area and get the J.R. stuff and meet me at my office."

"Yee-haw," Hunter howled as they both stood up. As they reached the area where they split up Hunter turned to Josh. "How do we make sure I end up on her dungeon sector?"

"Lucky for you, one of my old jobs was loading the schedules into the mainframe system plus I know the lady who does run the dungeons—and does the hiring. I work on everyone's systems and my office is in the same building as hers. I can manage that. It's a lottery which sector you get. I can make sure you get it though. No one wants that sector anyway, so it shouldn't be hard to get you in."

"Why doesn't anyone want it?"

Josh's brows furrowed as his lips pursed.

"Just tell me, man."

"It's hard for anyone who's a werewolf or shape shifter to go down there and see all the animals in cages—and the smell ain't too pretty either."

"Now, you're sure Valencia won't ever come across me. 'Cause wig or no, if anyone involved with Bravo Company comes into this area and sees me, I'll be toast. We've not listed that I have a red-neck identical twin brother with long dark hair and a fondness for chewing toothpicks on my file."

Josh put a hand on Hunter's shoulder. "I've never seen Valencia go down there and, unless anyone else in your company gets arrested, none of them will either. They don't work these kind of jobs. Y'all are soldiers. Those who work down there? They're not soldier material, to say the least."

Hunter let this sink in, then nodded. "How long will it take for J.R. to be employed?"

"Not long. Once we make his ID tonight you'll just need to bring him on into the office and apply for a job. He'll be a referral of mine. That'll help."

"Then let's get it done. See you shortly."

* * * *

"Hey. My name is J.R. and I have an appointment with a Mr. Brooks." Hunter said with a deep southern drawl. He wore a wig of dark hair cut in the shape of a mullet and he was chewing on a toothpick as he leaned on the secretary's desk, a young woman who he would refer to as unfortunate looking. As she gave him her attention, he touched the bill of his green John Deere baseball cap and gave her a nod and a wink.

"What time was your appointment?" she asked in a high twittery voice.

"I was told to be here at ten A.M. It's ten, right?" he asked.

"Yes sir. Uh, let me go check with Mr. Brooks."

"Thank you, ma'am."

The little woman got up and disappeared into the office behind her. A few minutes passed and she came out, followed by Josh, who was dressed for work now in his white dress shirt and blue tie. He carried a folder in one hand and put out the other to J.R.

"Thanks for coming in on such short notice, J.R., and on a Sunday." Josh shook J.R.'s hand.

"No problem a-tall. I was hopin' to hear from y'all."

"Good good—come on in to the conference room with me—I need to chat with you about the job we're considering you for. Denise? Could you please hold my calls?"

"Yes sir."

Josh nodded a thank you to her and they both walked into the conference room. As soon as he shut the door Josh let a chuckle escape his lips quietly.

"I forgot how funny you look in the full gear!"

"Dude, you saw it when we did the pictures last night."

"I know, I think it's the whole ensemble and the accent. I can't believe you wore the John Deere cap—put that away."

"What? It's stylin', dude," Hunter said with a laugh as he took it off. "So where do we stand?"

"Okay, so, I'm gonna bring in the woman in charge of the staff for the dungeons. Someone on that duty quit today so you're going to be her lucky star."

"Someone quit?"

"Yeah, darn shame, left us an email and didn't show up for work," Josh clarified with a wink.

"Oh yeah, damn shame. Hope they're okay," Hunter said with mock concern.

"Sure—they'll be fine. They'll just never come back here so, it's your job while you want it."

"Dynasty."

"The woman I'm calling in. Her name is Barbara. She's a nutcase. But she owes me a favor and we're short a dungeon worker so I'm hoping to get your ass in there by this weekend. She'll train you this week."

"Let's do this. The sooner I can get in there the sooner I can get to Jen and Eddie can find my foot up his ass."

"I'll go get her now."

Josh got up and left the conference room. As he shut the door behind him, Hunter opened the folder. It held the application he filled out last night, a photocopy of his Clandestine ID and his work ID for Superior Order Security Division. It all seemed to be in order, so he shut the folder and sat in the chair, finding a good J.R. type sitting style—legs spread wide and his hand on his large belt buckle. He took a deep breath.

Josh walked into the room with a tall, thin woman in her late fifties, pretty for her age. A touch of grey was showing at her temples, but he had to look hard to see it. Around her neck hung a pair of reading glasses on a gold chain.

Hunter stood up when she entered the room. She gave him a smile and shut the door. "Thank you so much for coming in on such short notice Mr…"

"You can just call me J.R., ma'am."

"Okay, J.R. it is. Thanks for coming in. Please, have a seat."

"Ladies first." Hunter said, motioning to the other chair at the table.

Barbara raised an eyebrow at him and took a seat. Hunter sat down afterward.

"J.R., I have an employee that has left us in the lurch and I need to fill his spot immediately. Are you free to start training this week?"

Bravo Company was on a two-week break from training so as long as Hunter could work the con in two weeks he'd be golden.

"Ma'am, I'm free to start today."

* * * *

"Are you sure?" Atlanta asked, looking at her surroundings.

It was about ten o'clock, cool for a Sunday morning in June, and they were in the Meatpacking District of Manhattan, at a building that was very non-descript and somewhat run down.

"Sure of what?"

She knocked on the door. "That this is the right address?"

"This is what I wrote down."

"So...is that a no?" she asked, pulling at her high ponytail and smoothing the front of her hair.

"Ha ha."

She grinned at him and the door opened. A lovely woman stood there, the skin obviously of a vampire. Atlanta concluded it must be the Mrs. she'd heard of, the sister to the prick who they bought the blood from.

"Sean and Atlanta?" Her voice was so sultry that even Atlanta melted.

"Yes ma'am," Sean replied.

"Hello, I'm Julietta, Bernard's wife. Right this way. He is expecting you."

They stepped through the door into another world. Standing in their apartment, you never would have believed what the building looked like on the outside. A large space, it smelled of a mixture of cinnamon and orange peel. The lighting was low with lit candles throughout, on surfaces and wall sconces.

Julietta noticed Atlanta's gaping mouth. "You like?"

"This is so not what I was expecting."

"That's the point. We don't want the building we're in to scream our location. Please, follow me back to Bernard's workshop."

The studio she stepped into was unlike most NYC apartments Atlanta had seen. To the right were three doors, with all but one closed. The primary space was warm, inviting and boasted high ceilings and a wide floor plan. The main room held a spacious living room, dining room, and kitchen in one space with room to spare. Julietta led her and Sean through this large space to the opposite side of the apartment where another closed door waited for them. Julietta knocked.

"Darling, your guests are here."

"Fantastic, show them in!" a deep voice from inside requested.

Julietta opened the door and stepped aside, motioning them into the room. This was a large, rectangular workshop with a generous tool table in the center and a glassed off board room area with a conference table and video equipment at one end. Atlanta wondered if Sean was as impressed as she was.

A tall man with short dark hair and a full beard got up to meet them, smiling. "Great to meet you two!" He put his hand out and shook each of theirs. He was wearing a dirty "I Love NY" shirt and ripped up jeans.

"Would you all like some coffee? Julietta asked. "I have some fresh beans ground."

"That would be lovely dear," Bernard said, crossing to her to kiss her briefly on the lips.

Julietta smiled as she touched his face, "I'll be back then." With that, she gently shut the door.

Bernard motioned to a couple of stools on one side of the rectangular table. "Do sit." Taking his working goggles off the top of his head he walked to the other side of the table and set them down. "My brother-in-law said you are hoping to do something new."

"We are," Sean told him, "We're not sure what though."

His eyebrows raced up his lightly lined face and his smile grew. "Excellent. I love work that gives me openings to be creative. Tell me a little about what you need it for."

Sean and Atlanta glanced at each other. They'd discussed on the way over how they didn't want to give too much away, but that they'd have to mention her specialty and hope money could keep him quiet. They also thought of testing him with her marking; hence why Atlanta's hair was up.

"Here, let me take your jacket," Sean said, giving her an excuse to turn around while he watched Bernard's face. "Now before we discuss what we are looking for and why, you see why this is absolutely confidential?"

The question hung in the air and Bernard let his gaze go to Atlanta and back to Sean and nodded. "I understand completely."

"Good," she breathed out in relief. "Then you understand also that we were never here, and you promise to make this item exclusively for us. We are willing to pay for your secrecy and the patent on the item."

Bernard pursed his lips. A tiny smile at the corner of his mouth showed that he liked this so far. "Lady, most of my weapons are exactly this sort of order." He sniffed the air and then looked at her with a slightly furrowed brow. "What kind of witch are you, lovely lady? You do not smell of the earth or of the water and you aren't running at a higher temperature, so either your friend here is diluting your scent or—"

"You already know."

He smiled. "Yes. You bare the mark, Air Witch." He must've seen fear in Atlanta's reaction. "Diana's daughter is always welcome in our household." His eyes watered. "I never thought I'd see this day or have this honor. Please, my hands are yours, my lady. What do you need? Something unique for both daily defense and battle I would think."

Atlanta relaxed. "Yes."

He nodded and sat quiet for a minute or so. Bernard got up to pace in thought. Finally he stopped and asked, "What hand to hand weapons are you good with?"

"Bo-Staff and a Bow," she replied.

"Good, good—" He started to pace again.

Atlanta's excitement became anxiety watching Bernard pace about his workspace talking to himself. She glanced at Sean and he took her hand. Bernard stopped his pacing and planning when he saw this.

"You two are together?"

Atlanta had no idea what that had to do with anything but she nodded. He pulled out some sketch paper, two feet by three feet in size and threw it on the table. He started sketching something and then caught her eye.

"You know, there's not many of us."

"Many of us what?"

"Not many of us," he said, motioning to himself and her. "You know, witches who are loved by vampires and vice versa. My lovely wife says vampires who do have a sadistic streak in them—a feeling of self-loathing or need of punishment."

Sean squeezed her hand a touch harder than she'd have liked. He eased up almost as quickly, obviously realizing his involuntary reaction. Atlanta didn't need

Bernard to tell her this about her partner. She knew how broken he was, loving him in spite of that, or possibly because of it.

Bernard didn't seem to notice the tension in Sean's whole being and kept on yapping. "I love my lady, and it pains her she can't spend eternity with me, but she said she'd rather have the time I have than no time at all. Even if it was legal, I'm too old."

"I'm sorry, I don't understand."

Sean answered this for him. "After a human reaches the age of twenty five, the chances of a successful vampire change are extremely slim. But, as he's a witch, he's not allowed to be changed anyways."

"Oh," Atlanta said, understanding part of what he was saying now. "Why is it not allowed?"

Sean again stepped in. "The Clandestine World frown upon the mixing of breeds. They call them abominations."

"Why?" she asked, the name alone giving her the chills.

Bernard leaned over his drawing paper toward them. "Because it's been told they are blood thirsty creatures with no control of their bloodlust."

Atlanta's whole body felt ill at the thought. She was almost positive she visibly shuddered. "Why would anyone even want to be that?"

"Isn't it obvious?" Bernard asked. "Immortality."

"It's not worth it," Sean said flatly.

"For love. Trust me, if I'd been young enough, I regret to admit, I'd have considered it."

Atlanta thought of how much Sean loved her, how much Roman loved her and how they both would live for hundreds of years past her. She rubbed her arms more out of her fear than of being cold. She remembered Celeste's warning. What if she took blood from them one too many times too close together?

"I won't let that happen," Sean said.

"Reading my thoughts again?" she asked in as lighthearted a tone as she could muster.

"No love, I can just read you."

Atlanta let her vision be filled by his honey colored eyes and for that moment, Bernard wasn't there. She felt the steadiness that was Sean. He did know her that well. How had she even been tempted to kiss Roman the other morning? Was that only yesterday?

Before that thought could take her down a path she didn't want to go down she turned the focus to their host. "How old were you when you met your wife?"

"I was thirty, so there wasn't a chance of temptation, but I love her dearly and she's pledged to be by my side until I go. We've been married now for fifteen years this summer."

Atlanta smiled, "That's wonderful!"

He smiled at her, "Thank you. We're very happy. She is a painter and I make legal items like furniture as well as what you're here for. We're well matched and mostly out of the public eye. We prefer it that way."

As if on cue, Julietta knocked on the door and came in with coffee, cream, and sugar. After she'd served it, she left them alone, again with a kiss for her husband and a smile for Atlanta and Sean.

He watched her leave and then revealed, "I will need three things from you in order to begin work. As soon as I have that, you can be on your way."

Atlanta sipped her coffee, considering it was possibly the best she'd ever had. "What do you need?"

"Hair sample for DNA, blood sample, and measurements."

"DNA? Blood?" she sputtered, almost choking on her drink.

"Yes, if you want this weapon to work for you and you alone it must be genetically engineered that way. I need the measurements to make the item to fit your build and size."

Atlanta thought about this for a minute, took a deep breath, and then nodded. He'd passed the test so she had to trust him. If she didn't trust anyone in this war, she'd get nowhere. Of course, it was a matter of trusting the right people. Bernard felt right.

Sean kissed her temple and they got to work. Bernard went to get her some juice and a cookie. He took a pint of her blood, a few locks of hair, and then measured and weighed her. Before she knew it, they were on our way out of the door into the room that smelled of cinnamon and orange peel again.

Bernard told them to come back in a week to discuss ideas. She told him they may not be in town in a week but they could easily do a conference call. This suited him fine, so they said their goodbyes and headed to the van. As the two of them headed to Brooklyn, the van was quiet. Atlanta could tell Sean was lost in thought so she reached over and put her hand on his, feeling his cool skin on hers, and wishing it wasn't rude to try and read his mind.

"Do you want to tell me what you're obsessing about over there, lover?" she asked, using the sweetest voice she could.

Sean didn't answer and she was about to ask him mentally, but he squeezed her hand and turned to her at the next red light and smiled. "Sorry. I only was thinking about what he'd said. How his wife will have to watch him die—how I'll have to watch you die. It's unsettling."

"We talked about this. Look, it's better than the alternative."

"I agree. I meant what I said in there. I'd never turn you even if you begged me to. As selfish as I am, I'd never put you through it. I'd rather watch you live to a ripe old age and die happy in my arms having lived an amazing life full of love and joy."

"And what would you do once I was gone?" she asked.

"I'd go on living the life that would've made you proud. Maybe you'll outlive me, who knows. This war makes things so uncertain. I'd like to think we'll all survive it, but I'm not that much of an optimist."

Now it was her turn to be silent. He kissed her hand and she gazed at him, the wind from the cracked open window tossing his curls about haphazardly. He mouthed the words "love you" at her and she returned the sentiment. He was right. This war very well could take the lives of any of them. It definitely was unsettling.

They changed the subject to her new weapon and they had fun coming up with outrageous ideas. They were still laughing and carrying on even as they walked up the stairs and into the main room where everyone sat. However, as they entered the room what they saw made the smiles fall from their faces.

Chapter Twelve

"As you can see, there are three different levels of the facility," Barbara was saying, "One for each classification. The top level is for vampires, the second is for shape shifters, and the third are for werewolves."

"I have two questions."

"Yes?"

"The top floor is the only one above ground and that's where you put vampires?"

"Yes. They can't tell if it's day or night out where they are. They do know they are on the top floor. So, if they misjudge the time and try to escape, they'll just be stuck indoors anyway. This way they don't have multiple floors to hide in, on their way up and out."

"I see. Where are the jail cells for witches?"

"The tower. You can't put an Earth or Water Witch underground...they'll cause a huge problem. So we put them all in the enclosed tower over on the east side."

"Okay then."

"As I was saying...werewolves are the strongest, so they're at the deepest level, followed by shape shifters. The level I need immediate coverage on is that level. Shape shifters are usually a docile group. However, it can smell and sound like you're the gamekeeper at the zoo when you are down there. That is, depending on how many are sedated during your shift. Most of the new ones trapped in human form so that they are less comfortable."

"I see."

Barbara must've heard a tone in Hunter's voice for she turned to him. "You don't have a problem with that, do you J.R.?"

"No, ma'am. If they're guilty then they deserve what they get."

This seemed to satisfy her and she nodded, putting her eyes up to the scanner for a retinal scan. As she did a computerized voice said, "Vannetta, Barbara. Full Authorization" and the door clicked open.

"Full authorization?" Hunter asked.

"This means I can move throughout each level without coming out onto the outside floor and going up and then scanning back into the next floor. You will have partial authorization. You are only assigned to the shape shifter level. If you do well, and move up, you'll obtain authorization to all levels."

Hunter nodded and smiled at her as he thought to himself that if he needed full access that badly, to save Jensine's life, per say, he'd just pull Barbara's eyes out of their sockets.

They entered into the dungeon area and as they walked along Hunter sniffed to see if he could smell Jensine anywhere close. Not a single person or animal's scent stood out to him. They all had been in here with each other for so long that they all smelled the same—and it was rancid, just like Josh had warned him.

"Wow, it does smell in here," he complained, his eyes watering.

"Yes, you'll get used to it. We pump a chemical in here to help make all the animals have the same scent so we cut down on the marking of territory."

"Ah. I see."

"We don't have that many in here currently of this species. Only about twenty or so. They're located in the area we just passed and then down here to our left. Follow me."

"Yes, ma'am."

As he followed her he saw all types of animals and humans curled up in corners of cages. All cages contained a base of straw, but also a small cot with a pillow and thin blanket and a toilet with a sink. They were no more than ten feet deep and five feet wide a piece. As they reached the end of the row he still didn't see Jensine.

"This is all of them…just the row as we came in and these?"

"No. We have a special room for the newcomers at the other end. It is a walled in room instead of bars. It's for privacy as we try to get information out of them. We have a girl in there now. However, I have orders today to move her down here. In fact, why don't you observe her transfer today?"

Hunter swallowed hard but put his best face forward. "Of course."

Barbara picked up the phone receiver on the wall at the end of the hall and dialed a number. "Yes. It's time to move Ms. Blackensdale to a regular cell." She paused and listened. "Do not argue with me…you've had enough time with her. Get down here and bring Brian. I have a new recruit for you to meet." She hung up the phone and shook her head.

"Problem?"

"Eddie is a problem. He enjoys the torture too much. He and his partner Brian will be down in a moment and you'll observe how this is done."

Hunter started his mantra now, saying to himself "I will not kill Eddie with witnesses—I will not kill Eddie with witnesses—"

She showed Hunter the schedule for baths and stall cleaning, which was every other day. Then she showed him the paperwork for cell monitoring. Shortly though, they were cut off by the arrival of Eddie and Brian. Eddie was thin but taller than Hunter, and Brian was a brute, easily over six foot and pushing 220 pounds.

Quietly he followed Barbara and her two goons down the hall to Jensine's cell. Hunter braced himself for the worst. Barbara opened the room and he stole a glance inside. Jensine was in human form and wore the usual prison attire. Pulled tight to her chest was a thin blanket as she shivered. He could tell her room was colder than the rest of the prison as the air hit him in the face. Jensine didn't even bother to look up as the door opened.

The first person into the room was Eddie, and when she either saw him or got a whiff of his scent a scream ripped out of her throat like Hunter had never heard. The words were unintelligible, but her body language made it evident she had been beaten by him, repeatedly. She was shoving herself up further into the back corner with his approach. As he grabbed her she wailed, the struggle caused her blanket to fall off. The bruises on her body were too many to count, and by the look of the circles under her eyes she either wasn't sleeping, or sleeping badly.

Brian stepped into the room and helped grab her, and before Hunter could see it happen the needle was in her and she went limp. Brian tossed the needle onto the floor and lifted her up and away from Eddie. Hunter wondered for a moment if Brian was fond hitting women too. He would need to find out. If he could get Brian on his side it could speed his mission along—not to mention it would keep Brian from a future filled with pain.

The group followed Brian as he headed down the hall into a clean, warm, barred cell and he laid her on the cot. He then took a moment to cover her with a better blanket. Hunter noticed a nicer pair of clean prison clothes in the corner. After Brian set her down, he pushed Eddie out the door and locked it up, handing the key to Barbara.

Barbara handed the key to Hunter. "Add this to the ring of keys on the wall, would you?"

Hunter wanted to pocket it, but knew he couldn't with all of them watching him. He put it on the ring and noted the number on it, 309.

"J.R., follow me up to my office so we can finish your paperwork and schedule your training next week. Eddie and Brian, you are free to head to the office." Brian started to walk away, but Eddie lingered. Brian stopped when he noticed and grunted out Eddie's name at him and he followed.

"When will I be working down here again?" Hunter asked.

"Next week. This week you need to do all the classroom work. Next week you'll be down here. Night shift on your own. Think you can handle that?"

"Yes, ma'am."

* * * *

"You sure about this?" Valencia asked, her long nails sliding down Jonathan's naked chest as they lay in her bed.

"I made the call, didn't I? I'm ready for this. I head to the airport in the next hour," Jonathan said.

"Good, it's time," Valencia said. "The final stages of our plan are finally in place. I need you back in Massachusetts."

"You have to promise to not kill him. That was our deal, neither of them."

Laying on her side, her hands fluttering in mild irritation, she huffed, "You have my word. I told you what I want."

Jonathan sat up, swinging his legs off the side of the bed. "I'll do it, didn't I already say I would?"

"Yes, you did. So yes, I promise they both stay alive," she said in a soft voice, "The only one I want is her. You remember the plan I told you, yes?"

"I do—though I do not understand why. I'd ask you, but I have a feeling you aren't going to tell me."

She thought about it for a moment and then sat up, wrapping her naked body around him from behind, hands on his chest. "Before I was a vampire, I was a very unhappy woman with a rich husband who loved me, but I didn't love him in return. He was a good man, just a normal mortal man with a good heart."

"What happened to him?"

Valencia removed herself from her lover and gracefully sauntered across the room, slipping into an emerald green satin robe before walking to the bay window and throwing the curtains open to let the sun bathe her sin. "I hurt him—though I didn't mean to—" She sat then, her head and heart full of many thoughts and emotions.

Jonathan must've sensed her emotional confliction and after sliding on his jeans he walked over toward her. "It's okay—you can tell me, Vee."

"I know I can, Jonathan. It's, well, it's that I've never told anyone this, so—" She took a deep breath, patted the seat next to her and then continued once he sat, his gray eyes intently on her face. "Mark was on a weekend trip for work so I went dancing at a club one night. That's when I met Dmitri. And I fell head over heels for him. I didn't know he was a vampire but he knew I had a witch blood. As you know, we witches smell different to vampires. Now, Dmitri was not a living vampire, he'd been created hundreds of years ago against his will and one of the things he wanted more than anything was a child.

"One night he asked me to get pregnant by my husband. He told me he'd marry me and the three of us would be a family. I was so in love with him that I decided I'd do anything for him. So I stopped taking my birth control and didn't tell Mark. It wasn't long before I was pregnant with Mark's child." She looked out the window. "The pregnancy was hard. I spent a lot of time in bed because the child took all of my energy for itself. Dmitri said that the baby was going to be strong if it was draining me that way."

She smiled and took Jonathan's hand. "Mark was so sweet and wonderful to me while I was bed ridden. He'd do anything for me. When our child was born, it was a wonderful time. We loved this child very much. I thought for sure Dmitri would keep his promise and we'd run off together. But he didn't. He preferred seeing me secretly. He didn't say it but he had problems with the fact that Mark was the father. He didn't think he'd care, but he did."

"Well that's just ridiculous. He asked you to—"

She put a finger to his lips, not only to stop him, but to sooth his temper. "For two years we went on this way. The child grew healthy, beautiful and strong. I should've been happy. I had a wealthy husband who loved me and a man I loved, but my world felt broken, like shards of glass. When I was with Mark I thought of Dmitri and when I was with Dmitri I felt bad for Mark.

"As my child started to learn to talk I worried that Dmitri's existence would leak out. I told Dmitri we needed to make our break for it soon. He told me I'd need to become a vampire to be with him. I refused. I was twenty five years old. I knew that I could lose my soul and even though I'd never seen myself as some saint, the idea of being soulless—disintegrating like a zombie until I fell apart. Well, as you can imagine, it bothered me immensely. He said that until I would change to be with him things would stay the way they were."

Valencia kissed Jonathan's hand, let go and wandered about the room. "I took my child to the babysitter's. Told her I was attending a function, but I was meeting up with Dmitri for a rendezvous. I picked him up and we were on our way to one of my favorite hotels when we got into a fight. Same topic as always.

"It was slick out, and I had to concentrate hard on the road, so I never saw it coming. He released my seatbelt and spun my wheel. The car spun out of control on the ice until it hit something with such force that I was launched through the windshield. I flew over the hood of the car and then I fell for what felt like forever. I finally hit ground and rolled, and before I knew it I was cold and wet and moving very fast. It took me a moment to realize I was in water. I couldn't move my legs or my neck and my arms did what they could to keep me from going under but it was a losing battle and under I finally went."

"That bastard let you drown?" Jonathan's face was enraged. So much so that she went over to him.

Slipping her arms around him, burying her face in his bare chest, she continued, his steady arms wrapping around her. "Suddenly I felt arms around me. It was Dmitri. He pulled me to shore. When he laid me onto the earth it was cold and I could feel my head bleeding. He looked down on me and smiled.

"Somehow I knew I was dying. I felt paralyzed and I was losing blood. Dmitri covered my eyes and whispered to me, *forever*, but in Russian. And then I felt it, his teeth in my neck. I started to scream *no,* because I didn't want to be like him. I tried to fight back, but I couldn't. I didn't know much about my powers to help me either. Before I knew it he'd drained me to the edge of death, then sliced his own wrist and put it to my mouth. The blood rushed out and down my throat before I could think about what was really going on."

Valencia untangled herself from Jonathan and sat down on the window seat, pulling Jonathon with her, holding his hands to give her the courage to go on.

"He picked me up and took me home—to Mark. He told Mark he was a friend of the family and that we'd been in an accident and he'd pulled me from the water. Mark wanted to rush me to the hospital but Dmitri told him I'd be fine. They put me in dry clothes and put me in bed and kept an eye on me. Mark couldn't see inside of me, or he'd have seen the bones mending at an alarming rate. What he did see were the cuts on my head start to heal. As I lay there changing I could say nothing but look at him with pain in my eyes—from my growing hunger. Hunger that was building so fast.

"I could smell Mark's blood and it smelled like my favorite foods all rolled into one. I couldn't move, but he was all I could watch. Luckily his family could watch the child overnight, so he was the only true human in the room."

Valencia paused.

"It's okay, love, finish your story, I'm here," Jonathan said, taking her hands in his.

She looked at his lovely face and continued. "The changes ended and a veil was lifted. I could see, and hear things I'd never heard before—smell things I never knew before—and the one thing I smelled more than anything was Mark. My sweet, wonderful, darling Mark. He was sitting in a rocking chair in our room, looking out at the night. Dmitri entered the room as he could feel I was awake. My head was swimming—I couldn't focus. Mark ran over to me and hugged me and said how much he loved me and asked how I felt and before I knew what I'd done—"

"You drank from him."

She nodded.

"It was Dmitri's plan all along, wasn't it? By doing this he was able to get rid of Mark and change you as he wanted."

Valencia paused. "Yes. Problem was that once my head was clear and I realized what he'd done, I was very angry and I left. I left him, I left the town, I left my child...I left. I couldn't trust myself near my human child. So I left. I jumped into an empty rail car on a train and let it drag me where it would take me. As you know, it was headed from Michigan to Canada. I've been here ever since. My child was given to Mark's family to be raised and once I was able to control myself around humans I'd watch the child from a distance. She had no powers for years and I was confused—until a few months ago—when she truly understood them."

Jonathan looked at her, his eyebrows furrowed together as if he was busy trying to put things together—trying to access information in his brain. Valencia didn't let him think on it long.

"Jonathan. Atlanta is my daughter."

* * * *

In the van on the way back to Massachusetts, they all sat in silence. They'd talked themselves to the point of exhaustion while at the safe house and then at sunset loaded up the van so as the sun dipped under the horizon they could start the drive to Boston.

While Sean and Atlanta had been out, Roman received a frantic call from Harmon. He said that Valencia planned to kill Phoenix, but that he was able to stop her. He convinced her to release him, but there were stipulations. He had been instructed to give those in person and was jumping on a flight to Boston at sunset. He assured them that his allegiance lay with them and that he was headed home to assist in getting Phoenix back.

Sean and Atlanta argued it was a trap. Stephan and Roman didn't think so. It was a horrible mess. They reached a point where they all were restating the same arguments over and over again, so they finally all stopped talking. Atlanta took the first shift in driving and Sean sat up front with her. Roman sat in the seat behind Sean so Atlanta could see him out of the corner of her eye. She and Sean had been having a mental conversation during the drive, but that too had drained to a close. So he reached out and took her hand, and they drove in silence.

The girls were sleeping in the back and Amanda sat with them and the cooler of blood and bottled water sat wedged between the front seats. Bianca would warm it with her hands and the boys and Amanda could drink it. But as witches need real food, Atlanta started scanning the highway for food signs.

Amanda moved to sit next to Roman as Stephan went to sit with Gray for a bit in the middle seat. Atlanta caught her eye. "You didn't have to come with us, you know. This is going to be dangerous."

Amanda didn't hesitate. "No choice."

"Everyone has a choice," Roman corrected her.

"Not really," she retorted, "I know who the good guys are. That's the side I'll be on."

Atlanta understood her. To Amanda it didn't matter who won or lost and it didn't matter what happened to her in the end. What did matter was what side she stood on when the chips fell. She'd rather die on the side of good than live on the side of evil—or worse, live because she'd done nothing. Atlanta could relate to that completely.

Everyone else seemed to understand and no one else commented. Again they all dropped into silence, lost in their own thoughts of the news Harmon would bring them and how much they'd believe. It was only a four to five hour trip but it was beginning to feel like forever due to the silence. Atlanta finally turned on the radio.

Two hours in, they decided to stop at a diner. Gray and the four witches went into the diner to get some food to go. They could've gone through a drive through but, unlike vampires, the humans had to use the restroom and stretch their legs. Atlanta was amazed at how the vampires could sit, unmoving, for hours. No changing position, no stretching, no nothing. It was a bit unnerving if she thought too much about it, which she chose not to.

After the pit stop, they loaded into the van. Stephan and Gray were took the front with Stephan behind the wheel. Sean and Atlanta tucked themselves into the rear section so that they could lie down after the greasy food fest. Atlanta knew her arteries were not her main concern.

Roman, Bianca and Celeste were teaching Amanda to play Euchre while Desi fell asleep in the space between the seats and the side door, cocooned up in a blanket to keep the draft from the sliding door off her. Once finished with her food, Atlanta curled up on the tiny square mattress in the back, with Sean wrapped around her, and dozed.

Finally, she turned toward him. He gently ran his finger along the sides of her face. It didn't take super powers to know he was upset about something more than the obvious issues they all had been discussing. Atlanta thought possibly he didn't want to share it with the whole class, but maybe he'd share with her. So she reached out mentally to him.

"What is bothering you? Please tell me." When he looked troubled she reached forward and touched his cheek. *"You are probably making a big deal out of nothing, so stop holding it in and tell me what's going on."*

He kissed her forehead and smiled. *"It's nothing. I'm just worried. When it comes to Valencia, all bets are off."*

Fear gripped her as a thought occurred to her. *"What if she wants to exchange prisoners? Him for you? I won't let that happen!"*

"Shhh." His lips met hers, soft and compassionate. *"One step at a time. If I have to run, I'll run."*

"I'd come with you."

He kissed her, pulling her in close. *"I know you would."*

He stopped kissing her to rest his forehead on hers. They stayed that way, kissing occasionally, until the van pulled into the driveway of the mansion.

"Harmon's car is here. We'll have the answer soon enough," Sean said to her, lacing his fingers with her as they walked into the house.

Harmon stood by the fire in the parlor, his black ensemble in stark contrast with his white blonde hair. Pepper was there, too, sitting on Atlanta's favorite chaise lounge. Seeing Atlanta's narrow gaze Pepper got up and moved. They introduced Amanda to Pepper and then she faced off with Harmon, mutual understanding of uneven ground in the silence.

Everyone took a seat either on the floor or a piece of furniture leaving Harmon the only one standing.

"Thanks for coming back so quickly. I know I took you away from something important, but I had to see you all. As I told you on the phone, I have been sent to give you information. Valencia will have one of her people bring you a letter soon. It will give you a location to meet where we won't be noticed by the human world. She will return Phoenix relatively unharmed in exchange for one thing."

"One thing? That's all?" Atlanta asked, her insides twisting as she held her breath.

"Yes," he said as he turned to look at her. "The deal is that Atlanta is to come, at a specified time and location to speak with Valencia."

At this the room erupted with people yelling different things from "the hell she will" to "why?" and "that makes no sense."

"Quiet!" Atlanta yelled. Everyone stopped talking and looked at her. She'd not even considered this. She'd been sure it would be Sean. Gathering her wits she continued, "Harmon, why trade Phoenix for me now? If she wanted to talk to me she could've done that at any time."

"I'm not sure. All I know is that she feels once you two can speak *alone*, things will change for both sides. This is more important than anything else."

"Alone my ass!" Sean shouted, standing up.

Roman stood as well. "Why alone? She can easily speak to her with us present. There's no need to put Atlanta in any more danger than she'll already be in."

Harmon spread his palms open and up. "That's the deal."

Sean stepped toward him. "We're not letting her go alone. Not—a chance— in hell."

"She will give us Phoenix back if she can only speak to Atlanta alone. That's the deal. If you don't do this she'll kill him, plain and simple."

"Why kill her trump card?" Bianca asked.

"Yeah, that seems like it'd be silly for her to do," Desi added.

"That is my brother!" Harmon yelled at Bianca. "He's no trump card and I suggest you watch your bloody tongue." Harmon seemed to be teetering on the edge emotionally. Atlanta wasn't sure if it was real or a great act. "He's my brother—my twin. We can't let her kill him. Trust me, she will if she is refused what she wants. She'll make it something showy, in front of human witnesses. That was her plan until I convinced her there had to be something she wanted more. She said Atlanta. If we don't bring her to the meeting, Phoenix dies in a way that exposes our world and as we know, all hell will break loose from there."

They all sat in silence for a moment. Sean and Roman sat down.

Atlanta took a cleansing breath. "Fine. I will meet her," Atlanta said, holding up a hand to Sean so she could finish. "The Great Order has no chance in this war without their leader. I refuse to talk to her alone, though. I must be in eyesight of everyone the whole time."

"No way," Sean started to say. "There's got to be another—"

"There isn't another way, Sean," she said softly to him as she took his hand.

"We can fight this war without him, but I'm pretty sure we can't fight this war without you," Sean said. "Roman, think about this."

"I am. I'm at a loss. Without Phoenix to pull all factions together, we can pretty much bet on most going underground and not being part of this fight at all. Valencia says she just wants to talk. I'm with Atty. We demand that she does so in view of us—can we do that, Harmon?"

"Probably. She'll be expecting a counter offer anyway."

Harmon may have addressed Roman, but he was staring at Atlanta in an odd way. She stared back and he looked away. What was his deal? He would look at her and waves of emotions wafted off of him in such a jumble that she couldn't read him. With a shake of her head she focused on Sean, who sat with his head in his hands. She heard nothing coming from him either, in a different way. It was like he was frozen. Where Harmon was the Emergency Broadcast Signal sound from TV, Sean was simply a fuzzy station with no sound, just static. Atlanta placed her hand on his back and realized he wasn't even breathing. It was if his whole body had shut down.

Atlanta turned attention to Roman, whose face held a mix of emotions. Everyone who she looked at seemed to be at a complete loss. They sat there for only a minute before Sean broke the silence, but it felt like ten.

"No." His voice was quiet at first. He stood up and said it full force. "No!" Roman stood up as well and opened his mouth. Sean stopped him. "You don't need to do this, Atlanta. This is the Prince that wouldn't even induct you into The Order. This is a Prince whose brother is working for both sides—" Harmon went to cut him off but Sean yelled at him. "Don't you say a word, or I'll drop you where you stand. I've taken you before, and I'll do it again. This time though, I'll make the damage permanent!"

Roman got out one word. "Sean—"

"Shut up! Everyone! This is unacceptable. I won't allow it. This girl is our only chance—don't you all see that? And you want to hand her over to Valencia? What is wrong with you people? Phoenix may be the cornerstone for the North Eastern Colonies but I'm sure they'll listen to Roman and Crone Brenner and the others. We cannot sacrifice the—we can't sacrifice who she is—we can't." Obviously Sean had almost said "the chosen child of Diana" but caught himself. She was sure everyone understood what he meant without saying it.

"Without Phoenix we can't even officially go to war, Sean," Stephan reminded him.

Gray finally stood up. "I'm with Sean. We find another way. It's too risky."

"Thank you, Gray," Sean breathed a sigh of relief.

"I don't think—" Harmon started to say, but that's all it took to put Sean in motion, and it was all over before it could begin.

Sean clocked Harmon in the face, causing his head to go crashing into the wooden mantel of the fireplace. Taking advantage of this shock he grabbed Harmon's hands and spun them behind his back, shoving Harmon down to the ground, his head hitting the brick hearth of the fireplace with a loud crack.

Sean sat on Harmon's back, pinning Harmon's legs with his own, holding one of Harmon's arm almost in the fire. "I swear on the goddess herself if you do not tell me the truth right now I will burn you to ash right here!"

Chapter Thirteen

"Roman! Get this wanker off of me!" Harmon yelled out.

Roman moved to touch Sean, but couldn't. He looked at Atlanta. "I can't, Harmon. There's a block."

"Bloody witch!" Harmon blurted.

Sean smacked his head into the back of Harmon's, and Harmon's head hit the bricks again. Blood flowed this time.

"This isn't helping any, Sean," Harmon said through bloody lips. "What she wants is what she wants. Killing me won't change her reasons."

"What are her reasons?"

"Like she'd tell me!"

"She would tell you, Jonathan. It's whether or not you'll tell us."

"There is nothing to tell!"

"Liar!" Sean bellowed in Harmon's ear.

"I can't tell you what I don't know!"

"You mean you only will tell us what you want us to know." Sean moved Harmon's hand into the fire further. It was close to catching on fire.

"Fine! I'll tell you how it is!"

Sean pulled the hand away from the flame, but not by much. "Start talking, you double crossing son of a bitch!"

"She took Phoenix for one purpose and one purpose only, to have the leverage to get an audience with Atlanta."

"Why not just call and ask her out for coffee?" Sean asked.

"None of you let her out of your sight and she figured this would be the only chance to talk to her. They're both Air Witches, you know. All she wants to do is talk to her. She doesn't plan on kidnapping her or anything like that. She doesn't want to kill her...that's the furthest thing from her mind!"

Sean pulled Harmon's hand back another inch. "Were you sent here or did you leave her?"

"Both. I begged for his life and she said for me to deliver this message to you all. If I did that he'd be safe."

"That's not leaving her," Sean pointed out.

"I have no plans of returning there if I can help it. No need to tell *her* that. She'd have changed her mind on this deal." Atlanta knew Sean wasn't convinced and neither was she, but what were they to do?

Atlanta tried another avenue. "If all she wanted was to talk to me why not take me that night at The Barn? This makes no sense."

"This is her second plan. I talked her out of her primary plan. Honestly, if using Phoenix doesn't work, she'd use Roman or Sean to make Atlanta come to Canada."

Sean loosened his grip a bit but Harmon still couldn't move.

"Roman, brother, I tried all I could. This is the best deal we'll get. He's our brother."

"Is that everything?" Sean demanded, his grip tightening again.

"That's all I have. I swear on Elizabeth's grave."

Atlanta caught Roman's eye and turned her attention to Sean.

"Let him go, baby."

"No."

"Please."

"He's lying." Sean squeezed Harmon's windpipe.

"I'm not," Harmon squeaked out. "It's all I know. If Phoenix is to live I had to come here and I had to bring you this message and you have to go meet her and Atlanta must talk to her. This is not negotiable. I'm sorry."

Sean still didn't let go. Teeth clenched he said, "You're not sorry."

"For all I know she told me more, but did a spell on me so I wouldn't remember."

"That's unlikely," Sean scoffed.

"But if she did we could do a spell to help him remember. We can do that, right Celeste?" Atlanta asked.

"Not sure we can. We'd have to know which spell she did to reverse it. I wouldn't know where to start—"

"But you could try," Atlanta begged.

"Yes."

"Sean, let him go. If deep in his psyche he knows the reason, we'll get it," Atlanta assured.

Sean leaned down and whispered in Harmon's ear, "You try to bolt or touch one hair on her head and I promise you will not see another day. Got it?"

"Yes."

Sean got off Harmon and Atlanta reduced the shield to just around Sean, in case Harmon lashed out. He did not. Instead he stood up and brushed off his silk black dress shirt. The blood on his head was dry already and the cut was healing. Even so, Celeste offered to clean it. He seemed as if he was about to wave her off, but he sat on the hearth. She fetched her bag and cleaned his wounds.

Roman placed a hand on Harmon's shoulder. "You haven't eaten in a while if you're not healing that fast on your own. Come, brother, let me get you blood."

"He stays here in my eyesight," Sean ordered. "You can go get him the blood."

Normally Roman wouldn't have taken commands from Sean. Atlanta knew he only did so because now was not the time to argue with him. Sean obviously was still on the verge of killing someone and Roman didn't want any more fighting. With a nod he left for the car to get the cooler.

Celeste packed up her things and Atlanta saw her glance up at Harmon with a look she'd never seen before. He returned the tender look and made an attempt to smile. She could tell they were having a private mental conversation. He finally reached out and touched her hair and spoke.

"Thanks, Ce-Ce."

She smiled and went to put away her supplies. "I'm going to go get books so we can start research. We can set up either in the study upstairs or down here in the parlor on the round table here."

"Down here," Atlanta suggested. "That way we have a better view of those approaching the house. Bring any books we'll need, down here. Let's put that in motion."

Everyone moved with purpose, except Harmon and Sean. Not that Sean needed to hover over him, as she'd put an air block on the entrances to the hall and the kitchen. She'd told him, but Sean stayed because it made him feel better.

Atlanta went to follow the other three girls when she saw Pepper. She'd not said a word and honestly, Atlanta had forgotten she was there until now. "You okay, Pepper?"

She didn't say anything.

"P.J., you in there?"

She seemed to snap out of it with Atlanta using her nickname. "That's the first time you've called me that since the night we met."

Atlanta went and sat down next to her. "It's hard to like a girl dating your ex, so you'll have to forgive me if I never use the nickname you ask your friends to use. I've never really seen you as a friend. But now, in this situation, you're going to have to decide if you are friend or foe. I know all this is probably not what you signed on for by getting involved with us, with Roman, but now is the time to make that decision. You can't stay here in the house with us unless you plan to stick with us through all that happens. You must understand why I say this."

She nodded and they were silent for a moment.

"I'm going to go for a walk in the woods and when I return, if I return, I'll let you know what I can handle. Is that okay enough?"

She placed her hand on Pepper's shoulder. "Of course."

Pepper nodded and left. She must've passed Roman on her way out, because as the door shut Roman walked into the parlor with the cooler in both hands. Atlanta opened it up and tossed a cold packet of blood at Harmon.

"You need any, hon?" she asked Sean.

Sean's voice, gruff with reined in anger and fear said, "Probably wouldn't be a bad idea."

"Ok." She took another packet out. "I'll go heat some up for you."

This insult to Harmon didn't go unnoticed, but instead of griping he bit into his bag and drank it cold.

"Harmon, I can go and heat that for you," Roman offered.

"I'm fine."

Roman seemed to share mental words with his half-brother, then left for the kitchen. Atlanta followed him with Sean's packet of blood, poured it into a mug and put it in the microwave. "What did you do before microwaves?" she wondered aloud.

"Pardon?"

"How did you heat up your blood before microwaves?"

"Same as humans heated food, on the stove top."

She couldn't help but find it funny so she chuckled lightly as she watched the mug of blood spin around in the microwave.

"That's funny?"

"Sorry, had a mental picture of a vampire in an apron and cooking at the stove."

Roman also chuckled as he finished putting all the blood into the secret fridge compartment and shut the door. He turned to her and his face became serious. He placed a hand on each of her shoulders.

"We won't let her hurt you. You know that, right?" She nodded. "Just because I wasn't as vocal as Sean in there, you need to know I feel the same way as he does about—"

"I know." Atlanta knew the unspoken word was *you* and not *this plan*. She also knew that where Sean only had her to worry about, Roman had more responsibility and that was why he couldn't be as forthright in the room with concern to his feelings about the situation.

"If anything happened to you I'd—it'd be Elizabeth all over again. My heart couldn't handle that. I'd walk out into the sun."

She put her arms out and hugged him. It was the first time they'd physically touched other than a hand or shoulder since before Jensine's death and she heard his intake of air in surprise as he wrapped his arms around her, pulling her close.

She kissed his cheek. "I'm going to be okay. We'll take all precautions, ok?"

Atlanta felt him nod. The microwave dinged to let her know Sean's blood was done. With one last squeeze she started to pull away. He took the hint and did the same.

"Do me a favor, okay?" He nodded. "Be honest with Pepper."

"I don't even know what to tell her. That is, if she even comes back. She looked a bit wigged out."

"She'll be fine. But I can tell she really cares for you. If you're not in a place to make that happen—"

"Which I'm not," he admitted.

"You need to be honest."

She grabbed the mug out of the microwave and cursed as it was too hot. Quickly she set it on the counter before she burned herself.

"I'm so sorry for what happened," he finally said.

"This isn't your fault."

"I don't mean this—I mean us. I destroyed your trust and in doing so ruined our relationship, and if Jensine is really dead it's because of my jealousy—" he blurted out.

Just the sound of her name made her body ache all over and her eyes tear up. Letting her head fall back she took a deep breath and fought the tears.

"I guess I pray someday you'll forgive me, 'cause until you do I'm not sure I can begin to forgive myself."

Atlanta brought her head back down to look at him. She wanted to tell him she forgave him, but she didn't and she knew that lying about it wouldn't solve anything. "I pray I will be able to, too—and someday I'll forgive you and me for that. But until then, know that I'm trying and I still care about you, that hasn't changed."

"But you don't love me anymore," he said in a whisper.

She pressed her lips together. It was so complicated. "Not the way I did," she finally said aloud. She added mentally, *"But I do love you."*

Atlanta cupped his face with her hand. His blue eyes were so sad and his beautiful face looked so torn. He put his hand over hers and leaned his head into her palm and nodded. For a moment she thought he was going to try and kiss her, but he didn't. He only nodded, leaning in to kiss the top of her head.

She heard him mentally say, *"I love you. That'll never change."*

"Can we get some help with getting books down?" Celeste yelled from upstairs.

He pulled away from her and they looked at each other for a moment. He gave her a slight smile and walked out of the kitchen to help Gray, Stephan and the girls get the books needed down to the parlor. She shook herself out of the trance she'd been in, took the mug, turned to head to the parlor and about dropped the mug in shock. Sean was standing there with an expression she couldn't read. She had no idea how long he'd been standing there.

* * * *

"How long have I been here?" Jensine asked aloud to herself. She ached all over and stretched. She tried to roll over, and fell to the ground with a thud. "Ugh."

Waking up fully, she realized she was in a regular cell with bars, and not a room with metal walls. She wore a pair of cotton drawstring pants and a long sleeved T-shirt. She wondered how she'd gotten them, let alone got them on. She decided to not worry about it.

Her head felt like she was coming out of a fog. They'd had her drugged since she'd been caught and now it seemed like she wasn't drugged for the first time in a while. She took in her surroundings. The cell was dark with a tiny light bulb in the hallway two cells away. With her feline sight, it was enough to see.

With a sigh, Jensine curled up on her bunk afraid to close her eyes. Each time she did, she'd see his face, smell his scent, or worse, think she heard him coming down the hall. She hoped that now that her cell wasn't isolated he was done being able to torture her. She wondered, how close were her fellow cellmates?

Pushing herself, she slowly rose from her bunk and faced the cell door. On the right was an empty cell, then a wall. Yet to her left were cells for as far as her eyes could see, a lone light bulb hanging every two to three cells.

"Hello?" she called out. There was no answer. "Is anybody there?" she inquired a little louder.

"Hello?" came a faint response.

Jensine breathed a sigh of relief. To know she wasn't alone in the dark was a comfort. "Who's there?"

"My name is Maria," the voice responded.

Jensine figured she must be a few cells away. "I'm Jensine," she paused, wondering how much she should say. Truncating her last name she said, "Jensine Black."

"Maria Dominguez. You're new here aren't you?"

"Yes."

"What did they say you did?"

"What they *said* I did? How do you know I didn't do something?"

"Honey, everyone in here is innocent—if ya know what I mean."

Jensine thought on this. She needed to stick to her story. She didn't know this girl or if she had an agenda. No more wolves in sheep's clothing for her. "I broke into the vampire dungeon to see a prisoner. I overheard the new camera system would be going online, that the system would be dark as it was installed, so I borrowed a key card from an employee—but I got caught, she ended up dead and they think I did it. They think someone helped me."

"Did they?"

Jensine leaned against the bars with her forehead. "No. I acted alone." She strained her vision to try to see the girl.

The slam of a door and approaching footsteps sounded in the distance. Jensine became silent, holding her breath as her heart began to race.

"He won't visit you here," Maria assured her.

"Who?" Jensine asked, playing dumb.

"Eddie."

Just his name made Jensine's skin crawl. "What do you know of him?" she asked, her voice hard and cold.

"Oh, I know all about Eddie. Every girl down here knows about him. He likes to hit women, not just the ones in interrogation. He seems to get off on it."

Tears came to Jensine's eyes and before she knew it, she was sobbing and sinking to the floor.

* * * *

"Sean," was all Atlanta could get out before her throat closed. She swallowed and took a breath.

Sean stopped her. "Do you love him?"

"I don't understand. Why are you asking me this? You know I love you."

"I do know that. It's just that he's still in love with you and I need to know if you're in love with him. I mean, I know you love him, I need to know how much." He leaned against the archway, as if steadying himself for her answer.

"Here, your blood is going to get cold," she handed him the mug. He took it but didn't look at her. She was stalling. He would know she was too. She'd be honest as always. "I don't know. He broke my heart. I'm not over that. I haven't forgiven him. My feelings for Roman are a bunch of pieces of glass, floating about in my head and my heart."

Sean still wouldn't look at her and she craved his beautiful honey eyes so she could read him, feel their connection. She needed him to look at her, so she took back the mug and placed it on the counter, coming to stand in front of him, making a decision as she walked toward him. She put her hands on either side of his head and pulled him to look at her. As she saw his face she realized his eyes were closed.

"Look at me."

He shook his head slightly.

"Please baby, look at me," she begged softly.

He opened his eyes and she wondered how horrible a person she was that she was causing two of the strongest men she knew to be so scared. She wondered how she could keep hurting them when all that was ahead of them was a questionable future. She heard music come on in the parlor. Desi was probably trying to keep the room calm with soft music.

"I love you so much—I wish you could see my heart," she said.

"But you love him too."

"I do. But it's not the same. He's not the kind of man I need to make me happy. I need you. I want you. Please, with all that's ahead of us, don't *you* start doubting me, too. I need you beside me."

His arms curled about her waist, yet he'd not pulled her in the way he normally did. "What happens when you can trust him again? What happens to me if he can be what you need?"

"Why are you worried about this? Are you trying to put distance between us because of what's coming? Is that what you want to do?"

He looked at the floor. "I don't know what to do, Atty. I know you still have feelings for him and he has them for you and I am going crazy with the idea of you going to meet Valencia. I know it won't be good—if I lost you—if you're thinking of leaving me—I need to—"

"Protect your heart, I know."

His eyes finally met hers with intensity. "I was going to say *our* heart. Mine is yours, and I want you to remember that you hold it in your hands and I feel helpless. I'm normally great with plans and strategies, but right now I can't even think about how to take my hands off you and walk across the room. It's like my brain is forgetting how to do anything. The thought of losing you, whether it's to him or to her, has my head spinning. I'm at a loss. I can't seem to get a clear head to be the protector I need to be. I feel absolutely frightened and lost because of it."

Atlanta moved closer to him until their faces were inches apart. "I hold your heart and you hold mine. Even if it's not all of it, it's most of it. That has to be enough for you, for now. You have to trust me like I trust you. You have to let life play itself out sometimes Sean and enjoy it as it takes you on its journey, even when it might end in a way that is painful. You can't run away or put a wall up to protect yourself. Pushing me away right now is the logical thing to do to protect your heart and if you need to do it, I'll understand."

He leaned in and kissed her, lightly. "I have no idea what to do. I've never felt this strongly about anyone in my life."

"Then don't walk away from me when I need you most."

Sean rested his chin on her shoulder and pulled her in close. "I can't be objective with you in the mix, I can't."

Atlanta felt her heart go into her throat and her eyes well up with tears. "And if you stepped away from me now, because of Roman and because of this meeting with Valencia, do you think it'd clear your head? Would you care for me less?" She barely choked out the words, fearing the answer.

He buried his head in her collar bone and pulled her tighter. Whatever he said was muffled by her body and shirt. Atlanta was about to ask what he'd said, when she heard him in her head.

"No, it'd only hurt me more—I hurt everywhere—"

Atlanta felt him shudder. Gently wrapping her arms now around him tightly, she murmured, "Come on. Let's go upstairs," she whispered.

He shook his head and muttered something about Harmon.

"He's not going anywhere and you can't be of any help down here right now. Come on."

No one said anything to them as they went up to their room. She shut the door and handed him the blood she'd brought from downstairs. He drank it down without pause and placed the mug on the dresser. The color returned to his face but he still looked utterly distraught. It was time for her to make her choices.

She sat on the bed and pulled him to sit next to her. She took his hand and he gripped it like a lifeline. "I may love Roman, but I'm *in love* with you." She could tell these words hit home.

He looked at her. "You are more than I deserve and I keep waiting for you to realize this and leave me. It scares me so much."

"I feel the same exact way. Come here."

She lay back on the bed, pulling him to lay next to her. He curled up on his side, encircling her arm around her waist tightly. Resting his head next to hers he buried his face in her hair, planting a kiss on her head.

He hurt. She'd hurt him and for what? Because of chemical attraction to a man who was never as good to her as Sean was. She needed to get her priorities straight here and now.

She couldn't hear his tears, but she knew they fell. Seeing him in pain she'd caused hurt her. The ache in her chest was almost suffocating. This had never been the case with Roman. Atlanta had never felt so connected with him that his pain was hers. They weren't one, not like this. She needed Sean to understand how she felt. She could say she loved him, but she'd already done that.

"Let me show you how I feel about you, if you won't believe my words," she said, pulling his face toward hers, letting her lips brush his softly at first, and then deeper as she pulled him close, hoping she could wash away his fear and pain.

* * * *

Jensine sat on the floor of her cell, her back against the door and her head resting on the bars to her side. It wasn't that it was comfortable, it just was better than moving. That would take effort and she'd have to care. Neither of which could she muster. In fact, she'd been on the floor for a while, crying until she had nothing left. Now she just sat in silence staring into the darkness.

"It gets better," she heard Maria say in the distance.

"I don't see how," Jensine mumbled.

"If you're good you can get moved somewhere with more people, get special food, get provisions like candles and matches. See?"

She heard the sound of a match striking and suddenly saw a glow in the distance. Jensine focused on the light and it revealed a girl two cells away. She held a candle under her chin yet in front of her face enough so that the light made it possible for Jensine to make out her face.

Maria was a Hispanic girl with long dark hair she'd tucked behind her ears. Her large brown eyes were doe-like while her other features were delicate. Yet even with these feminine features Maria's face held a strength Jensine had yet to see in a prisoner or soldier.

"It's nice to see you," Jensine said.

"Here, I have more."

Jensine watched as the candle and a tiny matchbook started coming toward her. At first, she thought the girl had thrown them, but soon she realized they were coming slowly. As it reached her face she put her hand out and gently took matches and the tiny votive. Quickly, she lit it.

"And now I can see you," Maria said with a smile.

"How did you do that? Are you a witch?"

Maria lit another candle. "No." With the extra light Jensine could see the dark circles under her new friend's eyes. "I'm telekinetic."

Jensine about jumped for joy. "Then can't you bust us out of here?"

The girl shook her head. "They keep me drugged up. Just moving that to you took all I had."

"I don't understand. I thought telekinesis was something—I don't know—in science fiction?"

Maria smiled. "I am the only one of my kind that I know of. Valencia keeps me for—scientific reasons."

"What does that mean?"

A tired laugh escaped Maria's lips. "She experiments with us. You'll see. She makes you, uses you, and breaks you."

A noise erupted in the corridor and Maria quickly blew out her candle. "Someone is coming."

Sadly Jensine blew out her candle too. She crawled into her bed, hiding her new item in her pillow, wondering about something new this time. What was Valencia experimenting on and why? This was something she hoped to dig into further.

* * * *

Sean and Atlanta lay in bed, entwined around each other. She knew they needed to head downstairs to be helpful but she didn't want to move. His fingers lightly trailed from her shoulder, down her arm, and up again as her head rested on his chest.

"We should probably get downstairs. This was really selfish of me," he said, kissing the top of her head. "Not that it wasn't worth it, but they need us."

"I'm surprised they didn't stop us."

"I'm sure it was evident I wasn't in the best state of mind."

"I'm sorry for how I made it worse."

"You didn't. I got jealous and I was already feeling scared to death and overreacted. I know how he feels about you...see it on his face all the time. The two of you try to avoid each other. I see it killing him every time I kiss you, or you me. He hates me..."

"He doesn't hate you."

"I wouldn't be so sure of that." They were silent for a moment then he continued his thoughts. "If I was feeling out of control with concern over all this, how could I expect him not to? I'm sure every minute we're up here he's feeling worse than I did down there, and to be honest, I hate that. Roman's been dealt a hand of responsibility I don't have to answer to. He's got things he deals with I could never comprehend, just like he can have no idea what's it's like to go through what I've gone through. I think we understand each other that way."

Atlanta pulled her head up to look Sean in the face. "It's going to be okay. We have to try and think like her. You're the best at that, so I trust you'll find a way. Ok?"

He kissed her nose. "I will try with everything I have."

She kissed him softly. "Come on, let's get dressed and go help them figure out the best action."

"Right now? We have to go right now?" he said, kissing her neck and then her collarbone.

"We should go help them..." she said, not sounding very sure of herself.

He kissed her neck, "You sure?"

"Uh huh," she said faintly.

He ran his tongue up to her ear and whispered, "I think thirty more minutes wouldn't change anything, do you?"

"Huh?" God, she couldn't think straight when he did this!

His hand caressed the curve of her waist to hip. "They can wait a bit longer, I think—"

"Yeah, a bit longer won't hurt them," she moaned out as his tongue touched her skin.

* * * *

The noise had been prison guards and they took Maria away for her shower. Alone again, Jensine thought about how silence paired with darkness makes everything feel worse. She tried to concentrate on the things Maria had told her. What could Valencia be up to? What kind of experiments was she doing?

Jensine jumped at the sound of a door closing in the distance. She heard footsteps coming in her direction but then, they disappeared. She sat up and looked around, tempted to light her candle. Her heart began to pound in her ears. The idea of Eddie coming down here now that she was alone had popped into her head and she fumbled for her candle and matches. "Who's there?" she demanded.

Something brushed by her legs, and Jensine screamed. She jumped up onto the bed and stared down into the dark, candle and matches now in hand. Hand shaking, she finally struck the match and lit her candle. Slowly she crouched down to see what touched her leg. She half-expected a ten-pound rat but instead there sat a cute gray tabby cat with big blue eyes, staring up at her.

Meow.

"Oh jeez—damn it, you scared the hell outta me!"

She got down off the bed and sat on the floor. The cat came over and rubbed up against her leg. She reached out tentatively at first, letting the cat sniff her hand. "Well hi, what is your name?"

Silence.

"You can talk to me you know, I'm like you."

Still silence.

"Weird. Even if you were a regular ol' house cat I could hear your thoughts so is it that you don't want to talk to me? It's okay, I understand. You wanna join me up here?" she asked, patting the bunk. The cat jumped right up and lay down. "If you take up the whole bed where am I supposed to lay down?" she teased. The cat seemed to understand her and moved over. "You sure you're not a shape shifter?"

Jensine slid an arm under the pillow and lay on her side. The cat curled up in the area between her arm and her body. Petting the cat she could feel her heart rate calm as her body relaxed. It's funny, Jensine thought; cute little animals had amazing powers of comfort. For the moment Eddie wasn't a thought, nor was the darkness. She blew out her candle and finally let herself fall asleep. The first sound sleep she'd had since being captured.

She woke up however to the cat licking her nose. Opening her eyes she found herself staring at a pair of blue eyes staring at her and thought, "Hunter—?"

Waking up fully she realized it was only the cat, staring at her and that it was wriggling. Seems she'd rolled onto its tail.

"Oh man—sorry kitty, I didn't mean to trap the tail."

She shook her head a bit and blinked a few times. "Wow, that was weird. For a moment, I thought I was back in the barracks and my friend Hunter was waking me up. Sorry kitty."

The cat rolled its eyes.

"I saw that. You do understand me don't you kitty?"

The cat lay down with a huff.

"You don't like being called 'kitty' I take it. Well, I suppose I need to give you a name—once I realize if you're male or female. I supposed I could check."

The cat started to back up but wasn't fast enough. Jensine picked up the cat and turned it around and lifted its tail.

"Oh, you're a boy—no wonder the name kitty wasn't appealing," she giggled, sitting him down. He looked horribly debased and sat with his back to her, angrily switching his tail back and forth.

"Oh come now. I know you can understand me so feel violated all you want. It's your own fault."

The gray cat still didn't turn around.

"I could've named you Tulip and you'd have be stuck with it if I hadn't done that. But now, I can come up with a manly name. Hmmm—let's see. You remind me of my mom's cat, but he was twice your size. He was a great comfort to my mom when she was ill and to me after she passed away—and now, you're being a great comfort to me too, even if I never see you again after this night. I'll name you Gato. I know, it's not too original—it's just Spanish for 'cat.' Maria will like that."

The cat turned its head to Jensine and meowed again.

"Plus, you're named after a special cat who meant a lot to my family when they were alive, so can you forgive me now?"

The cat turned around finally. Jensine was about to ask him to come to her when she heard a voice she'd never forget until the day she died. It was him. Without making any pleasantries about it Jensine snatched Gato and pulled him to her. "You need to run and hide. If he sees you, he could hurt you too." She set him on the ground. "Run! Go!" she whispered frantically.

Gato sat his butt down, his stance very solid.

"Shit. Stupid cat," Jensine threw her blanket over him, blew out her candle, hid it, and curled up on the floor, under the blanket with Gato, hoping to protect him from being seen. Her body involuntarily began to shake. She wasn't sure she'd make it through another beating. With the drug in her system, she couldn't really defend herself. So instead, she lay there shaking and trying not to make a sound.

She heard a cell door open down from hers and tears slipped down her cheeks. Jensine was appalled at her own fear but still found herself burying her face into Gato's fur. If he came in, she'd do everything she could to make sure Gato got out of the cell in time. She'd be damned if she'd let Eddie hurt a defenseless house cat.

"Come on Ed, we got work to do."

"You go on—I think I have some rounds to do down here."

For the first time in her life, in all of the hell she'd been through since leaving Massachusetts, Jensine felt her fear hit a new high. Her eyes opened and she looked directly into Gato's blue eyes. They looked sad and scared.

"I won't let him hurt you, I promise," Jensine whispered.

The cat butted her nose with his head.

"We have too much paperwork to do for you to go screwing around down here tonight," Brian complained. "Come on."

"I can stay down here if I want," Eddie said in the darkness, his tone defensive.

A door slammed. "Over my dead body. I'm not doing your work too. Either come up or I'll get Barbara. One more violation and you're on leave, pal. I'm tired of coverin' for your ass, now let's go!"

It was silent. Jensine held her breath.

"Fine. Let's go then. Later ladies."

Jensine let out her air and the tears began to fall down her face. Gato tried to lick them away and that's when she heard Maria. She too was weeping in her cell. The door to the cellblock closed in the distance and the only sound was of two girls crying in the darkness.

Chapter Fourteen

Sean and Atlanta headed down the stairs, she in black drawstring pajama pants and Happy Bunny T-shirt and he in his pajama pants and a black T-shirt. They both felt somewhat sheepish for leaving them all and Atlanta was worried they'd have to deal with comments.

"Hey, there you are," Celeste said.

"Feeling better?" Stephan asked Sean.

"Yeah. Sorry I freaked out, guys. I can focus now."

"That's all that matters. We got this delivered about an hour ago," Roman handed a certified letter to Sean.

They sat on the chaise and Sean opened it, Atlanta read over his shoulder. It listed longitude and latitude coordinates at the top and then in hand writing it said, "Meet me at these coordinates. Wednesday at sunset."

"Well, at least she gets to the point," Atlanta replied.

"Have we responded to this request?" Sean asked.

"Yes, the messenger wouldn't leave without a response. We told her yes but that she had to speak to her with us present. Just like we discussed," Roman said.

"I still don't like this," Gray whined.

"You and me both," Sean agreed.

Desi touched Gray's arm. "All of us don't like this."

Atlanta glanced around the room. Celeste was sitting next to Harmon, which interested her, and Pepper was back.

Turning to Pepper, Atlanta commented, "Made your choice then, I take it?"

Pepper nodded once. She said no more than that.

Amanda stood up. "We have a decent enough plan. The werewolves will arrive here Tuesday morning and we'll get them to come with us for extra back up."

"Good thinking," Sean said. "She'll bring her girls and some of her soldiers with her. If she doesn't get exactly what she wants from talking to Atty it could get nasty."

Atlanta tucked her leg under her. "What do you think she wants?"

"Probably to ask you to join with her," Sean said as he lightly scratched her back. "She'll tell you The Great Order is a bunch of liars."

"Something tells me she has something up her sleeve," Roman said.

"That's a given," Sean responded.

Atlanta pointed at the coordinates. "Where is this?"

"We already checked that out," Stephan answered. "It seems to be a spot where those reenactment dudes do their stuff way outside of town."

"That makes sense. No one will be out there right now. Their season doesn't start until August," Celeste said.

"Exactly. She wants us to meet Wednesday night. We'd be smart to drive out there Tuesday night and get a lay of the land," Roman suggested.

"How far out of town is this?" Atlanta asked.

"About ten hours," Stephan told them.

"Wow. Okay. Let's talk about what our strategy is so when J.J. and his crew get here Tuesday morning we have our ducks in a row," she said.

Sitting around the parlor, they discussed the best course of action until Atlanta felt her eyes were burning. She rubbed them and noted that Desi, Bianca, and Pepper had fallen asleep by the fire and decided they probably had the right idea. She looked at her watch. Sunrise of Monday morning wasn't far away. "I suggest we all call it a night, folks," she told them. "We can't plan or fight without some rest. It's four in the morning."

"True," Gray said, yawning.

Atlanta directed the newcomers to guest rooms, and everyone headed up the stairs except Roman. Instead he put another log on the fire. She pulled Sean close and nodded toward Roman.

He nodded and whispered, "I'll see you in the room."

"I'll be right there."

He nodded and kissed her hand before heading upstairs.

She tentatively walked over to Roman. "You not tired?"

He lay down on her chaise, which was nearest to the fire. "I'm going to stay down here by the fire and think for a bit. I don't like the idea of no one down here keeping a watch, for one, and for another, I went out to find Pepper and we chatted. I didn't want her staying here for me when I don't feel for her as she wishes I would. I can't right now."

"I know. I'm sorry."

He shook his head. "Don't feel sorry. This isn't your fault. This is Phoenix, and Harmon, and Devon, and Elizabeth, and Kat too. I think I need a night to sit here alone."

She walked over to him and messed up his already messy hair in an affectionate way, then kissed him on the top of his head. He took her hand.

"Well, try to sleep some okay?" she said.

"I will. You too."

She paused. "It's going to be okay."

He looked up at her, his eyes the window to a damaged soul. "I hope so." He kissed her hand.

With Sean, she felt *his* pain, while with Roman she only understood it. He'd lost so much it had to be difficult for him to just sit here and breathe in and out. She knew there was nothing she could do for him so with a light squeeze of his shoulder she headed up to her room.

If she were honest, she'd have admitted she really didn't think it was all going to all be okay, but she hoped she'd been a good enough actress so he'd sleep a little. Deep in her gut, she had a horrible feeling the next two nights were the last in her own bed. Walking upstairs though, she tried not to think of that. Slipping into the darkness of her room Atlanta slid into bed and wrapped around Sean to quiet her head.

"You okay?"

She decided to lie to him, too. "Yeah, just exhausted, but I'm too wound up to sleep."

Rolling over to face her, Sean caressed her from shoulder to hip. "Would it help your mind to think about something else?" he said, untying the top of her pajama bottoms.

"You're a maniac today," she said with a short laugh.

"I happen to be in love with you and this may…"

Atlanta put her finger on his lips, knowing what he was about to say. "Yes, take my mind off all this—please."

She kissed him before he could talk anymore. She knew she should be sleeping, but she was sure they weren't the only ones taking advantage of this time alone with those they loved.

* * * *

Jensine wasn't sleeping well. She kept waking up through the night. Then, when she finally would fall into a deep enough sleep to forget where she was, her psyche didn't. She started having a nightmare and woke up screaming out.

"You okay?" she heard Maria say.

Jensine looked around for Gato but he was gone. "Yeah. It was only a bad dream."

"What about?"

Jensine didn't want to say it aloud. "Nothing."

"It's better if you empty your head of it," she said.

With a sigh, Jensine figured it couldn't hurt. She got up and came over to the bars so she could see Maria better. That's when she noticed a darkening on her face. It was a bruise around her cheekbone at the eye socket." "Are you okay?"

"I'll be fine. Now tell me the dream."

"Okay. I was in the institute and I was lost, trying to get out, and I just kept getting more and more lost. Finally I came across my friend Hunter and he said he'd show me the way out. But as we continued around in circles I realized he was bringing me back down here."

Jensine lifted her candle, lit it, and stared into its flame. "I stopped following and turned around to go the other way but when I do the hallway is gone. It's now a wall—the wall of this cell. He shuts me in it and says horrible things to me through the bars. He asked me how I could pretend to be his friend and then betray The Superior Order. He says I deserved what I got." She stopped, tears threatening to spill. "And then, he smiles at me as he re-opens my cage door and lets Eddie in. And he comes in and beats the hell out of me, again."

"Is this guy, Hunter, the reason you're in here?"

Jensine shook her head. "No. It's just, I remember seeing the look on his face when I sat in the interrogation room. He was so mad, they all were. They believed Valencia's lies without question. He was my friend. If anyone should've given me the benefit of the doubt, he's the one that I'd have thought…" her voice trailed off. "Maria, I didn't come here to spy on and kill them. I didn't kill that girl."

"Are you sure he believes Valencia?"

"I don't know. In the dream he did."

"One thing to remember Jensine, the truth always comes out. Your innocence will eventually become clear and you'll get free of here and he'll know. You have to believe that or you'll go insane in here."

"What do you hang on to that keeps you sane?" Jensine asked wiping tears away.

Maria laughed. "I used to try to focus on being outside—the freedom of no walls."

"You said used to. What do you focus on now?"

Maria lifted the candle so Jensine could see her face a bit better. A large smile encompassed her face. "I felt the goddess touch my heart the day you arrived. She told me everything would be all right. You see? That's how I know without a doubt you will get out of here. And when you do—you'll come back and get me when you can. That, my dear Jensine, is how I stay sane."

* * * *

At nine o'clock on Tuesday morning, Roman was banging on everyone's doors. "They're here. Everyone up!"

"Jeez, they couldn't have come at noon? It's been, what? Five hours of sleep?" Atlanta muttered.

Sean's arms snaked around her. His skin on hers was warm, having taken on her body heat. It's soft, silky feel on her skin as he rolled lazily on top of her felt wonderful. She opened her eyes and stared at him. "I love you."

"I love you too." He pushed her scary morning hair away and held her face between his palms. "Morning, beautiful."

"Oh, I'm pretty sure right now I'm not beautiful," she said, touching her hair.

He lifted his body up enough to look down on her. "I totally disagree."

She ruffled up his hair and felt blood rush to her face as he laid back down on her.

"Are you blushing?" he noticed with a chuckle, "Really? I've seen every inch of you and you still blush when I look at you and compliment you?"

She reached out for a pillow, hit him in the head, and covered her face with it. "What are you doing?"

"Hiding my blushing face," she said in a muffled voice.

He laughed and pulled the pillow away. She opened one eye to look at him. His face was covered in a big smile. Something she hadn't seen in a long time.

"What are you smiling at?"

"You. I think you're cute when you get all embarrassed."

"Even with this hair?"

"Even with that hair. Besides...I gave you that mess of hair if I remember correctly."

She laughed and so did he. They then heard a knock on the door and both yelled out at the same time, "What?"

"Everyone downstairs in thirty minutes for breakfast and debriefing with the CPA," said Gray's voice.

"Ok."

"A real thirty minutes, Atty, not your version."

"Yeah yeah yeah…I got ya…thirty minutes," she yelled out.

"If you two aren't down in thirty, I'm coming in there for a three way," Gray shouted through the door. "So unless Sean feels like experiencing the softer side of Sears I suggest you make it down in thirty!"

"He means that," she said.

"Then let's get a shower and head on down for your breakfast. I could use some coffee and blood. You drained me last night."

"Oh, I drained you? You lie!"

He laughed again and threw the covers off her.

Thirty-three minutes later, they were dressed and walking into the large kitchen hand in hand, hair still wet. By the look of the goings on in the kitchen, you'd have thought it was a normal morning. Well, normal for them. The song "Dreaming" by OMD was playing on the radio and the girls were lip-syncing using spoons as microphones. Before she knew it, Sean grabbed her hand and twirled her into the room and they joined them, then Stephen and Gray joined in on the final verse.

The song ended and the radio station went to commercial. The girls went back to making eggs and toast, while Gray taught Stephan how to make banana pancakes. The entire kitchen was full of cheer as Desi sang about cream cheese, holding the English muffin out for Bianca to toast—by blowing on it.

Atlanta looked at them oddly.

"What? It's faster this way," Bianca explained.

"Morning, Atty, coffee is ready if you want some," Desi added, "Mugs are on the table there."

"You sure you don't want something with a bit more nutritional value?" Atlanta asked Sean.

"Oh, I can double fist it. If you'll pour me some coffee I'll get my breakfast."

"Coffee, comin' right up," Atlanta said.

Sean kissed her head, said thanks, and went to go heat up some blood. She poured coffee for them both.

Gray pointed her to the long table in the dining room. "We'll bring your breakfast, go sit down."

J.J., 2Doggz, Big Daddy Jay, Erik, and Lance were already collected in the dining room, with a new guy she didn't recognize. She could tell he was tall even though he stayed seated. Kicked back, one hand held a cup of coffee while other moved animatedly while he spoke with 2Doggz. He had really long strawberry blond hair and a goatee of a darker reddish version.

He must've felt her gaze because he turned his light blue eyes on her. "Good morning, ma'am." he said in a southern accent.

"Morning."

"Atlanta, I'd like you to meet our new computer specialist," J.J. said. "His name is Joe Gunn."

"Nice to meet you, Joe," she said and took a sip of her coffee, forgetting she hadn't put any milk or sugar in it yet and about gagged.

Sean laughed. "Here sweetie," he said as he handed her the milk carton and the sugar bowl.

"You'll have to forgive me, I didn't get a lot of sleep last night."

J.J. and 2Doggz shared a glance and both said, "I bet."

"Oh shut it, you two." Atlanta felt her face blush again and was saved by the food cavalry. Bianca, Desi, Celeste, Gray, and Stephan walked in with pancakes, eggs, toast, butter, jam, and syrup in their hands.

"Tada! Breakfast is prepared!" Desi announced with much pride in her voice.

They all sat down and dug in. Well, all but Sean and Stephan. They sipped on their blood and coffee and looked very content.

"Vampires drink coffee?" Joe asked.

"I loved coffee when I was human," Sean said. "I wasn't able to give it up as a vampire. It's an extra caffeine boost to the system."

"Amen," Stephan said, lifting his mug in a faux toast to Sean.

"Where are Harmon, Roman, Pepper and Amanda?" Atlanta asked.

"They've already had their blood and figured shower rotation was easier if they go while everyone else eats. Once they get down we'll head into the parlor to talk about the plan for the day and for tomorrow," J.J. said.

Atlanta nodded because she had a mouth full of banana pancake, but once she swallowed it, she looked at J.J. and said, "Thank you for coming."

"You're more than welcome, my lady."

As she glanced about the table and the kitchen it was hard to believe these were the same people she'd lived with all day yesterday. Monday had been a hard day. They'd all been very quiet, somber and focused. Now they were different. Everyone seemed lighter at heart and not so lost in their heads. For the first time since the call from Harmon on Sunday, they all chatted idly as they ate breakfast.

Once everyone was done, they cleaned up, poured themselves more coffee, and headed into the parlor for the CPA briefing. Atlanta sat with Sean on the chaise as Roman stepped up and began to address the group. For once, there were so many of them they took up all the furniture.

"Okay, first things first. A huge thank you to Celeste for the atmosphere and another huge thank you to the CPA for coming to assist."

J.J. nodded a thank you to Roman and Celeste blushed. Atlanta looked at her and then at Sean.

"Ah, now it makes sense," he said.

"What does?"

"The fact that we all feel so cheery this morning and everyone is focused and not stressed. She did a spell. Must've put some herbs in the air ducts. Smart girl. We all can concentrate better without getting all stressed out."

Atlanta glared at Celeste.

"What's wrong?" Sean asked.

"I don't like people messing with my moods without my permission."

"Let it go, Atty. She did it to help us all, not to go against your will."

She took in a deep breath and sighed. She wanted to stay upset but it was impossible. "I guess I wish she'd have told us."

"I'm pretty sure she didn't want to disturb us."

Atlanta nodded and went back to concentrating on Roman's speech, which was a good thing because he turned to her.

"—and now I give the floor to Atlanta since this plan was hers."

"You are more than welcome to explain—" she started to say but he sat down and everyone stared at her. Standing, she cleared she throat. "Okay. We will leave tonight after sunset," she started with and then reviewed the plan."

Amanda raised her hand.

"Yes?" Atlanta asked her.

"I have no weapons."

"Glad you asked that. Everyone will need to be armed. J.J. will be in charge of weapons, please see him before we head out to get your weapons of choice from the bunker."

She paused to look at her notes. When she glanced back up it was Gray whose hand was in the air. "Yes Gray?"

"That's one more than we can fit."

"Excuse me?"

"At max, the van fits ten and J.J.'s SUV fits six, and there are seventeen of us. With all our bags, we're going to need another vehicle. We can use my Jeep."

"We have sixteen," she said, "so we should be fine. We all are to pack a single backpack and that's all." Gray started counting and she cringed because she'd not wanted this discussion to be in front of everyone.

"I count seventeen, Atty."

Atlanta swallowed hard and looked at Stephan, and he took Gray's hand. "That's 'cause you're counting yourself."

It took a minute for it to set in and then his face showed he understood. He wouldn't be going. "Oh hell no! There is no way I'm staying behind on this."

She went to open her mouth, but Stephan beat her to it. "You're the only human in the group, sweetie," he said tenderly, "and even though you're a great fighter, you don't have the speed or strength to fight warrior vampires and werewolves."

"Atlanta and the girls don't have that either, and they're going!" he pointed out, his face starting to get red.

"But they have the elements on their side to fight with."

"Besides," she said, trying to help, "we need someone here to watch the kids."

"I'm going," he said stubbornly, "either in the van with you or in my Jeep." Tears of fear touch his eyes.

"You'd be in grave danger, and we couldn't protect you," Roman said. "It's against the law to give vampire blood to a Non-Clandestine person."

Atlanta cringed again, this time at the irony. For once she was glad Roman was sticking to Great Order laws. The last thing she wanted was Gray in harm's way.

Gray stood up. "My best friend in this world, my only family, is putting her life on the line and I refuse to not be there by her side. I refuse. So if you're going to put a spell on me then you better do it now, 'cause I'm coming!"

She sighed. Stephan stood up, too. "I can give him some of my blood—"

"You can't do that, Stephan," Roman said. "It's not allowed for combat and you know that—and you know why."

"Why?" Gray asked, his face and voice full of determination.

Roman explained. "The rule was set in place so that vampires couldn't make tons of familiars to do their bidding and die in wars. It's against the moral code we have, to protect the human race."

Atlanta thought that made sense, but Gray still looked upset.

"I wasn't going to give him my blood for the battle, sir," Stephan said quietly.

Everyone in the room became silent.

Atlanta stepped forward. "What do you mean Stephan?"

"Yes, what do you mean?" Gray asked.

Roman stood up, "There are three ways a vampire is allowed to give their blood to a human of Non-Clandestine decent. One is when they decide to turn them into a vampire, the second is to make them a familiar to protect them and do their bidding during the day hours, and the third is a bonding ceremony."

"Bonding ceremony?" Atlanta asked.

"It would be the equivalent to two witches being hand fasted or two humans getting married. A vampire is allowed to marry a human as long as they know who they are and the Head of the Vampire Clan gives consent."

"Oh," she said softly, then she heard Sean give a low whistle and a few other people whisper stuff.

Gray turned to Stephan. "So, can I assume, you don't want to change me or make me your bitch monkey, but you want to—marry me?"

Stephan looked at Gray and smiled. "I do." The whole room let out gasps and coughs and even a few whoops and hollers. "Will you marry me?"

Chapter Fifteen

Atlanta couldn't help herself, she was smiling from ear to ear. It was the proposal Gray had always wanted, where he was proposed to in front of everyone. Well, he probably hadn't dreamed of the blood part.

"Don't say yes just for this mission, Gray," Roman said. "The blood bond is permanent. It has magickal qualities to it and as long as you're alive you will belong to Stephan, body and soul, and he to you."

Gray looked at Stephan and smiled. "You would want to marry a man who's going to grow old and die on you, huh?"

"Call me crazy."

"Crazy man—" Gray said as he caressed Stephan's flawless face and then touched the corn silk blond hair that lay on his shoulders. "No more whoring days for me, then, I take it."

"That would be the case," Stephan said, his voice slightly tense. Gray still hadn't given an answer.

Gray kissed him with what one might call church tongue— just enough to make it more than a peck on the lips but not so much tongue action that those watching feel awkward. When he pulled away he said his answer very quietly, as if it were for Stephan alone, but they all could hear him. "Yes, I'll marry you."

The room cheered loudly, except for Roman who smiled nervously.

"You will give your consent to this, won't you?" Atlanta asked.

Roman spoke to her mentally. *"Will you feel better with him there at the battle or will he be a distraction?"*

"He'll be an asset, but I'll want special care taken for him, a guard. Please let them get bonded, Roman—for me—"

His look went soft and he nodded.

"Stephan, son of Ethan, and grandson of Parson Throneburg, do you ask permission to become blood bonded to this human, Grayson Alex Stoltz?"

"I do."

"Then, by the power vested in me as Head of the Vampire Clans of the North Eastern Thirteen Colonies, I grant you permission to become Blood Bonded."

The room became all in atwitter, and the primary reason of the meeting seemed to get lost for a few minutes. Eventually Atlanta had to bring everyone back to the issue at hand.

"Okay folks, let's sit down so I can finish my part of this meeting." People sat down and slowly, but surely became refocused on her. "So, if Gray is coming we'll need his Jeep, we'll use it for our luggage, making the van less jammed. Who do we leave with the children?"

"Kat's parents arrive today," Stephan said. "They were planning to just pick up Kat's ashes to take her home, but I'm pretty sure if I tell them what is going on they would stay for forty-eight hours. We can ask them when they arrive."

"I'm okay with that, are you, Sean? They're your kids."

"I'm good with that."

"Okay then. That's all settled. I now turn the meeting over to J.J."

She went and sat down with Sean, draping her legs over his lap resting her back against the head of the chaise. Sean tucked her red down blanket over them and took her hand under the blanket.

"Mr. Cameron, if you're getting ideas from the Gay Team of America over there, remember that I was raised a human girl."

"What does that mean?" he said with a slight chuckle even in his mental voice.

"That means I require a proper proposal with a ring and the whole nine yards." she playfully put her nose in the air.

"I would expect and do nothing less than exactly that."

Atlanta grinned and he squeezed her hand again as he laced his fingers in hers and they both went back to focusing on J.J. He talked about the weapons they had in stock. Then Roman stood up and reminded everyone of the laws about not being detected by humans, and how they should finish up whatever they'd not taken care of yesterday. It was a grim note to end on but he was right.

When the meeting broke, folks tottered off to their rooms to pack, nap, and put affairs in order. Atlanta went upstairs and grabbed their backpacks from under the bed, then turned to the large duffel bag that they'd taken with them to New York and put that on the bed too. It still wasn't unpacked. She put all the dirty clothes in the hamper and helped Sean as they packed up the few things they'd need. Neither of them spoke as they packed, other than to discuss what they wanted to take. It didn't take long to pack. Sean said he needed to run down and talk to the kids at the house about Kat's family coming and she needed to write some letters.

With a kiss he left and she sat down at her antique desk, pulling out some stationary. She sat there for a moment, and even the herbs in the air ducts couldn't help her thoughts from being what they were.

Atlanta had an overwhelming feeling that she may not be returning. Valencia said she meant her no harm, but since when had she heard anything about this woman that made her sound stable? If she was coming back, it might not be for a long time. Taking a deep breath, she concentrating on the magick in the air to make her words positive, and wrote letters to her grandparents and to her adoptive family. Both would be sent if she did not return. She even wrote a letter to Jensine in case some day it was found out that she was alive.

With her last three pieces of paper, she decided to write letters to Gray, Sean, and Roman. She cried through most of the writing process on those and it was evident from the splatters on the ink, but she really didn't care if they knew she'd cried.

Lastly she pulled out her graded thesis paper from her professor. He'd given her an A. Atlanta looked at the address on the envelope, flipped her computer on, and typed up a letter to her mentor. The letter made specific request that if she wasn't around to accept her degree that it should be mailed to her adoptive parents.

Once done she padded downstairs to put all her letters in the letter bag and then went up to the second floor to find Gray. He was in his room, lying sprawled out on his bed staring at the ceiling, listening to "Love Song" by The Cure.

"Hey you," she said from the doorway.

He motioned her over to him. She playfully crawled onto the bed with him and plopped down, curling up next to him, head on chest. He wrapped his arms around her and sighed.

"Rarely do you just lay and look at the ceiling, so—"

"I'm getting married," he said in a matter of fact voice.

She sat up enough so as to see his face. "And how does Mr. Whore-a-lot feel about that?"

His eyes alone moved to look at her. "I think I'm in shock."

"I would think so...hell, I'm in shock and I'm not the one who's doing a bonding ceremony tonight. Are we doing it before we leave?"

"Yeah. If the whole thing goes badly tomorrow night, I don't want that to be where I have to go to celebrate the day I got hitched."

"Good point."

He hummed an agreement.

She lay back down on her side, facing him. "I'm really happy for you, if this is what you want, Gray."

He too rolled onto his side so they could see each other. "What do you mean by that, baby?"

"I mean, as much as I want you there tomorrow night, I don't want you in harm's way. If you're coming because you feel you have to in order to protect me or whatever...I'd rather have you here, away from Valencia and her army. Once she sees you, you'll be on her radar and that bothers me."

"I'm going. I can't sit here while everyone else puts their life on the line for you when you're my family. I can't do that, Atty. I have to be there. Can you understand that?"

"Can you understand that if anything happens to you I'd be responsible?"

"You know that's not true."

"It'll be how I feel, Gray."

"I know. But I have to be there—the two people I love the most are going to be there so no matter what happens I have to be there as well."

She let out a sigh and nodded.

He kissed her forehead. "Will you give blood to Sean so he can fly again?"

She laughed. "I gave blood for that and other purposes yesterday. So yeah he has it on him."

"How much blood will I have to drink?" he asked, making a face.

"I only did it once, and I have no idea how much I had. It's a crazy intimate connection, though. Be forewarned."

"This is going to be intense then."

"Yes. It'll be very eye-opening for you about your mate...or shall I say...husband?" She giggled at the sound of the word.

He slapped her arm. "Stop that. I can't take it seriously if you don't."

She ruffled up his perfect hair. "It's just…my little man-whore is all growed up and gettin' himself hitched. I be so proud!"

"I'll tickle you till you pee!" he warned, making good of his promise.

"Stop!" She yelled, squirming and giggling.

"Not till you can say the word married without laughing!" he threatened.

"I'll pee on your bed!"

"For goodness sake please don't let her do that!" came Stephan's proper voice.

"Save me, Stephan!" she grabbed a pillow and hit Gray with it, but the tickling didn't stop and she seriously wondered if she might actually pee on his bed.

"What is going on in here?" they heard Sean say.

"Save me, baby!"

Sean quickly grabbed another pillow and start hitting Gray too, which meant Stephan grabbed a pillow. Feathers were flying as they were bounced around, laughing and hitting each other, until they heard a person in the doorway clear their throat loudly. Roman stood there with his arms crossed over his chest. He looked quite fit to be tied. Gray was the first to fall over laughing as he tossed the pillow at Roman.

"Why sir," Stephan said, "You look absolutely gobsmacked. I suppose there's a first for everything!"

"It's time for Gray to go and get Kat's family," he said curtly.

She stepped off the bed still laughing and walked over to Roman, "Oh come on, Roman, you're not mad we're having some fun, are you, really?"

He looked down at her, his face intense and his square jaw set. He pursed his lips. "No…I guess I thought you all would be taking this situation seriously."

She reached for him, touching his arm. "We do, Roman."

"Funny way of showing it. Some of us could be gone in the next forty-eight hours and you want to spend your last day having a pillow fight?"

Gray muttered, "Buzz Kill Bobby to the rescue."

Atlanta bit the inside of her cheek to keep from laughing.

"Actually Roman," Sean said, "Yes, that's exactly what we want. You're right, in forty-eight hours our entire dynamic of this group could be totally altered. No need for it to be that way already."

One lone feather floated down in front of Atlanta's face and she blew at it, making it float up and land on Roman's head. She saw it then, him trying not to laugh, and then as he looked up at the feather he crossed his eyes and smirked. She burst out laughing then, as did everyone else. Even Roman joined in on the laughter a little—which, considering his usual demeanor, was the equivalent of Atlanta rolling around on the floor in stitches.

Finally he said, "You do need to leave for the airport in five minutes, Gray."

"I know, I know."

Stephan tackled him to the bed and kissed him. Sean jumped off the bed in mock horror.

"You start that and he'll never get out of here," Atlanta teased.

"Right, right," Stephan said, helping Gray off their bed.

"Airport Shuttle Bitch is on duty, sir." Gray gave a smile and a salute, "I'll return in an hour or so. Anyone care to come with me for company?"

"I probably could go—" Sean said, giving her a questioning look.

"Only if Atty doesn't mind," Gray questioned faster than she could even nod or shake her head at Sean.

"I think that's probably wise," she said.

"She's right," Stephan said, "It's probably better if Gray isn't stuck answering all types of questions for the drive back. Sean can run interference and get them up to date on the situation."

"I agree. Plus, the girls and I have a Circle meeting in a few minutes anyway, to call on the goddess for guidance. You go help Gray." Atlanta affirmed. She wanted time with the girls to really get a solid focus on the situation, maybe consult their Book of Shadows for more things. They'd found a lot yesterday but fresh eyes today couldn't hurt. Plus they had to get the Bonding Ritual researched. She went over and gave Sean a kiss. "Just don't let Gray waste time, he has a bonding ceremony to come back here and get ready for," she added with a grin.

"Ah yes," Sean concurred, giving Gray a hardy slap on the shoulder.

"And on that note—"Gray said with a grin. He kissed Stephan and then snagged his keys off the dresser. "You comin', Sean?"

"Right behind you."

Stephan and Atlanta burst out laughing. "Now that just didn't sound right!" she said, trying not to snort while laughing.

"Thanks honey," Sean said as he shook his head at her. He came up and gave Atlanta a kiss and then headed off after Gray.

As she went to leave the room she reached up and took the feather out of Roman's hair.

"Thanks."

"I thought it was good there," Stephan added with a wink.

Atlanta put the feather in her pocket and went to her room to change into her ceremonial white dress and headed to the Wicca Room. Desi had beaten her there and had already begun the hunt for the bonding spell. As it was only the two of them in there, she took this chance to ask a question.

"Desi? Is there any romantic history between Celeste and Harmon?"

Desi looked over her shoulder and said, "Noticed that, did you?"

"I thought he'd been married to Elizabeth."

"He was. It's an unrequited love. She fell for him when she was fourteen—her first crush. Of course, she was too young for him to even think of dating, besides, his heart belonged to Lizzie." Desi put the book in her hand back and selected another, beginning to leaf through it. "When Lizzie died Harmon turned to Celeste for comfort for a while because they were good friends. I suspected Celeste was hoping that since she was seventeen and about to graduate from high school that he'd see her as a woman. I think secretly she saw herself taking Liz's place, but no one could ever do that."

Again she shut the book and put it back. This time she looked at Atlanta instead of grabbing another book. "They grew up together and Harmon's love for Lizzie was—I mean is, as deep as the ocean. Celeste's dream was something that could never happen—and deep down she knows it. It hurts, ya know…" Desi sighed and turned to grab another book. "…to not be better than a dead girl."

Atlanta went to the bookshelf and leaned against it. "He seems fond of her, though."

Desi too leaned her side against the bookcase, her look thoughtful and beyond her years. "He is. Probably cares for her a little bit more than friendship. However, his heart died with Lizzie. I think maybe Celeste still hopes. I'm not sure as she doesn't talk about it anymore." She stood back up and opened a book yet not reading. Instead she asked, "How'd you know?"

"He called her by a nickname I hadn't heard before, and she's been sitting by him a lot."

She nodded; her face slightly sad. "I wish she'd move on. He's not good for her."

"Tell me about it. I don't trust him."

"I don't trust him either, but don't tell Celeste that."

"I can tell he's hiding something from us. Sean said his mind is totally guarded. Is there a way we could get Celeste to see if she can get the information for us?"

"No way on this planet," came a voice at the door and Atlanta jumped. It was only Bianca. "Sorry, I heard what you all were saying as I walked up."

"It's okay, you just scared the crap outta me," Atlanta said with a smile. "Thought you were Celeste."

"Girl, please. All this black beauty could never be contained as a pale, tree huggin', doe eyed...she needs to leave that man alone. Bad news. Mmm."

Atlanta grinned, "Tell us how you really feel, Bee."

"What Bee is sayin' is Celeste would never pry for us with Harmon," Desi added. "We tried that road before. It's a shut case, Atty. Sorry."

Atlanta nodded and went over to the stereo system. "Well, I thought I'd at least toss the idea out there." She put an ambiance CD of the beach and nature on, turning the volume low.

Desi called out, "I found it!"

Atlanta and Bianca went to look over Desi's shoulder. It was a spell they could use for the bonding ceremony.

"Mark that and we'll take that book downstairs to make sure it's what Roman needs," Atlanta instructed.

Desi marked it and set it on the table in the corner. Then she and Bianca set up the athame, wand, water, candles, and incense on the altar while Atlanta grabbed their Book of Shadows. They were about to call for Celeste again when she walked in.

"Hey, sorry I'm late."

"Not a problem. Let's call the corners," Atlanta said. "Do your thing."

Celeste nodded. She got some dirt from the bag that was filled with soil from the back yard and put it in a bowl. She whispered some words over it and put it on the altar in the middle of the room, then grasped the chalk and drew a circle around the altar large enough for them to all to be inside of it.

Each of them, seizing a handful of salt, stepped into the circle. Celeste, last in, sealed the chalk circle with them inside. Each of them took a quarter of the circle line and put their salt on it. Then, they sat at their corners, Indian style, and closed their eyes and called upon the corners to recognize them.

The four concentrated on breathing in and out at the same time together, meditating and speaking to Diana on their own first. Atlanta asked for protection for her body and soul as well as Gray and Sean. She also asked Diana to let Jensine know she loved and missed her. Then, as if they all could feel they were all done meditating, Celeste stood up and they began the ritual.

******

Atlanta thought it was very likely the last time she'd get dressed up for awhile so she put on her favorite black satin Japanese dress. It came to her knees and had long, tapered sleeves. The black satin material contained beautiful embroidery of flowers in green and purple. "Very classy" is how Sean described it, and it was. She put on the full gear of nylons, heels, and her ceremonial jewelry. Sean himself was wearing the nice outfit she'd bought him—black dress pants and shoes and a dark purple dress shirt that made his golden eyes pop.

They headed downstairs so Atlanta and the girls could set up the parlor for a ceremony. There were sets of candles around the room to represent fire, and with a snap from Bianca they were lit. Atlanta set up a stick of incense for the element of Air and lit it. Desi put a small bowl of water on the mantel and Celeste put a small bowl of dirt.

"Now all the elements are represented," Desi sang out.

Once they were set up Sean leaned into Atlanta's ear. "Follow me."

The girls all turned curious face's to she and Sean.

"I guess I'll be right back."

He took her hand and led her out to where the sun was starting to set. The two of them walked out the back door and down the stone path he'd created that led down to the water. She didn't ask what he was up to but was glad she'd grabbed her purse. She'd wanted alone time with him too.

Finally they reached the deck he and the CPA built down by the water. It was a beautiful summer evening and he sat them down on the swinging bench, putting his arm around her.

"What are you up to, Mr. Cameron?"

"Nothing. I just wanted some alone time with you. Is that okay?"

"You just had a lot of me upstairs," she kidded as she kissed him, feeling her body tingle all over again remembering how tender and how attentive he'd been.

"I know, and that was wonderful as always, but I love it down here so it's where I wanted to give you this." He pulled a silver object out of his pocket and placed it in the palm of her hand. A silver ring lay there, gleaming in the sun and intricate in design. Obviously Celtic, the knots entwined in a graceful manner all around the wide band. It was both elegant, yet strong in its beauty.

"I'd planned on giving this to you on your twenty-fifth birthday. As it's not far, I thought maybe tonight would be better. This was my mother's. I want you to have it. It's delicate and strong like you are, like she was." He took her left hand and slid it onto her ring finger. "My father gave it to her as a promise ring before he went off to war. He came back safe and sound. I want you to have it. It's a promise ring from me to you."

She didn't know what to say. She was very choked up and she felt her eyes begin to water.

"No crying allowed—your make-up will run," he said.

"You sound like Gray." She blinked back the tears with a small bubble of laughter and then looked at the ring. It fit perfectly.

"Don't be too surprised, I cheated. I took one of your other rings with me and had this sized a few weeks ago."

She touched his handsome face with her hand, leaned in, and kissed him. "You like it?"

"I love it. Thank you so much. But you're not the only one with secrets."

"Oh?" He seemed pleased and curious, a wicked grin on his face.

She opened her purse, pulled out a long jewelry box, and handed it to him. "We're already past my birthday and I'm wearing your gift," he motioned to his suit.

"Oh shut up and open it," she said, smiling at him.

He slowly pulled the lid off. When he saw the necklace his face brightened, which made her smile and let go of the breath she'd been holding.

"Atty, this is beautiful."

It had been quite a find, actually. She'd just been browsing, killing time one day when she'd seen it. It was a short necklace made of black leather and silver. The leather wasn't only one piece but many pieces braided together tightly. In the center was a silver charm, the sign of the triple moon goddess, exactly like the one on the back of her neck. "You like it?"

"Do I like it? Are you crazy? Of course I like it!"

"Want me to put it on for you? It's been water protection treated so once I tie this on you could leave it on safely forever. I didn't want to get you one that had a delicate clasp—not with all the fighting you do."

He turned around and she wrapped it around his neck, tying its four strands of leather in a knot the jeweler had taught her. Once it was on, he turned around. It fell at the perfect length, the emblem falling below the hollow spot in the front of his neck. With his purple dress shirt undone by one button, you could see it perfectly.

She reached out and touched it. "I consecrate and bless this necklace in the divine name of the goddess. May the wearer's heart be blessed with love, may his mind be blessed with wisdom, may his soul be blessed with magick, may his life be joyous, long, and blessed with peace, freedom, and all that is good. Blessed be he, the love of the child of the goddess." She opened her eyes in time to see a white light shine from under her hand. Sean took a deep breath as it flowed into his body and his eyes finally caught hers.

"I felt your heart."

"Then you know that I am in love with you, and no one else."

He nodded and his eyes glistened.

She leaned over and kissed him and put her head on his shoulder. Again he draped his arm around her as they both looked over the water. They might have stayed there for a long time but she heard a mental message come in.

"Where are you?" came Stephan's voice. *"We are about to start! Gray is requesting Atty in our room."*

"Coming!" she said back, not shielding Sean.

"Guess we better go," Sean said aloud.

He took her hand and helped her up the walk because of her stupid heels, and after she'd slipped twice he picked her up and carried her at vampire speed up the rest of the way. As they reached the door he set her down and they calmly walked in. Sean went into the parlor and she headed up to Gray's room and knocked on the door.

"Come in."

Gray stood there, dressed in a light green ceremonial satin robe, staring at himself in the mirror.

"Don't you look pretty," she blurted out.

"You think?"

She smiled and nodded. "It's a nice robe. Did Stephan get it for you? It matches your eyes."

"Yeah, he said he got it weeks ago, he'd just hadn't gotten around to asking me to marry him yet. He'd not planned on doing in front of everyone."

"Not that you mind that he did."

"Oh hell no, you know me, make it a show!"

She laughed and hugged him. "Stephan said you asked for me...you're not having second thoughts are you?"

Gray took a deep breath and let it out slowly. Then he said, "Nope. I only wanted you to be the one to walk me down."

Chapter Sixteen

Atlanta and Gray headed down to the parlor hand in hand. The song "Somebody" by Depeche Mode played softly as they entered the room. With the heavy drapes pulled the only light in the room were the candles. She noticed bowls of fresh rose petals on all the surfaces as she walked Gray over to Stephan.

He stood erect, dressed in a similar robe in an amazing shade of dark blue. His golden straight hair hung loosely for once, softening his sharp features. Atlanta let go of Gray's hand as Stephan gently took Gray's other one.

Walking over to where Sean stood in the semi-circle of their friends she couldn't help but smile as Roman cleared his throat and began. "We're here to bear witness to the loving commitment made between Stephan and Gray. As many of you know, when a vampire gets bonded they do what they feel is the most intimate thing they can share, and that's the sharing of blood. In this act, each of the other knows their mate from the inside. The private thoughts of one become the private thoughts of the other. This type of bonding is a way to show your unconditional surrender to the other person. There is a token given to signify commitment to another. Do you each have an item?"

"Yes," they both replied.

Atlanta wondered when Gray would have been able to go get him something since it was that morning he was proposed to. Then she remembered—he probably would use the silver inscribed Beloved Ring he'd found in a magazine of hers that he'd bought for Stephan's birthday that was coming up in August.

Stephan pulled out a ring, also. It was a Celtic puzzle ring. Gray loved puzzle rings so this didn't surprise her. He wore a pinky ring that was a simple puzzle ring she'd given to him for a birthday once.

"Hand me your tokens," Roman asked as he held out a small velvet black bag.

They each dropped the ring into the bag and Roman pulled the draw string on it closed and handed it to Celeste.

"Ladies."

That was their cue. Atlanta let go of Sean's hand and the four of them stood in front of Stephan and Gray. Celeste held the bowl of dirt, Atlanta held the incense, Desi held the bowl of water and Bianca held a candle.

Desi and Celeste spoke first, "By the power of Water and Earth, West and North, these items shall be consecrated." As they spoke they put a droplet of water and a dash of dirt and salt into the pouch that held the rings and then handed it over.

Atlanta and Bianca spoke next, "By the power of Air and Fire, East and South, these items shall be charged." Atlanta put a pinch of incense ash in and Bianca put a piece of warm wax.

They all said, "So mote it be."

Atlanta took the pouch and lightly blew air into it and then closed the bag with the drawstring again. As they recited the next part they passed it from her down the line, each witch holding it for a moment of the ritual, shaking the bag slightly.

"Hail Mother Goddess and Father God, join us this eve, to take witness to your son's dedication of love for each other!"

At the end of the line Celeste opened the pouch and the rings were poured out onto a black satin cloth the couple held in their hands. The two rings dropped out onto the cloth and they were not dirty as one might think, but shiny and luminescent in their own way. As Gray put the ring on Stephan and vice versa they all continued the chant and they repeated after us.

"On this night of new beginnings," the girls prompted.

"On this night of new beginnings," Gray and Stephan replied.

"I, Gray and Stephan, dedicate my mind, body and soul to you, my partner, for the rest of this life, and for all eternity," the girls prompted.

"I, Gray, dedicate my mind, body and soul to you, Stephan, for the rest of this life, and for all eternity."

"I, Stephan, dedicate my mind, body and soul to you, Gray, for the rest of this life, and for all eternity."

Each witch then kissed the cheeks of both Gray and Stephan and went back over to where they'd been standing before, being sure to place their items on the mantle of the fireplace. Atlanta took Sean's hand again as Roman stepped forth.

"Now, with the sealing of blood will this promise be fulfilled."

One might think watching the blood exchange would be horrific, but it wasn't. Stephan stepped forward and with a wooden ceremonial knife he drew a line across his collar bone. The blood there swelled out of the wound and Gray hesitated for a moment but then leaned in and took some of the blood. Stephan's face was tense at first, and then, pure ecstasy. Once Gray had enough for the rite Stephan pulled him away. Atlanta could see the surprise in Gray's eyes that had probably been in hers after she'd drunk from Sean.

Then, as if on cue, Gray leaned his head to the right and closed his eyes in trust. Stephan stepped in and lightly bit into Gray's neck. Atlanta saw Gray's eyes flash open briefly from the pain of puncture, but then he was one with Stephan again and they shut. He didn't linger there long and soon he stepped away. Gray stood up straight, his eyes glistening with tears. Atlanta couldn't see Stephan's face but she assumed they were the same.

"As those who stand by, do you bear witness with me to this promise of love?"

"We bear witness," they all said in unison.

"Then, by the power invested in me, as Head of the Vampire Clan of the Northern Thirteen Colonies, I pronounce you blood bonded, husband to husband. You may kiss your spouse."

Stephan and Gray kissed each other quite passionately for having people watching, but they kept it short. Once they had separated the room erupted in a shout of joy and they all grabbed handfuls of rose petals from the bowls and tossed them into the air.

* * * *

Jensine had lost track of when it was day and when it was night. She slept whenever she felt tired and chatted with Maria whenever they both were awake. They had taken Maria away for what they called 'testing' and Jensine had fallen asleep again. When she woke up Gato was sleeping at her side, but she was worried about Maria.

"Maria? Are you back?" Jensine yelled out.

"Sort of," she said.

"What's that supposed to mean?"

"I'm here physically."

Jensine heard her grunt. "Are you okay?"

"Yeah. Just tired. They took a lot this time."

"A lot of what?"

"Spinal fluid."

Jensine shuddered. "Why?"

"Oh yeah, like they'd tell me. What was weird was they had me take this test and then I was put under."

"Like anesthesia?"

"Yeah. I have this tiny incision on my side. I have no idea what it's from but I feel really tired."

Jensine didn't have a good feeling about this. There were rumors that Valencia took women's ovarian eggs from them. Lifting up her shirt she saw a scar on her side. She guessed Maria's was in the same spot. Things were getting weird.

Reaching over she absent mindedly pet Gato as she wondered what Valencia would do with their eggs. Gato purred and rolled over a bit so his tummy and under his chin were exposed.

"Okay, okay, I can take a hint."

As she loved on Gato, she thought about what Hunter and Josh were doing. She hoped Hunter meant it when he said he'd come for her. She wondered if Atlanta knew she was alive yet, how Gray was, what new man he was chasing or if he was still with Stephan.

"Am I down here until I die?" she finally whispered aloud.

To this Gato sat up fast, bumped her head with his, and then shook his head as if his ear itched.

Just then there was a noise in the hall and they both turned toward it.

"Yo! J.R.! You down here? Valencia's gonna have my ass if you split early!"

Gato rubbed up against Jensine's body and then jumped off the bed and ran through the bars and was gone.

* * * *

The group had been walking for what felt like forever and a day. Atlanta's feet hurt and she actually considered trying to float. Thankfully she saw Harmon glance at his electronic device, of which she'd forgot the name of, and he said the words she was waiting for, "We're here. It'll be over this hill."

"Thank goddess!" she exclaimed. The other witches agreed with her and they all found the energy to push up that last hill.

As they reached the top, everyone holler in joy. It was a clear night and the moon and stars gave them enough light, along with their flashlights, of the area. Everyone else started to move into the large clearing, commenting on how they never thought they'd get here.

Yet all Atlanta could do was stand there, on the top of that ledge. Her feet wouldn't move and all she heard was the buzzing in her ears as she stared at the field. It was surrounded on all sides by hills. There were very few trees, only ankle high grass and rocks and a touch of underbrush where the earth met the base of the mini-mountains.

"Atlanta, you coming?" Sean asked, looking back at her as she stood motionless. "We need to check out the area."

"I don't need to," she said so quietly only vampire ears could've heard her.

"What? Why?"

She finally realized what the buzzing in her ears was. It was fear. It was adrenaline pumping through her veins at an alarming rate. She didn't need to explore this field for she knew every inch of it. She'd dreamed about this field since the night she'd met Devon. She died on this field.

"Atlanta?" she heard Roman whisper behind her. He'd been bringing up the rear of the group making sure they weren't being followed.

"Hmm?"

"You stopped," he said quietly.

"This is a trap," she whispered. "We need to go back. Now."

Sean walked up the incline to her. "Are you sure? What are you sensing?"

"Why have we stopped?" she heard Harmon say.

"She says it's a trap," Roman said. "Maybe we should go back. Everyone turn around and—"

"No!" Harmon said, "I'm not going back without my brother!"

"Like you care about your brother," Sean muttered under his breath.

Harmon went to hit him, but Atlanta blocked him with air. "Now is not the time."

Harmon cussed and turned to her. "We must follow through with the plan. If Valencia said Phoenix will be here then he'll be here and I think that's more important than some premonition you're having."

"It's not some feeling or premonition, Harmon," she said, and then she turned to Sean, "This is the place I keep dreaming about. Don't you recognize it?"

Sean's face fell and as he let himself really look at the field. As he recognized it, she saw it physically register in his whole body. The pain on his face was almost more than she could bear to look at.

"No. No, no, no—it can't be—"

She nodded and reached out for him. "It's the one Sean."

"Then we need to get you out of here."

"She's not going anywhere," Harmon said, now marching up the incline to them. "The deal Valencia made was that she comes with us. If she leaves, Phoenix is as good as dead."

"And that'd make you sad why?" Sean said to Harmon's face.

"I will kill you—you little maggot!"

"Bring it on, bitch! I'd like to see you try!"

"Sean! Harmon! Knock that shit off!" Atlanta yelled. "If you two want to battle this out when you get home great, feel free. But we have a job to do right now so I suggest you both calm down!"

Sean shoved his hands in his pockets and stepped away from Harmon to show he wasn't going to start anything and Atlanta let out a long sigh of relief.

"Atlanta," Roman started to say and she gently motioned him to be quiet.

"Will everyone be quiet for a moment?"

For that moment, she listened and concentrated on the task at hand. As she focused, the buzzing in her head disappeared and she could hear and smell the wind as it blew through the grass of the field. She watched the taller areas of grass ripple in the wind like the waves on the ocean and she knew what had to be done.

Atlanta knew Roman and Sean wouldn't understand. But this was her life, or what was left of it, and she needed to do what she felt was right. She looked at her watch. It was five-thirty. She touched the pendant around her neck and silently asked Diana's blessing on her soul.

"Okay everyone, listen up," she said, briefly glancing at the horizon one last time. "Sunrise isn't far off. We got about an hour, tops. We need to set up camp and get some rest. Roman, Stephan, Amanda, Pepper and Harmon? It should be pretty sunless in those caves so that'll be probably the best spot for you all to rest up—it saves us from putting up the UV tent. Sean?"

"I love my sky, honey—I'll stay out here with you," he said.

"Okay, but if you do I'm puttin' you to work. We could use your strength and speed out here."

"Of course."

"Everyone else? Set up the tents out here after we prepare the area for battle." She saw Harmon roll his eyes as he grunted in disgust. She flipped him off and continued, "In case this goes sour, we need to be prepared. The CPA are in charge of getting the area prepared. Men? Will that suffice for you all?"

"We're all over that!" J.J. said with a wink.

"Okay. We have about an hour until that sun comes up, so vampires make yourself useful until you cannot. The rest of you? Only work until eight and then get some rest. I want you all to have enough sleep for this. We'll all need to be up around two o'clock in the afternoon so we can eat and prepare. Let's take positions over by the northern caves.

"Celeste, Desi, and Bianca—we're going to need some of that tea. Could you get that started and then after I do a pressure check meet me up on that small little flat area above the caves. Also, plan on that warm up I mentioned being at three o'clock and you'll need to be in full Wicca battle attire."

"You got it, captain!" Celeste said. The girls headed off to do that, and everyone else took that as a cue to get a move on with it all.

Atlanta turned to head to the center of the field, but Sean caught up to her. "Atlanta, you can't stay. You're in danger. You know it and I know it."

"What's he talking about?" Roman asked, for he had followed her as well.

"Butt out of this, Pierce!" Sean said through clenched teeth.

She didn't need to answer, for Roman said, "This is the field from the nightmare isn't it?"

Sean looked at Roman and then at her. "What? How do you—"

"I did date the girl right around the time the dreams started, Sean. She told me about it. Don't get your knickers in a bunch."

They began to squabble, and Atlanta took the diversion as an opportunity to walk toward the center of the field again.

Roman ran up next to her, grabbed her and spun her toward him, placing both his hands on her shoulders. "Is it the same field?" His voice was soft yet strained.

To admit this, even to herself, was painful. Atlanta opened her mouth to say yes, but she couldn't. The utter terror she felt along with the alarms going off in her mind telling her to run, to be anywhere but here made speech impossible. So she nodded, holding the gaze of his blue eyes for only a moment. He sighed and rested his chin on top of her head. She felt Sean's anger so she pulled away and started to walk again. Unfortunately, they were faster than she was, and were next to her again in a flash of a second, one on each side.

"That field was covered in blood and you were—" Sean choked on the rest. Finding his voice, he added, "If this is the field, then you need to leave, hide—go far away—"

"For once, Sean's right. You have to go, Atlanta. We'll find another way to get Phoenix."

She stopped and faced them. "Do you both honestly really want me to do that? Just leave Phoenix and the rest of you high and dry? Abandon the mission. Great idea. Can't see why I didn't think of that. Oh wait, one little snag. Valencia will not let Phoenix go without me here, for whatever reason. I may not agree with Phoenix, but he is a leader of The Great Order, and though I do not have an official obligation, I have a moral obligation.

"Yet here you two are, standing there telling me to leave. I suppose you could force me to leave by strength alone, but if we go into battle the girls need me to make the circle whole. Their power decreases by half if I leave. Would you rather they die?"

"They aren't the Daughter of Diana," Sean pleaded. But what she heard in his tone was, "They aren't who I'm in love with."

"They aren't one of the last Air Witches either," Roman offered.

She took Sean's hand. "We don't know that for sure. Besides, I made a will. It addresses that." She went to leave but stopped. "Diana must have a reason. We have to trust in that." She kissed Sean's hand, let go, and walked away.

This time they let her go. She could feel the air around them not move as they looked at each other for a moment. Two men who wanted to protect the woman that they love, one woman who loved them both, as well others, enough to stay and fight.

Atlanta walked toward the center of the field and pulled all her jewelry out of her pouch and put them all on. She closed her eyes, stretched out her arms, took a deep breath and let it out, using it to push the air. It told her that no one but her team was in the space, which made her feel better. They had one human with vampire blood in him, six vampires, four witches, five werewolves and one Tiger Shape Shifter.

"Diana help us if that isn't enough for what was coming to meet us," she quietly said to herself.

Heading toward the caves she met with Bianca, Celeste and Desi. She pulled the wind to lift her and the girls up to the clearing above the opening.

"Protection Spell, ladies. Let's get a move on 'cause we need to get some tea made for everyone before they go to bed. I also need Celeste to have a chat with the earth here, see if it'll let us dig some traps, okay?"

"That's a good idea," Celeste agreed.

The four of them joined hands and began the protection rite. When they finished, Celeste went to go have a talk with the soil; Desi went to purify the water they'd gathered from the scary creek earlier that evening, and Bianca set off to help with the campfire. Atlanta went down to where Sean had finished pitching their tent. One look from him and she knew they had to have the talk.

"I'll be fine, Sean. I'm going to be extra careful, okay?"

His eyes narrowed as his brow furrowed. "If you say so."

She knelt down next to him, "I can't run, don't you get it?"

"No. No, I don't get it," he took her hands to face her. "You know damn well you *die* here."

"Maybe it's not today, though. Maybe it's another day. And even if it is today, there's nothing we can do about that. Fate is fate."

"I don't believe that."

"I know you don't, but I do, so honor that if nothing else. Okay?"

Sean nodded as he shoved the last pole of the tent into the ground so hard it almost disappeared into the ground completely. She tried not to laugh but she couldn't help it.

Sean sighed. "Sorry, I'll fix that."

"It's okay. I'll be back."

She grabbed her Bo-staff and concentrated on the air blowing past her, used it to lift her up to the clearing above the caves. After she worked with her staff for a bit she sat to watch the sun rise over the horizon. *This very well might be my last sunrise.* She snorted a laugh that held no humor, just realization. Was she really ready to die? No. No one is ready to die.

She looked up at the sky. "If we can save that hero-dying-for-the-world shit for later, that'd be great. Just a request." You never know, maybe God did take requests.

It was so quiet as she sat alone. Something she hadn't been in months really. Not since the beach at her grandmother's in October. That seemed so far away now. It was only seven months ago, but it felt like a decade had passed.

She was tired. Tired of no answers, tired of this anger and hurt she felt every time she looked at Roman. Not to mention, she was tired of ignoring the pain she felt every time she thought of Jensine. It was her fault. She knew that. Somehow it was her fault Jensine was dead, but she didn't know why or what to do to fix it, if she even could.

Questions plagued her mind. Did The Great Order never have an answer for those? Every time she asked something she got a partial answer and the run around. It got to be exhausting. How was she to save the Clandestine World from destroying itself and the world around it if she never seemed to know what was going on? Phoenix wouldn't swear her into The Great Order, yet in his absence she had taken over, not Harmon. That made no sense.

Harmon. That man wasn't right. She couldn't put her finger on it, but he wasn't stable. Roman said he'd never been quite the same since Elizabeth died. And there it was, yet another death she couldn't get all the specifics on. It seemed Harmon had finally picked a side, but had he? She didn't trust that he had.

With a loud sigh Atlanta watched as the sun finally escaped the edge of the horizon. She put her sunglasses on and stayed where she was, examining all the colors spread out like when watercolor paint spills on a paper towel.

The main question of all was the biggest one. Why did Valencia want to see her? Who was she to her? Was Sean right? Did she want Atlanta to join her? Would that be the only reason she wanted to see her? If that's all she wanted, couldn't she have just called and asked? That would have been a lot simpler than all this.

The thought of Valencia doing all this, including Jensine's death, just to get her to come over to work with her made Atlanta want to vomit. Ever since Jensine—that night—the pain of that would never leave her. How she wished she knew who was really to blame for her death. Was it The Great Order or was it The Superior Order?

"Care for some company?"

Atlanta about jumped off the mountain. "Sean! Don't do that!" She yelled at him as she hit him in the leg.

He sat down behind her, one leg on either side of her, and started to rub her shoulders. It felt so wonderful Atlanta couldn't get herself to tell him to stop. She should be alone, being pensive, making herself ready for death. But his touch right then was all she wanted deep down, so she let go of how she thought she was supposed to be and decided to just be. "You didn't come up here to tell me to go home again, did you?"

"No."

"You aren't going to try and take me away or anything, are you?"

"No."

She waited for an explanation. But he just sat there silently rubbing her shoulders. "Then why are you up here?"

"I thought I'd get some of this tension out of your back so you can fight better, and watch the sunrise with you."

"Okay." It was all she could say. She knew there was nothing for them to really talk about. She wanted to tell him she loved him, but she knew if she did she'd start to cry. Besides, he knew. If this was her last day, starting it right here is where she wanted to be. To sit in silence with him felt good. Eventually, she leaned into him and he wrapped his arms around her. As she fell asleep she felt his hand push her hair away from her face, petting her head. She opened her mouth to say something but he stopped her.

"Shhh—let your body go. Just relax—don't think—I'm right here—I'm—"

And that's all she heard. When she woke up she was in her tent, all warm and curled up with Sean and she realized he was saying her name.

"Hmm?" she hummed, still half asleep.

"We need to do the blood trade before it gets too late."

She took a deep breath and yawned as she nodded. Atlanta rolled over onto her side, which wasn't really that easy being as that they were both in the same double sleeping bag.

"You ready?" he asked.

"No. Yes. Maybe."

He smiled and cut his collarbone and she tentatively leaned in. She'd have thought that doing this once before would've made the second time easier, but no. She pushed past her slight nausea and let herself think of it as more of a sexual, loving thing, than a necessity.

She let her tongue touch him first and he moaned slightly. The blood on her tongue felt warm and full of life, almost tingling on her taste buds. She opened her mouth and covered the opening. That's when she felt his teeth glide into her neck, a pinprick of pain and then gone as his saliva numbed the area.

This time it felt different because they drank from each other at the same time.

Atlanta's mind drifted to the blood bond ceremony and pictured what it would be like to be bonded to Sean. He answered her with images of her in beautiful white robes and she felt his love for her. It was so strong she didn't know what to do with all the emotion but cry.

She saw his fear and pain along with the love. Then, just when she thought she couldn't take another second, he disconnected and pulled her away from him. Their eyes found each other and held. She knew now was the time. "When I was in the Carolina's I saw a doctor. I had some of my eggs taken and frozen. It's outlined in my will. If something should happen to me tonight..."

"Shhh...I know. I saw it in your mind. But it won't come to that. Let's pray it doesn't come to that. Please."

She nodded and lay her forehead on his. "We need to get ready."

Quietly he said, "Not yet. We have time for a little more rest. Just...please just lay here with me. Okay?"

She didn't answer verbally, instead she curled up with her head on his chest and they both went back to sleep.

Her watch alarm woke her up a bit later, but she was alone. She grabbed her bag and opened it. She pulled out the black outfit her grandmother had given her at Christmas and put it on. She then brushed out her hair, put it in a ponytail on the top of her head and snagged her boots. She slipped them on, grabbed her jewelry bag and stepped out of the tent. It was two o'clock in the afternoon and the sun was shining. Sean sat there by a camp fire with his eyes closed, the sun beating down on his face. She bent down and touched the top of his head. His eyes opened.

"Why are you sleeping out here?"

"Not sleeping," he said, pointing at the fire. "Cooking." She now noticed the food. "I was only resting my eyes as the food fries. I like the sun on my face. Did you sleep ok?"

She nodded and sat down next to him. "If it was my last sunrise and my last sleep—my last everything—they were worth being the last ones." She hoped he understood all that she meant. "And thanks for coming up there. I thought I should be alone and try to separate myself, but I was wrong."

He sat up and gave her a lingering kiss and then turned his focus back to the food on the pan. "What's that?"

"Your breakfast. Protein. I woke up only a little before you and came out here to put it on. Should be done in a moment."

"Looks that way. Thank you."

He smiled again and she rested her head on his shoulder as he flipped the eggs. Once they were done she ate them slowly, still leaning on Sean. Once done she shoved the paper plate into the garbage bag and said, "Go on in the tent and get some real sleep for the next two hours, okay? I'll have someone come wake you up at four o'clock."

"I got as much sleep as you, I'm fine. We have to go warm up with the girls, right?"

"Since when do vampires need to warm up?"

"It evens you out. Besides can't spar with five, love."

"You sure?" she asked, hearing footsteps behind them. She turned to see Gray.

"You about ready, Atty?"

"Yeah, let me grab my Bo-staff."

She stood and went back into the tent and got the Bo-staffs Phoenix had given them.

"Wow—what is that awesome smell? Eggs and bacon? Seriously? Where you'd get eggs and bacon? I got a bagel with cream cheese for my breakfast."

She stepped out of the tent and motioned to Sean. "It was his idea to pack some food. I put air protection spells on the eggs before we left the house."

"Sean? Impressive. You should eat some carbs later though."

"He's right," Sean said, handing her a roll he'd buttered.

"Thank you. I'll eat this as we walk over. Let's go."

When they got to the far end of the field the girls were already there. Each of them wore their outfits that matched hers—Desi in blue, Bianca in red and Celeste in green.

"Let's get to working this out, ladies," Sean said, winking at Gray, who laughed and pranced off to get into his spot in our normal circle formation.

Chapter Seventeen

As the sun set Atlanta braced herself in front of the caves with Sean to her right and Roman to her left. She held her Bo-staff tightly, as if to steady her resolve.

Harmon fidgeted. "She better come."

"She'll come," Atlanta assured him.

As if those words alone triggered it, a large air pressure change began to occur and Atlanta's eardrums felt like someone decided to step on them. It all released at once, an explosion of air occurring in the middle of the field, like a sonic boom. As Atlanta's focus returned a beautiful red headed woman stood in the middle of the field, in all her self-appointed glory, her hair billowing about her petite body.

There were three witches behind her, a large man next to her, and Phoenix bound and gagged in front of him. Atlanta had to admit, the small number surprised her. Something didn't feel right.

Everyone was quiet. Atlanta stared at the Air Witch and she gazed right back. Finally a smile crossed her face and for a moment Atlanta thought she almost looked lovingly at her. She truly seemed happy to see her. It made bile rise in her throat. She swallowed it down.

"Germondival, take him to them. They've brought what I want," she commanded.

Atlanta thought Valencia's face seemed familiar, like she'd seen her on TV or something. She blinked a few times.

"You okay?" she heard Sean whisper. She nodded.

The large man dragged Phoenix over to them and threw him upon the ground. Harmon dropped to the ground over his brother.

"Bring her to me."

"No," Sean and Roman said at the same time.

Valencia's eyebrows went up, "No? The deal was that I get to talk to the one they call Windfire, or Phoenix would get to take a sun bath on TV."

"You can talk to her from there," Roman said.

"You silly vampire. Do you really think I have to play these games with you?"

She raised her arm and before Atlanta knew it she was in the air, and moving toward Valencia. She tried to fight it, but Valencia had acted first and there was nothing she could do. She gently set Atlanta down in front of her and Atlanta calmly attempted to clear her mind. She looked into Valencia's eyes. They could have been her grandmother's—they could have been hers.

That was when Atlanta knew where she had seen that face. "Oh dear goddess—I remember where I've seen you—but it can't be—I must be wrong..."

Valencia smiled. She heard the witches behind her begin to chant as she said, "I don't want to have this conversation with anyone else listening in."

"What did you want to see me for?" Atlanta blurted out. "Who am I to you?" The panic gripped her chest.

"Right to the point, aren't you? Well, you get that from your mother. Your father would beat around the bush at everything. It was a trifle annoying, to be honest."

"You knew my parents?"

"Knew? I know your parents…well, your mother that is. She's not dead, Atlanta."

Atlanta blinked once or twice, maybe a hundred times for the time it took to process this. *Please goddess, let me be wrong.* "This is why you wanted to see me? To lie to me? Tell me you have my mother so I'll what? Come with you? Leave my friends? Not gonna happen, Red. After what you did to Jensine you're lucky I didn't come and kill you all."

She laughed and reached out and touched Atlanta's face. She was unable to move, to block her. "I can see why 'fire' is the other part of your name. That's good. That's power. You can use that. Problem is that you're misdirecting your anger."

"So you say."

"So I know." Valencia put her hands on her hips. "Don't you have questions? Questions The Great Order won't answer? I can answer those for you? I can give you your mother. I can bring closure to so many painful things in your life if you'll let me. Let me do this for you. Let me make up for the pain I've caused you." She gently reached up to brush some of Atlanta's hair out of her face. "You are so beautiful. You've got your father's high cheekbones and his mouth. I have to admit, I never dreamed I'd ever get to see you again. It broke my inhuman heart the day I realized I couldn't get you back."

"What are you talking about?" Atlanta asked, her voice trembling. *Goddess no! No, no, no,—she needed to be wrong—she had to be wrong—*

"Come now, Atlanta. You knew the minute you looked into my eyes."

She shook her head, which felt like it was spinning round and round like a top on a wobbly surface.

"You have the Setti family eye color, but you got his height, you lucky thing. I tell you, your father was so tall— six feet four. You even got lucky enough to evade this red hair."

Atlanta kept shaking her head, but now the tears fell down her face too. *The pictures grandma had shown her were black and white—the red hair had looked brown—*

"I'm your—"

"No. Don't you say it!" she yelled out at her. "My mother—"

"Died in a car accident, right? Well, yes and no. The woman who was your human mother died in that car accident. But the vampire that loved her saved her— made her—brought her back to life. He saved your mother's mind and body and it stands before you now, reborn."

"No—" was all Atlanta could say as the tears ran down her face freely.

"You do have to understand that by the time I was lucid it was too late to come get you. The transformation for me was hard, due to my age. It was months until I remembered my old self. I couldn't pop back up and claim you after so much time had passed. There'd be questions.

"Questions, questions, questions!" She clapped her hands at each word and laughed. "Oh love, what was I to do? They'd pronounced me dead and erected a tombstone for goodness sake!" She sighed. At least they assigned you to your Aunt and Uncle Hart. Always liked them, you know. Alas, I digress.

"I may have been gone...kept my distance. But I checked on you every now and again. Like on your thirteenth birthday on the hill..."

"You brought the wind!" Atlanta said without thinking.

She smiled and nodded. "No whiny cheerleading bitch was going to touch my daughter."

"So it wasn't me who did that!"

"You? No. Please, you were a teenager with no idea of your powers." She started to laugh. But the laughter died quickly and she continued, "She killed herself a few years later anyway. Why you saved her then I have no idea, you were only putting off the inevitable."

Atlanta's mouth dropped open. She wanted to say something, anything, but she could think of nothing.

"Life is painful, sweetie, especially for our kind and the humans we try to mix with. We weren't meant to be their friends. It only causes them more pain. Take your friend Jensine for example. What good did it do her?"

Clenching her teeth to hold her scream in Atlanta said, "You don't even have the right to say her name."

"But you could end that pain. Yours. Theirs. You could learn from me..."

"No." It was a flat voice that came out of her. A flat but strong voice.

"No?"

"I'm not like you. I've heard all about you. You're crazy."

"From who? Your lover, Sean?" she laughed lightly, waving her hand. "That boy has a twisted sense of history. Let me tell you and show you how it all really is, Atlanta. You've let The Great Order twist your mind to think like them. You have no idea about the truth. You have a fabricated story that has been told so many times that even they believe it now. I can teach you so much. I can show you the truth if you'll just let me."

Atlanta shook her head and emotionally reached out to find her witch sisters. She found them, but something was wrong.

"I can make you come with me, but I'd rather you wanted it on your own. My gates are always open to you. Remember that. I have a feeling I'll see you soon."

"I will never want to be what you are." Atlanta gathered the focus to slip her hand into a pocket and grasped the stones that were there, one from each of her girls.

"You have no idea what you're wrapped up in, my dear. Nor do you understand the truth. You have to listen to me. Your friends are not totally honest with you. The Superior Order can teach you, we can hone your craft and we will not lie to you."

"You killed my best friend!"

Valencia's eyes widened and then the look of pity came across her face. "Sweetie, Jensine was not attacked by us. Phoenix ordered the hit on your little friend by a rogue shape shifter and luckily one of my men got there in time to save her."

"Save her? They found her bones!"

"Those weren't hers. Those belonged to the shape shifter, the panther you saw on the tape. My man brought Jensine to me. She's been taken care of by my people since that night." She put out a delicate hand. "Come with me and you can see for yourself."

"You lie. You always lie! Grandma told me all about you—" The hope that Valencia wasn't lying opened the wound of Jensine's death like it had been yesterday. Tears filled her eyes, but she blinked them away.

Valencia's hand rested on Atlanta's arm. "I was able to save her you know. Of course, she is changed from how you knew her. There were things I couldn't fix. Her blood had been tainted."

"What are you saying?"

"She's no longer human, Atlanta, she was bitten. And might I say, she's not adjusting well. To see you would help her so much. Just come with me, you'll see for yourself. You don't have to stay, but at least come with me for a little while."

Atlanta thought for moment. She remembered that Sean had told her how Valencia was the queen of lies and of trickery. She started to shake her head. "You lie you lie you lie you lie!" She finally screamed. "I will not believe your lies! Jensine is dead and you're to blame!"

"No dear, you are. Jensine's death, the Jensine you knew, that is, was killed to convince you to support Phoenix's battle plans. So I removed him from your world for a time so you could get bearings on your own. Which you have. But you must listen to me. I am your mother and I know what is best for you. Now is not the time to argue about this. With the snap of my fingers you and I can disappear to where she is and you can see for yourself." She let go of Atlanta and offered her hand again. "It's your last chance. Don't make me take another route to this, please."

Atlanta couldn't comprehend all that she'd learned in a short time. She had to be lying to her. Valencia was manipulating her and she had to get away. Plus, something felt wrong and Atlanta couldn't figure out what it was. She had to focus her power if she was to break free. Inside her pocket she spun the ring Sean had given her on her finger, trying to link to him."

"*Atty!*" It burst into her mind. He was in pain. She had no go, now.

Focusing on his voice, pushing with all her power strengthened by the three stones in her pocket, throwing power into each word she yelled, "In Diana's name, Let—me—go!" The ground shook and a sound like the shattering of glass pierced the air and the bubble shattered, the sounds of the world coming back to her. Atlanta pushed with all her might and up she went, into the air, out of Valencia hold. As she came down she put out her hand to put a wall between her and Valencia.

"Leave," Atlanta said, "You are wasting your time. I know enough to know where my allegiance lies."

"Atlanta, help!" she heard a voice from her right yell.

Atlanta peripheral vision showed her a full-fledged battle in the field. Somehow Valencia's three witches and one werewolf had become more like thirty vampire soldiers. All of her friends were engaged in battle.

Valencia seemed more sad than mad. "I didn't want it to come to this. Know that. Remember that, later." Valencia stepped away, took hands with her witches, "Until we meet again."

Another sonic boom occurred and she and her three witches disappeared. Atlanta spun about in time to see Harmon kill a vampire.

"Where is Gray?"

Harmon swung his battle ax again, taking another vamp out. "Stephan sent him into the caves. He's injured."

Atlanta eyes scanned for the only other one who mattered. Where was he? She finally found Sean fighting a huge werewolf. He wasn't winning. The werewolf was poised over him with a stake.

"No!" she screamed and threw all her force at him. The werewolf, caught by the wind, flew back. By the time he stood up she stepped between him and Sean.

"You're gonna have to get past me if you want him!"

"You and what army?"

"Silver staff!" She yelled out as she reached up into the air. Her silver staff that had fallen flew from the ground to her hand. "I am the army."

The werewolf charged her and she jumped up into the air, hovered and came down behind him, thrusting the sharp point into his back, into his heart. He fell to the ground. Whirling about, sensing motion at her back, she caught sight of Sean as he picked up his sword. She stepped aside while he cut the werewolf's head off.

Out of breath he said, "You *are* the army?"

She smiled. "I didn't have time for a better line." He grinned. "Are you okay?"

He wiped dirt from his face. "I'm fine, or I will be."

"I have to go find Gray, he's been injured."

He kissed her. "Go, I'll be fine."

She then saw a vampire approach them. "You got this?"

"As Gray would say, I'm all over this like a bad hairdo on an eighties prom queen, honey."

She didn't stay to watch him fight, instead she ran off to see if Roman and the girls were okay. Unfortunately Harmon met her first.

"Gray isn't well. I just checked on him. He asked for you. You need to come stop the bleeding."

"Isn't the vampire blood doing that?"

"It's not *that* kind of wound."

She scanned the battlefield and the CPA had become bored with the hand-to-hand combat and had started the use of automatic weapons. It'd be over shortly. Gray needed her. "Take me to him."

Harmon took her hand and they ran into the caves.

"How far in is he?"

"Not too far...come on."

They ran further into the caves and soon were deeper than she thought they needed to be. "I thought it wasn't far?"

"For vampire legs it's not."

"Take me at vampire speed then!"

He stopped. "Hold on."

He picked her up and they were gone in a flash of a second. Before she knew it they were in the back of the cave. It was a cavern, with a ceiling barely high enough for Atlanta to stand up in. One of the oil lamps they'd brought lay on the ground next to a man. It was Gray. He lay there, unconscious, his leg bleeding badly at the calf. She noticed a tourniquet tied around his thigh and ran to him.

"Gray? Gray honey, can you hear me? Wake up, please."

"Atty?" Gray barely opened his eyes.

Pulling one open she examined it. "He's going into shock. How much blood has he lost?"

Harmon shrugged and went back to pacing.

"Atty?"

"Yeah honey, it's me. You're going to be fine. I'm going to get you out of here." She blew on his leg and stopped the bleeding with an air bandage. "Why isn't the vampire blood healing this?"

Harmon shook his head and said, "It's too massive of a wound."

"I was shot and it healed. It doesn't get more massive than that!"

"It's a magickal wound, Atlanta. It'll heal on its own soon enough. I just didn't want him to bleed out before it could. He got the artery by accident, stupid dog. He had one job…"

"What are you talking about?"

Gray groaned out her name and she turned back to him. "You'll feel better shortly. Just stay there, let me see the best way to get you out of here safely."

"They showed up out of nowhere and you were in that cocoon—we didn't know if you were okay—we had no choice but to fight."

"I know. It's okay. I'm fine, baby. Just hang on." She took his hand and he squeezed it.

"I feel so tired—so tired…"

"Don't you fall asleep, Gray—I need you to stay awake."

It was too late, he'd passed out again.

"Damn! Harmon?" There was no answer. "Harmon?" She spun around but didn't see him. "Where is he? How am I supposed to get out of here? I don't know the way back. Stupid Son of a—Harmon!" She heard footsteps. "Harmon? Is that you?"

"I'm right here," he said, stepping out of the shadows, his long blond hair now tied behind his neck.

"I need you to get him out of here and me back to the battle."

"That's not going to happen."

"Uh—why not?"

"My mistress has another plan for you."

"Your what?"

"You didn't accept her offer. I am to make you see."

"What the hell does that mean?"

"I didn't want it to come to this…she didn't want it to come to this…but you've left us no choice. I'm so sorry, Atlanta."

She thought for a moment and it came to her. "You didn't leave her to come to us, she sent you to us to so we'd come here! You unbelievable bastard!"

Harmon looked at her and with a tilt of his head the expression on his face confirmed her statement.

"How could you—to your brother—to Roman! What would Elizabeth say?!"

Before she could see it coming, a hand slapped her face so hard she heard her cheekbone crack.

"How dare you!? You know nothing of the truth of our world! You've only been a part of it for not even a year and you think you know it all. Well, you don't. You don't even know half because Phoenix and Roman keep you in the dark. They use you. The same way they use me and the way they used Elizabeth. Well, no more! It stops here."

Atlanta got up on her feet. She thought she'd try to run, but his speed was greater than hers and they were so deep into the cave there wasn't enough of a breeze to pull from to do anything defensive. She was trapped. The only thing she could think to do was to stall him and start to pull at the little moving air she could find. "How do they use me? Tell me what's going on, Harmon."

"Atlanta, there is no time for me to explain. She loves you so much, can't you see? This has to be done. The Superior Order are not the bad guys—they're just the honest ones. No one likes to hear the truth when it doesn't suit their fancy."

She felt the air coming. Would it get here in time? "I like the truth."

"Then you'll forgive me for what I'm about to do."

It was a flash—faster than she could blink. He wrapped around her with his hand over her mouth and the other around her arms and his legs around hers. She felt him mentally block her from crying out.

As she fell to the ground she heard him say, *"We are sorry it has come to this."* She then felt his teeth pierce her skin.

"No, Harmon! Please no," was all she said, trying to say but he wouldn't listen. She prayed that Diana could as she slipped into the darkness.

* * * *

"So, how's she hangin' in down there?" Josh asked.

"She's a little bit worse for wear. I gotta get her outta there, Josh. I think tomorrow night is the night."

"Dude, you don't even have access yet."

"Oh, but I will."

"What?"

"Would you gentlemen like to order?" the waitress asked.

"We'd love to," Josh replied. They ordered their food and as soon as she left Josh continued. "What half-cocked plan have you dreamed up now?"

"Been working an angle of my own for the past two nights. Nit-wit Brian took me up on an idea and as it seems, he's run with it a bit further than I'd dreamed."

"So, what's this angle?"

"Well, Brian's a slack ass. He'd rather sleep than work. Besides, he hates Eddie which is in his favor cause if I'd found out he'd been helping him he'd be taken care of too."

"True."

"Anyways, he's taken a shine to J.R.'s enthusiasm for his own gain."

"Gee, shocker," Josh said, his voice thick with sarcasm.

"I know, right? So the deal is he swipes me in and out for his shift and he sleeps while I work his shift for him. Told him I wanted to make sure I wanted the gig. You know."

"And he fell for this?"

"He and Eddie got one brain cell between the two of them, of course he did. Then, today he tells me even better information."

"Here you go gentlemen. One coffee and one ice tea?"

"Yes ma'am, ice tea right here." Josh reached for some of the sweeteners on the table. "Thank you very much." The waitress nodded and whisked off to another table. "As you were sayin'?"

Hunter wrapped his hands around his coffee mug. "So he had an extra key card made for himself, telling security he accidently washed his. So now, he doesn't even need to let me in or out, he just has to call me once he's signed in and I call him as I leave the facility." He grinned and added cream and sugar to his coffee.

"He's an idiot."

"Tell me something I *don't* know."

"So tomorrow is the night. I'm getting her out of there. I can't take a chance this is going to last. Plus, I won't be missed. I'm not really supposed to be there, I don't have class until the early evening tomorrow so by the time anyone notices anything she and I'll be on a plane outta here."

Stirring his tea, Josh asked, "Where will you go?"

"No clue. I can't take her home. The family and I still aren't speaking."

"Why not take her to where she came from?"

Hunter sipped the coffee. It wasn't the best, but it was caffeinated. "Probably not a good idea. Jonathan roams that area and he'd come across her for sure. I don't know. I think maybe we'll just buy a ticket to New York City and we'll stay there until she's in good enough shape to interact with people again. I know she hasn't been down there for too long but dude, she's a bit wiggy."

"I would be too if I'd gone through what she'd gone through. Do you have enough money?"

"Please. I have all that family money they moved over for my schooling which I then, in turn, moved into another account so I could jet, remember? I've been here ever since then, so it's all been sitting gaining interest. She has some special Visa and her passport hidden so I just need to take her to get it and we'll get out of here."

"How you gonna get past the guards? What about Eddie? Won't he notice you scan out?"

"Naw. Had a witch friend of mine make something special for his coffee, if you know what I mean."

"I'd say he doesn't deserve it, but he does," Josh said, sipping his tea.

"He deserves worse."

"I agree. But this way he will be the one that's framed instead of Brian. He may be a twit, but he's not as bad as Eddie so I'd rather he didn't take the full brunt of this. I'll leave him a note in his locker in the break room and when I call him I'll tell him to check it before he goes to the office."

"Good idea. So tomorrow night it is. That's what, Thursday?"

"Yes sir. As of this time tomorrow I'll be on my way back to the U.S. and Jensine will be safe."

Josh held up his sweet tea. "God willing."

Hunter touched it with his mug of coffee. "Yes, God willing."

* * * *

"Atty? Atty? Wake up—come on honey."

Atlanta opened her eyes to see Gray's face.

"Gray? Where—what—"

"Shhh—you need to save your energy—"

She looked around and they were in the cave still. Her spell on Gray had obviously worked, his leg stopped bleeding. In fact, it looked almost healed, which she thought odd. She tried to sit up but her head was swimming and then she felt this enormous pain in her chest and her stomach. She screamed out and doubled over. It felt like her insides were on fire, like she was burning from the within.

"Roman! Stephan! Someone!" Gray yelled out.

His voice echoed off the walls of the cavern. She glanced over and saw a pile of clothes.

"Did you kill—?"

"I found him looming over your body so I staked him."

All of a sudden Roman showed up, Stephan on his heels.

"I heard you yell—what's—oh no."

"A vampire got to her."

"Let's get her outside," Roman said.

He lifted her up and Stephan grabbed Gray and they whisked them through the caverns at vampire speed. Next thing she knew she was laying on the grass and all she could smell was blood and vampire dust.

"Did we lose anyone?"

"Only one. Erik. But—" Stephan started to say but someone interrupted him silently.

"What are you not telling me?"

"Nothing. You need to stay still."

Atlanta could hear people running over to her as her hands felt the wet grass under. She coughed. It felt like she was choking. She coughed again and thankfully something kicked out of her throat. She swallowed and it helped a bit but all she could taste was blood. It was like she was choking on it.

"Atlanta!" Sean yelled as he fell next to her, taking her head into his arms, cradling it. "Oh no. No, no, no—" he said as he wiped her face clean of what she'd coughed up. "You gotta hold on, honey. We're going to get you out of here and to a hospital."

Roman then came into focus. "Sean, give her room to breathe!"

She coughed again, and she saw blood spray Sean's face.

"I don't think a hospital can fix me, Sean."

Roman leaned down on her other side, looking into her face, "You have got to hold on, sweetie. Please—you just have to hang on. The elders of the Circle in this area are on their way."

She felt the world tilt and she turned to Sean, "Harmon, he said—"

"Shhh—save your energy," Sean begged her.

Roman reached down and pried her eyes open, looking at her closely, "Atlanta, did he give you his blood?"

"I don't know. I remember nothing after he bit me. I just kept saying no as I—" she stopped to cough again and realized she was having a hard time breathing. "Oh goddess I can't breathe! My lungs—they feel like they're on fire!"

"Roman! Sean! Gray!" Celeste was yelling, "They're here! The elders are here."

"You hang on, Atlanta. I have to go help them get everything down here…"

"I'm so cold—"

"Roman, we need you!" Celeste yelled out.

"I will be right back, you need to hang on."

She shivered. "I'll try."

He left and Gray handed Sean a blanket, which he calmly draped over her.

"Thanks."

He lay down next to her, cleaning her face and smoothing her hair. She opened her eyes long enough to see tears running down his face.

"Don't cry, baby, it's going to be okay. Its fate…there's nothing you could've done…"

He took her hand and pressed it to his face and kissed it.

"I love you," she said.

The tears fell down his face even more now.

She smiled. "Take care of Gray for me—him and the girls—and find my will—it's very important. Gray knows where it is—"

"Atlanta…"

"Promise me, please!"

He nodded. "I promise."

Roman showed back up—she could smell him before she heard him.

"Look at her. Please tell me I'm wrong."

One of the elders leaned down and took a pen light to her eyes. It burned like a hot poker. She wailed and tried to turn her head away.

"She's too far gone," he said, "You have two options, and you know it, Roman."

She let out a breath of air in relief and let herself relax into the grass…it felt so soft and she was so tired.

"Roman?" she said, but it only came out as a whisper.

He knelt next to her. "I'm here."

"Don't let them turn me. I don't want to be an abomination—I couldn't live like that. Let me go. You have to let me go. Let me die. I've done what I was here to do. Promise me you won't change me."

"Atlanta—I—"

"Promise me."

"He promises, don't you Roman?" Sean demanded, "Don't you dare let her go through what I've had to go through."

Roman dropped his head, "I promise none here will change you."

She forced her eyes open one last time and caught Roman's eye, "Goodbye beautiful, I—forgive you."

Roman's face contorted and his eyes brimmed with pink tears.

She turned to look at Sean, "Goodbye, baby, I'll always love you—"

She reached for him, but her hand fell and her eyes shut. She heard Sean and Roman scream out her name. Then it all was quiet and she let the earth take her back.

Chapter Eighteen

"Roman?" the elder said. "You need to cut off her head."

"What?" Sean blurted out, tears running down his face.

"Excuse me?!" Gray knelt next to her body, stroking her hair.

Celeste, Desi and Bianca started to cry as they hugged each other.

"Sean," Roman said matter-of-factly, "She's been given vampire blood to replace the blood that was taken from her. Look at her eyes, you can see the change starting. We can't stop it now, it's too late."

"Roman," the elder said, "If we don't burn her or cut her head off she'll wake up in the next twenty four hours as a vampire witch, and The Great Order has rules on that. They don't allow mixing vampire with other Clandestine breeds."

Roman stood there numb. His head was spinning. Then he heard Elizabeth's voice from that day in the rain, in the woods not so long ago. She'd told him, "even if it means the conversion," meaning save her life even if she must be changed into a vampire. Roman had wondered why he'd been sent that message, and now he knew. He had to allow the change. The goddess and the god had tasked him with this. The word of the goddess and god overruled The Great Order. He finally raised his head.

"I know the rules, Chartivon, I'm second to the Prince. Do you realize who she is? She's the chosen child of Diana, we can't let her die!"

Chartivon stood there for a moment, letting this sink in. "Does she bear the mark of the three levels of the moon goddess?"

"She does."

Chartivon began to pace as Sean held her body in his arms. "This doesn't mean she's above Great Order law. Only Phoenix can make this call," he finally said.

"The Prince has awoken from the spell Valencia had on him Roman," Amanda told him. "Why not ask him."

Roman nodded and prayed his half brother had his wits about him enough to remember the message from Elizabeth.

"I'll go get him," Amanda offered, and left the circle of people around her body.

Sean kissed Atlanta's head and laid her down on the ground. Standing up he crossed over to Roman. "You cannot be considering letting her become a vampire. Tell me you're not considering it."

"It's not my call."

"It is your call!" Sean shoved him. "You promised her! She said she'd rather die—let her be—hell, give me the axe! I'll do it if you're too much of a wuss to do it yourself! Death is better than being a made vampire! What if she were to wake up without a soul!"

"That won't happen."

"You don't know that!" Sean screamed.

Roman saw only too late Sean's plan. Sean used the element of surprise as well as his speed to his advantage and he ran for an axe that wasn't far from him. He grabbed it and turned toward his target before Big Daddy Jay and Lance got hold of him.

"Let me go! She had a last wish and we need to honor that! Roman, please!" Sean pleaded.

"She is the last of the Setti line, Sean—and the prophesied daughter of Diana—it's not my call."

"Bullshit!"

"It's not bullshit," came a voice from behind Sean. It was Phoenix.

"Oh, great, how convenient. You are here to ruin the day again."

"Sean!" Stephan scolded.

"What? I have no allegiance to The Great Order, nor did she. You never trusted her enough to swear her in. She doesn't fall under your laws officially and you know it!"

Roman caught Phoenix's eye. *"Elizabeth said the goddess foresaw this."* Roman mentally reminded him.

"I don't understand. This goes against all of our laws. But I'm not one to defy the god and goddess."

"Neither am I."

Phoenix rubbed his face. *"We'll explain it to everyone later. We don't have time now to explain this. How do I justify this?"*

"No bloody idea. I suppose you might say it's to make the sides even. Valencia is a witch vampire."

"No one is going to like that." Phoenix pointed out.

"And they're going to believe I had a vision of our dead sister in September and that's why we're allowing it?"

"Not a chance in hell."

Roman sighed. *"So we go with the war angle?"*

"We do." Phoenix then turned to Sean, his tone flat, "We can't kill her."

"We can, we can cut off her head and she'll stay dead. And as horrible as that is it's better than waking up an abomination!"

"Is it?" Roman asked.

The look on Sean's face mimicked how he felt. He could see Sean's heart breaking in multiple directions. To kill her or to let her change—either option was more than Sean would be able to bear.

"The only way we'll ever win a battle against a vampire witch, is if we have one ourselves," Phoenix pointed out. "Valencia is more powerful than any of us. If we let Atlanta become like her we'd have a fighting chance in this war."

"You're going to allow her to become an abomination so you can make her into some weapon? That's insane!" Gray yelled.

Roman saw Sean was close to breaking free and the axe was still in his range. "J.J. and 2Doggz, go help hold him steady!"

Everyone was quiet. The only sound was Sean screaming to let him go and the girls' crying.

"This actually is a stroke of good luck." Phoenix said, "Do we know who did this?"

"When I woke up I found a vampire leaning over her body so I staked him. I have no idea who he was. I didn't really think, I just acted."

Roman searched the group. "Where's Harmon?"

Everyone glanced around and started to talk to each other.

"Last time I saw him he was taking Atlanta into the caves," Sean explained. "If he did this—"

"Then he's dead, Gray killed him," Roman said.

"It didn't look like Harmon—I'd have recognized Harmon. It wasn't him."

"He's dead either way," Roman advised, "Great Order rules forbid this act and he is subject to those rules, punishable by death."

"Well hooray for one good thing today," Sean cried out.

Phoenix glared at Sean and walked over to him, "That is my brother you mock. Do it again and I'll kill you."

"Go for it! And while you're at it, kill her too! Because I don't know what you all think is gonna happen when she wakes up? But she's not gonna be at all happy to be an experiment you did to try and win a war."

Gray leaned over and kissed Atlanta's forehead and then stood up, "I've been quiet up until now because I'm not one of you, but I agree with Sean. If Atlanta wanted to stay dead then you need to abide by her wishes. She's not going to be on your side if you allow this. You think you've seen her mad before, it'll be nothing compared to when she wakes up and you've let her become this thing.

"You think you'll convince her it was for the good of the team? What team? She's not part of your team. All you have ever done is hide full truths from her," Gray's gaze fell upon Roman, "and take advantage of her skills and leadership. I know I have no power to stop you all. But I will not stand here and allow it. I will have *nothing* to do with this decision or any of you ever again…and I mean you too Stephan. Are you going to stand there and let this happen?"

"I have no choice Gray," Stephan told him.

"Then you can go to hell with the rest of them!"

With that he ran off in the direction they'd arrived from, heading for his Jeep.

"Gray, wait!" Stephan yelled out but Roman stopped him from actually going after him.

"J.J. and 2Doggz, I need you two to track Gray. He's going to need you."

Desi glared at Roman. "What are you talking about? He's not our main concern right now—leave him be."

"Can't. He was bitten by the head of the werewolves of The Superior Order. He's about to become a child of the head werewolf family. Germandival will come looking for him and I need J.J. and 2Doggz to make sure they find Gray first," Roman explained.

Stephan turned to face the direction Gray ran. Roman studied his best mate. Stephan was always hard to read but for once, it was apparent he was contemplating running after his husband. Roman reached out and put a hand on his shoulder. Stephan looked at him and then began to pace as everyone was yelling back and forth.

Finally he stepped up to Roman's right side and touched his arm. Roman saw what he was going to do.

"Don't." Roman said to him mentally.

"I must go. I will be back. Take her to our house instead of the mansion. It's safer."

"Stephan, don't go."

"Is that an order sir?"

Roman set his jaw and looked away, *"It is."*

"I'm sorry, then."

And with that, without any word to anyone else, Stephan turned on a heel and at vampire speed ran in the same direction Gray had gone.

"Where is he going?" Phoenix demanded, his tone curt.

Roman sighed. "He has to do what he feels is right."

"You gave him a direct order to stay."

"I did."

Phoenix shook his head. *"Roman, it's all breaking into a million pieces. How are we going to win this war if everything is shattered?"*

Roman saw tears in his brother's eyes for the first time in years and didn't know what to say, his own emotional pain rendering him useless.

"We don't have much time," Amanda stated as she approached them, "Look at her face. She's changing and fast. Her face is already smooth and flawless. She's changing way faster than normal."

"You know what that probably means don't you?" Roman pointed out to Phoenix alone.

"Yes. Royal blood-child."

"I'm sorry Phoenix."

"Not as much as I am. Damn it Roman! How could Harmon do this? It's the ultimate betrayal, going against everything we stand for."

Roman put a hand on Phoenix's shoulder. *"Maybe Harmon had a reason."*

"Maybe that reason was Valencia."

"Maybe it was something else."

"One can only hope."

"Chartivan," Roman said aloud, "can you take her in your vehicle and follow us home? Your van is without windows and no one else will ride with you but me. We can't take chances she's killed at this point. She needs quiet time to make the change. It's a ten hour drive. We need to get her home and fast." Roman instructed.

"I can. Put Ms. Hart on the gurney and tie her tight with vampire rope."

"No!" Sean screamed as he wiggled in the arms of the CPA.

"Sedate him, for the love of God," Phoenix blurted out. "This is bad enough without having to make sure he doesn't go rogue and attack you on the way home."

Chartivon walked over to Sean and reached into his pocket. He muttered some words no one could hear and tossed some dust on Sean, which caused him to pass out immediately.

Phoenix ran a hand through his long dark hair and took a settling breath of air. "Roman and Amanda, you carry the gurney. I'll carry Chartivon. We all need to go at vampire speed to Chartivon's van. J.J. and 2Doggz, follow Stephan and Gray's scent and get Gray to the safe house and bring Stephan to me. Lance—you, Joe and Big Daddy Jay take Erik's body and the witches. Drop the girls at Roman's home and then you three can take Erik to be laid to rest at your safe house. You'll meet up with J.J. and 2Doggz there."

"We're on it boss," J.J. said and he and 2Doggz were off running.

"Consider it done," Lance agreed, heading to lift Erik into his arms.

"I actually gotta be at work," Big Daddy Jay told them.

"Okay then, let's get a move on," Roman ordered. "By the time we get her home she'll have gone through most of the change if not all of it and we don't want her waking up in transit. It's time to break the speed limit people. Let's go."

With that everyone silently tied Atlanta to the stretcher and headed out of the field. Roman and Amanda picked up the gurney and just before they began their run, Roman looked back at the field one last time and he could see that it was covered in splotches of blood. Her dream had come true. How many more would?

He turned away and gave Amanda a nod. They ran Atlanta's changing body to Chartivon's van, loaded her up and began the trip home. Then, and only then, did he allow the tears to fall.

The End

TO BE CONTINUED

The next Windfire Novel: *Metamorphosis*

For more about The Windfire Series and pictures of the characters go to
www.tamsinsilver.com
.

Living Dead Girl

Author Biography

Tamsin L. Silver lives in New York City with her Border Collie/Lab mix, Keziah, but is originally from Michigan. She holds a BA in Theatre and Secondary Education with a minor in Creative Writing and Shakespeare from Winthrop University in South Carolina. She's taught both middle and high school drama, and now works in theatre as a freelance Director and Producer in New York City, where her writing has also been performed on stage.

Living Dead Girl

200

Made in the USA
Charleston, SC
17 August 2013